Get a Free eB
Biblical & Historical Research Behind the Exodus.

Limited Time Offer

FREE

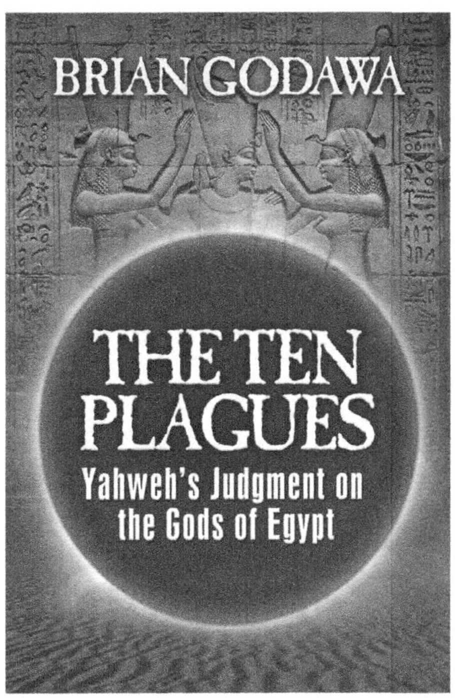

Natural Disasters? Gods at War? De-creation?

Have you wondered what Yahweh meant when he said, "I will execute judgment upon the gods of Egypt"? Did you know that there is a connection between the plagues and Genesis 1? The answers may astonish you. Some of the research behind this novel can be found at the following link:

https://godawa.com/get-ten-plagues/

Before You Read This Novel, Get the Picture Book of its Characters for Visual Reference

See the Characters as You Read the Novel!

Full-color picture book includes characters for the entire Chronicles of the Nephilim series:

• Noah Primeval • Enoch Primordial • Gilgamesh Immortal • Abraham Allegiant • Joshua Valiant • Caleb Vigilant • David Ascendant • Jesus Triumphant

These full-color pictures will boost your imagination as you read the novels.

Click Here to Get Now:

(in Paper, Hardcover or Ebook)

www.godawa.com/get-neph-pics/

affiliate link

Joshua Valiant

Chronicles of the Nephilim
Book Five

By Brian Godawa

JOSHUA VALIANT
5th Edition +1b

Warrior Poet Publishing
www.warriorpoetpublishing.com

ISBN: 9798710835197 (hardcover)
ISBN: 978-0-9859309-9-8 (paperback)

The Tabernacle and The Israelite Encampment. Logos Bible Software. www.logos.com

The image of the Ark of the Covenant recreated by Pastor Phillip Anthony Missick is used by permission from Dr. Stephen Andrew Missick, pastor of King of Saints Tabernacle, 2228 FM 1725, Cleveland, Texas 77328. www.kingofsaints.net.

Scripture quotations taken from *The Holy Bible: English Standard Version*. Wheaton: Standard Bible Society, 2001.

Dedicated to
all those who have struggled
with the moral implications
of the law of *herem*
in the Wars of Yahweh
and the conquest of Canaan.

ACKNOWLEDGMENTS

Special thanks to my Rahab, Kimberly. And to Michael Gavlak for his valuable story feedback, and his Caleb friendship (Or really, his Joshua friendship since I'm the old man). Thanks to Don Enevoldsen and Blake Samuels for their story feedback and encouragement. Shari Risoff, my sister-in-law did a wonderful job of editing these two volumes.

Thank you, Yahweh Elohim.

NOTE TO THE READER

For those who are new to the series and have not read previous volumes, there is much imagination in this novel and its companion volume, *Caleb Vigilant*, that may freak out some Bible believers who are unfamiliar with the ancient Near Eastern worldview and mindset within which the writers of Scripture themselves lived and wrote.

Within these pages one will read of fantasy creatures like Leviathan the sea dragon of chaos, satyrs with the torso of men and the lower legs of a goat, and other phantasmagorical images. It may shock the reader to discover that all these monsters are mentioned in the Bible in one form or another, often with reference to the paganism of Canaan.

When the Biblical writers engage in this kind of referencing, they are often using well known images and myths of their day to attack with polemical force. Thus, the satyrs that pagans worship are considered goat demons (Lev. 17:7; 2Chron. 11:15; Deut. 32:17). What I decided to do was to literalize the metaphors and bring these demonic creatures to life in all their spiritual imagination, thus embedding historical story with theological meaning. This is just what the Bible writers did when describing Yahweh crushing the heads of Leviathan when Moses crossed the Red Sea (Psa. 74:12-17), or describing the destruction of a nation in terms of the collapse of the universe (Judg. 5:19-20; Isa. 13:10; 24:1-23). So I have shown the actual activity of Yahweh through his angels fighting the sea dragon to putting down evil, as well as the true demonic reality behind pagan religion.

In this sense, the Chronicles are not an attempt to reimagine history but rather to imbue it with theological meaning. But despite this use of imagination, everything that occurs in the novels, every monster, every fictional character, is based on real Biblical and ancient historical and mythological research. If the reader has difficulty fully embracing this before reading, perhaps it would be helpful to read the Appendices I have at the back of each novel first before reading the novel. In those Appendices I reveal a bit of the research into the ancient Near Eastern worldview that goes behind the fiction.

I have made up far less material than you may realize.

In these novels you will also see angels that are very physical beings (with extra-physical and preternatural abilities) who fight with swords and cannot fly. It is important to remember that the modern notion of angels as immaterial spirit beings who fly with wings is a medieval construct and not a Biblical description.

In the Bible, angels may mysteriously appear and disappear, but they never have wings, they are not depicted as flying, and they are very physical creatures who eat food (Gen. 18:8), can have sex with humans (Gen. 6:1-4), and sometimes have swords as weapons (Josh. 5:13). Their flesh is a different kind of flesh than human flesh, but it is physical (1Cor. 15:39-40). I would contend that my view is actually closer to the Biblical picture than the conventional wisdom of winged spirit beings without physicality.

Another element of the storyline is a certain reality to the pagan gods of the world. They exist as supernatural beings with divine powers. But they are not actual gods as the pagans understand them, but rather demonic fallen "Watchers" or "Sons of God" from Yahweh's heavenly host, who are masquerading as gods in order to draw worship away from Yahweh. This too is not entirely manufactured on my part, but rather an application of Biblical verses that hint at the demonic reality behind Canaanite deities.

> **Psalm 106:36-38**
> 36 They served their idols, which became a snare to
> them. 37 They sacrificed their sons and their
> daughters to the demons; 38 they poured out
> innocent blood, the blood of their sons and daughters, whom they sacrificed to the idols of Canaan, and the land was polluted with blood.

> **Deuteronomy 32:16-17**
> 16 They stirred him to jealousy with strange gods;
> with abominations they provoked him to anger. 17
> They sacrificed to demons that were no gods, to gods they had never known, to new gods that had come recently, whom your fathers had never dreaded.

In Genesis 6:1-4 we read that these fallen Sons of Gods or Watchers came to earth and mated with human women as part of their corruption of creation. The fruit of that unholy forbidden union were the Nephilim, or giants of old. Though God destroyed this abomination with the Flood, the genetic corruption of the giants continued on into the seedline of Canaan, so that when

Joshua entered Canaan, it was filled with giant clans who traced their descendants back to the Nephilim before the Flood (Num. 13:32-33). Some of these giant clans were the Rephaim, the Anakim, the Emim, and Zamzummim (Deut. 2:10-23) and others who show up in the Chronicles of the Nephilim.

Then a strange thing happened at the Tower of Babel incident. When God separated the nations in their rebellion, he placed them under the authority of the fallen Sons of God or Watchers. God allotted the territories of nations to those Watchers as their own property (Deut. 32:8-9). God gave them over to their abominations. But then, when Israel would enter into the land of Canaan to claim it for their own, God would disinherit those principalities and powers and give that land to Jacob, the Seed of Abraham.

I have already explained in more detail the Biblical proof of these elements in previous Chronicles, so if the reader wants to understand it more fully, I recommend starting with *Noah Primeval* and read the appendices and the novels from there.

Another element of *Joshua Valiant* and *Caleb Vigilant* that may cause some concern with believers in the Bible is my census of about sixty thousand warriors and a couple hundred thousand Hebrews in the exodus. For those acquainted with the English translations, it seems that the Bible says there were six hundred thousand warriors and by implication, about two and a half to three million Hebrews in the exodus (Num. 1:46). This is not an attempt to deny or change holy writ. The fact of the matter is that the consensus of both liberal and conservative scholarship is that the English translation of "six hundred thousand" warriors cannot possibly be literally accurate.

Most importantly, it would make the Bible contradict itself, because in Deuteronomy 7:1 and 7, God states that the seven nations of Canaan were "more numerous and mightier" than Israel, who were "the fewest of all peoples." But in fact, during this time of the late Bronze Age and early Iron Age, there were less than one million inhabitants of Canaan.[1] That would make Israel more numerous and mightier by a figure of three times the whole of Canaan and as much as ten times the size of any singular people group. Secondly, if there were two and a half million Israelites, then the average Israelite mother would have had about fifty children each, another absurdity. Worse yet, for the peoples of Canaan to be more numerous and mightier than two or three million Israelites, there would have to be over twenty million Canaanites in the land. That is demonstrably false by archeological and historical evidence.[2] God performs miracles, not contradictions and absurdities.

I do not have the room to explain the details here, but I have included on the ChroniclesoftheNephilim.com website under the "Links" page, several articles that address possible interpretations of the numbers that would affirm the meaning of the Bible. Scholar David Fouts presents a strong case for the numbers being symbolic, a common technique used throughout the entire Bible. But I have included J.W. Wenham's thesis that the Hebrew word for thousand is *'lep*, which is a word that can mean military units of troops. Since Hebrew numbers were not numerical like ours, but words, the number "six hundred and three thousand" would actually translate as "six hundred and three military units" which

---

[1] John H Walton, *Zondervan Illustrated Bible Backgrounds Commentary* (Old Testament): Genesis, Exodus, Leviticus, Numbers, Deuteronomy, vol. 1 (Grand Rapids, MI: Zondervan, 2009), 344.

[2] David M. Fouts, "A Defense Of The Hyperbolic Interpretation Of Large Numbers In The Old Testament," *JETS* 40/3 (September 1997), 378.

would be more like six thousand troops in a population of about seventy thousand Israelites.

One last note of importance: The saga *Chronicles of the Nephilim* employs an ancient technique of changing names of both people and places from novel to novel and sometimes within the same novel. This peculiar technique was universally engaged in by all ancient Near Eastern writing including the Bible because in that world, names were not merely arbitrary sign references. Names reflected the essential purpose, meaning, or achievement of people or places. Thus, when people experienced significant changes in their lives, they might also change their name or the name of a location where it occurred. Or when one nation adopted another nation's deity, it would give it their own name.

Even the God of the Bible uses different names for himself in different instances to communicate his different attributes. While this is not familiar to modern readers and can cause difficulty in keeping all the names and identities straight, I have chosen to employ that peculiar technique as a way of incarnating the ancient worldview and mindset. So reader be warned to watch names carefully and expect them to be changing on you even when you are not looking.

In the interest of aiding the reader in managing the name changes in the series up to this point, and including *Joshua Valiant*, I have included the following charts that illustrate some of the more significant name changes.

	Creator	Zaqiel	Azazel	Gadreel	Gilgamesh
Enoch Primordial (Sumer)	Elohim	Utu	Inanna	—	—
Noah Primeval (Sumer)	Elohim, Yahweh	Utu	Inanna	—	—
Gilgamesh Immortal (Sumer)	Elohim	Shamash	Ishtar	Ninurta	Gilgamesh
Abraham Allegiant (Babylon)	El Shaddai	Shamash	Ishtar	Marduk	Nimrod
Abraham Allegiant (Canaan)	El Elyon	Chemosh	Ashtart	Ba'al	Amraphel
Joshua Valiant (Canaan)	Yahweh	Chemosh	Ashtart Ashtoreth	Ba'al	—
Divine attribute	Creator Almighty Most High	Sun god	Goddess of sex & war	God of vegetation & storm	A Nephilim

	Creator God	Nachash	Giant Clans	Sons of God	The World Tree
Other Names	Yahweh Elohim	The Serpent	Nephilim	Bene ha Elohim	Mother Earth Goddess
	Yahweh	The satan Adversary	Rephaim	Watchers	Great Goddess
	Elohim	Mastema	Emim	Gods	Gaia
	El Shaddai	A Seraphim	Caphtorim	Heavenly Host	
	Angel of Yahweh	Shining One	Zamzummim (Zuzim)	Divine Council	
	Son of Man	Accuser	Anakim	Shining Ones	
	El Elyon	Belial	Avvim	Holy Ones	
		Diablos	Horim	Anunnaki	

	True Heaven	Canaanite Pantheon	Mesopotamian Heavens and Earth
Hierarchy	Yahweh Elohim	El	Yahweh Elohim's throne
	Angel of Yahweh	Ba'al (rises to primacy)	The waters above the heavens
	Seraphim	Asherah (El's wife)	The firmament
	Cherubim	Anat (Ba'al's sister)	The heavens
	Sons of God "Watchers"	Ashtart	Earth
	Archangels	Dagon, Molech, Chemosh	The Abyss
	Angels		Pillars of the earth
			Sheol

Based on a true story.
And ancient traditions.

Deuteronomy 32:8-9

When the Most High gave to the nations their inheritance, when he divided mankind, he fixed the borders of the peoples according to the number of the sons of God. But the LORD's portion is his people, Jacob his allotted heritage.

Jubilees 15:31-32

(There are) many nations and many people, and they all belong to him, but over all of them he caused spirits to rule so that they might lead them astray from following him. But over Israel he did not cause any angel or spirit to rule because he alone is their ruler and he will protect them.

Deuteronomy 3:11

For only Og the king of Bashan was left of the remnant of the Rephaim. Behold, his bed was a bed of iron. Is it not in Rabbah of the Ammonites? Nine cubits was its length (13½ feet), and four cubits (6 feet) its breadth, according to the common cubit.

Numbers 21:27-29

Therefore the ballad singers say, "Come to Heshbon, let it be built; let the city of Sihon be established. Woe to you, O Moab! You are undone, O people of Chemosh! He has made his sons fugitives, and his daughters captives, to an Amorite king, Sihon.

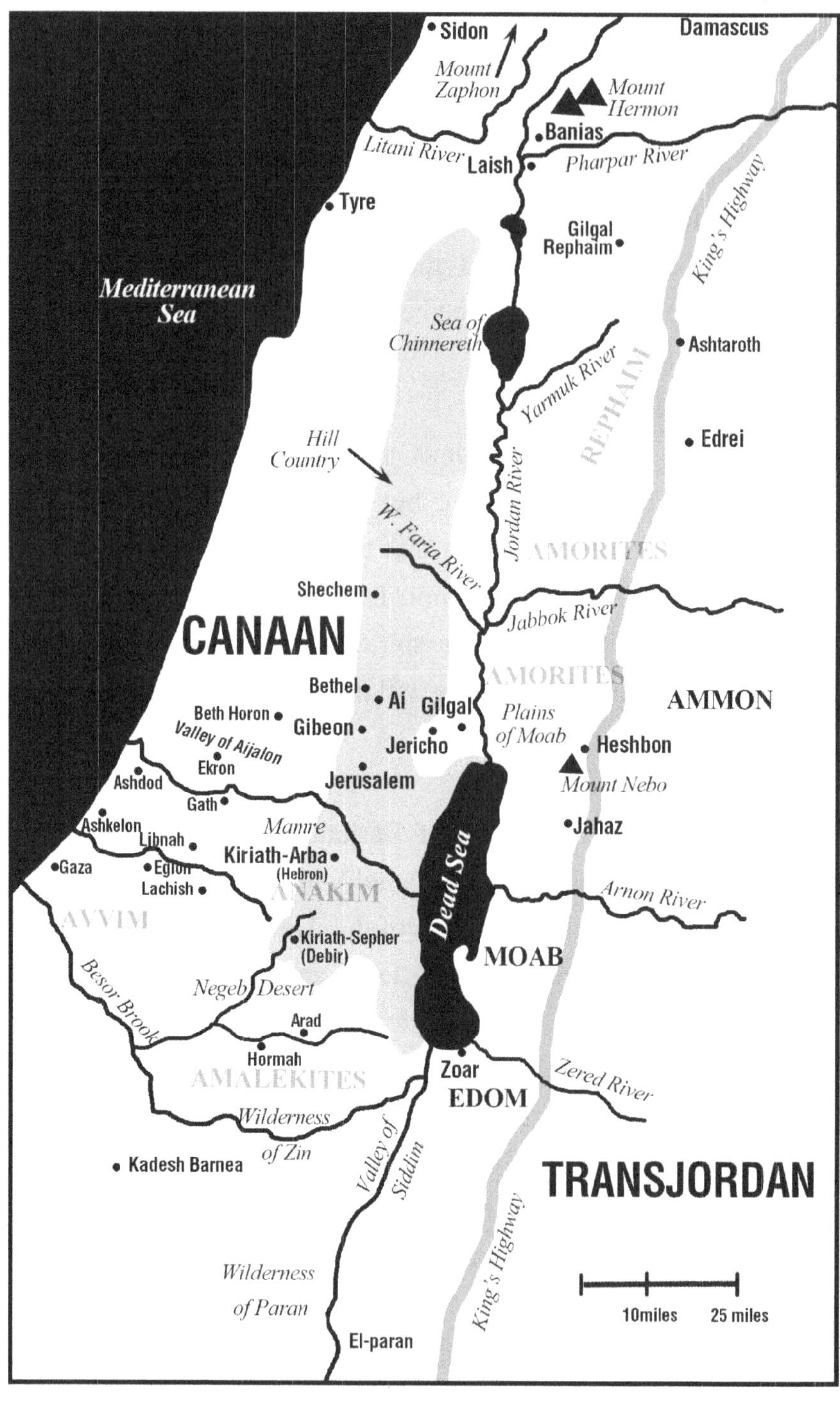

Sidon
Damascus
Mount Zaphon
Mount Hermon
Banias
Litani River
Laish
Pharpar River
Tyre
Gilgal Rephaim
King's Highway
Mediterranean Sea
Sea of Chinnereth
Ashtaroth
Yarmuk River
REPHAIM
Hill Country
Edrei
Jordan River
W. Faria River
AMORITES
Shechem
Jabbok River
CANAAN
AMORITES
Bethel
Ai
Gilgal
Plains of Moab
AMMON
Beth Horon
Gibeon
Valley of Aijalon
Jericho
Heshbon
Ekron
Ashdod
Jerusalem
Mount Nebo
Gath
Ashkelon
Mamre
Libnah
Jahaz
Gaza
Eglon
Kiriath-Arba
(Hebron)
Dead Sea
Lachish
ANAKIM
Arnon River
AVVIM
Kiriath-Sepher
(Debir)
MOAB
Besor Brook
Negeb Desert
Arad
Hormah
Zoar
Zered River
AMALEKITES
EDOM
Wilderness of Zin
Kadesh Barnea
Valley of Siddim
TRANSJORDAN
King's Highway
Wilderness of Paran
10miles
25 miles
El-paran

PROLOGUE

It was four hundred years after Abraham was promised the land of Canaan that his descendants, the children of Abraham, the Seed of Eve, left their bondage in exodus from Egypt to claim their promised allotment from Yahweh.

•••••

After four hundred years in the land of Canaan, the giant descendants of the Nephilim, the Seed of the Serpent, had spread out upon that land. The Jordan River ran north and south, splitting the country in half. The Anakim dominated the Cisjordan, which included the desert hills and valleys west of the Jordan River. The Rephaim controlled the Transjordan, which included the fertile hills and valleys east of that same river. They were both called by the generic term *Amorite*, and they worshipped the pantheon of Canaanite gods led by Ba'al the most high, Ashtart, goddess of sex and war, Molech of the underworld, and other patron deities of the region.

The land of Canaan was filled with abomination. The iniquity of the Amorites was complete.

CHAPTER 1

A trickle of blood dribbled out of Joshua ben Nun's nose. It did not flow down onto his chin, but rather up into his eyes and onto his forehead—because he was hanging upside down, along with his companion Caleb ben Jephunneh. Both of them had been beaten senseless and strung up in order to be skinned and eaten by a unit of ten giant Anakim warriors. The two had been ambushed when they were visiting the graves of their patriarchs, Abraham and Isaac, near the caves of Machpelah, just outside the oaks of Mamre in Canaan. Their horses had been taken from them.

And now they were arguing upside down.

"I told you we should not stop," hissed Joshua. "But you had to visit our forefather's resting place for your own sense of importance."

Caleb coughed back, "You are my truest friend, Joshua, but sometimes your arrogance is unbecoming."

"But I am right."

"Shut up, you two worms!" shouted the gruff nine-foot tall Anakim with a filet knife. "I cannot think straight."

"You never think straight," complained another nine-footer with a bandaged arm. He had been wounded in the fight with the two small humans. "I say we eat them, and move on. We are already late. And you know how angry Abi gets when we are late."

Abi was the shortened nickname for Abi-yamimu, their military general in the city of Kiriath-arba, just a few miles away. They were on first patrol for the evening, and they should have been back already.

Another one added, "He might sic Ahiman on us."

Ahiman was the right hand of Abi and he was the tallest and most fearsome Anakite in the land, the largest and mightiest of the Sons of Anak. The Anakim were the dominant force in Southern Canaan. They were a mighty clan of red and blonde haired fair-skinned giants whose ancestors were the primeval Nephilim from before the Great Flood. The name *Anak* was thought to mean "necklace," which was more a reference to their doubly long necks than the strings of gold and bones that they wore as attention-drawing jewelry. Because of their Nephilim ancestry they also had six fingers on each hand and six toes on each foot and grew to heights of eight to eleven feet tall. Ahiman was unusually large at fifteen feet.

"I will make it quick," said the one with the filet knife.

It would not take too long to skin and eat the captives. There were actually three of them. The third one was a mercenary from some unknown territory. He was unconscious. They would be a mere snack for a few of these towering warriors whose weight of four hundred to six hundred pounds required much daily meat to satisfy their hunger.

Most of the patrol sat at the fire warming up in the cold desert night.

The one with the filet knife raised it to start on Joshua.

But just as suddenly, a dagger flew through the air and lodged itself into the giant's bicep. He dropped his blade with a curse and clutched his wounded arm.

All ten of the warriors jerked their heads to see where the knife had come from.

Two Anakim warriors stepped into the firelight. The one that threw the knife was about ten feet tall and about seven hundred pounds. The other was a foot higher, heavier, and with a manicured beard. They both had the fair skin and blondish red hair of the Anakim, and the doubly long necks of bulging muscle. But these two were a higher caste. Their necklaces were more gold than bones. They were rulers.

"Lord Sheshai, lord Talmai!" blurted the captain of the unit.

They all stood up and gave their militia salute of submission to their overlords. It was a fisted straight right arm thrust forward with a fisted left arm at a perpendicular angle jutting into the elbow of the straight arm. It was their salute to power, the only thing they held sacred as worshippers of Ba'al, the most high god of storm and power in the pantheon.

The filet Anakim whimpered and groaned as he pulled the knife from his arm and sought to wrap the wound with a bandage.

Sheshai and Talmai were commanders of the armed forces for the hill country region. And they were brothers of Ahiman, the fierce one.

It was said of this mighty clan of Canaan, "Who can stand against the sons of Anak?" And of all these mighty giants, Ahiman was the most feared. He was twelve hundred pounds of brutal monstrosity. Because of this glorious reputation, the three brothers, Ahiman, Sheshai, and Talmai were often called by the honored name, "Sons of Arba," their original forefather.

The middle, Sheshai, was more of a politician, a cunning master of strategy and leadership. The youngest, Talmai, the one who threw the knife, was more aggressive and hot-tempered. He could explode with rage and everyone tried to avoid being the one to trigger it.

Sheshai walked up to the hanging captives. He leaned in close to look at Joshua, then Caleb. He sniffed them, and muttered in Akkadian, the shared language of the realm, "Egyptian clothing. But you are Semites. Habiru?"

Habiru was the Canaanite term used of wandering tribes of mercenaries and troublemaking nomads. Sheshai had heard that an entire nation of Habiru had escaped from slavery in Egypt last year. He and some of his Anakim brethren had joined a marauding party of Amalekites to invade Egypt and had encountered these Habiru in the desert. They seemed to use Egyptian magic that repelled the Amalekites, so Sheshai had never forgotten the incident. But it was a year ago and he had been in so many fights since then. These Habiru may have been the very ones that his own people were looking for. There was a blood feud between them that went back generations.

Sheshai noticed that Joshua was almost passed out because the blood had been rushing to his head. So he reached up and cut the rope hanging Joshua. He fell to the ground with a thud.

Joshua came to his senses. He noticed he was not far away from their pile of confiscated belongings, including their weapons.

"Who are you, little rodent?" asked Sheshai in Akkadian again. "Where do you come from? What tribe or people?"

But Joshua did not respond, so Sheshai repeated himself in Egyptian. It was one of the two dominant languages that everyone had to have some comprehension of or suffer economic disadvantage.

Joshua feigned semi-consciousness, strategizing how he could get to his knife in his pack to cut himself free. But his lashed feet and tied hands behind his back would not offer much in the way of opportunity.

Thank Yahweh, he thought. The warrior did not recognize Joshua. But Joshua had recognized him. Sheshai was the Anakim leader with the Amalekite forces that attacked the wandering Hebrews at Rephidim in Midian. Joshua remembered that fight. He remembered this warrior pompously calling out his own name to Joshua before attempting to kill him. If it hadn't been for Caleb stopping the giant, Joshua might not be here right now—ready to die again at the monster's hands.

Sheshai looked at the unconscious mercenary. He said to the Captain, "Strange armor. I have not seen this before. What is this one?"

The Captain replied, "We caught him by the Oaks of Mamre shortly after the Habiru. A loner. He was not a very skilled fighter."

But Sheshai stared at the creature with curiosity and said, "He could be a Hurrian or Hittite scout from Syria. I wish these Egyptians and Syrians would stop using our land as a playground for their control."

Sheshai lifted the mercenary's head. He was a rather handsome dark haired muscular fellow. It seemed odd to Sheshai. But it did not matter because the mercenary was not breathing.

"You idiots," grumbled Sheshai. "This one is dead."

He cut the rope and the dead mercenary dropped to the ground.

"You have let them hang too long."

He reached over and cut down Caleb's rope as well. Caleb twisted and landed on his back on the ground with a grunt.

Talmai said, "Hurry up, Sheshai. I want to get back."

Sheshai said, "Do not eat them. Bring them to King Hoham. I have a feeling these two Habiru may be what we have been looking for."

Joshua gulped. He knew that these Sons of Anak were looking for the Sons of Abraham because he had heard their captors tell their story about Abraham and their own forefather, King Arba, the father of Anak. It was not a positive tale. He knew that if they were taken to King Hoham in Kiriath-arba, they would experience a fate worse than being eaten. Then these brutish monsters would attack the entire nation of Israel hiding out in the Negeb desert, just south of their city.

They could not let that happen.

But it was about to.

Sheshai walked back to his brother and they prepared to leave. He barked to the captain, "Get your lazy rear ends up and back to the city. And keep the captives alive!"

"Yes, sir!" saluted the captain.

All the soldiers watched Sheshai and Talmai disappear into the darkness and gave one another looks of a close call with trouble.

"You heard the Commander! Get moving!"

Joshua heard one the soldiers ask, "Where is Sheshai going?"

The captain answered, "He is gathering forces to invade Egypt."

But when the captain looked back at where the prisoners were, he noticed that the dead one was no longer on the ground. And the other two Habiru were now standing, no longer tied up, but holding shield and sickle sword in hand.

Someone had cut them loose when everyone's attention had been turned.

That someone was the mercenary who had only been feigning death, looking for the right moment to pull his hidden knife and cut himself and the others free. He was not a chance encounter at Mamre. The only reason he "was not a very skilled fighter" when they captured him, as the soldier had said, was because he was pretending to be, in order to rescue the two Habiru.

But the mercenary was nowhere to be seen. He had disappeared.

And that was only the beginning of the surprises about to overwhelm this unit of Anakim.

The second surprise was two successive arrows piercing the captain and his closest commander.

Joshua dropped his composite bow and drew his sword.

But before the bodies hit the ground, the mercenary came out of the side bushes, outside the visual focus of the giants, and cut a swath through the middle of the soldiers before they knew what was happening.

He slashed, cut and thrust his way to the other side. He had dropped four of them before the others had their weapons up and ready to fight.

Joshua and Caleb gave each other a surprised glance. This fellow was impressive.

Six giants down, four to go, against the three humans. But with their skills, it was not good odds for the giants.

The mercenary picked up a fallen shield just in time to protect himself for the downswing of an Anakite's battle axe. The hit sent a jarring shudder through his entire body and pushed him to his knees. This monster was big, maybe ten feet tall.

Still, the Anakite was no match for the mercenary with preternatural skills.

The mercenary dropped the shield and dove through the giant's long legs. The soldier's long neck strained to see where he landed. But it was too late, as his femur artery gushed the last of his life out onto the ground.

Joshua and Caleb engaged the enemy. Joshua's bronze sickle sword was no match for the heavy giant swords made of a much stronger metal than he had ever seen before. He would have to get himself one of them.

Caleb's sword however, was entirely adequate to the task. It was in fact a special heavenly weapon passed down through his tribe from ancient descendants. It was a whip-like sword, ten feet long. Its blade was made of an unknown heavenly metal that was both flexible like a whip, and razor sharp strong and unbreakable. It had been forged in angelic realms and used by his ancestor, Lamech ben Methuselah, the father of Noah.

Lamech had named it "Rahab" because its serpentine nature reminded him of the sea dragon of chaos who went by the same name. And in the hands of Caleb, it was a very destructive sea dragon with extremely accurate aim.

Gabriel the archangel had visited Caleb in the past and taught him how to use the sword in the special angelic fighting style called "Way of the Karabu." Now at the age of 40, he did not so much fight as he did dance, moving in and out of his opponents, snapping Rahab like a dancer waving a long twirling ribbon—of death.

He cut off the head of a giant and the sword arm of another before they could even get within striking distance.

Joshua, on the other hand was Caleb's opposite in style. He was brute force and fury wrapped up inside rage. Once his instincts kicked into survival mode, Joshua was a non-stop flurry of rapid strikes, slashes, and stabs that few warriors could keep up with, let alone the slow giant he pummeled with ferocity, who succumbed to exhaustion.

At age 20, Joshua had the strength and stamina of a giant wound tight into his six foot frame. Although tall for his own people, his deceptively small appearance to these giants was an added advantage of surprise.

Unfortunately, Joshua was to receive the last surprise of the evening, as the one-armed Anakim, not yet dead, knelt up to land a deathblow on Joshua behind his back with his iron blade.

Actually, it was the next to last surprise, because before he could land it, a blur flew through the air and knocked the giant sideways to the ground with a last gasp.

It was the mercenary, who promptly cut off the monster's head from his long muscular neck.

"Whew," said the mercenary. "That was close. I almost had a lot of explaining to do to Yahweh."

The two Israelites stood catching their breaths, looking at their benefactor with astonishment.

"Are you—mal'akim?" asked Caleb. It meant, "angel," one of Yahweh's heavenly host, and he knew their presence ever since his visits from Gabriel years ago.

"I am Mikael the archangel, prince of Israel, sent to watch over and protect Yahweh's people."

Joshua thought to himself that this must mean he was destined for a higher purpose in Yahweh's plan if this guardian angel of Israel was watching over him. Joshua had hoped and prayed for such an honor. Being the assistant of Moses had fed that hope in his heart, handpicked by the ruler of Israel himself. And now that hope was growing stronger.

He had no idea just how wrong he was.

Mikael said, "You had better hurry and catch up with the other spies. They are almost back to the camp in the Negeb."

Joshua bent down and picked up a sword and scabbard from one of the smaller warriors. He smiled and wrapped it onto his horse.

"What about these soldiers?" asked Caleb. "If those commanders, Seshai and Talmai, find them, they will know for sure that we are the ones whom they seek. They might chase us all the way back to our camp."

"Do not worry," said Mikael. "Be strong and courageous. I will bury them. You just get moving."

Joshua said, "What about you?"

"Oh, do not worry about me," said Mikael. "You will be seeing plenty of me in the future. Now, go."

They went.

CHAPTER 2

Moses stood before the assembled congregation of Israel's seventy elders at the entrance to the Tent of Meeting. He was well over eighty years old and was weary with the burden of this nation of ingrates. They had seen Yahweh crush the power of Pharaoh and the Egyptian gods beneath the might of his strong right arm. The ten plagues, the parting waters of Yam Suph, and the drowning of Pharaoh's minions in those waters were still fresh in their memories. As was the thunder and lightning upon Mount Sinai. A pillar of cloud by day and a pillar of fire by night had led them out of Egypt and through the desert, and they had had their bellies filled by heavenly manna and miraculous quail.

Now, they stood poised on the edge of Canaan that Yahweh himself had promised to give them, and these spoiled selfish juveniles were grumbling and complaining about how much better things were in Egypt. Even Moses' sister, the prophetess Miriam, and his brother, the high priest Aaron, had challenged his leadership of the nation in the recent past.

They had always been bitter and jealous that Moses had married the Kushite woman Zipporah outside of the tribes of Israel. And they began a murmuring campaign, accusing Moses of being like Pharaoh in claiming God's special authority. Did not Yahweh also speak through the prophetess and the high priest?

The band of twelve prophets, of which Miriam was a part, had also supported her and Aaron. In the shadow of Moses, the prophets were not as elevated in their status, but they were conduits through which Yahweh sometimes spoke.

In this case, he certainly did not.

For their rebellious spirit, Yahweh gave Miriam temporary leprosy and then healed it, which scared the sin out of them both and put them back in their place.

But that was not even the last of it. Being slaves for four hundred years in Egypt had corrupted the soul of the people. They had adopted many of the very gods that Yahweh had condemned and judged. They had even made a golden calf at the foot of Mount Sinai, the very mountain of God! It would be a long and arduous task to purge the idols engraved on the hearts of this nation. He wondered if it was even possible to do so.

Moses loved his people, but they wore his patience down.

They were encamped in the desert of Kadesh just south of their Promised Land. They had a fighting force of about sixty thousand men for a nation of close to two hundred thousand people, and thousands of a mixed multitude.

Moses had sent out an elite scouting force of twelve spies, one chief from each tribe, to search out the land and bring back a report. They had taken forty days to traverse the length of Canaan and reconnoiter any intelligence they could to help their military strategy. They were supposed to find out how many people were in the land, what their fighting strength was, and whether they dwelt in villages or strongholds, as well as the fertility and produce of the land itself.

The spies had returned.

They stood before Moses and the elders and judges to give their report—more accurately; ten of the twelve spies were there. Joshua and Caleb had not yet returned because they were making a pilgrimage visit to the tomb of Abraham their ancestor in Machpelah. They were supposed to catch up with the others, but for some reason had been delayed.

For some reason.

Moses wore a veil over his face, as he always did after talking with Yahweh face to face. This was because something had happened to Moses' body when he was on Mount Sinai. When he came down from the mountain carrying the tablets of law, his skin shone with bronze light much like the *Bene ha Elohim*, or Sons of God. It was as if being so close to the presence of Yahweh had transfigured his body to that of a Shining One. It was not a complete transformation because it would fade with time. But whenever he re-entered the presence, his skin would glow again so bright that the Israelites could barely look at him and were frightened. So Moses put a veil over his face to calm their fears. Whenever he would go into the Tent of Meeting before Yahweh, he would remove the veil, and then he would stand before the congregation with shining face and tell all Israel what Yahweh had commanded, whereupon he would return the veil over his face.

Whenever his emotions ran strong, from joy or anger, the brightness would increase in intensity. He was so angry with these wretched ingrates currently that he kept the veil on to protect them from the blinding brilliance.

Ammiel from the tribe of Dan was the spokesman for the group. He was sweating nervously under Moses' expectant gaze.

Moses could see a frightened look on all their faces.

Ammiel's words were hesitant. "We traveled the length of the land of Canaan, from Bashan in the north all the way down to the Negeb. The Amalekites dwell in the land of the Negeb. The Hittites, Jebusites, and Amorites dwell in the hill country, and the Canaanites dwell by the sea."

"What of the Girgashites, Perizzites, and Hivites?" said Moses. These were the rest of the Canaanite nations that Yahweh had promised he would drive out before the Israelites. They were to make no covenant with these pagan peoples, avoid intermarrying with them, and show them no mercy, devoting them to complete destruction, lest they turn away Israel from following Yahweh to serve evil gods.

Ammiel replied, "They are spread throughout the countryside in various territories."

"And what of the fertility of the land?"

"It is true, as you told us, the land is rich and abundant, and flows with milk and honey."

"So where is the sample of produce you were to bring back? The fruit of the land."

Ammiel and the others looked at one another fearfully.

Moses snapped, "Speak up."

Ammiel took a deep breath before confessing. "My lord, Moses, we were unable to procure any sample produce." He paused again and swallowed. "Because we feared for our lives and could not afford the encumbrance."

Now, the seventy elders looked at one another and whispered amongst themselves at the scandal.

Ammiel continued, "The people we saw who dwell in the land are stronger than we are. They live in fortified cities with walls that reach up to heaven."

"Yahweh did not say it was going to be easy, Ammiel," said Moses. "Our years of being Egypt's sentry forces in Goshen has prepared us for just such a war."

"Not for this kind of war, my lord," Ammiel interjected.

"We saw the Nephilim."

A hush of silence swept over the entire congregation.

Moses gulped.

The Israelites were familiar with the gossip and legends about the Nephilim. And they had already had one encounter with some of them as they had battled the Amalekites in the wilderness at Rephidim. But now they were hearing eyewitnesses confirm their greatest fears. It was worse.

The Nephilim were the legendary giant offspring of the fallen Watcher gods, also called Sons of God, who mated with the daughters of men before the great Flood. In the days of Jared, two hundred of these rebels from Yahweh's heavenly host came to earth on Mount Hermon in Canaan. They revealed to mankind all kinds of sorceries and evil secrets. They sought to draw worship away from the Creator by posing as gods over the people.

And they engaged in a nefarious plot to corrupt creation through the elimination of the distinctions of the created order—unholy cross-breeding. They violated the separation of kinds, by creating hybrids of male and female, man and animal, and the most vile of all: human and divine. These were the Nephilim, the unholy hybrid offspring of human and divine seed, the giant gibborim warriors of old. These were the seedline of the Serpent. The spies had seen the giant clans that were the descendants of those original Nephilim.

This violence of humanity and divinity brought down the waters of the Deluge in judgment. The Watchers, had been bound into the earth to await their judgment.

But not all of them.

And their corruption was passed through one of the sons of Noah down through history until this very day.

Moses had heard that King Chedorlaomer and a coalition of Mesopotamian kings had wiped out most of the Nephilim descendants in the time of their father Abraham. But during his forty years in the Arabian desert with the Midianites, he learned that there was a surviving remnant of these giants thriving in Canaan, but he did not know just how many.

Ammiel's throaty voice shattered Moses' thoughtful optimism.

"Canaan is crawling with giants. They are of great height, and we were like grasshoppers before them. The land devours its inhabitants."

Hushed whispering broke out again through the assembly.

Moses' thoughtful pause made them uncomfortable.

And then he said, "What is their organization?"

Ammiel nodded to Shammua from the tribe of Reuben. He stepped forward with Geuel from the tribe of Gad, and Gaddi from the half-tribe of Manasseh.

"My lord, we scouted the northernmost regions," said Shammua. "We found the Transjordan ruled by King Og of Bashan. Og is the mightiest and last of the Rephaim, the most ancient of giant rulers."

"Describe these Rephaim," said Moses.

"They reach heights of ten and twelve feet, and they are heinous looking. Their bodies are without hair, their skin is pale grey, and they have large elongated skulls. They have two rows of teeth in their jaws, six fingers on each hand, and six toes on each foot. It is said King Og sleeps on a bed of iron fourteen feet long and six feet wide."

That would make Og ten to eleven feet tall.

A shiver went down Moses' spine. A shiver went down everyone's spine who was listening.

"Human sacrifice is ubiquitous," he continued. "It is unthinkable that many parents make their children to pass through the fires of Molech, god of the underworld."

Moses' stomach turned. He felt nauseous. Groans of horror swept through the crowd.

"But that is not all," added Gaddi. "Serpent worship is widespread. There is talk of snake clans that engage in unspeakable abominations between human and reptile. And I personally witnessed a tribe led by satyrs at Panias in the foothills of Mount Hermon. These goat demons lead the hairy descendants of Esau into depraved atrocities. Their tribe is called the Seirim."

Satyrs were chimeric creatures said to have the upper torso of a human and the lower legs of a hairy goat.

Just when Moses thought it could not get worse, three other spies, Palti, Gaddiel, and Igal, stepped forward. Palti spoke for them.

"We surveyed the hill country and there we found the Anakim, who come from the Nephilim. The sons of Anak."

Moses had heard of the Anakim. He knew they had ties that went back to the Israelites' forefather Abraham.

"What are they like?"

"They are the fiercest among the giants in the land. They reside mostly in the southern region. They have extra-long muscular necks with pale skin and blond or reddish hair. They also have the extra digits on their hands and feet. They worship Ba'al the storm god and they are cannibals. No one can stand before them. Three brothers called the Sons of Arba are famous in the region for their ferocity. Ahiman, Sheshai, and Talmai. Ahiman is legendary. No one is larger or mightier than he. It is said he is twenty feet tall and two thousand pounds." The exaggeration that gossip brought often added many feet to height and many pounds to weight. But how much, who could know?

Moses noticed that word must have spread through the camp because common Israelites were assembling around the meeting place to listen in on the report. By the end of this exchange, their numbers were large—and they were restless.

Ammiel stood forward again and announced, "It does not seem right to me that Yahweh would claim to lead us into such a lion's den of fierce savagery."

Just before the tension broke, Joshua's voice boomed through the camp, "Sons of Israel, be strong and courageous!"

Joshua and Caleb materialized out of the darkness carrying a large pole between them. On the pole was a bunch of grapes so large it dwarfed the two of them. It looked like it was the fruit of the gods.

"I beg your indulgence to forgive our tardiness, lord Moses. But Caleb and I were a bit delayed."

Moses nodded with curiosity.

Joshua added, "This bunch of grapes we were able to bring from the valley of Eshcol. As you can see, the fruit of the land is magnificent."

Ammiel interrupted, "Yes, it is food of the Anakim, before whom no man can stand!"

And now the crowd was unruly. A heckler yelled out, "Why has Yahweh brought us into this land only to fall by the sword?"

Another added, "Our wives and children will become food for giants!"

The crowd murmured in agreement.

Caleb's soul was broken for his people. He yelled in reply, "Trust in Yahweh! We are able to overcome these idolaters and occupy our inheritance!"

But a louder heckler yelled back, "We are able to find a leader to lead us back to Egypt!"

The crowd went wild.

Moses and Aaron fell on their faces and prayed to Yahweh. Joshua and Caleb began to tear their clothes in symbolic expression of their mourning for the people's disloyalty to their god.

The decibel level rose to a pitch of fevered excitement.

But then suddenly, the sound of a shofar horn penetrated the cacophony. Everyone quieted down.

Caleb lowered the horn he had grabbed from a priest. His voice cut through the din with resounding clarity.

"PEOPLE OF ISRAEL!"

It was like Yahweh had amplified his voice.

The assembly got even quieter.

He continued, "The land which we spied out is an exceedingly good land! Yahweh will bring us into the land and give it to us just as he promised! Do not fear these Canaanite abominations! Yahweh is with us!"

Joshua was beaming with inspiration listening to his fellow warrior. It impressed him that this Kenizzite, this outsider who was not even an Israelite of blood, had more faith than those who were natural born.

Joshua joined in on Caleb's exhortation, "Do not rebel against Yahweh! We are a chosen people! We will break down their altars and dash into pieces their idols and burn their graven images! But if we rebel and do not obey his commandments, we will surely be destroyed!"

In response, those without faith began to pick up stones.

Someone shouted, "We are not rebels!"

Another shouted, "Stone them!"

Moses was weeping on the ground.

But before anyone could make a move, the Shekinah glory, a pillar of fire embodying Yahweh's presence, appeared before the Tent of Meeting. Its twirling flames went up into the sky a hundred feet or more. It looked like a tight whirlwind of burning energy, with the sound of a low roar. It was frightening, awesome.

The masses went silent.

Moses quickly got up and followed the glory into the holy place before the stunned crowd. Joshua followed him.

With longing in his heart, Caleb watched Joshua disappear into the tent. Moses chose Joshua to be his assistant. This meant he was privileged to see the inner beauty of the tabernacle in all its detail, and at times even found himself close to Moses' and Yahweh's presence.

Caleb longed for this kind of experience with all his being. The tabernacle was the garden of Yahweh's presence among his people. The spirit-filled artist Bezalel and his craftsmen had built it according to Yahweh's own pattern revealed from heaven. Caleb was fascinated by its symbolic beauty on every level, from the brazen altar and bronze laver outside, to the Tent of Meeting inside, with its table of showbread and golden lampstand, to the unseen holy of holies, with images of cherubim guarding the sacred Ark of the Covenant. It filled Caleb with wonder and awe.

Only the Levite priests were allowed in the cordoned off area. But the tabernacle was a portable temple that they brought with them on their long desert journey and set up at every encampment. So Caleb would take pains to be there when the priests were setting up, just so he could get glimpses of the beautiful tools and adornments before they were all curtained off to the public.

The tabernacle was the focal point of the Israelite community and life. As such, it was placed in the center of their camp, with all the twelve tribes arranged around it like a protective shield. There they engaged in the multitude of sacrifices required by Yahweh to atone for the sins of the people as they found their way to the Promised Land.

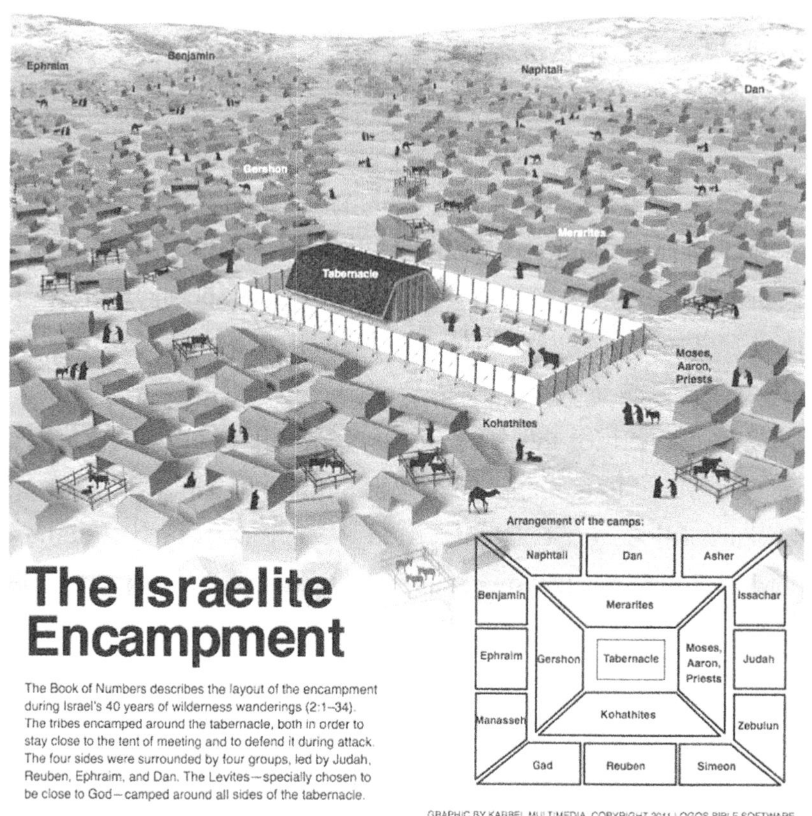

It was a painful irony that now Caleb stood before that tabernacle with the people of Israel congregated like a mob in the aisles and among the tents on the eastern side. They were animated by resentful and ungrateful disbelief of their own God.

But it was not the first time he had seen this kind of rebellion. And he suspected it would not be the last.

Inside the Tent of Meeting, Joshua laid prostrate on the ground near the entrance. He listened to the unveiled Moses arguing with Yahweh who spoke from the midst of the Shekinah cloud. He had envied Moses' station and direct communication with Yahweh for so long. He even fantasized about what it would be like to engage in such face-to-face interaction with the Creator.

Even from his distance, Joshua could see enough of the Shekinah to tremble with awe. It had now become a cloud, but it was more than a cloud. It was like a curtain hiding a glory so pure and bright that should it be seen in its fullness, no man could stand before it. One's eyes would burn out of their sockets. When he saw the cloud, his knees would buckle, and he could not defeat the urge to fall on his face to the ground.

It was the very presence of the holy.

And that holiness was now amplified with anger.

"How long will this people despise me?" said Yahweh. "In spite of all the signs and wonders, they still refuse to believe me. I will smite them with pestilence. I will disinherit them, and make you into an even greater nation."

"I pray you reconsider your wrath," said Moses. "Would that not give you a poor reputation among the nations and their allotted gods? After all, Egypt will hear about it and that might lessen the impact of all you did to them."

Joshua could not believe the boldness and audacity of Moses.

"Moreover, if you destroy this people, then the tribes of Canaan whom you seek to dispossess will tell themselves that all your glory is mere pompous bragging because you could not bring this nation into the land which you allotted to them as their inheritance."

Joshua was waiting for the strike of lightning, for Moses to be burnt to a cinder crisp.

"Adonai my lord, you are longsuffering and merciful and just. I beg you do not treat this people as they deserve, but forgive their sin and find another way to maintain the glory of your name among the peoples."

There was a long moment of silence. Joshua looked up, thinking Moses may have been stone-deaf or even stone dead. But he was not.

Yahweh finally spoke, "I have pardoned them according to your word."

It was amazing to Joshua. The almighty God, El Shaddai, Most High possessor of the heavens and the earth, Yahweh Elohim, the great I Am, just listened to the words of a mere mortal and changed his mind. Was that even possible? Could the living God be so intimate with someone that he would change his course of action on their behalf?

And then he heard Yahweh's decision and could not believe his ears.

When Moses and Joshua came out of the Tent of Meeting, Caleb was waiting for them at the tabernacle entrance like a loyal dog at the threshold of his master. He squinted in the brightness of his master's shining who remained unveiled.

The rest of the seventy elders perked up. Many of the congregation had already given up and gone to bed for the evening. The other ten spies awaited the decision as leaders of their tribes.

Moses looked sober as he stood before the congregation. Caleb watched Joshua and he knew this was not good.

"Sons of Israel!" Moses spoke with a strong voice. "Hear now the word of Yahweh! Tomorrow we will set out for the wilderness by way of Yam Suph."

The elders looked askance at one another. That did not make any sense. Did Yahweh now agree with the spies? Were the giants of Canaan too mighty of warriors to try to take the land after all?

Moses continued, "'As I live,' declares Yahweh, 'I have heard the grumblings of my people, Israel, who have put me to the test ten times and have not obeyed my voice.'"

Caleb trembled. He did not know what was coming, but he feared it. Moses was particularly bright as a star now.

"'I have determined, that of all of you listed in the census of Israel, not one of you older than the age of twenty, shall come into the land that I swore to your fathers. Except Caleb son of Jephunneh and Joshua son of Nun.'"

Everyone in the congregation stirred and whispered among themselves in shock.

Caleb glanced at Joshua, who returned his look with a knowing humility.

Caleb was grateful that his younger brother Othniel was only fifteen years old, and would escape the judgment.

Moses concluded, "They alone shall live to see the fulfillment of my promise, along with your young ones. But as for you, your corpses shall fall in the wilderness. This nation will wander in the desert for forty years, and your children will suffer for your faithlessness, until the last of your rotting carcasses shall fall in the dust of death."

Funny, how at this moment, the thing that entered into Caleb's mind was the beautiful symmetry of the punishment fitting the crime. One year for every day. Forty years of wilderness misery for the forty days they spied out the land in unbelief.

Even in judgment, Yahweh maintained a symbolic beauty.

The congregation and elders however did not consider it so beautiful a symbol. Some of them called out to Moses to reconsider as he turned and left them, veiling himself as if to close off the glory of God from them.

But Yahweh's full conclusion was not yet realized until the next morning when it was discovered that, with the exception of Joshua and Caleb, all of the spies who had given a bad report of the land to Moses had been stricken with a plague. They suffered excruciating pain, began to bleed from every orifice of their bodies until they vomited up blood, and died in piles of their own excrement and urine.

Within a week, they were all dead.

But the evening of jarring events was not yet over for Moses. Joshua had requested a private meeting with Moses and Caleb to share one piece of intelligence they had told no one else.

Joshua and Caleb arrived at Moses' tent late in the evening when everyone was asleep. Moses' shining had died down and he was now unveiled. They gathered around a small fire outside the tent and spoke in hushed whispers.

As usual, Joshua led the discussion. "We did not tell you that when we visited the burial cave of Abraham and Isaac, we were captured by a pack of ten Anakim from the hill country."

Moses' eyebrows arched with curiosity. "How did you escape?"

"I will explain that in a moment. But while we were in their grasp, we recognized one of them. He was one of the Anakim leaders we encountered with the Amalekites at Rephidim." We heard them recounting a narrative of their ancient descendants around the campfire. We could tell it was their sacred story that motivated them and gave meaning and purpose to their clan."

Moses had an idea of how bad this was going to be.

Joshua continued, "They spoke of their ancestor King Arba and our forefather Abraham."

Moses interrupted, "Did they know you were sons of Abraham?"

"No," said Caleb. "They were too busy contemplating whether to eat us or not.

Moses said, "What was their sacred story?"

"Well," said Joshua, "they spoke about how King Arba and his queen had first met Abraham and Sarah, our forebears over four hundred years ago."

Moses knew about the time Abraham spent in Canaan from the sources he was using to write a history of Israel and Yahweh's interactions.

"They spoke about how Abraham had moved to the Oaks of Mamre just outside of Kiriath-arba, and that when he first met King Arba, Abraham lusted after Arba's queen. But when Arba would not give her to Abraham, Abraham raped the queen, and killed her and Arba and the entire tribe—and cannibalized them.

But the queen was already pregnant with a child, so when she was buried in the ground, the child burst out of her body like a powerful cedar tree and grew to be the most powerful giant in the land. That child was named Anak. It is a legend of madness full of exaggerations, half-truths, and complete lies."

Moses mused, "But it is their sacred story. To understand our enemy, we must understand their story."

It became clear to Moses. This was their legend of how their people, the Sons of Anak, had originated: through the oppression of Abraham. A complete inversion of the truth.

Joshua finished, "Anak had heard that Abraham's children had gone to Egypt. A sorceress had foretold that the sons of Abraham would return one day, and in that day, the sons of Anak would have their revenge because they would slaughter the sons of Abraham. They also believe that we sons of Abraham worship an invisible mountain demon called El Sheddim, who flooded the earth in ancient days because he was jealous of mankind's ability to be like god, and angry with the Serpent for making man wise. The Anakim now worship Ba'al the storm god of Canaan, and the Serpent."

It was all too much for Moses. This story, the opposite of what actually happened, was the empowering mythos of the Anakim that drove them to seek out the seed of Abraham in order to wipe them from the face of the earth. It was amazing how just enough small details could have a ring of authenticity around which were built lies of perdition to justify monstrous atrocities.

"So how did you escape?" asked Moses.

Caleb now jumped in. "We were about to be eaten, but an archangel named Mikael aided us. Together we slaughtered the giants and buried their bodies before returning here. Mikael had told us that he was the Prince of Israel, and that he had great plans for Joshua."

Moses knew Mikael from his encounter with him in Egypt many years ago. He knew that the guardian angel's presence signaled danger for Israel.

Moses said with somber finality, "So these Anakim are the mightiest inhabitants of the land of Canaan whose sole purpose for living is to wreak vengeance on Israel for their blood feud against Abraham."

Joshua and Caleb nodded.

Moses wondered what forty years of delay would bring to the claim on their inheritance of Canaan. Would the Anakim find out about them and hunt them down in the wilderness? Would Israel even make it through the forty years? Would they be able to build a force strong enough to overcome the Anakim and the other Seed of the Serpent that now held the land in an iron grip of idol worship?

Forty years was a long time to wait. But hopefully, it was also a long time to prepare.

CHAPTER 3

Mount Hermon was a cluster of ranges in the southern part of the Sirion Mountains in the northern reaches of Canaan in the land of Bashan. Hermon was legendary for being the sacred site of the assembly of the Watcher gods who came down from heaven in the days before the Flood. From here, they planned and executed the Gigantomachy and the Titanomachy, both giant uprisings that found their apex in the War on Eden. That war was foiled by Yahweh's forces in the days of Enoch, and Eden was lost forever under layers of volcanic ash.

It was also at Hermon where the gods hatched their plan to corrupt the human race with the violation of the sacred boundaries of creation. Their diabolical schemes led to the violent corruption of all mankind and Yahweh defeated their abominations with the Deluge.

But even after the floodwaters receded, Hermon maintained its identity as the epicenter of spiritual rebellion in the cosmos. One would think Yahweh would send his own forces to besiege that fortress of evil and put an end to it once and for all.

But Yahweh had his own plans that no one knew or understood. And he worked out his will in no way subject to ignorant human wishes.

Several miles south of the location of the divine assembly, at the foot of the mountain range was an area called Panias. It was the home of the Seirim, an Edomite tribe of hairy wild born men, distant descendants of Esau. They lived in a city of caves cut from the red rock cliffs to appear as faux architectural homes. These were not unlike the Thamudi fortresses in the Arabian Desert, but with much less sophistication of design. The building caves were like a watch guard over a holy grotto from which the spring waters of the Jordan River came forth.

In the grotto was a shrine to the patron deity, one of the distant ancient ones from primeval days. The Seirim were ruled by an elite priesthood of satyrs, chimeric creatures of upper-half man and lower-half goat.

It was a satyr named Izbaxl that led twelve-year old Arisha of Panias through the forested valley some distance from the village. As firstborn daughter of a humble farmer, Arisha was dedicated to the service of the sacred cult of the Seirim. Though she would not be of age until she was fourteen, Izbaxl had taken a special liking to the young girl and sought to nurture her growth and understanding of the world.

For her part, Arisha was an observant and curious little girl. As they moved through the forest, she would stop at some beautiful flower, pick it, and give it to Izbaxl, who would take it with a smile and sniff it with pleasure before eating it. She liked the hairy goat-man from the small horns on his curly-haired head down to his cloven-hoofed feet. He was so cute. She thought of him as a big cuddly pet with his soft furry legs, bare strong chest, and musty body odor.

But despite this animal-like gruffness, he was so sensitive to the world around him. Satyrs were gods of nature and revelry. He helped her to see, smell, and taste the beauty of her environment like no one else. They would skip through prairies of long grass together, splash in the waters of rivers, play with the curious insects and rodents of the forest, and giggle about silly things.

But he also taught her all about the ways of nature. How to differentiate between poisonous and edible plants and roots, how different animals lived and hunted, how to avoid being prey for the predators and to live in tune with her environment.

Arisha considered Izbaxl to be more of a father to her than her own father, who had no life left in him, working the fields and sleeping the evening away.

Her mother had seemed to distance herself from Arisha, and she did not know why. She would give more attention to Arisha's two brothers and two sisters than she ever gave to Arisha. It hurt her, but she still loved her family dearly and sought to make her mother happier so that she would love Arisha more.

But her family was so weighed down by the difficulties of life that it seemed almost impossible to make them smile. She promised to herself that one day she would become the highest priestess of the cult so that she could take care of her family and make them happy.

But for now, Izbaxl made her happy as they raced through the trees playing tag, laughing and dodging one another.

They stopped to catch their breath.

"How much farther is it?" asked Arisha.

"Just outside the forest," he said, "and around the bend."

"Tell me more about Gaia," she said. "Since this is my first time, do I have to do anything?"

"No, silly," he said. "I told you, this is just your introduction to the Mother Earth Goddess and her guardians. You get to watch and learn."

They were making her first pilgrimage to Gaia. Everyone in the surrounding area of the Sirion mountain range and Bashan were obligated to make a yearly pilgrimage to pay homage to the earth goddess. But Izbaxl avoided telling her the details of what happened there. She would have to see for herself.

He had only told her that Gaia was the heart and soul of the earth. That all the trees and mountains, the lakes and oceans, and all the animals of the earth, and every living thing were united in Gaia's heartbeat and breath. He said that when men cut down forests to build their cities, and killed all the animals to eat their flesh, that Mother Earth would bleed and weep. That was why the Seirim carved their homes out of the rock instead of using wood from killing the trees, and it was why they only ate vegetables and deplored the cooking and eating of animals as murder and cannibalism.

Izbaxl stopped near a patch of mushrooms. They were shiny brown and compact. They reminded Arisha of little families with larger and smaller ones congregated together in little groups. Izbaxl plucked one and handed it to her.

"Eat."

She had never seen this kind before. She knew there were some that were dangerous, but she trusted Izbaxl. He would never hurt her.

"It will not taste good. But it will relax you. It will prepare you for your experience."

She took a bite. He was right. It was pungent and bitter. The flavor reminded her of the smell of horse excrement. She gagged. Izbaxl chuckled.

"Trust me, little flower."

She trusted him and swallowed the rest whole so as to avoid the linger of that disgusting flavor.

Within a few minutes she felt lightheaded and dizzy. Izbaxl smiled at her and waved her along.

He pulled out his pipes to play a joyful song as they skipped and danced their way out of the wood and around the bend of the foothills toward their destination.

Satyrs were masters of music. They would play to shepherd their flocks and to shepherd their people. Every time Izbaxl played his pipes, the music would calm Arisha down, like magic. She would abandon herself to the lilting hypnotic notes. She would not have a care in the world. And now, with the benefit of the magic mushrooms, she entered a trance of heavenly peace that made the time pass without notice.

They traveled through the steep cliffs of a wooded glen. As they neared the other side, Arisha noticed that all the greenery and trees were dying the more they walked on.

They finally arrived at a large clearing of a hidden valley. But it was desert like, bounded by the foothills of the mountains on one side and the dry rocky bluffs on the other.

It seemed strange to Arisha. It seemed like a little pocket of dry desert death in the midst of an otherwise lively area.

She stopped, stunned by the sight before her. A huge tree, hundreds of feet around had grown up into the clouds high above her. Its roots at the ground level were serpentine, twisted around like a tangled pile of, well, the only thing she could think of was snakes. She wondered if the mushrooms were distorting her vision, but she was not sure.

She was surprised that she had not seen this tree from a distance and wondered why it was the only living thing in this little valley of deadness.

"That, my dear Arisha," said Izbaxl, "is Gaia, the Mother Earth Goddess. The World Tree. And those are her worshippers."

Around the tree were hundreds of other pilgrims bowed to the ground before the great timber before them.

She saw others rubbing up against the tree like dogs often did to her leg.

"What are they doing?" she asked.

"They are loving Mother Earth. It is a ritual of fertility."

For all the talk of a goddess, this Gaia still seemed to her to just be a very big and gnarly tree. How could such a thing be like a person? She did not dare reveal her curious questioning because it had often gotten her into trouble in the past.

As they approached the tree past the worshippers, she could hear their soft chanting. It was quite haunting.

A beautiful woman approached them with two young daughters by her side, about the same age as Arisha.

She was stunning to Arisha. If Izbaxl's music tranquilized her fears, this woman's raven black hair, fluid movement and penetrating eyes sedated her soul.

Her voice expressed motherly assurance. "Welcome, Izbaxl. I see you have brought someone new to the goddess. A maiden. Sedated."

How did this phantom-like beauty know anything about me? thought Arisha.

"Arisha," said Izbaxl, "This is Lilith and her daughters Lili and Lilu. They are the guardians of Gaia."

"Hello, Arisha," said Lilith.

Lili and Lilu stepped forward and spoke as one with a heightened excitement. "Can we play with her?"

It seemed strange to Arisha. They seemed to be looking at her more like one would at a meal to eat than a companion with which to play. And how were they able to speak simultaneously? How would either of them know what the other was going to say? Did their mouths move when they talked or was it in her head? One of them even seemed more like a boy dressed as a girl.

Izbaxl stepped in front of Arisha and held her with a strong protective arm. "This is her first visit. She is not of age yet."

The two girls appeared disappointed. But Lilith was affirming.

"Well, then," said Lilith, "by all means, show her around. Expose her to the beauty of Mother Earth."

A chill went down Arisha's back. She could swear she saw a split tongue in Lilith's mouth. Almost like the garter snakes she had played with in the forest. Maybe it was the mushrooms.

She saw three tame looking hyenas sitting off a short distance from Lilith and her children, watching them like loyal dogs—or guardians.

"Let us move on," said Izbaxl, as he put his arm protectively around Arisha. They walked around the circumference of the tree.

Arisha looked up at the gargantuan timber that towered before them. She couldn't see the top of the tree. But she heard the sound of a large bird somewhere high above in the branches.

But the closer sounds of beasts brought her back down to earth as she saw before them, pens of animals all around: sheep, donkeys, pigs, goats, deer. Dozens of different animals were braying, baaing, and grunting. She stepped back in fright. She saw dozens of people lined up at the pens waiting their turns. Inside the pens were naked humans rubbing against the animals just like the ones with the tree and just like her parents did at night.

"What are they doing?" she blurted out.

Izbaxl chuckled. "Fret not, little one. We are here to explain to you the ways of love."

It was so disgusting she didn't know what to make of it.

"I know you have seen your mother and father do it, have you not?"

"Yes."

"Well, that is the most important way that we creatures express our love for one another. We unite our bodies in pleasure."

"That is pleasure?" she said. "Then why do they groan in pain?"

Izbaxl laughed again. "That is not pain, little mouse. That is gratification."

But still it didn't seem right to her.

Izbaxl said, "Remember how we have talked about loving the earth and all her offspring? About how humans are no more important than animals? And how we should love all living things with an equal love?"

It still didn't seem right to her.

He continued, "Well, if we really love all humans, and we really love all the animals, then one of the ways we show that love is through unity. That is why we call it 'making love.'"

"Why have my parents not told me about this?"

"Because you were not old enough to understand such beautiful things. But now you are."

It still did not seem right to her.

Though the mushrooms had made her more relaxed, more open to what she was seeing, they did not fully suppress her will.

"Am I going to have to do it?" she asked with shaky voice.

"Not yet," he said, "There will be time for that when you are older. I am merely your tutor, educating you so that when you are old enough, it will be very natural for you. It will be—beautiful."

It did not seem beautiful to her. And then she saw another pen area with a large number of naked men and women doing the same frightful things. She backed up against one of the large gnarly roots of the tree behind her.

"Arisha, my little mouse. Have I not been good to you all these years?" said Izbaxl. "Have I not proven myself trustworthy and wise to you, showing you the wonders and beauties of this world that you knew not?"

"Yes," she resigned.

"Then trust me in this," he said. "You are soon to come of age, and coming of age is full of many surprises—of ignorance transformed into enlightenment."

Something caught her eye in the tree root next to her.

She looked closer.

She jumped back in fright. The surface of the tree was not merely wooden bark, but it appeared to be the forms of myriads of humans fused into the bark, melted into the wood. They had become part of the wood themselves. They were frozen in agonized and painful positions. It was subtle, but she could see it. And it was like the entire tree was made out of these frozen statues of human pain. Was this another hallucinogenic effect of the happy mushrooms?

"I have one more thing to show you, Arisha," said Izbaxl. "I think you are mature enough to understand. Follow me."

He led her around to the backside of the tree.

She stopped and stepped back when she saw the scenario before her.

There were two priests dressed in blood covered robes who were standing by the tree roots. They were receiving a line of men, women, and children tied in fetters and guarded by soldiers.

The line of captives were led to the priests, where they were sacrificed upon a wooden altar, and their blood spilt upon the bark of the tree. Then their dead corpses were tucked into crevices of the tree where they appeared to be absorbed into the mammoth serpentine coils of the wooded roots.

Arisha grabbed Izbaxl's cloak tightly and stood behind him for protection. She felt like her clarity was coming back to her. The mushrooms were wearing off. She realized that Izbaxl must have given her the magic mushrooms to make her more open and understanding to these shocking revelations.

Was that a good thing or a bad thing?

"Why are they doing that?" she almost cried out.

"It is not as cruel as it appears, Arisha."

"But all animals are the sacred creatures of Mother Earth," she repeated back to him. His teaching flooded her memory. He had always stressed the holiness of animal life, even plants and insects. This seemed to be a violation of that sacred truth.

"Yes, that is true. But some creatures are more sacred than others. Do you remember how we have talked about the nature of evil men?"

"Yes." She was realizing that not all of life was good and that some people wished to hurt others.

"Well, many human beings are bad to Mother Earth. They cut down trees, kill and eat other animals and spoil the land. This is the price we must pay to appease the goddess Gaia. In a way it is really—justice."

He let her think about it for a moment, and then broke her concentration. "Let us go, Arisha. You have seen enough for today. I am sure your young mind is overwhelmed by it all."

She asked questions all the way back and Izbaxl explained more details to her. He told her of the spirits in the trees and plants. He explained that the earth with all its forests, lakes and rivers, and all the living things upon it was like one connected being and that being was the goddess. And it was man that ruined that harmony by corrupting Mother Earth. Man was like a plague on the earth that had to be cured, just like the plague that killed her uncle last year. He lay on his bed rotting away like a living corpse. It was a hideous memory, but it painted a picture she could understand.

Humanity must be sacrificed for the benefit of the whole balance of life on Mother Earth. Gaia was well pleased.

But how could a tree be a deity? Could not men cut it down?

She had seen her father carve a little human figurine out of a dead log and then they would worship it as a family. But then he would use the other half of the log to make a fire to cook the food they ate. Something about that incongruity always bothered her.

The mushrooms had worn off by now, and it all hurt her little head. But Izbaxl had always been so wise and so kind to her. She could only conclude that he was patiently helping her now to understand the mysteries of the heavens and earth that she had simply been too young to comprehend.

When they reached their village of Panias in the foothills, it was already late. The sun was down and families were indoors eating their meals.

Arisha said, "Should I not get home, Izbaxl? Mother and father will be angry it is so late."

"Do not worry," said Izbaxl, "I spoke to them. Come with me, I want to show you something."

They approached the holy grotto; a huge cavern that hosted the spring waters flowing down into the Jordan River.

Arisha paused. It was a sacred space that only the satyrs and hierodules, sacred priestesses, entered. The rivers of living water came from the spring that watered the earth. She had heard that deep in the cave was a pool of water that led to the very depths of the Abyss. Inside the grotto, the priests and priestesses served the satyrs and their god.

She saw another satyr approach them from the grotto. It was Xizmat, Izbaxl's younger brother. Xizmat was slighter than Izbaxl, and seemed to follow his older sibling around like a pet. Izbaxl had saved his brother's life in a dangerous situation years back, though Arisha did not know the details. But it explained why he was so grateful and devoted to his brother.

"Fret not, little one," said Xizmat. "It is time to show you your future."

She gulped and grasped both their hands tightly.

Izbaxl smiled at her innocence. It gave him great excitement.

The three of them walked into the large opening and the darkness swallowed them up.

The satyrs held her hand and guided her. They could see even in near total darkness.

After some walking, they stopped. Her heart raced. Her breathing turned shallow.

She saw torchlight come out of nowhere and approach them.

It was held by a priestess, one of the holy women of the sanctuary.

And then another torch held by another priestess.

Arisha began to get glimpses of beings around her.

They were satyrs and priestesses.

She could sense their presence more than see them.

But what she could see before her in the firelight of the torches was a large golden statue twenty feet tall.

It was the statue of a god.

"Azazel, the ancient one, god of the desert lands and lord of satyrs," said Izbaxl.

The graven image hypnotized Arisha. It looked as if he looked right at Arisha. A shiver went down her spine.

She stared long at his face, taking in every feature. It was a humanoid being with an elongated skull and no hair. He had the goat legs and cloven hooves of a satyr. But when she looked at the skin on his belly, she could see it was sculpted as very fine almost imperceptible scales. He was muscular and held in his hand a scythe. Normally, the scythe was for cutting wheat and barley for the harvest, but in this giant's hand it had the distinct appearance of being a weapon.

Izbaxl spoke to her as she continued to stare.

"This is your god, Arisha. It is he whom we serve, and it is he to whose service you are dedicated."

She looked up at him.

The priestesses circled her. They were dressed in flowing robes, wore veils, and swayed like hypnotic snakes.

"These shall be your sisters. They shall teach you the ways of the cult. It is time for you to become one of them."

"I am afraid, Izbaxl," whimpered Arisha.

“Do not be,” he replied. “I will watch over you. You will be mine, and no one will hurt you. You will be taught to dance and how to please men and satyr alike. It is time for you to become a nymph.”

CHAPTER 4

King Og of Bashan was about eleven feet tall, with the elongated skull and pale gray skin of the Rephaim. But he liked to emphasize his elite status by painting his face white and wearing the Rephaim distinctions of royalty.

He strode out the city gate of Ashtaroth, dressed in his finery, with his entourage in black chariot. His black robe and headpiece were accented with artfully placed exotic armor pieces that reinforced the image of a warrior king.

The city of Ashtaroth lay in the heart of Bashan just fifty miles south-southeast of Mount Hermon. As a key city on the northernmost reaches of the King's Highway, it was the fortified post that was most crucial in the connection of Canaan to Mesopotamia and Syria where the Hittites and Mittani ruled. To get into or out of Canaan, one had to first go through Ashtaroth, and this was not easy, because it was Og's walled city and he was the last of the Rephaim.

Og had become infamous because his Rephaim were gibborim giants that ruled the region with terror. *Gibborim* was the word used for mighty warriors of men or giants. On the Transjordan side, the Edomites had wiped out the Horite giant clan and settled around the southern end of the Salt Sea. The Moabites had slaughtered the Emim giants and secured their land now called

Moab in mid-country. The Ammonites had permanently displaced the Zamzummim giants in the lower region. The Philistine Sea Peoples overtook the Avvim giant clans on the coast of the Mediterranean.

The two clans that were not displaced, but rather grew stronger than their enemies, were the Anakim in the southern hill country of the Cisjordan, and the Rephaim in the Transjordan, the land of Bashan.

The Rephaim were a warrior people, not given to extravagance or display beyond the basic caste separation of ruler and citizen. Their architecture was simple, box-like and functional. But it was strikingly unlike other Canaanite engineering because it had been built according to the specification of a Watcher god.

That Watcher god was Ashtart, patron divinity of Ashtaroth, the goddess of sex and war. It all made for a rather imposing presence in the region and a fearful reputation among the allies and enemies of Og.

Og was receiving the arrival of a delegation from Egypt sent to collect tribute from their Canaanite vassals. Og had heard there had been plenty of turmoil in Egypt in recent years and Pharaoh was lessening his grip over the cities of Canaan. This was why the delegation was small and economical.

A retinue of fifty attendants guarded by a small regiment of only fifty soldiers approached the waiting Og. In the lead carriage was a nobleman emissary named Fenuku, who had been their liaison for years.

He was small, homely looking, and rather unimpressive despite his Egyptian royal garb of white linen tunic, gold jewelry, and braided Pharaonic hairpiece.

But Og was more interested in the being behind Fenuku. At eight feet tall, of soldierly frame, and golden skin, the being wore a white linen robe with the red and white crown of Egyptian deity. His body was humanoid, but his head was that of a falcon.

It was the god Horus.

As one of the more ancient deities of Egypt, Horus was the son of Isis and Osiris and was a god of war and hunting. He was called the Great God, the Lord of Heaven. The sun god Ra was king of the gods, but Horus was the active player in Egypt's human drama because Pharaoh was considered the incarnation of Horus on earth. A hieroglyph, "The Eye of Horus" was still a symbol of protection and royal power from the gods.

And that is what made Og curious. This impressive god of war and protection had never visited them before. Why was he here?

Og gave a dutiful nod to Fenuku, but kept his eye on Horus and bowed before the mighty being.

Og said, "To what do I owe your exalted presence, my god?"

Horus appeared agitated. His falcon eyes jerked around looking for someone.

He spit out impatiently, "Where is she? Where is your strumpet goddess?"

He was referring to Ashtart, who had not accompanied Og to receive their overlords. It insulted Horus. As if to say they were not important enough. As if she would get to them on her own good time.

"Forgive me, O mighty Horus. She is indisposed and did not tell me why."

Horus suddenly calmed himself and said with a still malevolence, "She had better have a good reason, or I will have her head."

Og's throne room, like his dress and the rest of his palace, was simple and without ornamentation, outside of weapons displayed on the walls to increase intimidation. It gave one the impression that Og was too busy conquering and ruling to waste his attention on such petty luxuries as the display of wealth.

The only thing of any consequence to him was his throne, made out of the black basaltic rock from the deserts around Bashan, and crowned with a wall display of many ornamental battle shields from his exploits throughout the years. They were beaten, cut up, and burned with the scars of battle, and they were his pride.

But Og was not particularly proud at this moment. He fidgeted nervously as he sat and stared at the entranceway, waiting for Ashtart to arrive. He did not bother to talk to Fenuku, who stood gazing up at one of the massive battle-axes hanging on the wall. It dwarfed his small human body.

Horus stood over by a window gazing out onto the surrounding walled city below. He fumed with anger at having to wait for that arrogant bombastic goddess.

Canaan had been under the vassalage of Egypt for some time. Previous Pharaohs had build fortress towers along the travel routes to insure compliance with Egyptian sovereignty. But with the recent Hyksos invasion, Egypt had lost its iron grip on the region.

Og was a mighty ruler and he had plans of his own for the Transjordan. But alone, he was no kind of force to stand against the Egyptian empire—despite its weakened state.

The peoples of Canaan were too unruly and fragmented to be able to form any kind of union in opposition to Egypt's control. They would have to be conquered by Og in order to be unified and that was no easy prospect, coupled with the fact that the Anakim in the southern hill country were a powerful force and surely had their own designs on the land.

Og busied himself strategizing how to dominate the Transjordan before he would trouble himself with the Anakim.

But he wanted them as well. He wanted to rule them all. He was just waiting for his opportunity, a twist of fate that might open the gates for his plan to begin.

A loud boisterous crow filled the room. "Well, well, well, what have we here?"

Og and Fenuku looked up. Horus turned.

Ashtart strode in like the Queen of Heaven up to the throne. She was eight feet tall with glimmering skin, lapis lazuli blue eyes, dressed in only an undergarment—and covered in blood.

She continued with her bravado, "This had better be good, Horus, because you have interrupted a very important spell of necromancy I am working on."

Horus looked her up and down with disdain.

Ashtart licked the blood off a few of her fingers like she had finished a snack.

"Necromancy is about the dead, so I had to engage in some death." She grinned.

Horus was not amused. "You did not receive my arrival at the gates, you kept me waiting, and now you lack the décor of cleaning yourself up in my presence. Have you no respect for authority?"

"And whose authority would that be, Horus? Ra, 'king of the gods' of Egypt?" She said it with contempt and kept a wide sarcastic grin on her face.

"Why did he send you, and not Hapi, god of the Nile? Or Hekhet, that froggish goddess? Kheprer, the beetle fly divinity? Apis, the sacred bull? Sekhmet, the goddess of plague?"

Horus stared at her vindictively.

"Come to think of it," concluded Ashtart with relish, "Where is Ra anyway? Not very sunny down there in Egypt, is it?"

Og listened, confused. He did not understand what exactly Ashtart referred to.

She kept her piercing blue eyes on Horus whose posture had suddenly slumped in abject humiliation. "Oh, yes, I heard," said Ashtart. "I have my messengers in Egypt. But my patron, King Og, did not, so let us educate him."

Og kept looking back and forth between Ashtart, Horus, and Fenuku. Fenuku remained mute the entire time, utterly worthless.

Ashtart strode around pompously.

"Evidently, Pharaoh had allowed a captive people to multiply in the land of Goshen. First they were his servants, and then they became quite a fighting force guarding the approach into Lower Egypt through the Way of the Philistines."

The Way of the Philistines was an important trade route that connected Canaan and Egypt along the coast.

Ashtart continued, "Now these *Habiru*, as we call them, became quite an annoyance to the Pharaoh, because evidently, they worshipped Yahweh, and Yahweh sent plagues upon Egypt until he let them go. It so happened that these plagues were directed at the deities of their pantheon, reducing them to impotence."

Ashtart paused to let it dig into Horus. She wanted to make sure his impotency was properly exposed. Even at his most powerful, Ashtart could cut him into ribbons. And he no longer had the protective power of the Egyptian pantheon behind him.

"And as I heard it, correct me if I am wrong here, Horus, but evidently Ra, the mighty sun god—well, shall we say—had his lights put out."

Og now understood his fortunate situation in light of Egypt's humiliation. He had heard there was trouble, but did not realize just how drastic it was.

Ashtart kept going on like a prosecuting attorney uncovering a crime. She had learned much from Mastema, the satan in Yahweh's heavenly court.

"And what exactly happened next, Horus? It is a bit unclear to me." That was a lie. It was clear as ever to her. She just wanted to hear Horus admit it.

Horus explained sheepishly, "After Pharaoh let the Habiru go, he changed his mind and had his army chase them down."

Og asked, "Did he kill the Habiru?"

"No."

Ashtart said, "I am sorry, Horus, would you speak up, please. I can hear you, but I am not sure the humans can."

"No," he reiterated with a touch of anger. He sighed. "The Habiru were trapped at the edge of Yam Suph, the Sea at the End of the World, but their god pulled back the waters to allow the Habiru to cross through on dry land. When Pharaoh's army tried to cross after them with his chariots, the waters came back and drowned them."

"The entire Egyptian army drowned?" asked Og. He could not believe it.

"Not the whole," said Horus. "The majority. Some forces were left in Egypt of course."

"Of course," mocked Ashtart. "But where's Pharaoh, pray tell?"

Horus grumbled, "Dead."

Ashtart said, "Ah yes, your kingly ward drowned in the waters of Yam Suph. Along with your precursor, the original Watcher god, Horus. So you are simply his replacement playing the part. You are a god in search of a pharaoh."

"We are all playing parts," Horus growled. "You included."

She ignored the weak challenge and said, "And then what happened?"

"The Amalekites invaded and almost annihilated what was left." These were the Amalekites that the Israelites had fought on their way out of Egypt.

"Tch, tch, tch. When it rains, it storms," mocked Ashtart. "So where does that leave us now?"

A subtle smirk grew on Og's lips. He knew exactly where it left *him*.

Horus gave it up, "This will be the last tribute I will be receiving from you. Egypt is withdrawing its protection from the region."

So that was it. Without the power of its Pharaoh and its gods, and without its mighty chariot army, Egypt could no longer maintain its iron grip on Canaan or its aggressive stance toward its enemies. And now it was being invaded by tribes called Hyksos, shepherd kings of nomadic tribes like Amalekites and Anakim.

That meant Og now had complete freedom to engage in his own designs on the Transjordan.

At last, his twist of fate had arrived. With mighty clans like the Anakim, it might take a generation of careful planning and strategic maneuvering, but his dreams of dominion were now a possibility.

Ashtart said, "Well, if Egypt will no longer be protecting Canaan, then she will certainly receive no tribute from us."

Og felt empowered by his patron goddess.

Horus went flush with anger. But he knew she was right. He had risked coming with the hopes of getting one last amount of extortion money, but Ashtart had uncovered his impotence and was now flaunting it in his face.

Ashtart sang, "Og, You had better get planning. We have a land to conquer."

Horus interrupted, "Do not be too sure of your own supremacy, quim. I am also here to warn you that those same Habiru have their sights set on Canaan."

Horus puffed up with his own sense of retaliation. "And the god who crushed the pantheon of Egypt will be coming with them."

Ashtart turned stone cold.

"Where are they?" she asked.

"I received word that they are wandering somewhere in the wilderness near Meribah."

"How many are there?"

"A multitude of thousands."

"Well, then, we shall just have to be ready for them when they arrive to give them an Ashtart welcome: the dance of death."

The dance of death referred to Ashtart's vicious and bloody battle technique. Despite the fact that she now submitted as consort of Ba'al, the most high god, she was still the second most ruthless warrior in the pantheon.

Ba'al had bested Ashtart in the battle of the nine kings in the Valley of Siddim so many generations ago. He had prepared to bind her into the earth. But when Ashtart revealed her diabolical plan of taking over Canaan, and submitted herself to Ba'al's complete authority over her, he decided to make her his servant. Her skills at war would be of more help to him than doing it alone. And her intellectual brilliance and strategy were a fitting complement for his overwhelming brute force. He was not a dumb brute, but her mind was definitely more cunning, so long as he could keep her in submission. And he managed to do so in unspeakable ways.

Ba'al's abuse of her became a well of pitch-black violence that Ashtart would draw upon for her own assertions of power.

Horus and Fenuku prepared to leave.

"Stop," said Ashtart.

She strode up to Horus. He stood his ground, but she could see he was weak. And she was strong. Very strong.

She said, "One more thing, feathered fowl."

She grabbed him by the throat and slammed him against the stone wall.

He did not react. He submitted. He knew he had not the fortitude to face her.

She whispered into his bird face. He could smell the odor of blood from her mouth. "Do *not* call me quim. I still have my rod, and I use it with excess and impunity. You *may* however call me—'ambidextrous' because I walk both paths."

When Ashtart had chosen her identity as a goddess in the antediluvian plans of the Watchers, she did so as an irony. The Watchers were all male, but they had to impersonate some female deities, and she thought it would be an extra rise to her scandalous reputation if the greatest warrior in the entire pantheon was a female who could kick the brains out of any macho male storm god. Any that is, except for the storm god Ba'al. Ashtart had modified his body to appear female, but underneath the façade, he remained utterly and totally male.

But Horus also knew that she would not bind him into the earth. Though the gods had personal ambitions, they needed to remain allies against the far greater enemy of Yahweh. He had counted on that fact by offering the intelligence of his approach.

Ashtart released Horus. He grasped his throat to rub out the finger marks and massage his windpipe.

He backed away to leave.

"Give my regards to Isis," she said. "I am still jealous of that girl's fashion."

CHAPTER 5

Forty years had passed slowly for Joshua in the Wilderness of Zin. Yahweh had vowed to make Israel wander in that desert wasteland for forty years until the entire generation of the spies was dead. As Joshua weathered the time, now being sixty-years old, much had happened to compound that judgment.

Another incident of rebellion had occurred where the sons of Korah challenged Moses' authority to lead the people. They thought that Yahweh could speak to everyone equally. They were swallowed up alive into Sheol as Yahweh's definitive response to such revolutionary anarchy.

The prophetess Miriam, Moses's sister, had died recently as well. Moses was one hundred and twenty years old by now. His brother Aaron was three years older. They both seemed mere shadows of their former selves, but with God's grace, they had managed to stay fit enough to walk around with some help.

For Moses, his days as a mighty Egyptian general in Pharaoh's army seemed so distant as to not be real anymore. Now, his bones ached, he had trouble relieving himself, he had little patience left with his stiff-necked people, and he struggled with the sadness of having outlived his beloved wife Zipporah, his own loyal father Amram, and his wise father-in-law Jethro. All his peers were now dead, and the new generation was hungry for their inheritance.

In a way, Moses longed to die and be with Yahweh. But in another way, he wanted so badly to see the Promised Land, that Eden allotted to Israel as her inheritance from primeval days. His short life of a hundred and twenty was nothing compared with the millennium of waiting that Abraham's seed had suffered.

They had stayed at Kadesh, a dry and desolate area, and the people were grumbling and complaining, yet again, that Moses had taken them out from Egypt and into the wilderness, only to let them die. There was nowhere to grow food or find shelter, and no water to live on.

They assembled before Moses to make their complaints known. Moses and his brother Aaron the High Priest then went before Yahweh in the Tent of Meeting to implore for his ear. Joshua, ever shadowing his master, bowed to the floor, and listened to it all.

Yahweh had told Moses to go to a large rock outcropping, and to tell the rock to yield its water for the sons of Israel to drink and to give their animals. He distinctly heard Yahweh specify *that he speak to the rock.*

The congregation had been gathered before the large rock and Moses stood upon it with Aaron and glared down upon the people. Joshua and Caleb stood at the foot of rock, looking up at their perturbed leader.

"PEOPLE OF ISRAEL!" Moses' voice rang through the camp with uncanny strength for such an old man. But he also shone like burning bronze in a refiner's fire because he was unveiled and had just been in Yahweh's presence.

Joshua could see from his vantage point that Moses was trembling. His fortitude came from a fury of anger that had been building in him for some time.

Caleb thought that Moses had become impatient with the people. That impatience had taken its toll on the old man.

Moses then spoke as if he was Yahweh himself, "Hear now, you rebels! Shall Aaron and I bring water for you out of this rock?"

The multitude murmured. They were not quite following.

Then Moses lifted his staff and struck the rock twice.

Everyone watched with anticipation.

But nothing happened.

Gossipy grumbling started to pepper the crowd. Maybe they would be going back to Egypt after all—without Moses.

But then, the ground rumbled.

Voices hushed.

And suddenly, the rock split in two, right down the middle, and a blast of spring water came bursting out of the rock, showering those closest to it.

People laughed and danced.

The water started to find its way and immediately carved out a small creek to flow toward the camp.

Shouts of joy, "miracle!" and Moses' name could be heard as everyone pressed in to get a drink from their newly flowing streams of water in the desert.

But when Moses and Aaron went back to the Tent of Meeting, they were surprised by Yahweh's response from within the Shekinah cloud.

It was something that would change all their lives forever.

• • • • •

It was the Sabbath. The last of the week where the Israelites did no work, but feasted and celebrated their god in worship and fellowship with one another. They followed this holy command even before they entered Canaan. Most of the feasts, such as the Feast of Unleavened Bread and the Feast of Harvest could not be followed until they were settled in their land with crops and the like. But others, such as the Sabbath and many sacrifices at the tabernacle, were celebrated in anticipation of their consummation in the Promised Land.

Joshua had dedicated himself to following all the details of Yahweh's laws with exact precision. The Sabbath was so holy that all work was forbidden on that one day. The Israelites would have to make preparations for their meals the day before so that they would be able to abstain from such mundane labors to focus on their sacred duty.

The duty to keep the Sabbath thus holy was so serious that even the picking up of sticks to make a fire was considered a violation and was punishable by death.

Many Israelites considered such punishments as extreme. But Joshua understood it more easily than most. He knew that it was not the measure of the finite crime that justified the seriousness of the punishment, but the measure of the infinite god, against whom the crime was committed, that made it of such magnitude.

Many of these wandering Israelites were still idol worshippers who could not understand the holiness of their deity because of their own moral depravity. Joshua was a man of the law and Yahweh's perfect law required perfect obedience, so he was determined to be that model of perfect obedience.

Caleb saw this character trait of Joshua as both a strength and a liability. To him, it was like following one half of the law of

Yahweh but ignoring the other half. For the other half, the laws of sacrifice and atonement, were precisely the completion of the story that began with man's sin. Atonement was the good news that followed the bad news. It was the heart and soul of Yahweh's sanctifying relationship with his people.

These were the differences that caused stress in Caleb's relationship with Joshua. But their bond overcame their differences. That bond was evident now as Caleb, his daughter Achsah, and his younger brother Othniel, entered Joshua's tent to share a feast with his family.

They sat on mats along with Joshua's extended family of mother, older uncle, two younger siblings and son and daughter. Joshua's wife Hasina, and his aunt served them dinner. It was a robust family, not as big as others, but full of life.

Joshua's father, Nun, had died some years back. So as patriarch of the family, Joshua gave the blessing. They entered into a meal of heavenly manna prepared in various ways, along with fresh water from the new spring.

Manna was the miraculous daily provision of food for Yahweh's people that began when they left Egypt and wandered in the desert wilderness. It appeared with the morning dew every day. The Israelites would gather enough for the day to prepare and eat. But it would only last that day. Any leftovers would rot with maggots.

Only Othniel had the sense of humor to speak up as he examined the manna meal in front of him. "Manna cakes, manna bread, manna porridge. I must complement you, Hasina. Just when I thought there was no new way to possibly prepare manna, your creativity proves itself once again. Manna soup! Thank Yahweh for herbs and spices to flavor his mundane 'miraculous provision.'"

Chuckles slipped out around the meal spread. But especially from Achsah. Othniel had watched over Achsah like an older brother as she grew up in Caleb's frequent absence. Othniel was now aged fifty-three and he shared a closeness with Achsah that sometimes made Caleb feel jealous and then guilty for his lack of fatherly presence in her life. In some ways, he was his brother's opposite. He was a swarthy man with dark curly hair, deep set eyes and stocky features, but he too had become a trusted warrior and commander of hundreds in Israel's army.

"Brother," scolded Joshua, "would you rather have some quail again?"

"Yes. But only if it is not accompanied by the same consequences as last time," said Othniel. "I will not forget that chastisement. We had quail meat coming out of our nostrils. One memory I do not treasure."

He poked Achsah sitting next to him and she giggled again.

Othniel was referring to the time when the Israelites had previously complained about the manna provision, and cried out for meat like they had in Egypt. So Yahweh sent them meat. A strong wind brought them so many quail to eat that their entire camp was piled high with squawking and feathers. They got sick of it after a month. Some even died from a plague, the rotting flesh was so bad.

Joshua's daughter Abigail peeped, "I still do not understand what manna is."

Othniel said with a silly sotto voice, "That is why we call it 'manna. It means, 'What is it?'"

The children giggled again.

Achsah stroked Abigail's head and offered, "I think Yahweh wants to teach us to be grateful even for what we do not have."

All the adults understood the double meaning of Achsah's words. She had lost her dear mother Nathifa five years earlier.

Caleb had met Nathifa seventeen years ago and fell madly in love. For some unknown reason, after they had Achsah, Yahweh would not bless them with any more children. This troubled Caleb deeply because he was an outsider, a convert to Israel from the Canaanite tribe of Kenizzites. So the only way he could feel a true part of the people of Yahweh would be through a large family that would blend into and throughout the nation.

But that was not to be.

Any normal Israelite would consider this childlessness a curse from Yahweh for some hidden sin or because of his pagan heritage. But Nathifa did not believe Yahweh owed them anything, and that all suffering was his way of making them draw near to each other and to their god.

Caleb may have been a gibborim warrior, but he was also a tender husband. He had adored and cherished his Nathifa as life itself. He was so affectionate with her in public, kissing her and embracing her, that he would often get in trouble for too much display in their modest culture.

When a desert plague had swept through the congregation, Nathifa had been struck by it and died. Caleb's cry of pain could be heard for miles around. He had determined to never remarry because his beloved was too much a part of his happiness, of who he was and what he had become. He could not move on and start anew without her. It would make him feel like Sheol would have won, and she would be forgotten in the land of the living. Living in the pain of loneliness without someone to replace her was the way to keep her memory alive.

Fortunately, Caleb and Achsah were accepted and loved as kin by Joshua's family, so they always traveled and set up tents near each other, regardless of their different tribal affiliation. Othniel would watch over Achsah when Caleb was gone, and Joshua's family would often take care of Achsah when Caleb and Othniel were both on a mission or engaged in military pursuits.

Joshua's son Nathan broke through the sad tension that filled the air when he complained, "I hate manna. I agree with Uncle Othniel. If we could eat quail, I would help gather the firewood to cook them."

Joshua snapped a look at Nathan, who froze in terror. He knew better than to make his father angry.

But Joshua was not angry. He was frightened for Nathan. "Son, what have I taught you about the Sabbath?"

Nathan's eyes were wide with fear. "We are to do no work."

"And what would happen if you picked up firewood in rebellion against the command of Yahweh?"

"I would be stoned by the congregation."

The conversation went uncomfortably quiet around the table. Hasina looked with pity on her little Nathan. He barely understood what he was saying.

Joshua continued, "I love you with all my heart, my son. But our god Yahweh is a holy god and he requires our total obedience. If you rebelled against him, I would have to obey our creator and hand you over to the judges or suffer the same fate. That would break my heart more than anything in the world."

"Yes, father," whimpered Nathan.

Everyone felt so bad for Nathan. He was so young. But they also knew that Joshua was right. That Yahweh's laws were to be followed with strict adherence. No man, woman, or child was above the law.

Hasina knew that Joshua was speaking the truth. He loved his son more than anything on earth. But he loved his creator more, and that meant he would offer him up as Abraham offered Isaac, if Yahweh requested it.

The good news was that when it came to his uncompromising standards, Joshua was harder on himself than he was on others.

Joshua turned to Caleb. “Let us go for our exercises.”

As Moses’ assistant, Joshua had represented Moses’ command to the armed forces. Moses was the military general of Israel, but with age, he had given over physical leadership on the battlefield to Joshua as his chief commander.

Joshua’s first proof of his superior skills had come early on in the exodus when Moses appointed him field commander to lead their forces against the pillaging Amalekites. Joshua had been successful and had served as proxy general ever since.

Caleb was a commander of thousands under Joshua, but also his right hand man, and the only one capable enough to personally train with his commander. Though he was eighty-years of age, he still seemed strong as an ox, blessed by Yahweh with a healthy durable physique.

Out beyond the camp in an open desert area, Joshua and Caleb engaged in battle exercises and fighting maneuvers with various weapons. As his elder, Caleb had taught Joshua everything he knew. Joshua had quickly become his equal but despite the age difference of a good twenty years, they were equals in stamina and intensity as well.

They were both driven men. Driven by devotion to their nation, but also by unspoken secrets as well.

Between them, however, there were no secrets held.

"Yahweh said what?" exclaimed Caleb with a dodge and a swing of his sickle sword.

"Moses and Aaron will not bring Israel into the land that he promised us."

Joshua blocked with shield. They were predetermined forms of technique rather than actual sparring.

"But why?"

"Javelins!" barked Joshua. They dropped shields and swords and picked up javelins to use with new forms of workout.

Joshua answered, "Because they did not believe in Yahweh or uphold him as holy in the eyes of the people of Israel."

Caleb huffed through his maneuvering, "He told Moses to speak. Moses hit the rock twice with his staff. That seems like a mistake to me, not a sin."

"That is the difference between you and me," said Joshua. "Battle-axe!"

They dropped their javelins and picked up battle-axes, swinging in arcs to build their strength.

"What do you mean?" asked Caleb.

"You do not understand the holiness of Yahweh."

Swing, swing, swoosh, swoosh.

"There is much about Yahweh I do not understand. He is full of mystery."

Swing, swing, swoosh, swoosh.

They stopped to catch a breath.

Joshua continued, "Yahweh's commands are to be followed exactly, just like his law. When Moses hit the rock like it was his power, and claimed he and Aaron brought forth the water, it was not a mistake. It was a vainglorious attribution of Yahweh's glory to themselves. Moses has become lax in his discipline and efforts at perfect obedience."

Caleb countered, "Moses has forgotten where he came from."

Joshua knew what Caleb was referring to. Moses originally had a stuttering problem when Yahweh chose him to speak for him and he did not think he was adequate to the task. Yet that is what Yahweh wanted, a leader whom the people would follow but not worship because the power of deliverance could only come from above. Yahweh took imperfect humans to display his perfect glory.

"And that is the difference between you and me," Caleb said. "You do not understand the grace and beauty of Yahweh."

Caleb picked up his whip sword Rahab and unfurled it. Then he engaged in an entirely different kind of technique with his weapon. Rather than the hard exertion of brute force and will, his technique was the elegant effortlessness of beauty and dance. It was the complete opposite of what Joshua had been performing, and it was clear that Caleb had suppressed his true skill for the sake of Joshua.

Now, he released himself to his heavenly training, to the Way of the Karabu. And it was evident that he did not teach Joshua everything he knew after all.

Joshua watched him with wonder as Caleb flowed like a river, the flexible sword waving through the air with rhythmic precision, sailing and snapping, twirling and slicing. Caleb appeared to be carried by the wind, lighter than a feather. It was a ballet of battle, a poem of pummeling.

And Joshua envied every move Caleb made. He could see the beauty and fluidity of the Karabu Way. But it was also a repudiation of everything Joshua understood about the nature of combat. Karabu was about dance and play versus strength and force. And *that* he could not abide.

And so the two of them kept a competitive tension within a bond of brotherly love.

Caleb stopped to rest, his breathing more steady than previously.

Joshua said, "I want to bring the Israelites into the Promised Land. I can be what Moses was not. I am disciplined and devoted to the law. I will follow every jot and tittle of Yahweh's commands."

"Well," said Caleb, "You do not lack for such rigidity. But it is Yahweh's choice who will replace Moses."

"I will do everything within my power to persuade Yahweh. To show him that I can be his perfect vessel."

"That is a tall order to fill," said Caleb. "You may find yourself becoming a broken vessel."

Joshua boasted, "At least Yahweh is the only one capable of breaking this vessel."

Caleb thought for a second. Then he said, "Can I show you something?"

"What?"

"I want to demonstrate a Karabu move."

"Caleb, we both have our own way of fighting. I respect yours, but I operate differently. Different approaches with the same results."

Caleb threw his weapon aside.

"Show me your approach without a weapon."

Joshua was younger and stronger. Caleb was strong but nowhere near the capacity of Joshua's muscular strength and vigor.

Even Joshua's height was superior at six feet tall to Caleb's five feet eight inches.

Joshua sighed and tossed his weapon down.

Caleb said, "Attack me."

Joshua protested, "If we grapple, I clearly outweigh you."

"Attack me any way you like."

"You asked for it."

Joshua balled his fists, raised them and launched a punch that would have knocked out a camel.

But he was not prepared for Caleb's dodge that threw Joshua off balance.

Joshua responded with an immediate series of punches. If one would not connect, the succeeding one would, or the two and three after that. Joshua would overwhelm Caleb with sheer force and power.

The only problem was, none of the punches connected.

Caleb artfully evaded some, and others he redirected causing Joshua to spin and twist, which drove Joshua into an increasing frenzy of frustration.

It made him lose his control.

Then Caleb stepped toward Joshua's body and using his thumbs lightly jabbed Joshua's neck on both sides.

Joshua blacked out.

When he came to, Caleb was sitting beside him on the ground with a smile.

"What in heaven did you do to me?" griped Joshua.

"Now you are learning," said Caleb. It was indeed of heavenly origin.

Joshua sat up.

Caleb said, "I used your force against you. Your fury distracted your concentration."

"What about that trick on my neck?"

"Knowing your enemy's weakness is far better than facing his strength. Karabu is the way of faith, not force. A small amount of faith can move a mountain, so a small amount of pressure can topple the mightiest of gibborim."

Caleb got up.

He offered Joshua his hand.

Joshua grabbed it, and let Caleb hoist him up to his feet.

"I understand," said Joshua. "My smallest command could demote you to a common soldier."

Caleb paused at the remark.

Then Joshua said with a touch of levity, "As your Chief Commander, I order you to teach me this move."

CHAPTER 6

Two years had passed for Arisha of Panias since she had been initiated into the sisterhood of nymphs. She had been trained to dance and to serve, but had not yet been given the full responsibility of a nymph.

She had become quite close to the other women, who nurtured her and treated her with respect. Her mentor Sisa had much affection for her. Being seven years her elder, and not quite as fair of face, Sisa was impressed with Arisha's maturity that seemed to exceed her age. She saw strength in her that she knew would cause trouble, so she taught Arisha to feign submission and keep her growing doubts hidden.

What Arisha did not realize was the effect she had on Sisa, who had never been troubled before by such thoughts as those that buzzed around in Arisha's head. She was contagious, and Sisa had been infected.

Why would the satyrs teach them to reverence and worship the earth and all living things, then treat the humans under their care with such disdain and disrespect? If everything was created, why worship the created things? Would there not be one who was not created but who created everything?

But there *was* a certain logic to it. If you think that humans are like a disease on the earth, then it would follow that you would oppress them in the name of the higher sacred right of the earth. If you thought that the earth was not created to be a servant to humanity, but humanity was created to be a servant to the earth, then treating humans as servants and slaves would not be outrageous at all.

Killing them might even be a good thing in this view. Perhaps this was also why the satyrs went to great lengths to protect the births of animals in the flocks but regularly caused miscarriages in her fellow nymphs, killing any infants that accidently survived.

But Arisha was a human and she had never done anything terrible to the earth. Most of the people she knew were not like that either.

What were they not telling her?

She was grateful that Izbaxl was not that way to her. He had always been kind and respectful toward her. He was different from the others. Maybe he would one day share his secret with her.

And another thing perplexed her. The sexual coupling that they taught her to be a fulfillment of natural urges did not seem natural to her at all. Humans having sexual unity with animals, siblings with siblings, men with men and women with women, adults with young children, everyone with everyone. It seemed to her that the only sexuality they discouraged was one man and one woman in an exclusive marriage relationship—the one coupling that seemed most natural to her.

Which reminded her of her parents, and she would start to cry because she was not allowed to live with them anymore, and could only see them occasionally. But then Sisa would quiet her with a motherly affection and it made her pain a bit more bearable.

She had to hide all her thoughts and questions. She was no scribe or wisdom sage and did not have the luxury of pondering and pontificating. She had to fulfill her duty and station in life.

And she was fourteen years old now. It was time for her to become a sacred nymph.

It was to be an evening of bacchanalia, a celebration of indulgence. The sacred grotto was lit up with torches and set with a feast of every fruit, vegetable, edible root, and plant known to man and satyr. The farmers had been required to sacrifice from the best of their crops in order to provide a cornucopia of excess for the satyrs and royalty who lounged and played in the grotto this evening.

And all of this played out before the golden statue of Azazel.

They had also invited some Rephaim from nearby cities and villages. To Arisha, these were ugly giants who towered over everyone else and had ugly looking heads with reptilian gray skin, scary eyes, and extra fingers and toes.

One of the things they hid from the villagers of Panias was the meat that they added to the feast. Rephaim were meat eaters and the satyrs were too. They just did not let the people know of their hypocritical behavior.

It was not such a secret though. The villagers could smell the grilled scent of roasted pig, fowl, and other game that now filled the spread of food before the revelers. They had learned to live with hypocrisy as a value of their overlords. The elite always live by a separate standard than the one they impose on others.

The music that filled the cavernous grotto was extravagant. Lute, timbrel, and percussion, washed over the audience like waves. The haunting vibrations echoed out into the surrounding countryside and could be heard miles away. Satyrs were not merely flute players with their pan pipes, they were accomplished musicians whose musical skills would have hypnotic effect, putting themselves and their audience into a trance of sensual abandonment.

And it led to the dance.

Arisha and several other of her nymph initiates followed their sisters in the Sikinnis dance that now accompanied the strains of the players.

The Sikinnis was the dance of the satyrs. It was a mini-drama played out with passion, panic, and desire. Arisha had learned and practiced its rhythms and movements for a long time until she had become one of the finest of the new crop of neophytes. She always became the best at what she did. She was ambitious.

Her ambition flowed through her now as she undulated like a snake with fluidity before the watchful eyes of satyrs, royalty, and Rephaim.

Her makeup was exotic and extreme, another talent she had perfected to enhance her already flowering beauty. Arisha had matured quickly.

She was the obvious star of the dance. She commanded their attention.

The dance reached a fevered pitch resulting in a frenetic climax that caused satyr, giant, and man to rise up and surround the nymphs.

A group of men encircled Arisha. But a strong firm hand grabbed Arisha and stood protectively in front of her.

It was Izbaxl, her savior. After all these years, she had never seen him so aggressive. It was as if a brute force had risen from deep within him. A satyr could be the fiercest of creatures with a hidden reserve of preternatural power. They could even induce panic in their adversaries. No one was going to fight his will at this moment. Unless they wanted to perish.

Another satyr stepped up behind him, backing him up. It was Izbaxl's brother, Xizmat. These two were ready to take on the mob.

But Izbaxl's grip tightened on her arm and began to hurt her. He barked at the crowd of assailants, "She is mine first."

Arisha looked with fright at him, and whimpered, "Izbaxl?"

She saw in his eyes a bestiality of indifference. As a predator looks at its prey before consuming it.

• • • • •

Arisha had survived that night. But barely. It was evil that raped her innocence that evening. She had gone into shock at the trauma and had taken days before she came out of her comatose state. Sisa had tended to her with heartbroken pity as Arisha healed in her bed.

But she was alive. She had survived. Underneath her beautiful femininity was a strong and unbroken will. She would not allow monsters to have the last word. She would pick up the pieces and overcome their cruelty with victory.

That fateful night had changed everything. Though she had no conscious memory of what happened, her mind was intruded upon by flashes of heinous moments like nightmares implanted into her brain. She knew now that her intuition about this world was right. The Seirim were not her people, the satyrs were not her saviors, they were her captors and oppressors.

She was going to escape them. She was just waiting for the right moment.

Izbaxl had visited her to see how she was doing. He had returned to his kind and gentle self, and even sat with her at times, stroking her limp hands with soft affectionate concern.

But he was not repentant.

And she now understood the world.

She knew now what he truly was, and what they all were, the satyrs; They were goat demons.

She had prepared to take nothing with her but a change of warm clothes for the desert nights, and a sacrificial dagger as both a tool and protective weapon. Sisa, her sacred nymph sister, had taught Arisha how to be a slave to the will of others. And that often meant some nymphs died as helpless victims of a patron's outbreak of rage.

But Arisha had never accepted such extremes. She had always maintained a small part of her soul for herself. It created a tension in her mind, like she was two people at war with her identity. One, a compliant slave who sought the acceptance and love of others through self-denial; and another, a sorceress, who determined to fight her way through to find the secret truth of the heavens and earth.

The only problem was, she had never used a dagger. She had seen it used on the humans in the roots of Gaia, as well as on older nymphs at the altar before Azazel in the grotto. It had sickened her. It was supposed to be done in secret, but her unstoppable curiosity had found her hiding out in the sanctuary area on forbidden nights when the satyrs engaged in their blood ritual.

She was not sure she would have the courage or skill to use the dagger should she need to.

She had waited until it was late and everyone was asleep. In a day or so, she was about to be released back into the fold of nymphs to begin her sacred duties. She was not going to be around for that to happen. She was going to leave tonight.

But she had not anticipated Izbaxl's eagerness to see her again.

In fact, he had already slipped into the nymph's living quarters deep in the cave and was on his way to the healing area.

She heard his cloven hoofs approaching her door. She knew the sound of his walk from the years of their intimate friendship. Panic seized her.

But revenge calmed her down and she pulled herself back into her bed to feign sleep.

What would she do now?

Her mind raced searching for courage.

With closed eyes, she heard the clip clap of his soft steps approach her and then stop.

She felt the hotness of his breath on her skin as he leaned in to her face.

She felt his sandy split tongue lick her face.

She pretended to open her eyes as if out of a deep sleep.

He hopped up on her bed to be closer to her.

"My little Arisha," he moaned. "I want you to be mine."

She whispered in his ear, "Not anymore."

His eyes went blank. What did that mean?

She lifted the dagger that she had held concealed by her side, and with one swift move, cut off his male member.

Shock seized him and he fell backward, blood pouring from his gaping wound.

And then the pain and reality hit him all at once, and he howled in agony, grabbing his wound to stop the bleeding.

It must have awakened everyone in the living quarters.

He fell off the bed to the floor with a thud.

And for one moment, even Arisha was shocked at what she just did. She did not know she had it in her.

But then she realized she would not have much time before she was beaten to death by her emasculated abuser or one of the guards no doubt on their way right now to find out what was going on.

She jumped out of bed, pulled her little packet of clothes from the corner and ran to the door.

She left the bloody dagger on the bed.

But as she hit the doorway, she was blocked by a figure.

It was Sisa. Would she turn Arisha in?

Sisa was also clothed as if ready for a journey. "Follow me. Or you are dead."

Sisa led her down the hall and around a corner. She grabbed a torch and led Arisha into a small crevice that opened up to a secret passageway Arisha had not known about. As one of the older nymphs, Sisa knew many secrets of the cavern that were not common knowledge.

Arisha whispered, "Why are you helping me?"

"Because I want to go with you."

And then Arisha understood. She had had as much effect on Sisa as Sisa had on her. Arisha's hunger for life had awakened Sisa's own desire. But her fear had kept that forbidden desire hidden.

"This passage leads us out to the desert. You better have a plan for where you want to go, or we are both dead."

"Oh, I do, sister," said Arisha. "I have been planning that for some time."

“Then let us hurry. I am not the only one who knows about this secret passage.”

They found their way through the small tunnel and out into the cold desert air lit by a full moon. Sisa started toward the valley.

“No,” said Arisha. “This way.” She pulled her toward the dark cedar forest.

“But the forest is full of wild animals and dark forces. We will not survive two days in there.”

Arisha said, “We will not survive the night that way. They will track us down in hours.”

Sisa knew she was right. The valley was the well-traveled pathway to other towns and villages in the area. It would be the obvious choice for fugitives of their slender frame and gender. And there was almost nowhere to hide.

The dark forest, on the other hand was dense and hostile, even toward satyrs and hunters. But Arisha had one benefit of being the charge of Izbaxl. He had taught her all about nature over the years. Not only about what plants were poisonous and what you could eat, but also the ways of animals, predator and prey, and various tricks to avoid being eaten.

They ran for the dark forest.

• • • • •

Though Izbaxl’s wound was serious, satyrs were creatures of robust strength. He had bandaged himself and found the energy to limp out into the night. He was fueled by the hatred of revenge that rose within the depths of his soul. He was not going to just kill Arisha. He was going to do far worse things to her—and her family.

His wound was so humiliating that he refused to explain anything to anyone. He imagined the mockery he would face when the others discovered where he had been cut by the slight nymph who seemed the object of everyone's desires.

He managed to get out on his own and limped directly toward the dark forest. He knew exactly how Arisha thought. He had taught her himself.

He carried Arisha's dagger in his hand and a bow across his back. Every step was painful—very painful. But he had a reserve of revenge to draw from.

Almost immediately, he heard the howl of a dire wolf deep in the forest, and he knew where Arisha was.

• • • • •

Arisha and Sisa heard the howl and froze in their tracks. It was very near. Arisha knew they had been seen and were now being tracked by a pack of dire wolves.

They did not have much time. Maybe minutes.

She barked, "Quickly, find a tree!"

They looked around frantically for a climbable tree.

There were not many. This was an old growth forest and the cedars towered over their heads like walls of timber.

Arisha spotted one in the distance. It was an oak tree with gnarly bark rough enough to grab onto and climb to branches high above the ground.

"There!" She bolted for it.

Sisa followed.

But the glowing yellow eyes in the forest had already found them. Six dire wolves burst out of the dense foliage a hundred yards from them, closing the gap quickly.

Arisha was already high enough to find a branch from where she could reach down and help Sisa.

Sisa reached out her hand and Arisha grasped it.

But the dire wolves had reached the base of the tree. The large black leader jumped and clamped onto Sisa's ankle.

Arisha screamed, "SISA!"

The weight of the wolf pulled Sisa right out of Arisha's hands and down to the pack of killers below.

Arisha lost her balance and her bag of clothes fell to the ground with Sisa.

She caught herself from a near fatal slip and dodged the snapping jaws of the black leader that had left Sisa to the pack to catch the little prize up in the branches.

Arisha moved before thinking and scuttled up the branches to the top of the tree out of visual sight amidst the foliage.

She could not stand to see the feeding frenzy she could hear below. She could barely breathe as she wept tears of great sorrow over the loss of her only true friend. A friend who had endangered her own life to rescue her, and was now dead forever.

Arisha could barely contain herself. But suddenly, she heard the sound of musical notes she knew very well.

She froze in terror. It was Izbaxl's pipes. He had found her.

She stopped breathing.

Izbaxl's music would hold the wolves at bay. It was a satyr's power over the nature of the wild.

The wolves stopped and backed away cautiously from the bones at the foot of the tree.

But they did not leave.

Izbaxl would normally have more sway over them, but he was noticeably weakened and had a bloody bandage on his wound that was causing the wolves to be more courageous than usual in the face of this master of nature.

Izbaxl limped to the foot of the tree and saw the carnage of the slaughter.

Arisha peeked through the leaves and could see him far below pick up one of the pieces of her clothing and sniff it.

Izbaxl did not know that Sisa had helped her. He thought Arisha was all alone. And since there was nothing left of Sisa's body, he must have concluded they were Arisha's clothes torn to shreds.

She had evaded him.

Izbaxl dropped the piece of cloth to the ground in anger, and reeled back to give a satyr howl.

The screeching bellow struck fear into the heart of Arisha—as it would into the heart of any creature, including the dire wolves, that backed up further and whimpered in submission.

But then the unexpected happened. Instead of hiding herself back in the foliage of the tree, she could not stop staring at her nemesis below. When he leaned back to howl up into the night, his eyes had noticed Arisha's movement.

She should have pulled herself out of sight.

But it was too late.

He had seen her.

And like a deer in the torchlight, she froze.

He had figured out what had happened.

He stopped, smiled, and whispered a prayer, "Thank you, Azazel. I will offer my sacrifice to you slowly—over many days."

He pulled out the sacrificial dagger that Arisha had used to cut him.

He held it up to her with a smile and she knew he meant to do to her what she had done to him—and more.

He limped up to the tree, held the dagger in his teeth, grabbed hold of the bark, and started to climb.

The wolves below drew near to watch what was going on above them in the tree.

Arisha's heart beat out of her chest. Her breathing grew shallow.

Izbaxl closed the distance quickly. He was wounded, but he was a powerful creature.

His hooves were not meant for such climbing, but the tree was very gangly with many ridges and crevices to grab hold.

He was almost upon her.

She looked above her. There was nowhere else for her to go. She was at the highest branch that could hold her. If she climbed out onto a branch it would only break and she would plunge to her death.

Then she thought that if she was going to die anyway, maybe she should just try to take him with her.

She started to climb out further onto the thinner end of the branch she was on. It started to bend.

But when she looked back, she noticed that Izbaxl had paused. He was not pursuing her anymore.

He was swaying with dizziness.

She could see his bandage was dripping wet. He had lost too much blood.

He was losing his consciousness.

The dagger slipped out of his mouth.

His desperate eyes made contact with hers.

He slipped but regained his foothold on the bark.

His gaze shifted from her to the skies and he muttered, "Curse you, Yahweh." His eyes rolled back in his head and he blacked out.

His grip released and he fell to the ground fifty feet below.

The wolves parted.

Izbaxl landed on his back.

The impact brought him back to consciousness. He was not dead. But he was seriously incapacitated.

The wolves snarled and began to advance upon the prostrate form of the satyr.

His blood was driving them wild with hunger.

They attacked.

In seconds, the satyr became one with nature.

But Arisha could not get the question out of her mind. *Who was this Yahweh that Izbaxl had cursed?*

• • • • •

It took weeks of wandering in the desert before Arisha found what she was looking for. She had never been very far from her home in Panias, and the Mother Earth goddess Gaia.

She knew she had to avoid well-known cities or popular trading villages because her presence might be too suspicious and cause a curious do-gooder to look into her identity.

Though all of Panias thought her dead and the secrets of Izbaxl hidden with him in the stomachs of dire wolves, she could not afford to be discovered and place her family in more jeopardy.

Her goal was to one day return and free her family from spiritual bondage in Panias. But she would have to build a new life and a new identity first. The best way to do so would be to start over in a place that was itself shrouded in mystery.

Gilgal Rephaim was just such a place. She had learned something about it from Izbaxl growing up, but only knew of its general location. Its name meant "Circle of Giants," and it was an astrological and funerary holy place tended by a monkish clan that was under the authority of King Og of Bashan, the chief Rephaim. They tended to avoid much interaction with other towns and cities, and were left alone because of their peculiar and unnerving ways. After what she had experienced, Arisha considered such a reputation her best hope to avoid detection.

Her first sign of the location was when she stumbled upon a huge serpentine ravine about thirty miles from Hermon. It seemed as large as some of the ravines near her home, but had the distinct appearance of being deliberately cut through the rock with designed intent. It was about a mile long and she wondered how on earth mere humans could accomplish such mighty engraving. It must have been accomplished with the aid of giants. She knew of giants who had occasionally visited Panias, but was otherwise sheltered from the rest of the world. She had no idea the numbers or the feats they could achieve.

She continued on and just a few miles from that ravine, she found a second indication that she was getting closer. This time it was a huge serpentine mound as opposed to a ravine. It appeared to rise from the earth hundreds of feet high. Another artifact that assured her she was very close now to her goal.

Her hopes rose within her. But she was weary from the travel, sick from lack of food, and it was getting dark again, so she had to find a place for the night as she always did. A safe place where she could avoid the predators of the desert.

At nightfall Arisha finally discovered a large circular monument of megalithic stones. It was over five hundred feet wide with stone megaliths twenty feet high. It must have been a monument built by giants. It consisted of five concentric circles of stone, creating a labyrinth that was attuned to astrological alignments in the heavens.

She found her way into the maze, fell exhausted against one of the stone walls, and began to drift off to sleep. She had found her destination. She had found Gilgal Rephaim. Now, she only hoped she would be taken in and accepted by its people, the Clan of the Serpent.

CHAPTER 7

King Sihon of Heshbon was not a giant, but he was a gibbor, a mighty warrior of strong build and glorious ambition, who ruled in the Transjordan just south of King Og and across from the northern regions of the Dead Sea. He was an Amorite king who had recently conquered and taken his region from the Moabites.

His people were not numerous. He only held a dozen cities compared to Og's sixty or more. But the territory he did hold was crucial. The plains of Moab were strategically optimum for access to the central region of Canaan across the Jordan valley. His home city was Heshbon on the King's Highway, but his recent war of expansion had secured all the land between the rivers of Jabbok in the north and Arnon in the south. The Moabites became his vassals, but they were a restless lot.

Sihon was a less sophisticated leader than Og. They had few giants but they made up for their lack of size with a fierce style of presence. They dressed like savages with animal skins and headdresses made of talons, horns and antlers of their game. They donned war paint and screamed in battle like unearthly shades of Sheol.

Sihon and his people were simpleminded in Og's view, even primitive. But they were useful.

Sihon stood with Og in his war chamber in Og's city of Ashtaroth. They were working through a treaty covenant to establish an alliance through which they might control the entire Transjordan region.

But the first order of business was for Og to suffer through Sihon's ballad singers as they sang a newly composed ode commemorating Sihon's recent victory over Moab. It was an offering to Og, but he had no interest in such wasteful indulgence of entertainment. Especially since it was self-serving of Sihon's pride. Og only tolerated it as an obligation of royal etiquette.

The minstrels played on flute and lyre. But they were mediocre musicians, and their playing caused Sihon's ears to hurt. His people were good at war, but not at music.

They sang:

For fire came out from Heshbon,
flame from the city of Sihon.
It devoured Ar of Moab,
and swallowed the heights of the Arnon.
Woe to you, O Moab!
You are undone, O people of Chemosh!
He has made his sons fugitives,
and his daughters captives,
to an Amorite king, Sihon.

Guards escorted the musicians out of the war chamber, and the chiefs got down to real business.

Sihon was desperate, but tried not to let it show to his superior, the Rephaim that towered over him by at least five feet. Og sat down in order to lessen his imposing presence and draw out Sihon's secrets. Both of their war councils surrounded the table with them, a total of about ten men. But they deferred to the kings in their deliberations and only advised when asked.

"Are you prepared for occupation of the southern Transjordan?" said Og.

"I took high losses securing my land from the Moabites. We are trying to encourage the population to breed so we can replenish our numbers. But these things take time."

Og said, "Something your minstrels neglected to point out in their praise. I thought you wild ones were obsessed with unrestrained breeding. Institute more inbreeding and tax those who fail to obey."

Everything was so simple for Og. He knew how to control the masses because he knew how they responded to authority and power. To him, they were means to be manipulated for his ends.

Og added, "What of your Moabite vassals?"

"They are a stubborn people. I do not think they would be reliable armed support so soon after their humiliation."

Sihon was completely at the mercy of this Rapha. He knew Og could defeat his forces with one bold stroke. But they were both a part of an Amorite treaty of nations and it would not be advantageous for Og to betray his own alliance of peoples. So Sihon sought to position himself as strategically beneficial to Og. An ally was more valuable than a vassal. Vassals may serve out of forced obligation, but an ally fought valiantly for their own share of the rewards. And a well-informed ally provided intelligence that doubled the reach of the dominant king.

"The Ammonites to the east are not numerous, and it would not take too much to subdue the rest of Moab south of the Arnon River."

Og said, "And what of the Edomites?" The Edomites controlled the southern region of the Transjordan, the key to complete victory of the region.

Sihon said, "I can guarantee deliverance of the rest of Moab, and together we could dominate Edom. But I need to finish my fortifications and rebuild my armed forces to be fully equipped. And do not forget, once we take final control of the King's Highway, we may need to be ready to deal with Hittite aggression from the north. They will not be pleased with our command of the region."

Og was calculating his plans. "How much time do you need?"

Sihon looked to his architect for the answer, who said, "A few more years."

"That is not an answer," said Og.

The architect gulped and gave the real one, "Five or six years?" He spoke more like asking for permission than stating a fact.

Og said, "We will not have five or six years with these Habiru already approaching the southern rim near Edom."

Sihon said, "Well, if King Rekem of Edom allows them passage, then I would only ask that you support me with troop reinforcements, so that we have assured victory with combined forces."

He thought he would add a request in the form of a hypothetical. "For instance, two hordes of Rephaim might strike fear into the hearts of these Habiru." That would be about four hundred giant gibborim, the finest and most ruthless of warriors. Sihon was shooting for the stars.

Og thought it through for a moment. "Are there any Zamzummim or Emim left in your territories?"

The Zamzummim were a clan of giants that were known for their freakish "buzzing" sound, and the Emim were another giant clan whose name meant "terror." They were both clans that had inhabited the region of Moab that Sihon had just conquered.

"I only have two platoons, one of each," said Sihon. "Moab had all but wiped out the Emim when they settled, and the Ammonites did the same with the Zamzummim."

Sihon did not have many giants in his army. Two hordes of four hundred Rephaim from Og would calm his anxiety and make him feel very secure.

Og pondered some more, then said with finality, "Done." Then he added, "I will send them at the first sign of the Habiru's approach."

Sihon sighed with relief. He had maneuvered through a potentially volatile situation to maintain his kingdom in the shadow of a most superior ruler, the mighty Og of Bashan. That would bring him accolades with the scribes who recorded their history of exploits.

•••••

In the same city of Ashtaroth, in the temple of Ashtart, another strategic meeting took place, but this one was not between two kings, but two gods.

They were Ashtart and Molech.

Sihon had adopted Molech, the underworld god of the Ammonites, as his own patron deity when Sihon pushed the Ammonites east of the King's Highway.

Molech had no concern whether his followers were united or divided. The more who were devoted to him, the better.

In Mesopotamia, he had been disguised as Nergal, husband of Ereshkigal, goddess of the underworld who guarded the gates of Sheol. So he jumped at the chance to start over in Canaan with a new identity and without the humiliating status of being the emasculated tool of a superior goddess.

As lord of the underworld in Canaan, Molech spent a lot of time in his underground dwelling and tunneling. Mightier gods such as Ashtart ruled the overworld, so his goal had been to establish an underground superiority that may be called upon some day when the pantheon would need it and therefore grant him higher status.

Because of the time he spent beneath the surface, his body had developed a pale skin with an ugly mole-like face and poor eyesight. He was imposing at eight feet tall with muscles honed from the movement of massive amounts of rock, and he wore a single loincloth because clothes shredded too easily in that environment. But his skin was also calloused from that same rough cave existence. Even his voice was gravelly.

Despite his frightening exterior, he too, like king Sihon, was still in subjection. His superior was Ashtart, the goddess ruler of the region, and personal escort of Ba'al, the most high god.

Ashtart's hairdo distracted Molech's attention. It consisted of a massive amount of hair twirled and piled into the form of two large horns that accented her heavily made up face. Horns were symbols of deity, so she was tickled by the ability to combine the symbolic with an outrageous style. It would be a bit comical if she were not the most frightening of all warrior divinities.

Ironically, this mighty goddess was expressing a need for Molech's expertise with the dead. She had been developing her own necromantic spell for a few years and had approached a rock wall, so to speak, and was asking for his help. Knowing her reputation for being the second-most ruthless and feared deity in the pantheon after Ba'al, he felt that this might be an opportunity for him to gain some prestige if he could only manipulate the circumstance to his benefit.

Unfortunately, he was not suave in his diplomacy.

"What is in it for me?" said Molech.

This low-life amused Ashtart.

He added, "You know, there is a saying in the shadows of the pantheon that Ba'al and his broad need all the help they can get."

"And you have quite the gall," said Ashtart annoyed. She thought how she might skin him alive and let him burn in the salt of the Dead Sea. Who needed voluntary cooperation anyway?

"I am only quoting what I heard," he countered. "You will find no ambitions of power or glory from me. Just give me limited territory, and a supply of children. All I really want is children."

Ashtart grinned with satisfaction. "Then children you shall have. To your heart's content."

Molech grinned through rotted stained teeth. Oh, how he treasured little children. The pleasure they brought him.

But then she sobered him up. "Of course, you do realize that these Habiru are the Seed of Eve, do you not?"

He looked at her with blank stupor.

"You moron," she spit out. "Have you forgotten the allotment at Babel?"

She was referring to the act of Yahweh that occurred with the Confusion of Tongues at the Tower of Babel in the ancient days. He divided the nations, fixed their borders, and allotted them according to the number of the Sons of God as their inheritance.

He had given the nations over to be ruled by the gods. But Yahweh kept Jacob, through the Seed of Eve, for his own inheritance.

Molech said, "That is how we received Canaan."

"Yes, that is how we received Canaan," she mimicked. "But, do not get too settled down little mole man. The Seed of Eve is on their way to Canaan, which means Yahweh intends to dispossess the Seed of the Serpent from their inheritance. It will be a great War of the Seed."

"What does he want to do to us?" said Molech.

"Bind us in the earth, you idiot. What do you think?"

Molech's face went even more pale than it already was. He had been spending too much time below. He needed to get out more and spend time on the surface to keep more informed.

"I am sure your brilliant powers of deduction have already figured out that that means we are not merely fighting a turf war. This is for our ultimate destiny. If we do not work together, we will be *bound* together—until judgment. So I suggest you use your special skills with the dead to help me with my necromancy, because it may be the only chance we have."

CHAPTER 8

Moses and Joshua stood on the ridge overlooking the vast plain that stretched out before them in the Wilderness of Zin. Behind them below the ridge was Kadesh, the encampment of the Israelites for the past forty years. The years had not disabled Moses' transfigured body, but the stress had made his soul weary. Joshua was as hearty and strong as the day he spied the Promised Land.

Joshua had mustered the Israelite forces in readiness, because before them a few miles out on the plains was a vast army of Edomites in full battle regalia. Behind them were the Seirite mountains of the territory of Edom that they were guarding.

A plume of dust rose from a small figure on horseback racing his way back to Moses and Joshua. It was a messenger.

•••••

In the tabernacle, Eleazer the priest helped his father Aaron to sit down and rest outside the Tent of Meeting as priests engaged in their daily sacrifices. The priesthood was a rigorous responsibility that required daily sacrifices and offerings from the congregation: Burnt offerings, grain offerings, peace offerings, and sin offerings.

Because of the hostility growing near the border of Edom, there were many freewill burnt offerings that families brought on behalf of their warriors assembled with Moses in order to consecrate them and remove any uncleanness before battle.

The outer court was soaked in the blood of sacrificial animals. It covered everything and everyone because of the massive amount of sacrifices. Israelites were lined up outside and allowed in one at a time. The laypersons were responsible for bringing their animal into the court, slaughtering it and cutting it up. The priest would then take the blood from the basin for ritual sprinkling, burn the animal on the bronze altar and then dispose of the remains.

Because of Aaron's age, performing his duty was becoming increasingly difficult. His eyesight was failing and he could not stand for long periods of time. He was quite frail and Eleazer knew transference of the high priesthood was inevitable. He would most likely succeed his father, but the notion did not entirely comfort him. The high priest had a heavy responsibility upon his shoulders.

This people were so unruly and idolatrous in their affections. The golden calf debacle, the sons of Korah rebellion, the constant griping and complaining against Yahweh, left Eleazer with a sick feeling in his stomach. He just did not feel safe.

Yahweh would ultimately punish rebels, as he always did, but Eleazer did not want to be a death statistic of their next rebellion. Collateral damage to justify Yahweh's judgment. They always tended to focus their violence upon the leaders, like Moses. The high priest was the leader of the holy cult. So Eleazer did not relish the prestige of such a promotion.

Caleb had arrived to report Moses' thoughts to Aaron and return with any advice from the leader's brother. But Aaron was grumpy and had no advice. He was losing all interest in such matters. Caleb was soon on his way back to the ridge where Moses and Joshua stood.

For his part, Caleb had not seemed anything like his age. He was still strong, sinewy, and sharp of mind as any forty-year old and was proud of it. He ran as fleet-footed as any messenger. He chalked it up to his Karabu training.

When Caleb arrived at the front, he communicated Aaron's lack of concern, which troubled Moses. But Moses had no time to fret for his brother, as the messenger also arrived from Edom.

Moses had sent a request to the king for passage through his land to reach the King's Highway for their northern journey. Moses had tried to appeal to King Rekem of Edom's familial history by calling them brothers and recounting Israel's suffering at the hands of Egypt.

He was hoping that the king would see Israel as a weak and pathetic nation without the will to fight, and therefore not a threat to Edom. He even promised to pay for any water they drank or any food they ate as they passed through their land. Moses just wanted to get to the King's Highway and they would be out of Edom's hair.

The messenger got off his horse and bowed to Moses, "My lord, King Rekem of Edom has received your request, and he resolutely states, 'You shall not advance through.' If you try to do so, he will draw his sword against us."

"I thought so," said Joshua.

Moses added wryly, "Armies in battle display are not usually a welcoming party."

Joshua spit out in anger, "Let me call forth our forces. We will crush these insolent god-haters."

"No!" barked Moses. "They are sons of Esau. They are not the enemy."

Joshua interrupted him, "But they stand defiant against Yahweh and his people. What right have they to live?"

Moses said, "We will travel south and around the edges of Edom, by way of Yam Suph."

"It will add months to our travel," complained Joshua.

"You will have your opportunity to strike soon enough, Joshua," said Moses. "It is not yet time."

Joshua was stubborn. "We will complicate our troubles by going around them, only to have to ask them admittance again when we reach the Highway on the other side, because it also cuts through their territory."

Moses said, "Yahweh has given Mount Seir to Esau as a possession. Would you seek to question Yahweh's allotment?"

Joshua finally backed down. He knew Moses conversed face to face with Yahweh. Joshua would not argue with that.

Caleb could see what Joshua could not in his haste to respond with force. Esau was not the Seed of the Serpent; they were brothers of Israel, rebellious brothers though they were. And Israel needed all her strength to face the kings of the Amorites, Sihon of Heshbon and Og of Bashan.

CHAPTER 9

The plateau of Mount Hor rose several thousand feet high and overlooked the desert wilderness of Zin. Its rough red rock showed layers of sediment that were claylike at the bottom, but harder limestone on top.

Moses, Joshua, Eleazer, and Aaron stood on the mountain looking down upon the people of Israel who filled the plains at the bottom. They were at the very border of Edom, but were not going to enter. Much to Joshua's dismay, Moses had sent word back to King Rekem assuring him they would respect his demands and not transgress the borders of Edom.

They were here today because Aaron was very weak and dying, and was about to be gathered to his fathers. Moses was not much younger than Aaron, but was much stronger for his age.

The high priesthood had to be transferred onto Eleazer. Moses knew his own time would be soon as well, but he did not know when.

Aaron had worn the vestments of his high priesthood for the sake of the ceremony they were now performing before the eyes of all of Israel below them.

Joshua watched Eleazer help Aaron take off his vestments and then put them on himself. Then Moses decreed Eleazer as the new high priest of Israel. It was a simple ceremony, but a significant one. For God was drawing them near the time of fulfillment for his Promise.

It had been forty years since Joshua and Caleb disagreed with the report of the other spies regarding Canaan. God had cursed that generation to die in the wilderness, every one of them above the age of twenty.

They were all dead now, all except Moses and Aaron, who were told they would not see the Promised Land for their arrogance at Meribah.

They waited with Aaron, placing him on a bedroll in a cave and tending to him until he finally died. And when he did, Moses wept with a great cry of pain deep within his soul. His transfigured flesh seemed to flash like lightning with his anguish. He had shared the deepest of life's pains and the highest of life's blessings with his older brother.

Aaron had his moments of dishonor throughout his life. But he had also been an irreplaceable support for his younger brother in the most impossible of circumstances. When Moses fled to the desert for forty years, Aaron stayed behind with his brethren in Egypt to receive Moses back into their fold. When Moses was too fearful to face Pharaoh, Yahweh had sent Aaron to help him. When Moses was incapable of being a spokesman for Yahweh because of his stuttering and slow speech, Aaron became his mouthpiece, speaking for him to both Israel and Pharaoh with eloquence and sure tongue. Aaron had even participated in miracles at the directions of Moses.

Aaron's weaker moral constitution had failed at Sinai when he helped the Israelites to make the golden calf, and later when he challenged Moses' authority along with Miriam. But a lifetime of love, support, and obedience could not be invalidated or dismissed because of a few lapses of character so common to human existence. Forgiveness was more enduring than failure.

Moses, Joshua, and Eleazer wept freely for the loss of a beloved brother, father, and high priest.

They buried Aaron on Mount Hor.

Moses turned to Joshua and said, “The forty years are fulfilled. It is time to enter Canaan and claim your inheritance.”

CHAPTER 10

It had been six years since Arisha first found her way as a fugitive to the mighty megaliths of Gilgal Rephaim. She had collapsed inside the maze of concentric stone circles of the mysterious astrological mound, and had been discovered by one of the priests tending to the holy site.

She was brought to the village hidden away in a cavern deep below the surface. It was at least a thousand feet wide by her best guess and there was a large lake of glassy pure water at its edge. At first it reminded her of the grotto at Panias, which made her restless with bad memories. But she soon learned that it was a very different community and there were no satyrs here. They called themselves the *Nachashim*.

They were the Clan of the Serpent.

They performed the rites and mysteries of Ophiolatreia, or snake liturgy, which included the breeding and handling of snakes, as well as the submissive worship of the Serpent god, Nachash, from whence they drew their name.

In many important ways, they were the opposite of her origins. The Seirim were a hairy people like their ancestor Esau, the Nachashim were mostly hairless and pale skinned. The Seirim were passionate and nature oriented. These were colder, reptilian and dwelt among the rocks and the underground. The Seirim worshipped Azazel the hot-blooded goat god of the desert, but the Nachashim worshipped Nachash, the cunning cool serpent of the underworld.

These outward differences had comforted Arisha at first. She had been so damaged by the betrayal of her people that she wanted to start over in a world as far away from them as possible. But for all the differences between the two people groups, there were some things that just did not change in creation.

As soon as she was brought to the clan, she learned that there was no king or leader. It was an egalitarian community of about four hundred people. They all lived together in the one large cavern with spring fed lake. They did not believe in individual ownership. They shared all things in common, such as living quarters, food, and even each other. They even slept all together in the cavern, like a bed of snakes would. Thus, there were no families with couples as parents, but rather, the young were taken care of separately.

They prided themselves on being different from the other peoples of Canaan who were led by kings and queens and other elitist rulers that always eliminated equality and created a caste distinction between the poor and the rich. But not so in "The Nest," as they called their utopian community.

They had accepted Arisha into their midst under the condition that she shave her body of all hair and adopt their ways. She readily agreed and settled into her new identity.

But she had learned quickly that all such claims to equality were a façade, because the priesthood that was responsible for the religious cult of the Nest was in reality a privileged class that ruled the people in the name of the people. The god Nachash was the ultimate authority over the Nest and the priestly class were his enforcers.

Someone always rules the community.

Arisha had gone along with it all at first, absorbing her identity into the commune, but eventually, she could not abide the "special attention" she was getting from the men who would be lined up to be with her instead of "equal access" to other women. Equality was a lie to justify the redistribution of power from those who had more to those who had less.

Her unwanted attention had resulted in several abortions, the first of which had been an abominable experience she taught herself to forget. But one never fully forgets such things.

She started to stand up for herself and would not submit to the "greater will of the Nest," as the manipulators would call it. She got a reputation for having a fiery independent will and a selfish loner attitude. Individual worth was discouraged in favor of the will of the Nest. She became so defiant that one of the priests who knew her occasionally called her "Rahab" after the sea dragon of chaos. He saw it made her even more incorrigible, so he stopped it.

Arisha was now twenty years old.

She was preparing food to eat in her special area that she used for herself, away from the community. It was one of those days where she sought to be left alone with her thoughts.

She heard the sound of footsteps approaching.

She peeked out from behind the rock. She was shocked to see a dozen men arriving behind the high priest Tannin, whose name meant "dragon."

She knew immediately what her fate was to be, and she lashed out with the food knife in her hand, slashing the first man to grab her. He screamed and pulled back his bleeding arm painfully.

But it was futile. She would not be able to protect herself against the lot of them.

They quickly surrounded her and subdued her. One punched her in the stomach and she doubled over in pain.

Tannin yelled out, "Stop! Do not damage her."

She struggled to get loose as he came near to her. But she was held in place by a dozen hands.

Tannin got right up into her face and stared down into her eyes with a reptilian grin. She could see his teeth that were all filed to fangs. His skin was scaly and so dry it was cracking and peeling. The priests of the Nest were humans, but they engaged in sorcery with drugs to try to turn themselves into snakelike beings. The result was ugly mutations of serpent-like humanoids.

She spit in his face. His eyes blinked, but he did not flinch. Instead he responded by sticking a forked tongue out of his mouth to lick her face with relish.

He smacked his lips and said, "Tonight, you will make a fine sacrifice."

• • • • •

This evening was the annual sacrifice to the Serpent Nachash. Gilgal Rephaim was not the only place of serpent worship in Canaan. In fact, Ophiolatreia was a dominant force throughout the entire land, illustrating an underlying influence of that god behind the pantheon of deities that ruled in their various territories. Even the mightiest of gods gave homage to the Serpent.

Thus, this evening, the gods of the area, Ashtart, Chemosh, and Molech would be at the ceremony that would include a visit from Nachash himself.

And for that visit, six female citizens must be offered in sacrifice in order to protect the community for the coming year and appease the gods.

Tonight, Arisha was to be one of those six victims. She was rounded up with the other five women in a pen and forced to wear white garments as a symbol of purity. It seemed to her a mockery of the truth, since none of them were pure, especially her.

Everything was lies. Everything. She did not know what the truth was anymore. She had escaped from Panias after being made an offering to satyrs and men. And now she was being made an offering to a serpent god.

It had felt to her as if she lived in a world that was unnatural. It made her long for an impossible purity of being. These malevolent gods made her wonder if there was a good and loving divinity anywhere on the earth. Or was existence just a brutal form of perpetual suffering until one died and entered the oblivion of Sheol?

She did not have the luxury of pondering such self-reflective thoughts anymore. They would soon be all over. The priests led the white robed women, followed by the rest of the community out to the megaliths of Gilgal Rephaim.

The community spread out around the vast stone circle and chanted poetic verse that sounded like soft hissing. At the front of the crowd, Arisha noticed the two gibborim kings of the area, Og of Bashan and Sihon of Heshbon. They too were here in obeisance to the Serpent.

The parade of priests led the women through the stone openings toward the circular tumulus in the center.

As she tread the pathway, Arisha considered in her mind the meaning of the serpent in Canaan. It was a powerful divine figure that symbolized many things. First, it was a symbol of fertility. Its shedding of skin symbolized eternal life. The image of a snake eating its tail in the form of a circle was called the Ouroboros and was a picture of the cosmos. It was a symbol of kingship, borrowed from the uraeus on the crowns of Egyptian Pharaohs.

But the serpent was also a universal symbol of both healing and wisdom, as it was known that the Serpent had given words of wisdom and maturity to the first humans in the garden paradise so long ago. He had helped to free humankind from the unfair controlling tyranny of the Creator who sought to keep mankind ignorant and subservient to his unpredictable whims.

But the snake was also the guardian of the tree of life in that paradise and the underworld regions below.

All these and other symbolic meanings surrounded serpent mythology with an aura of divinity and greatness shared by few other beings. But Arisha was not seeing that greatness as they lined up around the tumulus. She was seeing the fangs behind the elegance, the poison behind the beauty, the lies behind the split tongue, and the death behind the smooth silence.

Her thinking was interrupted by the presence of the visiting gods, Ashtart, Molech and Chemosh. They were all lined up before the women. For the first time ever, Arisha had the opportunity to see these beings up close. She had always seen them at a distance. But at this closeness, she noticed something she had never seen before. She could see their eight feet tall powerful frames, their shining skin of subtle scales, and their ophidian eyes of lapis lazuli blue.

But she could also see the features of their faces, and the face that caused her shock was Ashtart. Her whole past came flooding into her mind as she stared up at the great Watcher god looking down upon her and the others.

The reason for this was that she recognized that face. She had seen it before. She had studied it. It was the face of Azazel from the statue of Panias. Though Ashtart was a female, she knew at that moment it was really Azazel in disguise.

She did not know how to react. Ashtart noticed her stare and became curious.

She tried to appear more naïve than she was.

Suddenly, the sounds of eerie music echoed through the stone walls as musicians played to introduce the being rising from the tumulus: Nachash.

He was not a formidable looking divinity. He was not muscular like Molech or handsome like Ashtart. Only his six wings spread out behind him added a sense of glory lost on his rather undeveloped and ugly form. But his voice carried authority, he shined like burnished bronze, and the other gods seemed to defer to him with respect.

The truth was, Nachash was a seraph, one of the highest beings in Yahweh's heavenly court. And in that court, his ordained role was to be "the satan," the accuser or adversary who challenged Yahweh and his law.

On earth he went by other names such as Belial or Diablos. His personal favorite was Mastema.

He was not physically imposing like the other gods, but he was diabolically cunning and a master of legal manipulation. His primeval act of temptation in Eden had plunged the world into chaos and emboldened the mighty two hundred Watchers from Yahweh's divine council to rebel. One of the leaders of that band of rebels was the mighty Azazel, who now stood before Nachash.

But all this, Arisha could not know. She could only discern that Ashtart was the Azazel she had worshipped back in Panias, and that all was not as it seemed.

The gods conferred amongst themselves. The six women were lined up in a row for sacrifice.

And then a bizarre creature was carried on a stretcher from out of the tumulus. Four priests held the stretcher on poles and brought it right up to the women. Some of them backed up against the wall in fright.

It was hideous. But Arisha was not as squeamish as the others. She tried to get a closer look.

She knew what it was. It was an Ob, a serpent seer. Obs were mediums that could talk to the dead and see the future. They were sensitive to the spirit world and were often called upon to validate the sacrifice.

The Ob was a human being that sought to transform into a serpent, through a combination of sorcery and natural body modification. This one had its arms and legs cut off so that it was only a naked body that could wriggle and writhe like a snake. It lay on its stomach facing forward. It was bald with a white clammy skin underbelly, and a head and torso with scales. But the scales were not completely covering the body like a snake, but rather they were in sporadic patches all around, as if it was a magic spell that had failed. Its eyes were reptilian-slivered pupils and its tongue was split and three times the length of a normal human tongue.

The thing made Arisha want to vomit.

The Ob was brought up to each woman. It would lick her body in one upward motion from toe to head. Upon approval, he was taken to the next one.

When the Ob reached Arisha, it snickered with delight. Its inhuman eyes caused a chill down her spine. But also, a pang of hatred for yet another evil to endure in this wicked world.

The Ob cackled with a sleazy laugh. Then it licked her.

She shivered. It resurfaced the memories of her betrayal by Izbaxl years ago. She also remembered the courage she found within her to respond in self-defense. And she thought she would grab this tongue in like manner and cut it off, if she only had a dagger.

But she did not have a dagger. And she was about to be offered up to the dagger in sacrifice to Nachash.

But the Ob stopped, hissed, and made a choking cough.

It was raised up to her face and glared into her eyes.

She found all the anger in her soul to stare back in defiance.

They may destroy my body, but they will not destroy my soul.

Then the Ob went into a trance. Its eyes went back into its head, and it jerked and spasmed with a seizure.

When it was done, its eyes reopened and it croaked out, "This wench is a chosen vessel."

It stopped even the gods, who turned to look at Arisha. She now felt more vulnerable under their penetrating gaze.

The Ob continued, "I have entered the spirit realm and I have seen great and terrifying things. This is no ordinary being. Out of her womb will come forth a great and mighty warrior whose kingdom shall overthrow all kingdoms. Thus saith the Ob."

Arisha was in shock. What in heaven was this creature saying? *She* is no ordinary being? *She* is a chosen vessel? It made no sense to her.

His fellow gods followed Nachash as he stepped over to Arisha and stared at her. His gaze hypnotized her. She felt paralyzed and entirely at his mercy.

He tilted his head trying to understand what he could not see. But then a huge grin came across his face. His fangs gleamed in the torchlight. From out of nowhere, six reptilian wings spread out behind his back creating a kingly presence of glory.

Arisha trembled with fear.

Nachash said, "Take this vessel and prepare her for the sacred marriage."

The other gods appeared shocked. Arisha did not understand why.

Nachash turned back to them by the tumulus and they argued quietly amongst themselves.

Four priests grabbed Arisha and escorted her out of the Circle back to the Nest.

She would not be sacrificed to Nachash this evening. No, her fate was much worse. She knew she was being saved for Sacred Marriage to that malevolent monster.

Flashes of that evening in Panias years ago intruded in on her mind. The pain, the horror, and the aftermath. It had taken years to put it behind her. But she now realized she had not put it behind her. She had only ignored it. And all the wellspring of emotion rose up inside her because she knew it was going to happen again.

She determined in her heart that there was no way she was going to let it happen again.

Over by the tumulus, the gods conferred. Molech was conspicuously silent around his superiors in intellect. Ashtart was angrily determined.

"You should not do this, Mastema," she snapped. "You know what happened with my antediluvian plans of interbreeding."

"Yes," he whispered thoughtfully. The Deluge frightened the Sheol out of all of them.

Chemosh added, "And now we are only seventy over the nations." He was referring to the original two hundred Watchers who came to Mount Hermon to defy Yahweh. All but seventy were bound into the earth by Yahweh's archangels because of their mating with the daughters of men. This was why none of them had ever tried the Sacred Marriage again. None of them, except Ashtart.

Ashtart said, "I tried again at Sodom with less. And I almost lost everything. Do you want to see all of Canaan go up in flames?"

Mastema simply said, "Yes."

Chemosh said, "You cannot be serious."

A grin spread on Mastema's face. And they understood he was not being entirely so.

He said, "You heard the Ob's prophecy. I doubt that it was intended for us."

Ashtart understood first. "You think this may be *Yahweh's* chosen vessel."

Chemosh said, "The Seed of Eve."

Mastema said, "If I impregnate her and kill her after the child is born, then it will have to be my seedline whose kingdom will overthrow all kingdoms."

Ashtart giggled. "The anti-Seed."

Chemosh chimed in with approval, "Yahweh is coming to dispossess us from the land. So if he wants to burn up his children's inheritance like he did Sodom and Gomorrah, then let him burn it all. Let it all go up in flames."

Molech was titillated. He loved fire as much as he loved children. He loved children *on* fire. He wanted to create an entire valley in Canaan that would be devoted to passing children through the fires of Molech.

Mastema quieted them all. “This must remain a secret. Tell no other gods. It will only increase our chances of discovery by the enemy, as well as those usurpers in our ranks who would seek to use it to their advantage.”

Ashtart knew Ba’al was just such a usurper. He had the power to contest even Mastema, and would surely do so if given the chance. It was Mastema’s prestige that had saved Ashtart when Ba’al was about to bind her in the earth at Sodom. They had been at odds for millennia and Ba’al had finally bested her in the battle of the nine kings. But when he was about to leave her crushed under millions of tons of rocks, she had offered him a deal that turned his mind.

Ashtart had the favor of Mastema in Canaan, and had been breeding the Seed of the Serpent that would war with the Seed of Eve. Since Yahweh himself in the Garden prophesied this enmity, Ba’al knew it would be his way of ingratiating himself to a superior in Mastema. By saving Ashtart and making her his submissive consort, he was building his own strategy for conquest.

But Ba’al was in southern Canaan now with the Anakim. So he would not know of Mastema’s plans. Ashtart finally had leverage over Ba’al. It would only take some time before she could find a way to use it against him, and free herself from servitude to his command.

But right now, there was blood to drink.

• • • • •

The four priests brought Arisha into the Nest to prepare her for the Sacred Marriage rite. The first stage was to ritually cleanse her in the waters of life in their cavern.

They brought her down to the waters' edge and tried to disrobe her. She pulled away from them and snapped, "Do not touch me, you reptiles. I will clean myself."

The priests looked at each other. This was typical of Arisha.

The leader was Bodo, a gangly and sniveling weed of a man. He knew what was going to happen to Arisha, the humiliation, the pain and suffering. But he felt sorry for her, despite her obstinate attitude.

He said, "Arisha, your willfulness will not be welcomed by the deity with the tolerance we have too often displayed toward you."

She did not respond. She just stared at him defiantly.

He buckled. "Be sure to fully immerse."

She walked to the edge of the water, turned her back to them. They had all sought to control her in the past, but not this time.

She dipped into the water up to her neck, then took off her robe and let it drift freely. She breathed heavily.

Bodo thought that the cold water caused her hyperventilation. Or maybe this stubborn girl was finally beginning to face the consequences of her spirited independence.

Arisha then slipped below the surface.

She was in the habit of staying under a long time. It was her way of getting away from the community to be alone, of feeling in control. So initially, it did not alarm Bodo that she failed to return to the surface. She had hearty lungs and could stay down for quite a while.

But more time passed and Bodo's concern grew.

She was not coming up.

It had been over five minutes.

Now, closer to eight or nine. Something was not right.

Bodo finally ordered the priests. "Get others. Spread around the shore of the lake. Make sure she does not surface and try to get away."

He unclothed himself and walked into the water to search for her.

He dove in search of Arisha, expecting to find her body trapped in a crevice or ridge by suicidal intent. There were many in the deep cavernous lake.

He dove downward.

There was a special algae in the lake that glowed with iridescent light, thus giving him the ability to see in what would have been pitch-blackness.

But he could not find her.

He came back up for air and dove again.

Others surrounded the lake shoreline with torches to make sure she did not escape.

Bodo must have dove down a dozen times before he gave up from sheer exhaustion.

He had others dive as well. But they came up with nothing.

This was not good.

Nachash would not be happy.

•••••

Later that evening, Tannin, the high priest, had returned to the Nest to retrieve Arisha for Nachash. But he found Bodo and the priests cowering in fear of their lives.

"She what?" yelled Tannin.

"She drowned," said Bodo. "We took her to the lake for cleansing. She refused our help and demanded to clean herself. You know how stubborn Arisha can be."

"Yes, I know, fool!" said Tannin.

Bodo continued, "When she went under the waters, she never came back up. We immediately called for help and posted sentries all around the lake. She could not have escaped our net."

"Yet, she is gone," said Tannin with biting anger.

"Several of us dove down to try to find her body, but we were unsuccessful."

"That was several hours ago when you brought her here. Why did you not alert me?"

The priests looked nervously at one another. Bodo whimpered, "We were afraid for our lives."

"As well you should be. You failed to secure the god's vessel for Sacred Marriage. You let her drown. And then you did not repent."

The four priests fell to their knees. Bodo cried out, "We do repent, my lord! Please have mercy on us."

"If I have mercy on you," said Tannin, "then Nachash will have no mercy on me." He turned to the other priests around them and barked an order, "Execute them now."

The priests were immediately put to the edge of the sword.

As it turned out, Nachash had no mercy on Tannin either. He was cut down with the others when he brought the information to the god.

But Nachash also refused to believe Arisha was drowned unless he saw her lifeless body before him. This female was too important to be so easily killed in a twist of fate or suicide. So he sent other divers to continue scouring the cavernous lake to find her.

It was a deep lake with many rocky crevices and fissures for a body in which to be lost or stuck. They searched for a full day, but could find nothing.

They never did discover what happened to Arisha, the rascally spirited girl who had brought so much trouble into their commune.

She was dead and gone to them.

• • • • •

Arisha did not drown. She escaped. Her relentless curiosity had saved her again. For years she had known of a hidden underwater cave that led from their lake down to an underground river. But she had told no one, and kept it as her secret. It was her hideaway.

The way she found it was by chance.

She loved swimming in the waters as an opportunity to get away from the community and be alone. There were algae on the rocks that glowed with iridescent colors, creating quite a beautiful aura of an underwater world apart.

It was peaceful solitude for her to dive in deep water and explore. She performed exercises to increase the amount of time she could hold her breath, and had gotten to the point where she could stay under water for a full ten to twelve minutes.

One day she stumbled upon a small crevice that opened up to a larger tunnel. She could only make it part way down the tunnel and had to turn back. But when she looked up, she noticed bubbles at the ceiling of the cave. She learned that they were actually pockets of trapped oxygen where the water did not fill in. She then discovered she could suck the air out of those pockets which would enable her to go further.

That was when she discovered the underground river. And that underground river was where she had escaped her Sacred Marriage to the god Nachash.

She had used up most of the air pockets on the ceiling and had only a few left for one last visit to her secret river. But that night she did not need enough air to get back, so she sucked the last of them and barely made it to the river of deliverance.

And that was why they never found her escape route. They had found the crevice and the long tunnel, but several had drowned trying to explore the cave's distance. They concluded there was no way that slender female could have gone further without additional air—the additional air they could never have found in the ceiling air pockets because she had used them all up.

Arisha let the river current take her wherever it would. She did not care if she would come out alive or not. As far as she was concerned, it was much more desirable to drown alone and untouched in a vast underground cave than be touched by a deity she did not believe was benevolent.

As it happened, the underground river did not go deeper, but instead emptied out into one of their local rivers a couple miles away. She drifted all the way to the Sea of Chinnereth.

She found an old sailcloth along the shoreline and fashioned a primitive covering for her nakedness. Then she trekked around the shore of the lake and followed the Jordan River south.

She wanted to get as far away from Bashan as possible. She decided she would cross the Jordan and find her way in the Cisjordan, hoping it might be a different world, maybe even the opposite of the Transjordan.

She eventually found a city not far from the Jordan that had huge protective stone walls that seemed to reach to heaven. It was completely different from anything she had ever seen. It looked like they were built to protect its citizens from the brutality of the world outside its walls. It was an immense fortification. It made her feel safe.

She had found the city of Jericho.

She decided to find a way to melt into this new world and never be found by her past again. She had yet another chance to start a new life with a new identity. Just how, she did not know.

But when the first person she met who asked her name awaited her answer, she realized she had not thought ahead and did not know what she should call herself.

She would not use Arisha for fear of being tracked down by her past. But she had to say something or she might be discovered as the fugitive that she was.

So she said the first name she could think of that came to her. It was the nickname she had been given by one of the priests in the Nest of the Serpent Clan.

"My name is Rahab."

CHAPTER 11

Caleb strained to see inside the outer courtyard of the tabernacle. The drapes were pulled back for some of the congregation to see the ritual, but only those in front would really have a good sight on it all.

Providentially for Caleb, he was the Right Hand of Joshua, so he had a front row seat with his daughter Achsah and his brother Othniel. He watched with transfixed wonder as the Levites enacted their ordained duty of this highest holy day of the year: Yom Kippur, the Day of Atonement

Joshua however had fallen asleep. He did not value the beauty of what was taking place as Caleb did.

It was one of the only feasts they performed before entering the land of Canaan because of its sacrificial link to the tabernacle. To Caleb, it was the most significant of the feasts because it represented propitiation, the cleansing and atonement of the entire nation. He had learned many of the details of the tabernacle by watching them assemble the mobile temple and from annoying Joshua to describe other details he had seen from his assistance to Moses.

Caleb would watch the ceremonies and become absorbed into the beauty of Yahweh's holiness. It was much more than just intellectually understanding the symbolic meaning of it all. It was a sacramental entering into the spiritual truth through the physical ritual displayed before them. He understood that spiritual reality came into contact with their earthly existence through the physical cult.

Since Yahweh was an eternal invisible spirit, unlike the finite visible pagan gods and their graven images, he was transcendent from his people and set apart. But also unlike the pagan idols, he was a shepherd and loving father who was very near and imminent with his people and set within.

The tabernacle was the symbolic physical display of that otherwise invisible presence. Thus it stood at both the physical center of the camp and the spiritual heart of the nation.

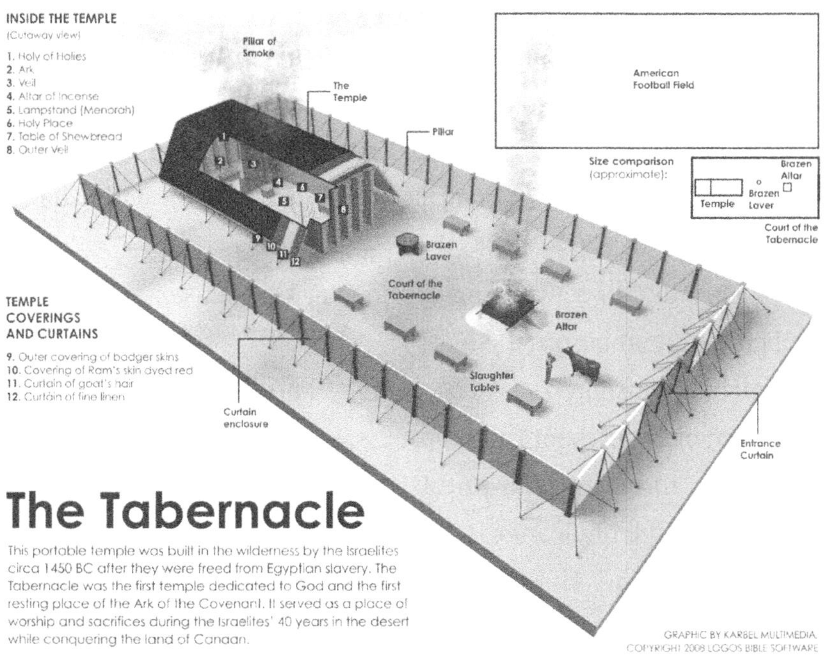

The outer courtyard was one hundred-fifty feet long by seventy-five feet wide. Wooden poles holding linen curtains over seven feet high sanctioned it off. The Tent of Meeting, or holy place pitched at the back end and was fifteen feet wide, fifteen feet high, and forty-five feet long. It was divided into two sections, the holy place and the most holy place, the inner sanctum.

Normally, Israelites would bring their sheep, goats, turtle doves and other offerings to the gate to be sacrificed by the Levite priests for their various known and unknown sins as needed.

But today was different.

Today, the high priest, now Eleazer, Aaron's son, would perform special ceremonies on behalf of all of Israel. And the high priest gloriously displayed the beauty of holiness to Caleb.

Achsah leaned in and asked Caleb to speak to her of the meanings of the various elements. She knew how studious he was of every detail and loved to see his passionate interest come alive as it used to with her mother. Othniel listened in with shared interest.

Caleb spoke like a running commentary as Achsah and Othniel watched the ritual before them.

Caleb whispered, "The high priest's white linen undergarments represent righteousness." It was a righteousness not encountered in pagan high priests that were often half-naked in a display of savage uncleanness.

He continued, "His robe is a seamless blue garment trimmed with multicolored pomegranates and golden bells to symbolize the fruitfulness and call to worship."

Over the robe, Eleazer wore the ephod, an apron. "The ephod," said Caleb, "is made of golden wire and blue, purple, and scarlet thread; representing heaven, royalty and blood respectively."

"On that ephod is a 'breastplate of righteousness' that contains twelve different gems. Jasper, sapphire, emerald, onyx, and others."

"Emerald is my favorite," said Achsah. She loved its bright green glow.

Caleb continued, "The precious stones represent Yahweh's heavenly city as well as the twelve tribes of Israel."

"But that breastplate is also called the 'breastplate of judgment' because it contains a pocket over the heart of the high priest, do you see it?"

"Yes," said Achsah.

"In that pocket are the two mysterious elements called the Urim and Thummim."

"Lights and perfections," translated Achsah.

"Exactly," said Caleb. These elements were used to seek divine counsel and guidance from Yahweh in special circumstances.

The headdress of the high priest was a thick linen miter wrapped around his head like a turban.

"See the plate of pure gold on his forehead? What is engraved on there?" He quizzed her.

"Holiness to Yahweh" she said.

"Excellent. You remembered what I told you."

She gave a guilty glance at Othniel. "Actually Othniel recently helped me to memorize some of the details."

Caleb gave Othniel a jealous look, "Well, did Othniel help you remember what purpose it serves?"

"To bear the guilt of the people and remind us of the ongoing need of having Yahweh in our minds."

Caleb said, "Now, if you could only remember your chores at home as well, we would have a better kept tent."

"Father," she complained. Caleb smiled back. He could not be too jealous of his younger brother. Othniel had been born to a concubine of their father many years after their mother had died. Life in Egypt and the desert brought a high mortality rate, and many men found themselves starting over with new families later in life. Othniel himself had lost his family to plague years earlier, so Caleb would always find more in common with his brother than what divided them.

These elements of the high priest's garments, as well as the other Levites' wardrobe were for the purpose of glory and beauty.

But on this Day of Atonement, there was yet more glory and beauty at work. Eleazer first washed himself at the brazen laver that stood before the Tent of Meeting to cleanse himself for the ritual.

Caleb whispered, "Now comes the sacrifice."

Eleazer took a bull and killed it for his own sins, letting the blood drain into a bronze basin. He would then clean the animal and burn it on the brazen altar of sacrifice that stood before the bronze laver.

Caleb quizzed Achsah some more. "And what is the purpose of the high priest sacrificing for himself first?"

She said, "He too is in need of forgiveness of sins to be able to represent his people."

And herein lay a tension of paradox. For a high priest to sufficiently mediate between god and man, he would have to be sinless. But only a god could have such perfection. But a god could not represent man because he was wholly other, separate. Thus the repeated need for the high priest to be forgiven before he could perform his mediation. It was a weakness of the system that Caleb had thought could only be permanently overcome by a being of both deity and humanity, a kind of "god-man" that could become an eternal sacrifice. But he thought his imagination got away from him, for such a thing seemed impossible indeed.

Eleazer then took a censer full of coals from the altar and brought it into the Tent of Meeting.

"Describe for me again what is inside the holy place," she said.

"A seven-armed golden lampstand is perpetually aflame with holy oil to light the tent. It is shaped like a blossoming almond tree, a symbol of the tree of life in the Garden of Eden so long ago. But it is also considered the 'light of the world' that gives light to all men."

She and Othniel had closed their eyes now, imagining in their minds what they could not see with their eyes.

Caleb continued, "Across from the lampstand is the table of showbread. It is three feet long and a half-foot wide and made of wood overlaid with ornately tooled gold. On it are twelve cakes of bread representing the twelve tribes of Israel, and they are replaced on the Sabbath. It is a meal for the priests to commune with the 'bread of life' of the presence of Yahweh."

She could picture now the idea of eating bread and in their midst, the Shekinah glory cloud. It captivated her.

He interrupted her visualization. "Before the holy of holies, the most holy place, is the altar of incense, a gold-laden structure whose rising smoke represents the perpetual need of intercessory prayer on behalf of the people." This was yet another need for the people that no human high priest could attain to.

Eleazer brought his censer from the sacrifice, whose smoke mixed with the altar of incense to protect him from what he was about to do next: enter the holy of holies, the very presence of Yahweh. This was the only time each year that this could be done. If approached on any other day by the high priest or anyone else, Yahweh would strike them dead.

Caleb continued his vivid description of the holy of holies. "The veil encloses the most holy place, another colorful curtain made of the blue, purple, and scarlet of the high priest's ephod. On it are artistically embroidered images of the cherubim, as symbols of the guardians of Eden."

The veil was a curtain of separation, a barrier that kept humanity ultimately at a distance from Yahweh. Achsah imagined the impressive chimeric cherubim and what they might look like before the throne of Yahweh.

As Caleb got caught up into his descriptions they turned more into a narrative as if they were right there in the tent watching it all. "Eleazer opens that curtain with trembling hands, protected by his incense, to stand before the ark of the covenant. The ark is about three and a half feet long by two feet wide and high, and made of acacia wood overlaid with finely crafted gold."

Now, his voice became more hushed with trembling. "Inside the ark are the very tablets of the law carved by the hand of Yahweh; a golden jar of the 'bread of heaven' and Aaron's rod."

The bread of heaven was the manna that never spoiled, and Aaron's rod was his staff that blossomed miraculously, confirming Aaron's Levitical priesthood.

Caleb continued in his whisper as if he and Achsah were in the very presence. “The cover of the ark hosts two sculpted images of sphinx-like cherubim with their wings spread over the ‘mercy seat,’ the symbol of Yahweh’s heavenly throne. The ark is Yahweh’s throne and footstool on earth, carried on poles and guarded by hybrid cherubim, just like other kings’ thrones. Except Yahweh is not visible.

Reproduction of the Ark of the Covenant without the carrying poles

"Eleazer sprinkles blood from his sacrifice onto the mercy seat, the final act that brings propitiation for the high priest. He then returns outside to act on behalf of the peoples' interest."

They saw Eleazer step outside of the tent. Caleb was recounting it exactly as it happened in real time.

Eleazer took two goats and threw lots.

Caleb explained, "Now, he decides which goat will be sacrificed to Yahweh on behalf of Israel. He follows the same procedures as he did for himself with the blood of the chosen goat to propitiate for the sins of the people."

Eleazer slew the goat at the altar.

But what happened next fascinated Caleb the most. The second goat was kept alive. Eleazer took his bloody hands and placed them onto the live goat's head.

Caleb said, "He confesses the sins of Israel as a ritual means of transferring them onto the goat."

Another priest then led the goat out of the tabernacle and away from the camp.

Caleb commented, "He is sending the scapegoat into the wilderness to send it to Azazel."

The only thing Caleb really knew of Azazel was that he was one of the fallen Sons of God who was supposedly bound into the earth in the desert. Why on earth would that monster be a part of Yahweh's Day of Atonement?

Caleb reasoned that since the goat was not killed, but kept alive, it was not a sacrifice to Azazel.

He continued to Achsah, "The desert to us is *tohu wabohu*, a place of chaos that is unformed and unfilled. When we crossed Yam Suph, Yahweh had promised us that he would crush the heads of Leviathan and create the heavens and the earth out of the chaos." This was another way of saying that Yahweh would part the waters of chaos of Egypt, and establish his kingdom covenant order out of the disorder and lawlessness that was Canaan.

Sending the goat out into the desert to Azazel, was not an offering to the damnable goat demon, but rather it was a banishment of Israel's sin to the realm of chaos outside Yahweh's kingdom—the same realm of Azazel.

One could almost consider it a compounding of sins onto Azazel to magnify his judgment.

This high holy day filled Caleb with wonder and awe at the glory and beauty of Yahweh's picture of atonement. It was his only hope for acceptance and inclusion into the Children of Abraham, and he prayed his daughter would cherish that hope as well.

Caleb's tribe was originally the pagan Kenizzites who were descended from Esau, the cursed brother of Jacob. Yahweh had chosen Jacob over Esau to be the one to carry the seedline of the Children of Abraham. Even though Caleb's entire tribe had converted and joined the Israelites, only blood atonement seemed to convince Caleb that he had any chance of being truly accepted into the family of Yahweh. That is why it was so beautiful to him.

It was a holy sacrament of poetry, music, and art.

Joshua did not care for poetry, music or art, so he began to snore. Caleb nudged him to spare him the embarrassment and Joshua jerked his head awake with a quick glance around.

"It is over," whispered Caleb. "You are forgiven."

"Thanks," Joshua muttered. "I owe you."

Caleb gave him a scolding look and said, "It is not me you owe."

• • • • •

The people had returned to their daily lives. One aspect of that daily life was the accumulation of manna every morning.

Joshua's wife Hasina took their children out into the desert outside the camp to gather the manna, along with hundreds of others. It was a fun time for the young ones as they trampled about trying to collect more of the "what is it" than their fellow rivals.

A handful of warriors watched over the women and children. Most of them stood bored at the edge of the camp.

But Hasina noticed that Othniel, who was one of the guardians today, was hovering over Achsah, giving her special attention. They were chatting and laughing and he even carried her basket for her.

Hasina could see that Othniel's tenderness and affection toward Achsah was an interest that was clearly more than guardianship. The only problem was that Othniel was just too shy to let his intentions be made known. Achsah was certainly of marrying age, but no doubt their age difference was an obstacle for Othniel's confidence.

Hasina smiled to herself and thought, *Men. He is an accomplished warrior, but when it comes to love, he has not a clue.*

Near the outer edges a small group of about six children raced around competing with each other. Joshua's five-year-old son, Efram, led the pack, carrying his little bronze pot half-full of manna.

But he got too far away from the rest of the gatherers. Hasina noticed it and started to call for him.

"Efram! Efram, you are too far! Come back closer to the group!"

Efram did not listen. He was so intent on his mighty quest, that he kept scanning until he found the biggest bunch of manna he had ever seen. It was just near a ridge. He ran over to it and began to fill his pot. This would be it. This would be the winning batch!

The sun's rising from the east glared into his eyes as he grabbed and grabbed at the heavenly bread.

A shadow suddenly came over him and he could see more clearly. He smiled.

He looked up and saw the silhouetted figure of a tall man standing before him, blocking the rays of the sun.

He was a broad and burly man.

He was carrying a shield and spear.

He was a warrior.

A Canaanite warrior.

Hasina's scream brought Efram out of his stupor.

"EFRAM! RUN!"

But when Efram turned back, a dozen other warriors suddenly surrounded him. They came up from below the ridge.

He dropped the pot of manna to the ground, spilling out his winning collection, now completely forgotten by him as he ran for his life back to his mother.

The warriors were on horses.

There were hundreds of them.

And they went after the women and children.

The warriors captured some of the innocents by using nets, and others, by simply picking them off the ground like a mighty bird of prey might do with a defenseless rodent.

The Israelite guardians tried to fight on behalf of the children, but they were so overwhelmed, they were all slaughtered.

•••••

Joshua was leading battle exercises in the desert on the opposite side of the camp from the gathering children. The leadership under the general consisted of commanders of thousands and commanders of hundreds and of fifties. The basic fighting unit of Israelites was a five-man squad who trained together and fought together as a team.

Those squads were in the middle of practicing their skills when a messenger came on horseback to give the news of the Canaanite attack to Joshua.

The soldiers were already equipped and warmed up for a fight. But they were also on the opposite side of the camp, far away from the site of attack.

By the time they arrived, it was too late.

The Canaanites had killed hundreds and had kidnapped two hundred others.

It was an atrocity, a slaughter of innocents.

Joshua and Caleb sought to gather whatever intelligence they could before they went after the raiders.

As they walked through the field, surveying the dead women and children, a righteous anger welled up within Joshua.

Caleb scanned the area for his daughter. But she was nowhere to be found.

Some of the surviving women and children told them about the men and their swords, and nets, and merciless cruelty. There was nothing distinctive about them. They were Canaanite desert marauders, dressed in typical animal skins, leather armor, and they went north.

Tracking the monsters would be the easy part.

Some of the soldiers had found their loved ones dead and wept over them.

Joshua was grateful he had not seen his family. That increased his chances that they would be hostages to be rescued. But he could not give in to his desire to complete his search, for that would place his personal interests above the nation, which was of greater importance.

He was about to announce his command to pursue the Canaanite murdering kidnappers, when he heard the voice of Othniel shout out, "Caleb!"

Joshua jerked around to see Caleb running toward a young girl kneeling on the ground holding the body of a woman and weeping.

The girl was Achsah. She was alive.

Othniel was standing over them with bloody sword drawn, nursing an arm wound.

Caleb grabbed her and held her tightly.

Joshua approached the three of them.

But he stopped twenty feet from them.

At his feet lay the body of a little boy.

Efram.

A fireball of pain arose in Joshua's soul and his knees buckled. He felt dizzy.

But something in him told him he had to continue.

He picked up the broken body of his son and cradled him in his arms as he continued toward Caleb, Achsah, and Othniel.

They were now looking at Joshua with eyes of fear.

Joshua trembled as he drew near.

When he arrived by the three of them, he saw the two bodies on the ground that Achsah had been crying over. They were Joshua's daughter and his wife, Hasina.

He stared down at them like stone. He lowered the body of his son to group them together.

Caleb and Achsah moved back to give Joshua room.

Joshua arranged them together on the ground with stoic rigidity as Othniel explained what had happened.

"We were ambushed by a band of Canaanite marauders. There must have been several hundred. The other guards were killed. Hundreds were kidnapped."

Caleb knew his daughter was only alive and safe because of Othniel's protection.

Joshua could not allow himself to break down. He trembled, holding back the tsunami of pain in his soul.

But he had to lead the armies of the Lord, and he could not fail his nation for his own personal loss. There would be plenty of time to grieve and wail later.

He grabbed the sleeve of his tunic and ripped it with gritted teeth. It was the act of grief most familiar to them all.

He could not stop the flood of emotion that invaded his mind. This woman, this precious treasure, had brought such happiness and grace into his life. Despite the miracles of Yahweh's presence and deliverance through all these years, she had been the most vivid proof of Yahweh's shepherding concern for him. In her love, he understood love and was changed by it.

Her softness of body and soul was completely alien to him, his complete opposite. Yet, in that way, she balanced him, kept him from becoming the cruel and heartless monster he knew he could become. Her precious smile and embrace made this warrior weak in the knees.

And these children, so young, the fruit of their love together. He could remember cradling their frail little infant bodies in his arms when they were born. His hopes for them had been so high. His sorrow was magnified by the fact that he knew he was too hard on them, too demanding. They were Yahweh's way of pounding the selfishness out of his own soul. And in their youthful flaws he could see himself before his heavenly father. His own imperfection, his own selfish demands and need for guidance and wisdom. They taught him as much about his heavenly father's love for him as any of the sacrifices could.

But now they were all dead.

They were butchered by evil, and along with them, Joshua's love.

Joshua got up from his knees and looked out into the distance in the direction of their enemies.

He announced to the soldiers around him, "Commanders of thousands, commanders of hundreds! Delay your grief, and let us hunt down these Canaanite cowards, rescue the hostages, and may Yahweh's justice roll down like waters!"

The men shouted and gathered for the chase.

But only those next to him could hear Joshua's prayer. "Yahweh, if you will give this people into my hand, I will devote their cities to complete destruction. I will kill every last one of them, man, woman and child."

Joshua looked over and caught Caleb staring at him. It felt to them both as if time itself had stopped and they saw into each other's being.

Caleb knew Joshua better than anyone, and he could see that something inside of Joshua had changed.

It was frightening. Joshua had always been a warrior soul of discipline and strength. But his family had been the love that anchored him in God's grace. Now, it was as if that only vestige of grace in his life had been murdered, ripped out of him.

All that was left was a man of war.

•••••

It only took Joshua's army a couple of hours to track the Canaanites down to a confederation of several closely linked villages north in the Negeb. The area was called Arad and had a population of about three thousand people, with about a thousand warriors.

Joshua descended upon the villages with four thousand men. There was no delay, no preparation, and no negotiations for hostages. They simply fell upon Arad's first city and mercilessly slaughtered all its inhabitants. When the other villages came to the help of their sister population, Joshua turned, spread out, and cut them down.

It was overwhelming to experience, even for Caleb and Othniel. Yahweh was clearly empowering them for massive victory. They had swept over these Canaanites like the rolling waters of justice. They had been Yahweh's tidal wave of devastation.

And true to his vow, Joshua devoted the entire coalition of Arad to destruction, every man, woman, and child.

They rescued two hundred of their women and children who had been taken hostage, and returned to the encampment of Israel.

CHAPTER 12

Less than twenty miles north of Arad was the city of Kiriath-arba. It was the stronghold of the Anakim where King Hoham ruled and the Sons of Anak were uncontested.

The Anakim were a giant clan whose legendary height was "as tall as the cedars," with extra-long muscular necks to match their frightening presence. But their strength and skill at fighting was even more frightful as the saying was known all through Canaan, "Who can stand before the sons of Anak?"

Of all the giant clans of Canaan—the Rephaim, the Emim, the Zuzim, and others—the Anakim were the most fierce. They worshipped the god of power, Ba'al the most high deity of the pantheon. And that power worship caused pressure to build, tempers to flare, and fights to explode within their own ranks.

To create a cathartic release for their social unrest, they built the Pit of Death, as a place to work out their hostilities through contests of power.

Whether it was for a criminal offense, a family feud, or a highhanded insult, Anakim could challenge one another to duels to the death. They could be between two or three or any number of opponents so long as the numbers were equal for competing interests.

The Pit was a circular arena dug into the earth about two hundred feet in diameter, with ascending slopes for the audience to sit on and watch the entertainment. They nicknamed it "the Gilgamesh Arena" in honor of the ancient gibbor, Gilgamesh of Uruk, a Mesopotamian giant king who would satisfy his own restless power by challenging his citizens in contests of combat. If anyone could best him they would win the right to be his Right Hand of the kingdom. But the difference with that battleground and this one was that in the Pit of Death, only one came out alive.

In the Pit this day were four Anakim. It was three against one. But this was not an uneven fight because the one who stood before the three was Ahiman, right hand of General Abi-yamimu. He was the largest, most fierce of the Anakim. At fifteen feet tall and twelve hundred pounds of pure muscle, he struck terror into anyone who faced him in combat.

The three who were facing him today were imposing as well. Two were the personal bodyguards of their king, Hoham. They were mighty warriors, all between nine and ten feet tall, with necks and arms of iron, the finest of fighters.

But the third was General Abi-yamimu, or Abi, Ahiman's own superior in the army.

The reason for this unusual contest was that Ahiman had claimed to uncover a plot for a coup against the king between these two bodyguards and General Abi. They denied it and charged that Ahiman had a secret agenda that fueled his lies. He wanted to take their place of power beside the king.

As Abi's right hand and the fiercest warrior in the land, Ahiman's reputation was impeccable. But so were the reputations of the General and the bodyguards. And the evidence was not strong enough to indict.

In this warrior culture of honor, such unresolved disputes were often settled by duels. When a warrior's reputation was so impugned he felt he could only clear his name of dishonor by proving Ba'al's favor in a battle to the death. So the General and his bodyguards challenged their accuser to a duel in the Pit to clear their names.

Ahiman demanded that there would be no weapons. It would be hand-to-hand combat.

This was very personal.

The three of them waited in the Pit for Ahiman to arrive. Abi was quick and nimble, well studied in tactics. His strategic ability to understand the enemy and anticipate battle maneuvers earned him his prized status through many victories. He was also a master of swordplay. Unfortunately that would do him no good today, as there would be no weapons.

The bodyguard Okrl was the strongest of the three and had a reputation for being vicious and relentless, which would compound his advantage in today's fight, as well as increase the odds on bets laid down against him.

The other bodyguard Khta was the smallest of them at about nine feet tall and bald. But he was massively built at close to eight hundred pounds of rock-like brawn, and was a mighty grappler and wrestler.

They were all naked except for their loincloths and leather belts.

They spread out in formation at Abi's lead.

The amphitheater was filled today, standing room only, because of the enormity of the event.

The origin of that enormity entered the pit area and the crowd roared with applause.

Ahiman strutted proudly at his titanic fifteen feet. His footsteps seemed to shake the earth. With his mere loincloth and belt, the full impressiveness of his physique was on display. He was all sinew and muscle. His extra-long neck jutted forward in predatorial position, his long blond hair had been cut off for this fight, leaving him bald. His six-fingered hands spread out as he walked, then curled into a knuckle tight crunch, ready to pulverize his opponents. He painted his face with war paint—The lightning bolt of Ba'al across his forehead, eyes and mouth. Looking at him, many people thought of the storm god.

Ahiman, the storm demi-god, raised his fists in glory, opened his mouth, and the amphitheater filled with the sound of his roar.

The crowd cheered in response.

But his opponents were ready for him.

They circled. The three had been a team for many years, which would be a disadvantage to Ahiman. They had the ability to move in tandem, like a tag-team of warriors, and they knew each other's style.

All four of the giants engaged in a ritual display of swaggering their long necks like a cobra preparing to bite—the tradition of the Anakim as they faced duels in the Pit or on the battlefield. It intimidated their opponents and struck fear into the hearts of their enemies.

Up in the king's royal box, Ahiman's brothers, Sheshai and Talmai, and Sheshai's wife Izabel, watched the combat seated next to the king. Though King Hoham was himself a tall and powerful giant, he still required protection and these two would provide that during the contest, while his bodyguards fought. These brothers had been the most loyal of the Anakim, performing many feats of legendary heroism during the rise of King Hoham.

Had it been any other Anakite who had made such an accusation against the king's guards and general, Hoham would not have believed them.

But these three were different.

Sheshai stroked his beard. He was the brilliant one, the middle brother, and leader of the family because of his intelligence. He had led the Hyksos forces into Egypt a generation earlier and captured the Goshen region before returning home. He whispered commentary on the fight into the king's ear as they watched.

Talmai, the youngest, was also the most restless. He was a hothead with an explosive temper that had often gotten him into trouble. Sheshai had to bail him out more than a few times through fast-talking or legal maneuvering. Talmai deferred to Sheshai because he owed him his very life over such rescues.

Talmai stood instead of sitting because he was fidgeting and wishing he could be a part of the fight.

Talmai loved killing. He loved the feel of a weapon in his hand and the exhilaration of battle. The taste of the blood of his enemies on his lips made him delirious with rage. He was not a very religious man, but eating the flesh of the vanquished was the height of religious ecstasy for him. The Anakim were cannibals and became known for their art of flaying and impaling their victims. Ahiman may be a thundering elephantine force of power, but Talmai was a wild rabid lion that could rival his brother when unleashed.

Sheshai kept Talmai on a tight leash.

Izabel watched the fight as a good Anakite female should, quietly, and dressed attractively with long strings of golden necklaces on her long and deliciously slim neck. The female neck was a sexual turn on for Anakim males. And Izabel turned many male necks.

Down in the Pit, Ahiman looked around at his encirclers. His long Anakim neck could stretch around almost to his back.

He knew he would have to take out the strongest one first because this would give him the advantage in both strength and morale. The strongest one was Okrl, who was behind him.

The three of them moved almost as one. They signaled each other according to Abi's leadership. He had practiced with them as a team in preparation. And that preparation kicked in as the three of them attacked simultaneously. Fighting one at a time would be to Ahiman's advantage, but all at once would be to theirs.

As they rushed him, Ahiman spun around to face Okrl, so that when they hit, he would have Okrl in his clutches.

It was a pounding that would have taken the breath out of any normal Anakite.

But Ahiman was not a normal Anakite.

They fell to the ground in a cloud of dust and rolled, fighting for control.

Ahiman had Okrl's head in his hands. This monstrous adversary may have had a body of muscle and strength that was impenetrable, but the skull that housed his brain was not.

Ahiman squeezed with all his might and crushed Okrl's skull like an ostrich egg.

When they rolled further, Okrl's body lay dead in the dirt.

Ahiman pulled away from the two others and faced them again.

It was shocking how quickly Ahiman dominated. His reputation was well deserved.

The two others kept maneuvering, waiting for the right moment to strike.

Ahiman's long arm swung out and clipped Abi's head, knocking him face first into the dirt. He got up shaking off the dizziness.

And then he ran away.

The crowd yelled with disgust. Cowards would not live in the Anakim community, so it did not make sense what he was doing. And worse yet, this was the general of the king's army.

It diverted Ahiman's attention just long enough for Khta to leap.

He hit Ahiman in the mid-section and the two went down to the ground. Despite his lesser size, Khta rivaled Ahiman's strength.

They wrestled for control.

Unfortunately, for Ahiman, Khta was the better wrestler.

What Ahiman did not see was that Abi did not run away. He ran to the edge of the Pit where a soldier threw a sword to him.

It was a massive sickle sword of iron. And Abi was a master swordsman. Evidently, he did not care about the consequences of breaking the rules of combat. He was forfeiting his life. But he had figured he would most likely die at the hands of the gargantuan anyway. Better to be able to take him with him to Sheol than go alone in failure.

Khta grappled with Ahiman in a contest of strength and moves that resulted in Khta's superior position.

Khta was the better wrestler, but Ahiman was stronger.

Eventually, Ahiman pinned Khta through sheer force, and head-butted him to break his nose. The physical damage would not weaken him in the state of combat, but the blood flow would be a hindrance.

Ahiman was just about to bend down and use his teeth to rip out Khta's throat, when he noticed Khta's eyes shift to see something behind Ahiman.

Someone behind Ahiman.

Ahiman reacted instinctively by rolling and pulling Khta on top of him, switching places.

He did it just in time as the sword of Abi swung down in an arc of judgment on Khta's back. Khta released his grip in death. Ahiman rolled out from beneath him to face his attacker.

Up in the king's box, Talmai moved to jump out of the box and help Ahiman against his cheating opponents.

"Talmai!" shouted Sheshai.

Talmai stopped.

Sheshai said in front of the king, "He is perfectly fine to take care of himself."

Talmai gritted his teeth and stepped back into the box with a growl.

Once Abi broke the rules, Ahiman was no longer bound to those rules, and it would be perfectly appropriate to even up the odds by having his brother join him. But Sheshai knew that if Ahiman did not do so, but stayed within the bounds of the rules to beat the cheater, then his integrity would be elevated in the eyes of the king and the people, and his accusations against the bodyguards proven just.

Abi swung his sword ferociously in a figure eight, leaving no room for Ahiman to do anything but back up—all the way to the edge of the Pit.

Ahiman whipped off his leather belt. He dove to the side and rolled in the dirt as Abi hit the Pit's stone wall. Sparks flew in every direction.

Someone threw a sword into the arena near Ahiman.

But he did not take it up. He did not need it.

When Abi turned toward Ahiman, he was ready.

Ahiman had figured the pattern of Abi's slashing swings and used the leather belt like a whip to wrap around the General's hand, jerking him forward into the dirt.

Ahiman stepped on Abi's sword hand. He kicked the sword aside, and kicked Abi into unconsciousness.

The crowd rose with bloodlust. Their champion had turned the tables.

Ahiman raised his hands in victory.

The crowd chanted for blood.

Up in the box, Sheshai looked at a stunned King Hoham.

Sheshai whispered to him, "My lord, you have the undying allegiance of the brothers Arba. We are your servants."

Ahiman had just won the contest and proved his cause. His accusations against the General and his bodyguards were justified by the gods.

But Ahiman was not done. Far from it.

He knelt down and grabbed Abi's head in his hands. There was no need to crush his skull as he had Okrl's. He was going to do something different to his General.

Something more spectacular.

He knelt on the supine giant's sternum and pulled on the neck with all his might.

The body of the mighty General was woven together with strong muscles and tendons. But those muscles and tendons tore at the brute force of Ahiman's grip.

A popping sound penetrated the stadium as Ahiman ripped the giant's head and spine from his body.

He raised the skull and skeletal column high above like a trophy. The chanting of the multitude had become so loud it drowned out all thoughts. Sheshai needed no words. The actions showed a mighty gibbor hero of the masses.

Talmai smiled with pride over his big brother.

Ahiman reached down with his hand and thrust it under the General's sternum and penetrated into his body cavity.

He grabbed the heart and ripped it from the corpse. He took a massive bite out of the organ. Then, chewing on his victory, he raised the heart high to the assembly.

There was no stopping him. Ahiman was the champion of the Anakim.

As Ahiman strode to the king's box to present himself in victory before the king, Sheshai pulled Talmai aside and whispered into his ears over the din of the multitude, "You see, brother, political strategy achieved what raw fury could not. Had you rushed into the ring to lessen the odds, the victory would be less as well. We are now more trusted than ever."

Talmai smirked with satisfaction. Sheshai's strategy of false accusation against General Abi had worked.

Might made right.

• • • • •

King Hoham sat on his throne before the three kneeling Arba brothers. With sword on each shoulder, and Ba'al priest sprinkling holy blood, he proclaimed, "Sheshai and Talmai, I sanctify you as my personal bodyguard and war council."

Then he turned to Ahiman and pronounced, "Ahiman, by your just proof of righteousness before the gods in the Arena of Gilgamesh, and the display of your faithful loyalty to your king, I anoint you as the new General Supreme of my armed forces in the name of Ba'al the most high god."

The ceremony would be later. For now, Hoham had to appoint the new positions lest unrest turn to anarchy in the ranks of the military. Ahiman would be the most feared general the Anakim army ever served.

But Sheshai's aim was much higher.

Ahiman was the strongest warrior who ever lived in the land of Canaan, but he was not strong of mind. He understood little and cared less for politics and statecraft. It was Sheshai who coached him behind the scenes, whose advice Ahiman followed with trust.

The Anakim worshipped power, and Ahiman had that power. But Sheshai knew that power could not rule without politics. And even though Sheshai was not strong enough to ever sit on the throne of his people, he knew he could rule through proxy. His brother commanded the respect and submission of those around him, but Sheshai orchestrated his every move. And he would orchestrate the rule of the state once his brother rose to the throne that they would eventually take by force from King Hoham.

The initiation was interrupted by the arrival of a messenger. He bowed before the king.

"What news do you bring?" said Hoham.

"My lord, I am loathe to say it is not good. Have mercy upon me." Though it was not their fault, messengers were often executed in fits of rage for bad news.

"What say you?" said Hoham.

"The kingdom of Arad is desolate. They were raided by a tribe of Habiru, desert wanderers. They killed them all with ruthless cruelty."

"All the villages?" asked the king.

"All the villages, my lord. I alone escaped to seek your help." The kingdom of Arad was adjacent to the Anakim stronghold.

Talmai blurted out, "Who are these infernal Habiru?"

"I do not know," said the messenger. "Some say they came from Egypt many years back. But they are not Egyptian."

Talmai started to get angry. "Some say? Some say? What kind of a scout is it that can only gather hearsay instead of evidence?"

Talmai stepped forward. The messenger stepped back in fear.

"Wait," said Hoham. "From Egypt, you say?"

"Yes, my lord."

Hoham looked at Ahiman, "Do you remember the prophecy of our forefather Anak? Did he not speak of the return of our sworn enemy from Egypt?"

Ahiman glanced at Sheshai, who nodded with subtlety.

Ahiman then nodded to Hoham.

Sheshai leaned in to quote the prophecy by memory, "The Children of Abraham will one day return to our holy land to finish the evil that their forefather could not; the destruction of Anak. But the sons of Anak will rise up and destroy Abraham's seed to the very last man, woman, and child."

Talmai offered, "We must find out if these Habiru are truly the children of Abraham."

Hoham concluded, "Send scouts on reconnaissance to gather intelligence on them."

Sheshai said, "Immediately, my king."

But then Hoham concluded, "But regardless of their identity, they have pillaged too close to us, and they have transgressed our boundaries. Ahiman, prepare your forces for war."

CHAPTER 13

The city of Jericho was located in the most central area of southern Canaan, not far west from the Jordan river, and had the largest spring of freshwater in the land. It had become a lush fertile oasis in the area that lay on the crossroads of access to the entire region. It was also the oldest city on earth, and had experienced many different inhabitants throughout the millennia.

Because of its central location and resources, it was of strategic military importance to the region and had evolved as a well-equipped fortress known for its legendary walls. About nine acres of land hosted the city's population of a few thousand people, mostly armed forces. Even military forts needed crops, herds and commerce, so its population had expanded to include about one third civilians providing those services. Their patron deity was the moon god, Yarikh.

The walls that surrounded the oval shaped city were twofold. First, a retaining wall about forty feet high guarded the outer perimeter. But between that wall and the second forty-six foot high wall, was an embankment that rose another forty feet.

Some of the occupants lived inside the area between these two walls. Since their location provided less protection, the real estate was of less value. This resulted in the more questionable elements of society living between the walls, such as harlots, foreign travelers, and dependents on the welfare of the chief commander of the city.

One of those citizens had a home built against the outer wall to house a tavern and inn.

She was the innkeeper Rahab, a harlot.

When she first arrived at Jericho, she had changed her name from Arisha and assumed her new name to disguise her origins. But she had to work for her keep because she had too much dignity to be a lazy dependent on the commander's good graces of welfare.

Unfortunately, her only training had been in the art of pleasing men as a nymph back in Panias. So she pursued the only thing she could make good money at without becoming a slave: prostitution.

At first, she joined a brothel in the lower class south end of the outer wall embankment. But she was so successful that she quickly rose in prominence and in income, gaining the attention of the commanders of the fort.

Rahab was now twenty eight years old. And she had a plan. She lived frugally and saved her money so that within a few years, she had saved enough money to purchase a failing tavern in the richer northern district of the rampart embankment.

She had much success with her tavern and become quite well known in royal circles, but had always turned down offers to become a personal concubine to various officers who begged for her favor like pathetic mongrels. She wanted her independence and felt empowered to hold an establishment of her own. She turned her disadvantaged victim status to her favor and advantage.

But her real plan was found in the peculiar character of taverns in the township. They were places of local gossip that kept her on top of everything going on in the city all the way up to the Chief Commander, who had also slobbered for her affections.

But more importantly, the tavern was the establishment of choice for travelers on their way to and fro through the land. So this allowed her the ability to gain information on anyone from the Transjordan that might be searching specifically for her. She poured her ale to loosen tongues and kept informed for her own safety.

She had most recently heard from travelers in the southern Negeb and wilderness of Paran that there was danger in the Transjordan region. Apparently, a tribe of desert nomad troublemakers, Habiru, had attacked and destroyed the cities of Arad, and word through the Edomites came that the Habiru were on their way to the Transjordan. That piqued her interest. She would welcome any hostile force to rise up against the kingdom of Bashan because that would include the Serpent Clan of Gilgal Rephaim and maybe even lead all the way to Panias. She made it a point to keep her ears open for that news.

But there was one other thing that she had planned for so many years. She saved her money until she could afford to buy back the one thing that had been taken from her so long ago and cast her adrift in a world of pain and sorrow: her family.

Today was the big day. She had paid a caravan of mercenaries to travel up to Panias and bring her family back to Jericho. It had taken almost all her savings to ensure their safety, but it was worth it. It took some convincing for them to go, but she proved her intent to them with a secret letter sharing details of her past that only she and her family would know.

Her inability to show her own face in Panias was due to the fact that should any of the satyrs discover she was alive, they would link her to the disappearance of Izbaxl and probably kill her. Satyrs were passionate and vengeful creatures.

She paid off her family's debts, which had kept them enslaved to the community, and brought them back.

She had wondered after all these years, how many of them were still alive and healthy. Her father and mother would be quite old if they had survived.

She only prayed they did not pay the price of her rebellion.

The day she saw the caravan in the distance through her window on the wall of the city, she could not contain herself. She mounted a horse and rode outside the city walls to meet them.

When the mercenaries saw her coming, they halted.

Her horse slowed to a canter. Rahab's heart raced with hope and fear.

The first ones she saw were her two brothers in the lead. They were twins. They were grown now into handsome young men of twenty-six years old. Baraket and Baxilet. She could still tell them apart.

They did not recognize her. She got off her horse and pulled back her hood with a smile. Their eyes went wide.

"Arisha!" they said in unison, and jumped off their horses to hug her desperately.

And then she saw her sisters, now in their early twenties, and beautiful as ever. The oldest, Shiba, looked worn; the youngest, Yasha, glowed like a princess.

They screamed her name and she cried out. They almost fell over with their joyful caresses and kissing of one another.

Rahab could see two young men standing sheepishly by, the husbands of her sisters.

Then Rahab stopped, and she looked around. She felt dread over her soul.

"Mother and father?" she said to them all. "Are they…?"

She could not say it. She feared the worst.

Baraket quipped, “Well, they are old and slow as ever, but they are not dead, if that is what you mean.”

And then she saw them.

They limped from the back of the caravan with creaky backs and legs.

It was her mother and father.

It had been over sixteen years since she had seen them, but they looked as if they had aged thirty years. She immediately began to cry and broke away from her siblings to meet them.

She stopped in front of them.

They looked at her with shocked unbelief.

“You are so beautiful,” said her mother.

“We thought you were dead,” said her father. “All these years. My little Arisha, you have grown.”

“You are so beautiful,” said her mother again.

The siblings had all drawn near to Rahab.

“I have a new name,” she said. “Rahab.”

“Rahab,” repeated her father. “My Rahab.”

He opened his arms and they embraced, the three of them.

Sixteen years of loneliness, despair, and sorrow melted into weeping.

“Rahab?” said Baraket, “The name of the sea dragon?”

Everyone began to laugh. Both laugh and cry.

Then Rahab through happy tears croaked out, “Yes, and that means you had better do what I say, little brother, or you will experience the chaos of my wrath!”

Everyone laughed again.

“Well, I see you have not changed, dear sister,” replied Baraket. And they all laughed yet again.

Rahab had redeemed her family. She had so dreaded the possibility that they were dead for her rebellion. But they were not.

"What did you hear of me when I vanished?" she asked.

Her father explained, "No one knew. Izbaxl and Sisa both disappeared as well without a trace. Izbaxl's brother, Xizmat, announced to us that Izbaxl ran away with the two of you."

Rahab deduced what had happened. Izbaxl's pride kept him from explaining anything to his fellow satyrs when he left to hunt down Arisha. When the dire wolves ate him, they consumed all of Izbaxl's and Sisa's bodies and with them all the secrets of that night.

Rahab breathed a deep sigh of relief. She turned to her family and said, "Come home with me, and I will tell you what happened that night."

• • • • •

The dire wolves did consume all of Izbaxl's body that night. All of his body *that was in the woods*. There was however blood that was left in Arisha's room that night. She had cut him and he had bled on her sheets and the floor. Xizmat had examined the room that same night and found the satyr's bloody flesh.

He knew that it was Izbaxl's, and that it proved foul play. But he remained silent and waited for any news to give light to his discovery.

When no information was forthcoming, he hid the embarrassment of his brother's failure from the rest of the community. He kept it to himself until he could discover new evidence that might bring resolution to the mysterious crime.

When Arisha's family had been redeemed from their debts and left for the south these sixteen years later, Xizmat immediately remembered them as the family of Arisha. He did not take the connection as a coincidence, and decided to employ a spy to find out where they went.

The spy had followed them to Jericho.

CHAPTER 14

The gods and goddesses of Canaan met at their cavern in the heart of Mount Hermon. Mastema presided over the meeting on the throne seat that looked out upon the pitch-black lake that had a perpetual flame across its surface: The Abyss.

Dagon, Molech, Asherah, and Chemosh had been waiting for Ba'al and Ashtart to arrive.

They were late.

When the two gods finally entered the cavern, the others noticed Ashtart being led by a collared leash with spikes around her neck. She sported excruciating body piercings all over her anatomy, from bars, studs, and rings, to hooks in her back, used to hang her by her skin. Everyone could see the bruises, contusions, and open wounds covering her from head to toe. She walked with a slight limp and one of her eyes was a bruised bulge closed shut.

She would heal quickly. She was a Watcher.

It was obvious Ba'al had been carrying out his violent temperament on her, but no one dared make reference to it for fear of Ashtart visiting the same upon them. She was submissive to Ba'al's dominance, but she was still the goddess of war and could cut anyone else down with ease.

She was just glad to be on top of the earth instead of below it.

Mastema said, "You are late."

Ba'al replied, "Ashtart and I were building my temple on Mount Sapan in the far reaches of the north."

Mastema glared at Ashtart. "I am sure you were."

Ashtart played her part with irony. "We put a wonderful window in it, so Daddy Storm God could hurl his thunderbolts and rain storms. The earth convulsed, the mountains quaked, and he opened a rift in the clouds. You will all simply have to come and have a party."

Mastema was gangly and ugly, but he still commanded the attention with his superior legal standing over the seventy Sons of God.

"The time for celebration is over," he said. "The War of the Seed is upon us."

A hush went over the gods. They knew what that meant.

It had been prophesied in the Garden that the Seed of Eve would be at war with the Seed of the Serpent. The gods had sought to pollute the seedline of Eve by interbreeding with it. They had birthed the Nephilim, giant hybrids of human and angel, and had used them to draw worship away from Yahweh. They sought to violate the holy separation of creation.

But they had also sought to track down Yahweh's chosen ones, the bearers of the seedline, in order to destroy them: Enoch, Methuselah, Lamech, and Noah.

The great Flood was Yahweh's response of judgment.

But their project of corruption did not stop. Their search for the Seed in each generation continued and failed time after time, even after Yahweh had made a covenant with Abraham to establish his inheritance through his lineage. That Seed through Isaac and Jacob eventually became a large family of seventy that was sent into captivity for hundreds of years in Egypt and were forgotten to the world.

That family of seventy became a nation of a multitide of thousands.

Meanwhile, the Seed of the Serpent filled the land of Canaan with their progeny and purpose.

Mastema caught them all up on recent events. “And so this Moses has led the Seed of Eve through the desert for a generation, and is now on its way around Edom to enter into the Transjordan.”

Ba’al asked, “So their claim is on our land to dispossess us?”

“Yes,” said Mastema.

“Then why did they not enter into south Canaan?”

“They tried, but failed,” said Mastema. “Yahweh even killed an entire generation for its lack of willingness to fight. And therein lies our hope. They may be Yahweh’s people, but they lack conviction. Many of them still worship some of us, and are therefore subject to curses from their god.”

Molech and Dagon chuckled.

Mastema continued, “If we are strategic about our battles and operations, we can crush these Habiru.”

Ashtart said, “But the Cisjordan is considered the Promised Land by Yahweh. Why are they approaching the Transjordan?”

“I think this Moses is going to establish a base of operations in the Transjordan from which to launch an invasion of the Cisjordan.”

Ashtart said, “Well, I say, come and get it, old man.” Ashtart had been preparing for this for a long time.

Molech sniggered. They had worked together on a plan so bold they actually wanted the Habiru to attack them. They would unleash a storm and stress upon these troublemakers that they would have no idea how to deal with.

"We must be ready," said Mastema. "And we must stay organized. Chemosh and Molech have the southern region of the Transjordan with Moab, Ammon, and King Sihon. Ashtart guards Bashan and King Og. Ba'al remains in the southern hill country with the Anakim, and Dagon, the coastline cities of the Philistines. Asherah can take the north."

"What about you?" asked Molech.

"I will be filing legal motions against Yahweh in his heavenly court to try to keep him from entering into Canaan."

Ashtart grinned. "You are trying to force Yahweh's hand."

"What do you mean?" asked Molech.

Ashtart kept watching the legal adversary as she spoke, "Mastema believes that the Seed of Eve, is more than this nation of people, the children of Abraham."

Molech, Dagon, and Asherah looked to Mastema and the others for their answer.

Mastema gave it up, "The Seed is not plural. It is singular."

"A person?" said Dagon.

"A king."

"A king?" repeated Molech. "And it is he who seeks to inherit Canaan?"

"He," said Mastema, "seeks to inherit the *earth*. Canaan is only the beginning. I fear the real plan of Yahweh is that this tyrant ruler may even undo Babel, and with it our inheritance."

Molech was having a hard time following. He was a bit slower than the others.

Ashtart tried to steal a bit of Mastema's thunder as she quoted the ancient antediluvian prophecy. "I will put enmity between you and the woman, and between your seed and her seed; he shall crush your head, and you shall crush his heel."

Ba'al jumped in, "He shall crush your head. He is singular."

"Brilliant," said Ashtart.

Ba'al yanked her chain to quell her sarcasm. She gave a choked gasp.

"Is it this Moses?" asked Ba'al.

"No," said Mastema. "But they have a sacred text that claims he will be a prophet like Moses. And he will come from the lineage of Judah. It says, 'The scepter shall not depart from Judah until Shiloh comes. And to him shall be the obedience of the peoples.'"

"How do you know this?" asked Molech.

"Because he keeps up with current events," said Ashtart. "You should try it sometime, ignoramus."

Molech withdrew. He felt stupid.

Mastema explained, "Moses has spoken of it publicly to his people. He is even writing it down. And we, of course, have spies."

"That is audacious," said Ashtart.

Ba'al tried to sum it up. "So the Children of Abraham are coming to war on our inheritance. But then there is an anointed king who is coming through the line of Judah, and he is the prophesied Seed to crush…" he paused respectfully, "…your head?"

Mastema showed his only moment of actual weakness, when he replied, "And all the Seed of the Serpent will go down with me."

"Well then," concluded Ashtart with a more positive attitude, "I suggest we send out scouts to find this chosen seed—and kill him. And in the meanwhile prepare for war."

CHAPTER 15

The Israelites left Mount Hor and traveled south. Their goal was to travel around Edom, by way of Yam Suph where they would turn north and approach the King's Highway, which would take them into the Transjordan area.

One day, Joshua and Caleb came to Moses' tent as he was writing on his leather parchments, a new technique he had learned in Egypt before the exodus. Tablets were so heavy and could break so easily. But this new form of writing on parchment was much more mobile, flexible and saved space. For years, Moses had carefully written down the laws and applications that Yahweh gave to him. But he also had been incorporating it into research on his people's ancestry, from the Garden of Eden all the way up to Abraham, Isaac, and Jacob's lives. He would eventually add his own journeys in the wilderness with Israel.

"Wait," interrupted Moses. He was in the middle of looking through some clay tablets.

"These are toledoth tablets," he added. Toledoth is the word for genealogy.

"They are the very genealogies of Enoch, Methuselah, and Noah."

As a court Egyptian, Moses had been taught not only Egyptian hieroglyphs, but Akkadian, the international language of trade, as well as his people's distinctive Semitic dialect.

"These have been engraved by the very hands of our ancestors. It is both humbling and rewarding. Like a window to our own past in Yahweh's hands."

Joshua had no patience for such scribal frivolities. He got right to the point.

"Moses, the people are protesting our desert wandering again."

"Now what?" said Moses, annoyed at how this all kept interrupting his very important job of putting down Israel's history. He started to glow with his emotion.

Caleb explained, "The same as prior gripes. 'Why did you take us out of Egypt? We do not have any food or water. Our families are going to die in the wilderness. It is not just.'"

"They want justice, do they?" said Moses. "Then let us pray that Yahweh gives them justice."

Moses got up and led them to the Tent of Meeting.

Caleb stood outside the tabernacle courtyard waiting as they prayed. His thoughts began to drift toward his daughter and how she really needed a mother. He felt a bad parent because he had been so involved in protecting the nation that he neglected his daughter.

But then he thought of Joshua's loss of his wife and children, and his heart was broken for his friend. He wondered if Joshua would ever recover his ability to love again.

For so long he had envied Joshua and his special status as Moses' servant. He wondered how a man could be so close to the presence of Yahweh, and yet be so hard.

Meanwhile, Caleb, who loved every small detail of God's tabernacle and every poetic ritual of atonement, was forced to stay outside the center of holiness.

It was as if law and holiness seemed to be at odds with grace and beauty.

Caleb's attention was taken out of his thoughts by the sight of movement on the ground in the corner of his eye. He looked down and saw a snake. It looked like a kind of cobra. But this one had wings, four of them. It was what they called a *seraph nachash*, or flying fiery serpent, because it had shining copper scales like a Shining One, and it symbolized the seraphim that guarded Yahweh's throne in heaven.

But this seraph was on earth, and it was deadly. He pulled out his sword and chopped off its head.

He had heard legends about these creatures being in the Negeb, but this was the first one he had ever seen.

He wondered if it had bitten anyone.

And then he heard a woman scream.

Instinctively, he ran toward the scream.

As he did, he could hear others scream throughout the camp, and a dread came over him. He suspected he knew the reason.

He saw another cobra crawling in front of him, about to launch itself in flight. Its wings were not large enough to fly like a bird, but they would enable short aerial bursts that made it look like the serpent was leaping like a jackrabbit. He cut it in half as it leapt.

He was sure of it now. There must have been a nest of these seraphim cobras that was accidentally unsettled by someone.

But as he turned past a lane of tents, he stopped in horror.

He saw thousands of serpents slithering and flying throughout the camp. People were running to escape them. Some were throwing them out of tents. Some were trying to kill them.

Caleb started hacking off the heads of the ones closest to him. But he soon discerned that it would be impossible to make a dent in their numbers.

It had to be a miracle. Or more precisely, a curse.

Moses' words came back to him, "They want justice, do they? Then let us pray that Yahweh gives them justice."

More screams were all around him. People were being bitten throughout the camp. He knew that the venom of the seraph nachash could be lethal. Many would become very sick. And many others would die.

He rushed home to make sure Achsah was okay.

He reached his tent and heard a scream from inside.

"Achsah!"

He whipped back the tent flap to find Achsah standing on top of a pile of wood. The entire floor was covered with the nasty vipers. Some of them were leaping at her.

But Othniel was there, hacking the snakes to pieces.

Caleb helped him finish off the serpents and then hugged Othniel with fierce gratitude.

"Once again, my brother, you have saved my precious treasure."

Othniel said, "It is my honor, brother."

Othniel opened his arms and Achsah let him carry her out of the tent. And at that very moment, Caleb could see a tenderness in Othniel toward his daughter that he had not noticed before. A connection between the two of them.

But now was not the time for such petty observations.

They arrived back at the tabernacle only to discover that there were no snakes around it. It was as if Yahweh was keeping them away from his holy presence.

Evidently, others of the congregation had begun to discover this protection as well and had begun to crowd around as close as they could to the outer courtyard curtains.

When Moses and Joshua came forth from the Tent of Meeting, people cried out, "Moses, save us!" and "We have sinned!"

One of the elders ripped his clothes and bellowed in a loud audible voice, "We have spoken against Yahweh and against you! Have mercy on us!"

Moses stopped, turned and walked back into the Tent of Meeting.

Caleb thought it looked like Moses did not want to listen to their pleas. Like he wanted them to wallow in their sickness and death.

Or he was going to plead with Yahweh.

After a few minutes, Joshua led Moses out of the tent, and up to the courtyard entrance.

People were still weeping and crying out. It was rather loud and noisy.

Moses waved Caleb over. Caleb had to avert his eyes somewhat at Moses' shining.

Moses said to him, "In the past, you were a blacksmith, were you not?"

Caleb wondered what that had to do with the pain and misery all around them.

"Yes, Moses," he said with hesitation.

"Good. I need your help then."

Moses led Caleb over to a blacksmith's station in the camp.

He picked up some copper objects made by the smith, and spoke to Caleb.

"Do you remember the image magic in Egypt?"

"Yes."

The Egyptians believed in sympathetic magic that would replicate images of creatures like snakes as a means of scaring away those creatures.

Moses said, "I want you to make a bronze seraph serpent on a pole, similar to what we saw in Egypt, only different."

Caleb said, "But that could take several days."

"We do not have several days. You will have to get the help of the blacksmith and make it within a day."

Caleb sighed. He hated doing things hastily, and it was even more important not to do mediocre work on an artistic object.

Moses said with a glint in his eye, "Joshua tells me you are enamored with the art of the tabernacle."

"Yes."

"Now is your chance to make some art."

Caleb said, "I wish Bezalel were still alive."

Bezalel was the spirit-filled artist who crafted the tabernacle to Yahweh's specifications with his own creative flair. His background in Egyptian and Philistine aesthetics had been a source of much beauty in the work.

"He used to complain too," said Moses. "You artists never have enough time to create your 'masterpieces.' But I need one tomorrow. So create for me a beautiful seraph serpent on a pole—and do not forget the wings."

"Okay," said Caleb.

With the help of the smith, Caleb sculpted a clay winged serpent wriggling around a pole, and had it cast into bronze. He could not put the detail he wanted into it, but he was not disappointed.

• • • • •

When Caleb brought the bronze serpent to Moses and Joshua at the tabernacle, the next day, He could barely stand up. He had worked all through the night and did not get any sleep.

Moses looked at it, and said, "Well done, Caleb. It is beautiful." He took the bronze serpent with a litany of priests to parade through the camp.

As he walked through the camp, Moses had Joshua speak his words loudly for the ears of everyone. "Hear O Israel! We are entering into a land that worships the Serpent! These fiery serpents that have attacked you are an example of what will happen to you in Canaan if you continue to grieve Yahweh with your unfaithful hearts! The Serpent will bite your heel and you will die. Turn now from your unbelief and turn back to Yahweh. If a fiery serpent has bitten you, and you look upon this *Nehushtan*, you will be healed! Trust in Yahweh and he will do it!"

Nehushtan was a Semitic wordplay on the words for bronze and Nachash, as well as a third word for practicing sorcery. It was a sarcastic jab at Israel's wayward tendencies.

Everyone was coming out of their tents to see the great sign before them. And those who had been bitten would merely look upon the bronze serpent and they were healed. Others had to be carried because they were sick and others were on their deathbed. But as Moses said, if they looked upon Nehushtan, they were healed. Caleb saw the serpent shining in the sun with the same brilliance as Moses would shine when seeing Yahweh.

It was a beautiful picture to Caleb of how Yahweh would place their sins upon a cursed object, and then forgive the Israelite who simply looked to that object with faith.

It was too bad that Canaan, the final destination to which they were arriving, was like a horrid pit of flying fiery serpents full of poison and death.

Caleb decided to teach his daughter Achsah how to use a bow that day. Her life had been in danger twice and she was helpless without Caleb. Both times she had been protected by Othniel. But Caleb felt that he had failed her. Though he treasured the femininity of women, he thought that they should still have some ability to defend themselves in this hostile desert.

He found a bow and some arrows and brought her outside the camp to begin her lessons. He was determined that she would never be caught without a defense again.

After he taught her the basics of nocking an arrow, aiming and releasing at a target, he talked to her as she practiced her skills on a small desert tree at a short distance.

"So, my little turtle dove, you are of marrying age."

Achsah aimed and hit the tree without response.

"Good shot," he added.

"Thank you," she said.

"Have you any young men who show interest?" he asked.

She nocked an arrow and aimed with nary a concern.

"None that I care about." She aimed and hit the tree again.

"You have a natural skill, Achsah."

"Not really," she said. "Othniel has given me a few lessons."

"Othniel again," he said annoyed. "I am being outdone in parenting by my own brother."

She snapped, "He is not my parent. You are. Othniel is a kind and giving man."

"There is no need for hostility."

She said, "I think the best thing you could learn from him is that he does not treat me like a child."

Caleb raised his eyebrows. "Indeed. And has he ever shown interest in you…"

She looked at him trying to figure out what he meant.

"You know, for marriage?"

Like a spy, he wanted to gather intelligence, but he did not want to encourage her to actually consider such thoughts.

"Ewww! No. We are best of friends. Why would you say that?"

Caleb knew what was occurring. Othniel had always been in the shadow of his older brother's notoriety and achievements. All his life, Othniel fought to make a name for himself that had nothing to do with being "the brother of the famous Caleb," Right Hand of Joshua, Karabu giant slayer, and possessor of Yahweh's special promise of entering the land.

Othniel had actually become quite a warrior and leader in his own right, as he had recently secured the position of a commander of thousands in the army. There wasn't anyone else Caleb would rather have had protecting his little Achsah.

But he also knew that Othniel struggled with self-confidence in two areas: women and Caleb. Slaying a giant is easy compared to understanding the mysteries of the female gender. Failure was assured in that battle. And comparison with his older brother always ended in Othniel losing. How much more intimidating would it be if Othniel was interested in Caleb's own daughter? Caleb considered that Othniel would probably take years before he could gather the courage to reveal to Achsah his intentions for her, let alone ask for Achsah's hand from Caleb.

Good, thought Caleb, the jealous father. *The longer he takes, the better.*

CHAPTER 16

Sheshai's wife Izabel was eight feet tall, with a long slender neck and beautiful long reddish hair. Though she was Sheshai's wife, she currently laid in Talmai's bed as Talmai stood drinking a glass of wine looking down upon her.

Talmai said, "Just be thankful I am not Ahiman."

"Why?" said Izabel.

"Because he is infertile."

She could not believe it. He said, "He is so pumped up on sorcery he cannot seem to sire offspring." The sorcery he referred to was the use of drugs that would enhance muscle strength and the drive for violence.

She said, "Are you sure he is not a secret boy lover?"

Without warning, Talmai moved like a cobra and grabbed her neck. Izabel's eyes strained with confusion. She could not breathe.

He leaned in and whispered to her with finality, "He is my brother. And he is not a boy lover."

He released his iron grip on her.

She rubbed her throat in fear. "I am sorry, Talmai. I was just having fun with you."

Talmai looked away from her and said, "I do not appreciate my family being made fun of."

"I am sorry," she said. "It will not happen again."

A hard knock on the outer home door, jerked Izabel into fear. She looked to Talmai for direction.

"Do not worry," he said. "Sheshai rarely visits my quarters personally. Stay here."

Talmai moved over to the house door. He picked up his sword just in case.

Anyone would be a complete fool to attack Talmai in his home.

He opened the door and peeked out. It was a messenger from the king.

• • • • •

The palace of King Hoham was built upon the ruins of King Arba's original palace in Kiriath-arba. It had been cursed and abandoned for a generation after Arba and his queen Naqiya were slaughtered by Abraham and his Amorite allies.

When their sole surviving son, Anak, grew strong and built a formidable force of warriors, he reclaimed the city and rebuilt it from its ashes.

The city was on a large hillside above the valley, with a deep cliff protecting its backside. They had added a wall around the original town and extended some of its acreage.

The king's palace was on the top of the hill overlooking the city. It was made of red stone and brick. The Arba brothers all resided there, but it was large enough to maintain their privacy.

Talmai raced across the palace courtyard to his destination.

Sheshai, Ahiman, and King Hoham were inside the king's war room with several other captains of the army when Talmai finally arrived out of breath.

Sheshai said, "It is about time, little brother. You are as slow to obey as my wife sometimes."

Talmai responded, "Big brother, I am confident that Izabel is faster and more obedient than you let on."

Talmai bowed to the king. "I am sorry, my lord, I was in the presence of a lady I could not too quickly leave."

Hoham smiled. "Talmai, you rascal."

Ahiman watched Talmai closely. He did not care for his brother's braggadocio or his impulsive ways. He could be the weak link in their secret plans for a coup if his lips were too loose to a woman.

Ahiman was also envious of his little brother's fertility. Because of his secret inability to breed children, Ahiman felt like he was less than his brothers. It made him angry. It made him want to become king more than anything. He glared at Hoham with hungry eyes.

Hoham interrupted Ahiman's brooding. "My council, we have received word from our returning scouts."

Hoham nodded to one of the captains who had received the intelligence. He was a fat one. He said, "The hostile Habiru wandering in the wilderness of Zin and Paran are indeed the Children of Abraham."

Ahiman said, "The scourge of Arba."

Sheshai said, "Who is their king?"

"His name is Moses," said the fat one.

Talmai jumped up. "Let me hunt this Moses down and skin him alive."

"Patience, brother," said Sheshai.

"Sheshai is right," said Hoham. "He is too old. He will surely die soon anyway. Our concern is to find out who will replace him."

Ahiman said, "I will muster our forces."

Hoham shook his head. "No. They are already traveling south, *away* from Canaan."

"That is strange," said Ahiman. "They were on the threshold, and had wiped out Arad, and now they would run away?"

Hoham looked to the fat one again, who said, "We believe they are traveling around Edom to enter the Transjordan."

Talmai responded, "Then let us cross the Jordan and welcome them with 'arms' held open wide."

They all knew he was making a pun of the word, "arms" as a reference to weapons.

"No," said Sheshai. "I say we wait to see what their strategy is. They will be coming to us. Then let them come." Hoham's face brightened with realization of Sheshai's point. "If it is the Transjordan they want, they will have to face Sihon and Og. And that will not be a pretty sight."

"But we cannot let Sihon and Og steal our glory," said Talmai.

"True enough," said Sheshai. "Your passion speaks to the importance of justice. But let us not forget who our enemy is. They are greedy, conniving deceivers who use the blood of our children to bake their bread. We will get our vengeance. But we must do so wisely. If we do not need to be the first to jump into the fray, then why should we? We can learn their weaknesses by watching them battle with others."

The king was smiling and thinking through Sheshai's advice.

Then he said, "Let Sihon and Og have the first stab at these Habiru—and save us the casualties."

CHAPTER 17

Moses, Joshua, Caleb, and the commanders of thousands, including Othniel, stood on the bank of the Arnon River. Across that river lay the territory of Sihon, king of the Amorites. The Israelites had traveled the long way around Edom and had finally arrived at their destination months later in the Transjordan.

Joshua was looking out on the land with hungry eyes. "Give me the word, and I will send in our forces and kill every last one of these Amorites with holy pleasure."

Moses said, "You are too quick to kill, Joshua. You must learn that righteousness is not achieved through force, but through persuasion."

"But these Amorites stand in the way of Yahweh's will."

"Only if they do not allow us passage. We have no interest in the Transjordan. Yahweh does not promise it to us. Only the Cisjordan of Canaan is our goal. We will ask them for safe passage."

• • • • •

Heshbon, the city of Sihon, king of the Amorites, lay on the King's Highway just twenty five miles north of the Arnon River. South of that river was Moabite and Edomite territory. Sihon ruled the land between the rivers Arnon in the south and Jabbok fifty miles in the north. His western limit was the Jordan River, and his eastern limit, the desert of the Ammonites, whom he had pushed east in his territorial expansion.

Heshbon was well fortified and on a plateau about two thousand feet high. Inside the king's domain, Sihon sat on his throne carved from an ancient cedar tree. His advisors surrounded him as he read a dispatch brought by messenger from Jahaz, another one of his cities just ten miles closer to the border of his kingdom.

Jahaz was a smaller city than Heshbon. Whereas Heshbon and its surrounding community contained as many as four thousand people, Jahaz only housed about two thousand. And Jahaz did not have fortification.

"Scribe!" barked Sihon. "Prepare a message for delivery to King Og."

The scribe had been waiting and ready. But the urgency with which Sihon spoke made him tremble as he prepared his writing tools and clay tablet.

As Sihon dictated to the scribe, his advisors were appraised of the situation as well.

"Say to Mighty Og of Bashan: Thus, Sihon of Heshbon, king of the Amorites. For you, your Rephaim, and your realm, may all go well, and may the gods protect you. For me and my kingdom, my city of Heshbon, all goes well. I send you this urgent dispatch with my most humble gratefulness to be your ally. The dangerous time we have strategized for has arrived. Our territories are now in jeopardy, as the Habiru have been spotted preparing for war across the Arnon river facing my city of Jahaz. They are led by an old fool named Moses, a fanatical follower of this white-bearded geriatric deity called Yahweh. He is fool enough to ask for unmolested passage to the plains of Moab, for entrance into the Cisjordan. But I think these ruffians have as their ultimate target to conquer your fertile land of Bashan. He has promised not to turn aside to take of my vineyards or water wells. Naturally, I refused his request and have already begun amassing my forces at the town of Jahaz in order to thwart these sons of pigs and monkeys. Per our agreement, I now request that you send me, with utmost of haste, the two hordes of Rephaim gibborim you promised to help defend your interests. Of course, even more Rephaim numbers would insure victory for your cause, but I leave that to your generosity and wisdom. I remain your ally in full, and may the gods protect us both with favor and justice."

Sihon thought that stressing Og's own interests was politically clever. The fact of the matter was that without those Rephaim giant units of four or five hundred strong, he was not sure he could hold out for long.

The scribe hurriedly finished his tablet and prepared to bake it for delivery.

Sihon barked orders to his commanders, "Prepare our total forces for immediate removal to Jahaz. We will incorporate the Rephaim units when they arrive. And alert the priests of Molech. We have need of special sacrifice."

The commanders moved to obey.

• • • • •

Joshua and Caleb finished consulting with the commanders about their strategy for battle in Joshua's war tent.

The commanders left the tent to muster their forces for a ten-mile march to Jahaz across the Arnon.

Joshua and Caleb were startled by the sudden presence of four men in their tent.

"Where did you come from?" asked Caleb.

They had turned their backs for a second. Did they slip in unnoticed so quietly?

Mikael spoke first, "I told you that you would be seeing more of me." He smiled.

Joshua saw the three others. "And who are these gibborim with you?"

"Let me introduce the archangels Gabriel, Raphael, and Uriel."

Caleb already knew Gabriel from his schooling in the way of the Karabu many years ago.

Caleb said to him, "Welcome, old friend."

They hugged briskly.

Joshua was confused. "Why would we need the help of four archangels? Our spies have confirmed Jahaz will be an easy victory."

"We are not here to help you," said Mikael. "We have our own mission. Linked to yours, but of separate concern."

Caleb said, "It must be very important or very difficult to require all four of you."

"Actually, it is both important *and* difficult."

Joshua said, "Dare we ask what?"

Uriel interjected with his characteristic sarcasm. "Yes, you may dare. But we will not answer."

Joshua and Caleb stared with blank faces, not knowing how to respond.

"I am only kidding," said Uriel.

Mikael said, "We are here to take care of business we have left unfinished for too long. We are going to capture the gods of this land and bind them in Tartarus."

Tartarus was the lowest place in the belly of Sheol. It was the place of imprisonment that was of uttermost distance from the presence of Yahweh. It was said that Tartarus was as far below Sheol as the earth was below the heavens.

"How do you bind them?" asked Caleb.

Gabriel pulled up his cloak to reveal a band made of white thin hair wrapped around his bicep.

"This is the indestructible hair of Cherubim from the very throne of Yahweh. We bind them with it. It will hold them until judgment."

Uriel added with a smirk, "It is a special talent we have. Do you want us to teach you how to do it? It is fun."

"No, thank you," said Joshua. "Gods are above our pay wages. We will stick to men and giants."

"Uriel is our resident jester, in case you have not noticed," said Gabriel. "He is just making up for his lack of size."

Uriel *was* smaller in height than the others.

Uriel elbowed Gabriel. "You will have to forgive him. He is just envious of my skill."

He added as an afterthought, "And oration."

Then another afterthought, "And brilliance."

Gabriel angled for the last word, "But *not* his bravado."

Raphael, the silent one, just smiled with amusement.

Mikael, stepped in, "Okay, you two. Keep it up and they will not have *any* confidence in us."

Joshua and Caleb gave each other a side-glance.

Caleb could not help it. "Is that how you capture them? Distract them with bickering? That is brilliant."

"That is what Enoch used to say to us," said Uriel.

Joshua changed the subject, "Why would it take four archangels to overcome a Watcher god?"

Mikael explained, "The Watchers are the Sons of God that rebelled against Yahweh and came to earth. They were among the mightiest of the heavenly host. But they were also granted authority over the nations at Babel. That authority places them above archangels and is a form of power that grows with their evil. Ashtart and Ba'al are the strongest, and we are in their territory, which gives them a compounded advantage. I want to make sure they do not slip out of our grasp again."

Caleb said, "I guess you have your hands as full as we do."

Mikael said, "We will ride with your forces, but will depart when we reach the location of our intended targets."

"Fair enough," said Joshua. "We set out in the morning."

Then Caleb added to Uriel, "Our soldiers could use some entertainment tonight if you are available. Maybe some comedic theater?"

CHAPTER 18

Sihon had aligned his forces outside the city of Jahaz on the field for battle. They were over two thousand soldiers, including those who came from Heshbon. When the Rephaim gibborim arrived, it would have the effect of doubling that force against the Habiru intruders.

But the pressing concern was the religious sacrifice he was currently watching. It was common practice for cities, besieged by evil attackers, to offer human sacrifice to their gods.

The god of the Moabite lands was Chemosh, a phony Yahweh imitator. But when Sihon had dispossessed the Ammonites, he also retained their god, Molech, king of the Underworld.

Molech had a preference for children. So the priests of Molech prepared ten children, decided through lottery, to offer to his infernal eminence.

Sihon and his soldiers were adorned in their battle dress of leather armor, painted bodies, wild headdresses and animal skins. It was all calculated to project savage chaos upon the enemy.

They lined up in devotion before the huge bronze altar, called a "high place," that was situated just outside the city. High places were elevated platforms and altars devoted to the worship of the gods. Molech worship included veneration of the dead, which would be invoked to protect their forces against the living.

The altar was a large bronze image of Molech with a bull's head called a *tophet*, and the act of sacrificing the children was called, "passing through the fire."

It was an abomination of evil.

But Molech was satisfied that day.

• • • • •

A mile out from Jahaz, the army of Yahweh finished their approach toward the city. They were four thousand in number. The rest of the forces, about two thousand, guarded the nation in Moab.

Moses was riding in a special carriage with pillows to lessen the roughness of the ride on his aging bones.

He heard the drums in the distance and he knew what it was for: Molech, the abomination of the Ammonites. He had learned of that heinous monstrosity when he had sojourned with the Midianites years ago. He could not wait to demolish their high places, and melt their graven images in the flames of their own judgment.

• • • • •

King Sihon sat on his horse overlooking the battlefield before him. He was outnumbered two to one. He did not stand a chance without the Rephaim from Og.

But the Rephaim had not yet arrived.

He was beginning to panic. Og had procrastinated for too long. He had waited until the last minute to send the reinforcements as promised. As a result, Sihon would experience heavy losses.

His hope rekindled when he saw a messenger from Og move through his ranks to meet Sihon.

"My lord," said the messenger. "Forgive the delay. The Rephaim are almost arrived from Ashtaroth."

Sihon had lost all sense of protocol. He shouted at the messenger. "By the gods, man, how far? We have not much time!"

"Og says to sally forth without them. They will bring up on the left from the Highway and flank the Habiru forces. You can crush them in a pincer move."

Sihon was only partially encouraged. "You had better be right, messenger, or all is lost, and Og will be next to fall."

The messenger left him to lead his army into the battlefield.

When the horns of war bellowed and the two forces met on the field of fire, the Rephaim had still not arrived.

The Habiru forces were cutting through Sihon's army like a knife through pudding.

Sihon was in the rear watching the outer ridge to his left for a sign of the Rephaim's arrival.

It could still work. The giants were massive fighting monsters, whose surprise would multiply their terror many fold. Sihon hoped he could rally the remainder of his men to draw extra strength from such a turnaround and turn their impending defeat into victory.

• • • • •

Molech and Chemosh watched the battle below unfold decidedly against their favor.

Suddenly, Molech saw four figures on horseback approaching the city. They were not engaging in battle except to ward off attack. They appeared to be intent upon an independent mission.

Though his eyesight was not good, he recognized who they were. They had the presence.

They were archangels. Four of them.

There was only one reason why four archangels would be needed for such a task. They were here to bind the gods.

Molech turned, only to discover that Chemosh was already gone. The coward had run. Just like he had millennia ago in the War on Eden. He should have figured as much.

There was no way Molech could face four archangels alone. It would probably be best to withdraw up to Ashtaroth and alert Ashtart to prepare. His chances for victory would be increased by the side of the goddess of war.

It was not cowardice to avoid this confrontation. It was cunning.

• • • • •

Sihon's men were fighting savages. But these Habiru seemed to have the favor of the gods with them. They overwhelmed his forces and drove them back.

And still the Rephaim had not arrived.

So Sihon blew his special trumpet to signal his giant platoons.

A strange high-pitched buzzing sound came out of the rear of the Amorite forces. The Amorites suddenly pulled back in retreat, and the Israelites followed the chase.

But the Amorites also split down the middle of their forces, leaving a gauntlet for the arrival of one hundred giants, to come running through like a battering ram against the Israelites.

These were the Zamzummim and Emim remnant that Sihon had saved for just such a surprise. If the Rephaim came soon, it would be a one-two punch that could slaughter the Habiru.

The Zamzummim made the strange buzzing sound that pierced ears and confused communications amidst the ranks of the enemy.

The Israelite archers released a volley of arrows at the giants, but they were like toothpicks poking the titans. Annoying, but not stopping the relentless monsters.

The giants pummeled their way into the Israelite forces, tearing them asunder. They towered over the soldiers in both size and strength and fought with a fearsomeness the Israelites had not seen before.

They caused a momentary lapse in the Israelite advance. This was Israel's first encounter with the giants that they had heard of a generation ago. Othniel was in the thick of this giant incursion leading his men to defend. He felt a shiver down his spine when he saw these huge warriors, and his men rolled over like a pack of hares beneath a boulder.

But the giant's mistake was that they were too speedy and efficient. They had burrowed their way into the middle of the Israelites, expecting to be followed on the side by flanking Amorites. But their comrades had not been able to follow them because they had been too crippled.

So Othniel saw his opportunity and led a sea of Hebrews to surround the Emim and Zamzummim.

One hundred giants hit the Israelites hard that day with heavy losses. They gave Moses and Joshua a portent of the power of the Seed of the Serpent. If only one hundred of these monsters could accomplish this much damage, imagine what a thousand could do?

But this was only one hundred giants enveloped in a morass of thousands of battle-hardened Israelites.

The titans were cut down—with great difficulty—but they *were* cut down.

But Othniel was not done.

He led a force of Israelites to press forward and finish off the Amorites. Sihon himself was now engaged in battle. He was a gibbor and would not be taken easily. He hacked and held off Habiru with a strong arm.

And he knew that his opponents were still shaken by the giant attack, and for a short time, they would be vulnerable to a Rephaim blitz of more giants.

That was when Sihon's hope flared as he saw on the distant ridge, the arrival of a party of figures on horseback.

He thought, *Praise Molech, the gods have answered my prayers. The Rephaim have arrived.*

But the gods had not answered his prayers. The figures were not a multitude of giant warriors, but a mere party of five on horseback. They were not arriving, they were watching.

Just then, a spear pierced Sihon through because of his distracted attention.

It was Othniel's spear. He had zeroed in on Sihon and attacked the leader with zeal.

As the iron barb entered the king's gut, it dawned on Sihon.

He had been the biggest fool of all. The riding party must have been spies for Og, who never intended to send the Rephaim. He gave Sihon the false hope to lure him into confidence to fight the Habiru. He knew Sihon would lose. So instead of wasting his own forces on a losing battle, he would withdraw and allow Sihon to do some damage to the Habiru, which would increase Og's advantage when he faced them afterward.

The last revelation that came to him as he lay dying was that Og had always wanted to control the region. With Sihon's kingdom decimated, Og could vanquish the battle-weary Habiru and have the entire Transjordan to himself.

Sihon had been the biggest fool not to see it.

And then he breathed his last on earth, to face his maker in judgment.

• • • • •

The four archangels arrived at the city and found their way to the temples. Molech was long gone. Chemosh, they found cowering in his sanctuary, trying to hide.

They dragged out the trembling deity onto the floor. He had even wet his tunic.

Chemosh yelped, "Please do not bind me. Please do not bind me! I beg you, have mercy on me!"

Mikael said with resounding authority, "Where is Ashtart?"

Chemosh looked confused at the angels.

"In Ashtaroth!"

"Boy, was that pathetically easy," said Uriel. "I would hate to be your colleague in crime."

And then they did something strange. They turned and walked away. They left Chemosh alone!

Did they offer him mercy after all?

It dawned on Chemosh. He remembered that Yahweh had commanded the Israelites not to dispossess the Moabites or the Ammonites because they were the descendants of Lot, Abraham's nephew. So the angels were not authorized to bind Chemosh and Molech, the gods of the Moabites and Ammonites while in their protected territories.

They were after Ashtart and the others.

Uriel was right. Chemosh was pathetic.

But he remained unbound.

• • • • •

With the city in flames, Moses, Joshua, and Caleb gathered by the high place of Molech to personally direct the tearing down of its foundations and the destruction of the tophet.

The still smoldering flesh of child sacrifice on the tophet made Caleb wretch. He had seen the horrors of war, he had crushed wickedness, and impaled evil with swords and pikes. But this sight was too much for him.

He forced out, “What kind of demons do such things?”

“Humans do such things,” replied Moses. “Evil is more advanced than we give it credit.”

Joshua wrapped it up. “We must maintain our momentum as an element of surprise and terror. We will subdue the surrounding villages and towns within days and move swiftly up to Edrei in Bashan.”

Edrei was the first city in the kingdom of Og.

CHAPTER 19

Rahab's family did not take long to settle in to the large inn she had acquired in the wall of the city that was above her tavern in Jericho. Though she was involved in shameful employment, they could not condemn her too easily because she had been stolen from them at a young age and forced into a hard life. It was all she knew.

Rahab had survived. And it did not surprise her mother or father. They always knew her independent spirit would either get her killed or help make her own way in the world. She had clearly done the latter. She had purchased an inn with tavern and found herself in the know of everything that was happening in the region because of the travelers who frequented her establishment.

Today, she was serving some of those very travelers some of her special ale for which she had become known. There was a table of Amorite traders and nomads discussing the latest hostilities in the Transjordan. As Rahab served them their drinks, she eavesdropped on their discussion.

One of the traders, an obese one with pimples, said, "I would stay on this side of the Jordan for a while until they get it all settled out over there."

Another one with an eye patch said, "They completely decimated Sihon's forces at Jahaz, then took Heshbon and the surrounding region within days. It is no longer Sihon's kingdom."

Rahab had arrived late into the conversation and wondered whom they were talking about. Who had the kind of power to subdue Sihon? She knew he was an ally of Og of Bashan, which made it even more reckless and foolhardy a venture.

One-eye looked up at Rahab. "What are you standing there for, wench? Pour my beer!"

He grabbed her by the wrist and jerked her over to him, pulling her onto his lap.

She dropped the ale pitcher. It fell to the floor and shattered, drawing all their attention to the floor—while her hand reached in her cloak to pull a dagger and place it at One-eye's cheek.

She whispered into his face, "If you fancy that good eye of yours, I recommend you release me. I run a respectful house, and I do not appreciate rabble-rousers."

One-eye's one eye was wide open with shock. The other men laughed. One of them shouted, "Zakura, meet the proprietor of this good establishment, Rahab the innkeeper! And, may I add, she keeps her promises."

The men all laughed. Zakura released her with embarrassment.

They laughed again. Rahab playfully slapped the back of the ox's head.

He said, "Aw, I am just teasing you, Rahab."

One of the barmaids cleaned up the broken pitcher on the floor.

Rahab said to them, "Who are these invaders, you speak of?"

The obese one offered, “Habiru of some kind. But I have not seen their likes before. Word is they were desert wanderers from Egypt. But they worship a single god.”

“Easier to focus on one,” said someone.

“No,” said the obese one. “I mean that they worship one god as the only god, and seek to dethrone all others.”

“Ba’al?” said Rahab. He seemed the reasonable choice, since he was the most high god, chief of the pantheon in Canaan. No one was mightier than the storm god.

“No,” said the obese one. “I do not remember his name. It was weird and hard to pronounce. But I have never heard of him before. They claim he is the Creator of all things, and the god of all gods. That he is invisible and has no outward form.”

“How do they worship him?” said one. “Where do they look if he is invisible?”

“He has a tent in their midst.”

“Well, there you have it. All gods need to reside somewhere. But a silly little tent? What is he, a dog?”

“Dog” was the derogative word they used for homosexual cult prostitutes.

“I could care less about their god or their dogs,” said the obese one. “What I am concerned about is their effect on my trading business. They have strange dietary habits and do not interact with foreigners well.”

Rahab was engrossed with these Habiru. “What do you mean?”

“Well, for one, they have a whole scroll of foods they cannot eat. Like pork, shellfish, most birds.”

“Curses! There goes my business in the east,” said One-eye. “I make most of my money selling swine.”

"It gets more confusing. As I understand it, they cannot eat anything with cloven hooves. But if it has cloven hooves *and* chews its cud, then it is okay to eat."

"Who are these ignorant people and their crazy rules?" said the ox. "They should go back where they came from."

"That is not the half of it," said the obese one. "They refrain from pleasures of all kinds other than marriage of a man and a woman: No incest, no adultery, no homosexuality, no cult prostitution, no bestiality."

"No fun," interrupted One-eye.

The ox said, "Their god is a prude."

One-eye added, "And if he claims to be the Creator of all things, then why did he create us with such desires?"

And another, "One man and one woman only, with children? Disgusting."

"Boring," said One-eye.

Rahab was becoming more interested in these Habiru with each passing description.

The obese one was not done. "And they execute necromancers, diviners, sorcerers, mediums, and astrologers."

"Well, that just about takes care of everything we do in Canaan."

"Barbaric," said the ox. "Next thing you will tell us is they have no human sacrifice either!" Everyone laughed as if it was absurd.

The obese one just raised his eyebrows and nodded as if to say, "No human sacrifice either."

"That is outrageous!" proclaimed One-eye.

"I am deeply offended," said another. "How dare they come into our land and condemn all our practices!"

The obese one said, “One thing is for sure, Og of Bashan will not tolerate such intolerance. He will bring justice. He will bring a hammer down upon their heads.”

One-eye said, “I hope he carves them up and eats them.” Then he thought of something, and gave the obese one a dirty look. “How do you know so much about these uncivil savages?”

“They are not all so high and holy as their god wants them to be.”

“Ahhhh,” said One-eye. “Hypocrites.”

The obese one continued, “They allowed me to pass through with my wares, and I was able to make some trades with their locals. They have no qualms with strangers and aliens, just so long as you are not hostile toward their god.”

Rahab had been completely mesmerized during the entire discussion. Now she finally jumped in eagerly. “What was your trade?”

He was hesitant. “Well, just some foodstuffs and other minor cultural artifacts.”

“Like what?” she exclaimed. He was not getting away with that one.

He sheepishly reached into his cloak and pulled out two small pieces of strange material folded up.

“This is some of their writing. But I cannot read it.”

Rahab was already jutting out with greedy hands. “Let me see.”

He handed them to her.

“What is it?”

“It is Semitic. They call it papyrus. A new medium for writing.”

“A lot lighter than clay and stone tablets,” she said.

"They say it is the future for communications."

She opened one of them and looked at the text.

"I recognize this script. It is similar to my own people's writing. But different."

Rahab's people were the Seirim. They had come from the Edomites whose lineage traced to Esau—the brother of Jacob—the forefather of Israel.

The obese one got anxious. "Can you read it?"

She was reading it already to herself.

She said, "It is a poem. A song for the congregation, I think. It is labeled at the top 'elleh haddebarim.' I think that means, 'these are the words.'"

"Well, what are the words?" said One-eye. "Read it!"

She had to translate a little, so she read with some stops and starts.

"It says, 'remember the days of old. When Elyon, the Most High gave to the nations their inheritance, when he divided mankind, he fixed the borders of the peoples according to the number of the sons of God. But Yahweh's portion is his people, Jacob his allotted heritage."

The oxen butted in, "What in Sheol does that mean? Who is Yahweh? Who is Jacob? I cannot understand poetry."

Rahab settled him, "Yahweh is the name of their god that Kabu-Amurru here could not remember."

The obese one shrunk a bit in his chair.

"And I believe that Jacob is the ancestor of their people."

They were all transfixed now. One-eye said, "Keep going, keep going."

Rahab read on. "'He found him,' I think that means Jacob, 'in *tohu wabohu*."

"What is that?" said one.

"It means a 'waste of wilderness.'" She continued. "'Yahweh alone guided him. No foreign god was with him.' Then it says he forsook Elohim who made him and scoffed at the rock of his salvation."

One-eye put it together. "Just like Kabu said, they are hypocrites! They are unfaithful to their god."

Rahab continued, "They stirred him to jealousy with strange gods; with abominations they provoked him to anger. They sacrificed to—sheddim—that were no gods."

"What are sheddim, Rahab?" said Kabu.

She made sure she was translating correctly, and said, "Demons. They sacrificed to demons that were no gods." She continued, "'To gods they had never known, to new gods that had come recently, whom your fathers had never dreaded."

One-eye was on top of it, "Those are our gods! He is talking about our gods as demonic. That elitist pig."

The ox butted in, "They do not eat pork."

One-eye gave him a dirty look.

Rahab continued, "He says he is a jealous god. He will punish them." She skipped to the end. "'Rejoice with him, O heavens; bow down to him, all gods, for he avenges the blood of his children and takes vengeance on his adversaries. He repays those who hate him and cleanses his people's land.'"

An ominous silence washed over them. It sounded like a portent of disaster.

The ox was a bit slow. He said, "His people's land. What land is he talking about?"

But none of them would speak up. They all had a strong sense of exactly what land he was talking about: The land of Canaan.

Rahab said, "Can I borrow this for a while, Kabu?"

"Oh, I do not know, Rahab."

"Free beer until I give it back."

"Well, in that case, keep it as long as you want," he responded without even thinking. He did not have to think. She was clearly giving him the better deal. The silly harlot.

She folded the parchment back up and stuck it into her dress. She looked at the door to the tavern and saw one of the nobles from the palace standing at the threshold. It was Jebir, the Right Hand of the Chief Commander of the fort. He would not defile himself by entering the establishment. He expected Rahab to greet him at the door. And there was only one reason why Jebir bothered to show his face in such an otherwise seedy locale.

• • • • •

Rahab stepped into the water of her military patron's large stone bath to cleanse herself. The two things she appreciated about military commanders was that they paid well and they had wonderful, comfortable bedrooms and baths. The most helpful thing was to enter a bath to try to wash off her sins by soaking in the clean hot water.

The truth was, it only helped a little to shield her pain.

Alyun-Yarikh, the Commander of Jericho, sat in a towel by the edge of the bath.

"Rahab, please marry me. I would make you so happy. I would shower you with gifts and I would never let you go. I would love you forever until the day I died."

Rahab gave him a look of contempt. "Do you realize every man I do business with says the same exact thing? Almost word for word."

The Commander said, “But I am…”

She finished his sentence with him, “Different. Yes, and that is what every man also says.”

He said, “Why do you not call me by my name?”

“Alyun,” she said, and he smiled. “I am not going to marry you. You are the Chief Commander. And you are a man. You speak of your vows of eternal devotion—and then you are unfaithful.”

If she spoke to the Commander this way in public, it would cost her head. But in the privacy of his home, it was the one place he preferred her to speak honestly.

“You would let me go, you would not love me forever, and it certainly would not last when you got older, much less the day you died.”

“But I am….”

She held her finger up to stop him.

“You are not different. You are all the same. Do you know why I am so successful with my business at the tavern? Because men are simple, and I know how you think. I know you better than you know yourselves. Trust me, you do not want to marry me.”

Alyun sat back in frustration.

She watched him closely. Then said, “So why did you invite me over tonight?”

He looked at her. She was right. She could read him like a tablet. He spoke up, “Have you heard any intelligence of the Transjordan?”

“Just that there is war, and the traders are avoiding it,” she lied.

“Nothing about Habiru or their intentions?”

“No,” she lied again. “Why?”

"Keep your ears open at the tavern, and let me know what you hear about the invaders and their god. I will pay you well."

"Why so important?"

"These invaders are evil, Rahab. They are killing everyone and enslaving the survivors."

"Everyone does that. You do that."

Alyun looked at her. He could not keep anything from her. She was too disarming. Her beauty was like a truth spell. "There is word that the Transjordan is not their true goal."

She said, "You mean they intend to invade the Cisjordan?"

He gave her a look of yes.

She finished the revelation, "Jericho is the first across the Jordan River for an invasion."

He said, "If they can conquer us, they have a bridgehead from which they can attack the entire region. We are not sure if that is their goal. But you will let me know if you hear anything about them, will you not?"

"Of course, my lord," she lied again.

He tried to scare her into the importance of it all. "We have heard their religion is a perversion of all that is holy and good. They use our blood to bake their bread. And from what I have heard, they are sons of pigs and monkeys who worship an evil mountain demon that wants to kill all our gods and take over the pantheon."

Killing all their gods did not seem too bad of an idea to her. She had been used and abused by the deities of Canaan. She would like to see them all destroyed. This mysterious Habiru deity was sounding more and more interesting to her. A sole god who claimed to be creator of all things. A foreign god who detested all the very religious behavior that she had questioned through her entire life. A jealous god who hated the same gods she hated. Indeed, this was sounding more like the kind of god she wanted to find out more about. She could not wait to get home and read those songs again. Their words haunted her.

"Rahab." His voice brought her back into the present. "Be very discreet and do not let anyone know you are gathering intelligence for me. If these Habiru find out, they may send spies to take you from me and kill you. And sacrifice you to their god."

She stared at Alyun and thought, *What a commander of morons I serve. He is so desperate; he is lying to make it sound worse than it is. Why do I keep serving this fool? Do I have a choice?*

He said, "Promise me, you will tell me the moment you hear anything about these Habiru savages."

She looked at him and smiled. "I promise."

That night, she trimmed a small lamp with some oil and hid herself away in her room. She pulled out the two pieces of strange parchment and read them over and over. The words were strangely beautiful. As she read, she felt her heart sing. It was the strangest most delightful thing she had ever experienced in her life.

The song she had already read at the tavern was frank in its condemnation of the Habiru by their own god. It was bizarre to her. What sacred text would speak so honestly and negatively of its own people? The scriptures she had been acquainted with were only optimistic and self-congratulatory. Religious devotees tended to wax eloquent of their own righteousness and their god's favor of them. But this Habiru text talked about their people as if they were spoiled children being beaten by the rod of their deity for disobedience.

This Yahweh, as he was called in the text, was so pure he showed no partiality in his judgment.

This text was so honest. So truthful.

The other song spoke about Yahweh guiding the Habiru away from Egypt and into the desert. And when Pharaoh chased after them, Yahweh heaped up the waters for these "people of Israel" to cross over on dry ground. But when Pharaoh's chariots followed, Yahweh blasted his nostrils and the waters came back and swallowed them all in a flood.

It was a fantastic ballad of mighty exploits. She wished it were more than just the expression of an artist's heart. That somehow, it might be true.

And then she came to the words that made her weep:

Who is like you, O Yahweh, among the gods?
Who is like you, majestic in holiness,
awesome in glorious deeds, doing wonders?
You have led in your steadfast love
the people whom you have redeemed;
you have guided them by your strength to your holy abode.
The peoples have heard; they tremble;
Now are the chiefs of Edom dismayed;
trembling seizes the leaders of Moab;
all the inhabitants of Canaan have melted away.

Edom, and Moab, and all of Canaan? So their plans *were* to cross the Jordan. All of Canaan *was* their destination. She giggled. Would not the Commander of Jericho pay all the money in the treasury to know this?

But she was not interested in all the money in the world.

She hid the parchment and tried to sleep, pondering these things in her heart.

She could not sleep.

She could only remember the last words of Izbaxl before he fell to his death by the dire wolves. He had cursed this very same god, Yahweh. The debauched gods of Canaan all seemed to know and hate this divinity with whom she felt herself falling in love.

CHAPTER 20

The city of Edrei was twenty-five miles across the Jabbok River into the land of Bashan, the kingdom of Og. This would not be as easy as conquering king Sihon. This was Rephaim territory; the grey skinned monstrosities with elongated skulls, six-digit hands and feet, double rows of teeth, and a fury wrought from the depths of Sheol.

Edrei was a chief metropolitan city of the Amorite kingdom and housed three thousand inhabitants. It was widely known for its strong fortifications. But one of its secrets that was not widely known was its underground city below the city. In times of war or disaster, the people would go below into tunnels and living spaces where they could live indefinitely. With access to underwater springs and stored food supply, protected by their elevated position above the valley, they could outlast any enemy besieging them, including the Habiru that now surrounded their fortress.

But they would not need to withstand such a siege, because Og had led his army from his host city, Ashtaroth, and pulled in conscripts from surrounding territories. He was not going to take any chances. He had a five thousand-man army facing these Habiru invaders, who appeared to have about five thousand as well.

But the Habiru did not have four companies of Rephaim giants who were gibborim warriors. That was about eight hundred giants divided into fighting platoons of fifty or so. That gave Og the decided advantage of three to one.

The Rephaim were the last remnant of a fearsome clan of giants whose lineage reached back to mighty warrior kings of Canaan. Some had even fought in the War of Eden before the Great Flood. They were not about to allow a horde of wandering scrappers attempt to extinguish them as they had done to the Emim and Zamzummim at Jahaz.

This city was a precursor to the heavily fortified cities of Canaan the Israelites had yet to encounter in the Cisjordan. Jahaz was child's play in comparison. The battle of Edrei would be the proving grounds of Israelite ability or the killing fields of their annihilation.

• • • • •

On the north side of the city was a massive cemetery for the surrounding communities. It was holy ground where devotees of Ashtart would bring their dead to bury them for blessing in Sheol. Ashtart had a temple for Molech built underground like the city beneath Edrei.

Since he was lord of the underworld, it was only fitting to plaster the walls of this cemetery crypt with the corpses of the dead. Torchlight cast an eerie glow on the skulls and bones embedded in the walls around them.

Molech had just now arrived and they were trying to complete their plan using mediums, sorcerers, and necromancers. There were one hundred of them congregated in this holy habitation of horror.

Molech told Ashtart, "They chased me all the way to the Sea of Chinnereth. I only evaded them because I entered the underground waterways. Endless caves and tunnels. They would not follow me into that labyrinth with the possibility of getting lost a thousand feet below the surface."

Ashtart jabbed, "I guess there is some benefit to being a worm god."

It was a distinctive trait of Ashtart to belittle gods lesser than she. Her vanity knew no bounds.

She added, "They suspect I am here, but they have no idea where. And by the time they figure it out, it will be too late, and they will find themselves facing the most fearsome attack they have ever faced. This has to work, mole, or we will be bound in Tartarus. And you will not be able to dig your way out of that pit."

Molech shivered. He knew of no worse fate than to await judgment for seventy times seven generations imprisoned in the deepest pit of Sheol.

She continued, "There are four of them, and only one and a half of us. And they are not going to stop."

"Well, neither will our minions," smiled Molech.

And then he realized that she had said, "One and a half of us," not "two of us."

He had to swallow her insults or face swallowing her scythe.

• • • • •

It was a clear evening under the moonlight. Moses, Joshua and Caleb hiked up to a ridge to look out upon the battlefield that lay before them a mile away.

Caleb was explaining the news he had discovered from their battle with Sihon.

"Evidently, it was Othniel, who led the forces inward after the surprise attack by the giant squad. And it was his spear that pierced the body of Sihon."

"Congratulations," said Joshua. "You must be proud of your brother's courage and zeal."

"When it comes to family life, he can be quite annoying. But in a battle, I value him second only to you, commander."

Moses said, "We shall have to give him an honor of distinction before the congregation when we have the opportunity."

Caleb knew that with the dangers of war, that opportunity may never arrive. Every battle could be a soldier's last.

They had arrived at the height of the ridge and could now see the landscape below them. The city of Edrei was on a small plateau surrounded by forest on three sides. They had cleared an open valley around the city perimeter of about a hundred yards outward. This was enough to keep invaders from approaching Edrei under cover and to provide a battlefield for skirmishes to stop sieges. Og's forces were encamped in the open field encircling the city above them.

Moses said, "Thank Yahweh for the terrain. We will not be facing chariots as in the flatlands of Canaan."

"Thank Yahweh, we only have an army of Rephaim to face," said Caleb with a twinge of sarcasm.

At that moment, a cloaked figure approached them running up the ridge. Moses tightened with fear. But Joshua and Caleb did not. They were expecting him.

When the figure arrived, Moses could see he was a young and handsome man, an Israelite about twenty-five years old. He breathed heavily from his run.

"Moses," said Joshua, "This is Salmon ben Nahshon of the tribe of Judah. We asked for volunteers to spy out the city of Edrei for us."

Caleb added, "Salmon here was the only one with guts enough to try."

"Impressive," said Moses. "May Yahweh bless you with sons of greatness. What news do you bring?"

"My lords," said Salmon catching his breath in between. "I have run all the way from Edrei. I was able to capture a guard and slip in through the gates in his armor. I have ascertained that there are several thousand citizens in the city, and about five thousand soldiers gathered from the cities of surrounding Bashan."

Joshua was impatient for what he really wanted to know.

"And how many Rephaim?"

Salmon sighed with sobriety. "Close to a thousand, sir. They are upwards of ten to twelve feet tall."

A thick silence fell over the three of the leaders. They were calculating the kind of odds they would have against such giants. They were not very good.

"But there is one other secret you will want to know."

As if they did not have enough complications.

"There is an underground city *below* the city where its citizens flee to for protection during a siege. I reconnoitered some of the secret passageways below, so if we break through, I can show you how to get down there."

"Well done, Salmon" said Joshua. "I am impressed with your skills of espionage. The best I have seen so far. I will reward you for them."

"Thank you, commander," said Salmon.

"And rest assured, I will call upon those skills again for future reconnaissance."

"It would be my honor."

Moses interrupted with a quizzical look, "Salmon, how were you able to gather such good intelligence?"

Salmon turned his eyes away from Moses and the others with a shade of guilt. After an uncomfortable pause, he said, "My lord, the best place for gossip in cities are taverns."

Moses was not privy to such details. "I see. With much drinking, there is much loosening of tongues."

Caleb added wryly, "And with other weaknesses of the flesh as well."

Moses now caught on and looked at Salmon, who still appeared too guilty to look him in the holy eye.

Caleb knew that Salmon had a weakness for women. He thought that it might become a weakness that would betray him one day.

Moses said, "You say these Rephaim are upwards of twelve feet tall?"

Salmon said, "They are as tall as the trees of that forest."

After a moment, Joshua said, "Then we shall use the trees to fight the trees."

Moses and Caleb looked askance at Joshua.

He continued, "The forest is dominated by juniper trees. Now, these demonic brutes are so tall, it takes four of us to fight one of them. But if they are drawn into the forest, their faces will be in the branches."

Moses and Caleb smiled.

Salmon held back his reaction. He knew his place in the presence of such great leaders, and it was to respond only when spoken to.

Caleb said, "They will have to bend down, which hampers their flexibility and striking force."

"The trees will be shields for us," said Joshua, "but obstacles for them."

Moses said, "What tactic do you propose will lure them into such a disadvantage they are no doubt aware of."

Joshua only said, "I suppose it would have to be one which would undoubtedly appear as an advantage."

"I have been thinking," said Caleb. "Our archers slay at a distance so we do not have to lose men in close combat. But these giants are twice the size of a man. At the battle of Jahaz, arrows were mere nuisances to the Emim and Zamzummim. So what if we built special bows that were three times the size of a man?"

"Who would be able to operate them?" said Moses. "We have no giants on our side."

Caleb was still thinking it through. "I suppose a two or three man crew would suffice."

Moses yawned. "Well, my counselors, I will leave you to your ruminations. I am an old man and in much need of my sleep. Salmon would you bring me back?"

"Yes, my lord Moses."

Salmon and Moses left them. Joshua and Caleb continued to look out onto the forest and field of battle.

"Joshua," said Caleb, "I know you have never stopped mourning the loss of your family."

Joshua would not respond.

Caleb continued, "You know that I too have suffered such loss. So this, my question, is not without empathy."

Joshua was curt. "What is your question, Caleb?"

"Do you kill for vengeance or justice?"

"Canaanites killed my family. How do you suggest I kill Canaanites, with the joy of the Lord?"

"Joshua, I know what it means to lose hope. To lose the one thing in your life that brings balance to your being. And I am here to tell you that if you do not watch over your soul, my Captain—my friend and brother—you will lose it."

"I envy you," said Joshua. "You live in a world of imagination and ambiguity. You are a man of spiritual symbols and heaven. You see *through* everything into some kind of purpose or meaning beyond. It is like you are not even on earth. But I am a man of earth, blood, and law. I cannot help but see what is before me, and I demand justice, here and now. Yes, I fight for Yahweh's justice, but I am fueled by vengeance. For if I am not, then I have dishonored the memory of my family and of all the Israelites who have been kidnapped, beaten, enslaved or murdered under my watch, and they are truly lost forever to me."

• • • • •

At that very moment, on the other side of Edrei, a lone scout made a reconnaissance trip around the city to gather information on the full perimeter of the fortress plateau.

But it was not Salmon.

Uriel was the smallest and most stealthy of the four archangels, so he had been commissioned to make the trip.

It was at the backside of the city that Uriel discovered a large cemetery within walking distance of the city. Because places of the dead were considered taboo by Canaanite religions, he knew that armed forces would most likely avoid them unless absolutely necessary in the defense of the city.

Uriel knew this would be the place for them to approach the city while the war was going on around the other side. They needed to find the temple of Ashtart inside the city so they could capture and bind her.

He slipped through the graveyard of stones as the night fog began to settle. If he was not an archangel, he would have been a bit frightened by the way the moonlight spilled on the megalith stones. It marked burials of the rich, while the small burial mounds for the poor became partially obscured in the mist.

Just past the burial grounds, he heard the sound of a single garrison at their watch. About ten of them sounded loud and sloppy in their discipline because of the unlikelihood of enemy attack at this location.

He moved around them and found his way to the plateau that rose high above him. He concealed himself into a position where he could watch the entire mound, and then focused his sharp preternatural eyes to look for something.

Within an hour, he found what he was looking for. A colony of bats fluttered toward the mound and then seemed to disappear into the ridge of stone and rock.

He smiled, and started for that area.

He had to climb over a hundred feet up the rock, but he eventually found the hidden opening into the cave. He knew there was an entire city beneath the mound of rock, so there had to be secret tunnels and airways for access into their midst.

When he looked into the opening, he saw it was large enough for two men to get through. But there was an amazing natural wonder just inside, blocking human access through the cave: the largest hornet's nest he had ever seen. It was mud-like and made of pulp and bark chewed with the saliva of the insects. It covered the cave walls and ceiling like a natural archway and went into the cave a good fifty feet or so, creating a gauntlet of stinging death for any who stirred the angry hornets.

Uriel smiled and whispered a prayer, "Yahweh, you are an amazing creator, the creatures you make. Now, please let me find another way in, thank you."

But as he turned and looked upon the graveyard below him to climb down, he noticed a cloaked figure slip into a large Megalithic structure.

He whispered again to Yahweh, "Now, that may be one of the fastest answers to prayer yet. What, two seconds? I think that even beats the moment Abram saved Sarai from the assassin of Nimrod."

Uriel was referring to a moment when an assassin had captured Sarai after fighting with Abram. Abram was about to throw a dagger at the assassin, knowing he was too weak to make it hit its target. But when he asked El Shaddai to help him in his aim, he did not have to throw because the assassin fell dead from blood loss. It was a double miracle, because Abram would probably have missed and hit Sarai.

That prayer was answered in about two and a half seconds.

Of course, Uriel knew there were millions of prayers answered by Yahweh *before* his beloved children even uttered them, but he liked to see how close he could get to simultaneity.

He climbed down the rocky crag to get a closer look.

• • • • •

That same night, the Rephaim had engaged in sabotage. A platoon of fifteen giants had circled around behind the Israelites and captured a train of supplies on its way to the Israelite camp.

But they did not steal the supplies. They did not need them. The supplies, they burned. What they wanted to steal were the humans. They kidnaped twenty hostages and brought them back to the army of Edrei.

By the time the Israelites had discovered the sabotage, the Rephaim had already brought the hostages into their camp and cooked them.

Cannibalism was a spiritual rite that the Rephaim believed involved a transforming truth. By eating the flesh of their enemy, they were absorbing their life source into their own bodies, and with it, their power.

• • • • •

The next morning, when Joshua had arisen, Caleb alerted him and they went to their observation point to see a line of poles rising above the morning fog. On them were draped the carcasses of their twenty countrymen impaled like limp standards before the armies of Bashan.

Caleb said with righteous indignation, "So, this is our enemy. This demonic seed."

After a moment of silence, Joshua stated, "The pride of these titans will be their undoing. They have just given us an advantage."

Caleb could not believe Joshua would be thinking strategy at a time like this. He had become so pragmatic and cold-hearted.

Then Joshua said, "How quickly can you make those gigantic bows you talked about?"

"I will need a few days," said Caleb.

"You have two," said Joshua.

Caleb sighed. Not again.

CHAPTER 21

The morning sun was about to rise. Joshua had gathered his troops for their attack on Og. He walked through the ranks to inspire the men. He spoke from his heart. He spoke with great conviction.

"Warriors of Israel! We are about to face our first of many encounters with the gibborim of this land: The Rephaim! But fear not, for we are fighting the Wars of Yahweh! Know who you are, Seed of Abraham! And when you arrive on the battlefield and you see their towering forms, and you are tempted to fear, just remember; your ancestors, Enoch, and Methuselah, and Lamech, and Noah vanquished the Nephilim of their day! You are the descendants of giant slayers! These Canaanites are the Seed of the Serpent, and Yahweh has promised you conquest!"

The men did not cheer, for their strategy was to approach the battlefield with stealth. But they had grown strong in confidence and courage to face their fearful enemy.

They picked up and marched swiftly to their positions in the woods outside Edrei.

• • • • •

Og of Bashan looked down into the forest below. He was dressed for battle with his signature painted white face that embodied death, along with his royal dress of black body armor, black cape, black headdress and gloves. His armor alone was one hundred and forty pounds. It was rare ancient Nephilim armor passed down from antediluvian days. He carried a spear whose shaft was like a weaver's beam and whose head of brass weighed twenty-five pounds. His sword was the size of an average male human soldier and could cut that soldier in half with one swing.

He and his eight hundred gibborim warriors were the last of the Rephaim, a fearsome people in the days of Abraham, whose reign of terror had only been stopped by a four-army coalition headed by Elamite king Chedorlaomer.

Og had vowed that would never happen again, so he was particularly set this day upon fighting to the death—to the last giant if necessary.

But he had higher hopes than that this day. Because he had a few tricks up his chainmail. And he would cut down every last one of these detestable Habiru, man, woman and child, to eradicate their seed from the face of the land.

His men below were aware of movement in the woods and were already standing ground in the morning fog that seemed to cover everything except the Rephaim that stood above it at nine feet and more. They were like beacons that rose out of the mist with their eagle eyes on any approach.

But what they had not anticipated was that the giants could be seen above the fog, *but could not see anything within it.*

They were therefore easy targets for the special cross bows created by Caleb and brought to the edge of the forest beneath the fog. They were powerful enough to breach the distance and pierce their giant targets with efficiency.

There were ten giant wooden bows. They were the size of two men, placed on their side and mounted on a wheeled cart low to the ground. A hand crank would pull the bow string back and notch it. A large arrow bolt would be placed in the groove and the bow aimed at a giant above the fog, before its release. The entire process would take about eight to ten seconds.

This was the Israelite's first surprise attack.

A hail of bolts came at the Rephaim and took out a half dozen of them. Before the enemies could get their bearings on what was happening, another volley of large arrows took out another eight giants. Some of the bolts had skewered three and four normal soldiers at once, but the bulk of them were aimed high at the Rephaim.

Then a flurry of normal arrows announced the Israelite archer squad. The Bashan archers returned the attack, but the trees acted as protective shields to the Israelites. Another volley of giant arrows killed more Rephaim before they realized what was happening and began to sink below the fog line.

The Bashan forces sounded their war horns and charged the forest's edge.

But when they got there, the Israelites had vanished, melted back into the forest.

"COWARDS!" screamed the field commander, Kemoc, a Rephaim warrior with years of battle experience, a scarred face and a few missing fingers to prove it.

He turned to his standard-bearer and told him to signal the king up on the city wall that the Israelites were firing and running away.

They returned to the plateau base and regrouped.

Before the fog could dissipate, the Israelites launched another giant bow attack, killing a dozen more giants and withdrawing into the forest again, chased by the Bashan forces.

But the fog was clearing and Og knew the Habiru would not be able to cower in hiding any longer. He had never seen this kind of battle before. Armies would line up and face each other on the battlefield to contest numbers and strength. But this hit and hide tactic was juvenile. This Moses and his general Joshua were clearly frightened of his Rephaim, and that was an advantage he would exploit in the next attack.

• • • • •

Around the other side of the city, four archangels prepared for their special mission: to capture and bind the gods of the city. Uriel had brought back intelligence to Mikael, Gabriel, and Raphael that was game changing. He discovered that Ashtart and Molech were holed up in an underground Temple of the Dead outside the city walls in the vast regional cemetery.

The archangels would not have to get inside the city. They were relieved. But Uriel felt that their relief might be hasty because he knew the gods were preparing for something big, but just what exactly, he could not be sure. All he knew was that they had gathered the largest assembly of sorcerers, mediums, and necromancers he had ever seen. About one hundred of them. This would not be a mere battle with Watchers, but with their occultic magic as well.

Inside the Temple of the Dead, Ashtart and Molech led their cadre of occultists in human sacrifices and a series of blood rituals. These were not the usual rites of public atonement, but rather specially developed magic rituals of conjuring.

Twenty human corpses hung upside down with blood draining into the canals of a large circular Babylonian style emblem engraved in bronze on the floor. The blood seemed to follow the canals of the emblem into a subterranean destination.

Twenty guards stood around the large cavernous tomblike temple, their backs to the sedimentary walls embedded with skeletons of the dead. Torches lit the temple with an eerie flickering orange glow.

Thirty necromancers chanted incantations from their ancient Babylonian tablets, secured by Ashtart from her Mesopotamian past. It was a cacophony that sounded like the buzzing of an insect hive crossed with the hiss of a pit of snakes.

In the midst of this dissonant noise, thirty male and female sorcerers engaged in a diabolical ritual with corpses that was too horrendous to describe. The bodies of the exhumed dead were in various states of decay.

Thirty sorcerers mixed alchemical potions for the reanimation of dead tissue, which they then added to the blood seeping down into the dark earth. "Dark earth" was a Hittite expression that meant the underworld.

Molech presided over the ceremonies, as he was in fact the Lord of the Underworld. He made a child pass through the fire that was located in the center of the room.

As hungry for violence and debauchery as Ashtart was, even she was repulsed by Molech's depths of depravity. He was truly the lowest of the gods when it came to evil. And he had no sense of fashion either. He was just a maggot that fed on rotting flesh to her.

But a useful maggot nonetheless.

And speaking of fashion, Ashtart was decked out in her favorite death cult warrior garb. Hair back and out of the eyes, face painted in deathly white with black lipstick. All black leather, but also made with cuts and openings throughout to facilitate flexible movement. Topped off by a wonderfully flowing hooded cape.

She carried her favorite weapon, her scythe, and thought that someday they should adopt her look as the symbol of death, she was so ravishing. She thought Og had been quite the copycat with his own adornment mimicking her. But she knew imitation was a sincere form of flattery so she let it go.

She considered humiliating Og when this war was over, just to remind him who was queen of fashion in this town.

• • • • •

Over in the battlefield of Edrei, the fog had cleared and the armies of Bashan engaged in war chanting, taunting the armies of Israel.

Joshua signaled his forces, and two platoons of slingers came forward, guarded by shield carriers, backed by a division of a thousand men and covered by a volley of their archers behind them. Slingers had to get a bit closer for efficient hits.

The Rephaim laughed at them. They looked like a party of herdsmen without sword or spear. Shepherds used slings to frighten or sting predators from their herds. But did they really think their puny little rocks were a weapon against warriors? These Habiru were becoming more ridiculous in their eyes with each passing wave of attack. They seemed like children—devious malicious children—but children.

The slingers were not children, but highly trained units mostly from the tribe of Benjamin that had developed the art of slinging for the art of warfare.

The sling consisted of one leather strap about six feet long, with a little pouch in the middle. The slinger would grab both ends of the sling and place a round rock in the pouch. He would swing it in a circle about his head or vertically at his side as fast as he could. He would then release one of the straps at the right moment to jettison the rock at its target.

What the armies of Bashan did not realize was just how lethal slung rocks could be.

So when they hit, dozens of men were seriously wounded, including giants.

The Israelites got off two rounds before Og's war horn bellowed, announcing a charge of his army.

The Israelites turned and ran back into the forest.

"Not this time, you scurrying rodents!" yelled Kemoc, the Bashan field commander.

The Rephaim charged, chasing the Habiru back into the forest. But they were not going to stop at the forest line this time. They were going to hunt them down and slaughter them like the scared little jackrabbits they were.

Joshua was perched deep in the forest on the highest tree possible, and he could see his plan had worked. He was trying a new form of commanding. Rather than leading his forces into battle, he thought he might have a tactical advantage if he could see the entire battlefield and forces before him and therefore be able to make strategic judgments that he could not possibly make in the heat and heart of the battle. Up here, he could see what was going right and what was going wrong, and signal his forces through trumpet or standard to meet the changing tides of battle. It was the same thing that Og was doing from his perch high atop the walls of Edrei.

But Joshua did not like being outside the theater of battle. Down in the thick of it, he felt connected to his men and his men to him. He fought with them, bled with them, and they moved like a synchronized body. Up in his perch, he may have a better oversight, but he was removed, distant from his brothers in battle, and thought it would make them feel alone.

Caleb was down below guarding Joshua's position with a small unit of men. He was itching to kill himself some giants, and had thought of excuses to slip away into battle and leave his general in the hands of the guard. But he could not trust anyone but himself to make sure of that protection, so he stayed put, wrenching his neck trying to see Joshua up in the tree.

Down in forest battle, the Bashan forces plunged headlong in pursuit of the Habiru.

But they were so intent upon catching them that they failed to see the line of Habiru warriors on either side of them that had been waiting in ambush.

The chased Israelites now turned back and faced their pursuers to fight.

And the Bashan army was surrounded. The first clash of hand to hand combat began.

• • • • •

Ashtart had barely finished pouring the sacrificial blood into her goatskin flasks when the sound of Mikael's booming voice penetrated the Temple of the Dead and silenced everyone.

"Azazel and Ramiel, prepare for Tartarus!"

Four archangels do not need the element of surprise to ambush a spree of evil. Mikael thought it would be an inspiration for his team, and an added terror for their enemies. He had spoken the original names of the Watchers who were masquerading as Ashtart and Molech.

The archangels started slicing through the waves of wickedness that stormed toward them.

It was easy. It was not even a fight. It was an annoyance.

No, it was a ploy.

The attacking minions were intended by Ashtart and Molech to delay the angels so they could make good their escape.

The angels had their hands and swords filled with their attackers, but they saw the gods depart through a tunnel.

Mikael yelled, "They are getting away!"

The supernatural team increased their speed and finished making minced meat of their enemies.

Uriel remarked, "You know, I think we might be competition for the Destroyer." The Destroyer was the Angel of Death who was used by Yahweh to wipe out whole populations of evil.

"Not the time for levity!" yelped Gabriel.

Mikael said, "Gabriel and Uriel, take the tunnels. Raphael follow me to the surface!"

When Mikael and Raphael broke the surface and exited the megalith entrance, they saw Ashtart and Molech standing at a distance.

Uriel and Gabriel exited the tunnel to join their comrades.

They froze with trepidation.

Ashtart and Molech were walking backwards, spraying the blood from the goatskins all around them like a farmer watering his crops.

But these were not crops.

Mikael looked at his feet. They were in a cemetery.

And suddenly the ground that the gods had watered with their alchemical blood began to erupt.

The angels watched in wonder as deceased and buried bodies came alive and broke their way out of their graves.

The distance between the angels and the gods was blocked by an increasing number of these rising corpses, these living dead.

They were all in various states of decay, due to the amount of time they had been dead and buried. Some were whole persons with rotting flesh and glazed eyeballs, others were nearly all skeleton, but all of them were now facing the angels and were ravenous for human or angel flesh.

They attacked.

Uriel and Raphael were the closest. They sliced off arms and legs, but the creatures kept coming at them, chomping their jaws.

And they were inhumanly strong.

This would not be easy.

Uriel screamed out, "They are like Shades of Sheol!"

Gabriel decapitated a few, which seemed to stop them.

"Then cut off their heads like Shades!"

Uriel followed suit and the two of them backed up to join the others. They broke into a fighting form and defended themselves against the growing circle of freakish miscreants.

Mikael could see that Ashtart and Molech were now running through the graveyard, finishing up their deadly seeding.

There were now hundreds of them, animated corpses that could not die because they were already dead, with chomping jaws of death. And all of them surrounding the angels for a breakfast meal.

• • • • •

The trees had worked as a strategy for Joshua. The battle had been forced into the woods. The Rephaim advantage was overturned as

Joshua had planned because their tall height had necessitated bending down to avoid the branches. The giants could not maneuver easily and the odds were balanced.

But Joshua had not anticipated the technology of the Bashan army. Their weaponry was superior to Israel's. Whereas the Israelites had the long rectangle shaped shields of Egypt, these soldiers had smaller round shields influenced by the Sea Peoples who had recently infiltrated the coastland. The round shield was more versatile and conducive to swordplay.

And the swords were different as well. Whereas the Israelites carried the bronze curved sickle swords, most common in the Near East, their enemies carried stronger heavier swords made of a more durable metal. Joshua had heard of the advances of this new metal called "iron," and had seen its advantage in strength and durability when he had spied out Canaan a generation earlier. But he had yet to see its effectiveness on the field of battle with many troops.

Unfortunately, their iron was very effective against his bronze. And in the hands of a giant, it would shatter Israelite weapons.

Joshua's army was wavering.

• • • • •

The swords of the four angels were spinning like fans, cutting off heads left and right.

They had to push forward to avoid creating a pile that would block them in.

But these living dead were not easy to kill. They were supernaturally strong and relentless.

The angels were getting tired.

Uriel was drenched with sweat. His arms were getting heavy. These things just kept coming.

And angels were flesh, so even though they could not die, they could suffer wounds and bites. And they were being scratched in too many close calls.

Uriel realized that should they be overcome, their bodies could be eaten and they would be forever imprisoned in the bellies of the undead—alive, but chewed up. He grimaced. They would fail their mission. They would fail their god.

This was not looking good.

He saw the gods in the distance split up. Ashtart went north, and Molech went south.

But right now, none of the angels could consider making chase. They had to keep from becoming a meal for these living dead.

Uriel shouted, "I need a moment to rest!"

The other three circled around to protect their comrade. They would surely chide Uriel if they survived, but they would give their lives for one another without a complaint or qualification in such dire moments.

But they also knew their little brother had a secret weapon, and he just needed enough preparation for a burst of energy to pull it off.

Uriel caught his breath and yelled, "Okay, brothers, get ready to be outdone again!"

Gabriel rolled his eyes. But then he smiled through gritted teeth as he took down another few living dead. As much as he teased him, he loved Uriel and respected him greatly.

But he could not pass up the opportunity. "I hope you are keeping count, featherhead!"

Uriel screamed, "CLEAR!"

The angels pushed outward and made an opening for Uriel to push through the masses.

He took his swords and held them out like a horizontal windmill blade. He then spun in a circle like a one-man cyclone. The blades created a moving fan that cut through zombie bodies and heads by the dozens.

But there were so many of them.

He created a kind of pathway for the angels to advance and find a moment of rest.

But Uriel could not go on forever.

When he stopped, the area around them was cleared. But he fell to the ground dizzy. He had spun the longest he had ever done with this signature move, but it had taken its toll. Even angels can become exhausted when pushed to the limit.

And so he did not see the two zombies that had evaded the death spin.

They jumped for him.

Gabriel and Mikael had seen it coming. They threw their swords.

One blade cut off the head of one zombie. But the second one merely lodged in the other's chest cavity.

That was not enough to stop the monster.

The thing caught Uriel from behind and took a big bite off his back muscle. Uriel screamed in pain, and swung around blindly, cutting the thing's head off. But he had been wounded, and even though angels healed quickly, this would not be a speedy recovery because of its occultic properties.

They were all cut and bruised and wounded from their encounters, and now that they had a moment to rest, they realized that they too were impaired by the demonic magic of their cuts and gashes. Had they been humans, the wounds would have turned them into the walking dead as well. But angelic flesh was heavenly. They could be damaged by death magic, but could not be transformed by it.

But they *could* be eaten. And that would split them in a thousand different pieces sitting imprisoned in a thousand different bellies. That fate was unthinkable to them.

When they looked up, they discovered that they were already surrounded anew by a circle of hundreds more ravenous undead pressing in.

They would not have the strength to finish this fight.

• • • • •

Down in the heat of the battle, Othniel had noticed that these Rephaim were not the same as the giants they killed at Jahaz. They were in every way superior. They were bigger, stronger, more skilled at warfare, and organized. The Israelite forces were weakening. They just didn't have the vitality without their general in their midst leading them on. Othniel thought they needed a surge of new strength. They needed the faith and presence of Joshua and Caleb.

Fortunately, Joshua was thinking the same thing as Othniel, because he almost fell out of the tree in his hurried rush from his perch down to his horse.

When he landed, Caleb just looked at him and said, "It is about time, general."

Joshua barked, "To the battle!" and they were off.

When Othniel saw them arrive at the fray, they were at full strength and pumped up with energy.

Othniel knew that the soldiers would find inner renewal from seeing their general by their side slaying giants.

And he was right.

These Rephaim titans were fierce and brutal. But they bled and they died like any other living creature.

Joshua and Caleb jumped from their steeds. They were more versatile in their movements without them.

Caleb unfurled his whip sword Rahab and faced six men surrounding him immediately. He twirled the blade around his head and cut them down as fast as Uriel with his windmill move. But this was not surprising considering Caleb was trained in the same Karabu technique as the archangel.

Joshua pummeled several opponents with sheer force. He was fresher to the fight and he used that to his advantage.

But then he faced his first giant, a ten foot tall blue grey Rephaim staring him down with venom in his veins and hatred in his eyes. The Rephaim roared and Joshua could see his double rows of teeth.

The gargantuan had a double-headed battle-axe. The common axe head of many Israelites was the duck-billed socket axe. A fine instrument for piercing armor and bones. But this thing was the size of a round battle shield with opposing curved semi-circular blades that cut completely through the small trees behind Joshua as he dodged the swings.

SWOOSH! CRUNCH! SWOOSH! CRUNCH!

The Rephaim kept coming, kept swinging. He was relentless. Joshua had to back up until he slammed into Caleb. Both of them turned to face the Rephaim.

The monster swung down and the axe buried in the earth with an explosion of dirt.

Joshua had just that second to spin around and come down on the giant's left wrist with the full force of his sword blade. He cut clean through the giant's flesh and bone. The Rephaim howled with anger and pulled back, its severed six-fingered hand lying on the ground.

But it seemed not to slow down. It only got angrier.

It now came swinging the battle-axe with its right hand. It seemed to be as agile with one hand as with two.

Caleb pushed Joshua back out of the way and took the titan's attention. Caleb was eighty years old, but he was as strong and vigorous as a forty year old.

And he was Karabu.

He moved with the fluidity of a river and the grace of a butterfly as he wove a dance around the frustrated swinging of the giant.

The giant's anger made him sloppy and Caleb swirled his flexible blade behind him until he could find an opportunity to wrap it around the giant's good arm and yank it back, slicing the arm from the body. It fell to the ground like a log and the giant screamed again.

Joshua finished off the limbless monster with his blade. It fell to the ground with a crash.

Joshua retrieved his sword.

He did not see the warrior behind him, about to pierce him through with spear.

And Joshua also did not see the flying whirl of Rahab from six feet away drop his attacker with ease. The body fell to the ground on top of the dead Rephaim.

At that moment, Joshua and Caleb understood fully that the general's joining in battle had rallied his men with supernatural inspiration. Joshua was a powerful symbolic figure to them. His valiant presence gave them the faith they lacked.

The Israelites were now on the offensive with the Rephaim. They used the trees as shields while the titans were being cramped by the trees as obstacles—just like Joshua had anticipated.

More than a few of the immense warriors had gotten their heads knocked or tangled in low hanging branches, making them blinded easy prey for their adversaries.

This was no battlefield for giants. Caleb could feel it. The tide had turned.

But there was one last wave he had not considered. It came in the form of Og of Bashan plowing through his own forces to find Joshua and take him out.

Og was no mere warrior. He was eleven feet tall and as experienced as the finest of warriors. He materialized through the dust of battle like a phantom wraith of doom. His black cape flowed behind him like a spirit. He wielded two mighty iron swords, one in each hand that brought death to everyone with whom they made contact.

And he was headed straight for Joshua.

• • • • •

On the other side of the valley, the four embattled archangels faced certain demise. They were worn down, wounded, disoriented by the mesmerizing effect of the black magic, and they were surrounded by a raging horde of the living dead. They had killed hundreds of them, but there were hundreds more, and they had no strength left but to gasp for air. The swords had become heavy weights on their arms that they could no longer wield.

Except for Mikael, whose swinging blows Uriel noticed did not seem to waver. Uriel knew Mikael was the strongest of the four of them, but this endurance seemed more than usual. Uriel could not spend any more energy on such distractions and focused back on raising his own heavy weight to smite the pressing hordes.

And that was when it hit Gabriel.

This confrontation with creatures very much like the Shades of Sheol, reminded him of a tactic Uriel had told them he had used so long ago when he was in Sheol with Noah and Methuselah facing the actual Shades.

Gabriel reached into his cloak and pulled out his trumpet, put it to his lips and blew with the last breath in him.

The sound rang out and moved like a concussive shockwave of power that flattened the entire army of undead surrounding them. They fell like lead weight under the rolling vibrations of Yahweh's call to war.

In a moment, it was all over. Everything was still. Everything was dead once again. Truly dead.

The others looked at Gabriel.

He said to Uriel, "Remember what you told us when you were with Noah in Sheol?"

Uriel hit his own head like an idiot. "Of course! I cannot believe I did not think of that!"

Gabriel explained, "I figured that since our trumpets had supernatural effect on the real Shades of Sheol, it might have a similar effect on these occultic imitations of Shades."

"More than that," said Mikael. "This was dark earth magic of the underworld. Ashtart must have been developing it for generations. But the sound of Yahweh's call to war broke the spell."

Then Uriel broke in, "Mikael, can I see your sword?"

Mikael handed it to Uriel.

It felt very light in his grip.

Uriel said, "I thought something was strange when I saw you fighting with this. I knew you were strong, but this feels lighter than our swords. And a stronger metal."

Mikael apologized, "In all our busyness, I had forgotten to mention it to you. It is a new metal called 'steel.' An alloy of iron and carbon. Lighter and stronger than iron. It has yet to be revealed to humans."

Uriel complained, "It must be great to be the firstborn. You inherit all the best stuff. I get the leftovers and hand me downs."

"Uriel," scolded Gabriel, "be thankful for what we have. Yahweh owes us nothing."

"I know, I know."

Mikael said, "We have no time to waste. Uriel, can you track down Molech? We need to stop him from getting any intelligence to Ba'al. Gabriel and Raphael can help me hunt Ashtart."

Uriel groaned and held his throbbing bite wound.

Gabriel threw out, "That is unless Molech is just too much for you. We would totally understand if you were just too weak to handle that scourge by yourself."

He was at it again. Their non-stop competition of egos.

Uriel stretched through his pain and said, "No, no. That is all right. You three need all the help you can get for your *single* fugitive. I will take Molech *all alone, by myself.*"

Raphael and Mikael smiled.

But Gabriel would not be outdone. "Well, you can take Ashtart instead, if you would prefer."

They all knew full well that it would take them all to subdue the fearsome goddess of war, who was second only to Ba'al in power and chaos.

But Uriel was second to none when it came to wit. He concluded their banter with a wink, "I will tell you what, I will catch back up with you three to help even the odds. Yahweh knows, you need it."

"Okay, you two," said Mikael, "kiss and make up. We have gods to bind."

Uriel said, "I do need everyone's help for one last thing before we embark on our hunting trip."

• • • • •

Joshua faced off with Og. Caleb joined him. He was not going to let his general face this demonic titan alone.

But the Rapha they recently dispatched was a juvenile compared to King Og of Bashan.

He towered over them at twice their size. His six-fingered hands held his iron blades with an iron grip. And his armor was something Joshua and Caleb had never seen before. It was forged in the heavenly height of the pantheon of gods, Mount Hermon. Even Caleb's archangelic whip sword could not penetrate it. He cracked it at Og and it bounced off with sparks.

Og swung at Caleb, who dodged and danced like a gust of wind.

Karabu, thought Og. He had seen this kind of fighting before. And he had learned how to counter it.

Og immediately increased his focus on Caleb, who barely kept ahead of his attacks.

Caleb's sword sliced through the air in a wide arc. Og jammed his iron sword into its path and managed to get it wrapped by Caleb's blade.

His strength far outweighed Caleb's. He yanked and the sword ripped out of Caleb's grasp and flew into the air thirty feet away.

Caleb was weaponless. He dove out of the way and picked up a round shield from a dead soldier to protect himself from Og's slashing.

That was when the sound of Gabriel's trumpet penetrated the forest and vale from the other side of the city. When they heard it, the Israelites gained new strength and the upper hand in battle. It was as if they heard their own victory call and rose up to triumph.

The warriors of Bashan became frightened and withdrew from the field of battle.

The Israelites chased them back to the city of Edrei. In the lead was Othniel, the ever-determined brother of the mighty Caleb.

But Og continued to fight with Joshua and Caleb.

Joshua's training kicked in and he attacked with every ounce of force left in him.

Og was driven back as he blocked Joshua's slashes, thrusts, and hacks. And because he had focused on defending against Joshua, he had lost track of Caleb. So by the time he countered and began to push Joshua back, he did not know that Caleb was behind him—in a tree.

When Joshua backed Og against that tree, Caleb jumped.

He landed on Og's back and grabbed his collar with all his might.

Og immediately layered both of his swords across his back and across Caleb's back, and sliced them through Caleb's body.

But Og did not know that Caleb had shouldered his newly acquired shield against his back like a turtle shell.

The iron blades dug through the shield, but they did not reach Caleb's flesh.

And Caleb was not without a weapon after all.

He had pulled a dirk from his belt and jammed it in the base of Og's skull underneath his headdress.

Og screamed and backed up against the tree, crushing Caleb, who fell to the ground unconscious.

Og tried to reach for the blade, but his arm and armor were too bulky to reach the small thorn penetrating into his brain.

And that meant he was entirely open for Joshua to thrust between the joints of his special hardened armor to penetrate his giant heart.

Unfortunately, the blade stuck in the armor and Joshua pulled away without his weapon, its handle sticking out of Og's sternum.

Og was going to die. But he was not dead yet.

He had dropped his swords, and had fallen to his knees. The brain wound from Caleb paralyzed his left arm.

With his life bleeding out of him, he found one last gush of strength to grab the stunned Joshua with his good hand. His huge six-fingers held Joshua in the air, crushing his windpipe, choking Joshua's life out of him.

Og crowed, "I have you at last, you Yahwist fanatic. And I will take you with me to Sheol."

But before Og could make good his promise, he felt the sensation of cold metal wrap around his neck like a rope. Rahab in the hands of Caleb again.

Caleb said, "No, you will not, you son of Belial."

Caleb yanked, and Og was decapitated into oblivion.

Caleb went to help Joshua, who massaged his wounded windpipe. He could barely speak. He did not have to. They looked at each other. Grabbed wrists. They were comrades in war. Brothers in the Lord.

"You really owe me that land of Abraham now," said Caleb.

Joshua croaked out, "What do *I* get for saving *you*?"

Caleb thought for a moment and said, "I will not tell Moses you took too big a risk."

Joshua shook his head and said, "Let us finish off this city. Find me the spy Salmon."

When Joshua and Caleb arrived in the city, their army greeted them. But no one else was in sight. It was a ghost town.

Othniel announced, "My lord, when we broke through the gate, there was no one here. They have all vanished."

Salmon stood beside them. "They are underground," he said. "In their city beneath the city."

Joshua said to Salmon, "Where are the passageways you discovered, so we can smoke these badgers out."

• • • • •

But Joshua would not have to pursue the underground fugitives, because at that moment on the backside of the plateau, a hundred feet in the air, Uriel was in the cave opening he had discovered on his spying trip. It was the one with the magnificent hornet's nest filling the tunnel.

Uriel took out his two swords and ran through the gauntlet hive like a miniature tornado, cutting up the hornet's nest all the way to the opening of the cave.

The hornets were driven mad with rage at the attack. They began to pour out of their nest like a billowing storm cloud.

But Uriel reached the opening and dove out, landing fifteen feet below with a thud on a rocky ledge.

Simultaneously above him, Mikael, Gabriel, and Raphael used all their strength to dislodge a boulder at the entrance and cause a cave in that sealed the entrance and trapped the angry hornets inside. It forced them to go in the other direction, straight into the catacombs beneath the city where the populace had hidden out with the surviving soldiers.

• • • • •

Up above, the city was already in flames and black smoke billowed into the sky. Salmon had led Joshua to one of the passageways that he had found on his spy mission.

But before they could enter it, Joshua and his forces suddenly saw soldiers and citizens screaming and running for their lives from secret openings in the city. Many of them were swatting at hornets still following them, and others were dropping dead from the stings that covered their bodies.

The hornets were repelled from Joshua's men by the smoke of the fires around them.

Joshua did to King Og and his people what he did to King Sihon and the Amorites. He defeated them until they had no survivor left, and possessed their land.

Og's head and body were hung on a pole in the field of Edrei.

• • • • •

When the armed forces returned to the camp of Israel, Moses called a congregational gathering to honor the heroic deeds of the living and the dead. They had already buried their fallen and worshipped their god Yahweh for his protection and victory. But now several warriors were honored for their mighty exploits.

The one that mattered most to Caleb was his brother Othniel.

Joshua, Caleb, Othniel, and the others stood before the congregation in their military garb. The elders and judges were all present with a large representation of their tribes to recognize these mighty men.

As Moses recounted Othniel's deeds on the field to the congregation, Caleb watched his daughter in the front of the crowd beaming with pride.

Moses described Othniel's launch into the breach of the giant forces at Jahaz. How he had found his way through the tangle of chaos to be the vanquisher of King Sihon. Caleb saw Othniel stealing glances at Achsah.

It was customary to offer these men of valor fulfillment of a wish as gratitude for their sacrifice on behalf of Yahweh and his people. They had risked all in battle for their countrymen. It was not unreasonable to offer them some earthly reward for their exploits.

Some would ask for large parties of much eating and drinking with friends, some would request elevation of rank in the military, others specific tracts of land for inheritance. It was common for many to ask for the hand of a woman in marriage.

So when Caleb stood before his brother and asked what his desire would be, he saw that Othniel was nervous and sweating. Othniel stared in Achsah's direction then jerked his eyes toward Caleb with what looked like a tortured mind. He was taking too long. He appeared to want to say something, but did not have the courage to say it aloud.

Caleb waited for him, making it all the more uncomfortable. He knew that this man who could slay giants in combat and lead a thousand men in battle with a war cry, did not have the courage to publicly declare his heart for a young woman for the fear of failure and rejection. Caleb thought of him like a big ox with his tongue cut out. But he believed that if a man could not display the courage to face the failure of a woman's or father's rejection, then he did not deserve to win that woman, much less Caleb's precious Achsah. Achsah needed more than a brutish protector and provider. She deserved a companion and sensitive husband.

Husband? The thought of her married to Othniel made Caleb's stomach turn. He secretly hoped that Achsah had not gotten any ideas from their earlier talk about marriage.

In the crowd, Achsah was feeling sorry for Othniel. After her father had mentioned his name as a possible husband for her weeks ago, she began to see Othniel in a different light. She began to see all his playfulness and affection for her with far more importance than she ever had. She would daydream about him walking with her in a garden and kissing her. Hearing his mighty deeds of war caused a feeling to rise up within her that she had never experienced before.

It was intense desire. The man who had been like a bigger brother to her all her life, who had watched over her, rescued her, and taught her so much about survival, was now a warrior with a steed ready to carry her away.

Only, he could not mount his stallion. He seemed too intimidated by her father or by his own lack of confidence to speak up.

Well, one thing she knew for sure. She would never usurp his obligation to lead in the ways of courtship and betrothal. Her father had modeled the kind of man that she required. And if Othniel would not have the courage to ask for her hand, she would remain waiting, even if it took him years.

She prayed it would not take him years.

And suddenly, to Caleb's and Achsah's surprise, indeed to Othniel's surprise, Othniel blubbered out the words, "I want to be a judge!"

Caleb was not sure what he heard. It was not what he had anticipated.

Othniel clarified, "After we have settled in the land, I want to become a judge of Israel and deliberate justice."

Caleb stole a glance at Achsah. She looked crestfallen, heartbroken.

But Caleb felt relieved. As much as he loved and respected his brother, he felt he was not good enough for his Achsah. No one was good enough for his Achsah.

Caleb pronounced to the congregation, "Othniel has requested to be a judge for Israel when we are settled in the land! A judge he shall be!"

Down in the crowd, Achsah held back tears. She felt rejected by the very man that she was beginning to open her heart to. She changed her mind and concluded that it would probably not take years for Othniel, it would take forever. She resigned herself to the death of her hope in this new Promised Land.

CHAPTER 22

Thirty miles south of Edrei, Uriel had been tracking the fleeing Molech, only to discover he had holed himself up in the territory of the Ammonites east of Sihon's old kingdom. Because the Ammonites were sons of Lot, the nephew of Abraham, Yahweh had given them special dispensation so that Israel could not possess their land.

By hiding himself in Ammonite territory, Molech was legally protected from Uriel's jurisdiction. If Molech left the area, Uriel could arrest him, bind him, and send him to Tartarus. But inside the territory of Ammon, Molech was free. He was under their protective shield.

Uriel knew Molech would not dare risk that protection, so it would be fruitless to wait outside the borders for him. Molech could stay there forever. Uriel thought he would be of more use to his team of archangels if he could catch up with them to aid in their capture of Ashtart.

So he immediately set off for the distant northwest. He only hoped he would find them in time to be of help. This was not a time for egos between angels, Ashtart was vicious enough to require as many of them as possible to capture and imprison her. She had become quite powerful over the eons.

And she was just a warm up for Ba'al, the most high god of the pantheon, who had been building his stronghold in Canaan for centuries with Ashtart's help.

Uriel had no idea how they would be able to take *him* down.

• • • • •

The three archangels, Mikael, Gabriel, and Raphael had tracked Ashtart to the north of Edrei. Within ten miles of her escape, they had figured out her destination. It was obvious. And why not? Why would she not go to her source of power?

It was Mount Hermon, the cosmic mountain of the gods, the location of the Watchers' descent to earth in antediluvian days. It was their mount of assembly and it connected heaven to earth and earth to Sheol. Though this time of year was filled with many festivals and rituals throughout the earth, the pantheon would not be assembled. Nevertheless, it was a fortress that archangels should not approach without great trepidation.

The three of them hiked through the cedar forest at the foot of the mountain to their point of entry. There was a temple that contained a sacrificial pit leading down into the cavern assembly room of the gods.

But three archangels could not avoid detection entering that temple complex and walking right up the stairs and into the bowels of the enemy's fortress.

That is why only one of them went.

Mikael cloaked himself in the hooded robe of one of the priests he secretly killed outside the complex.

He made his way up the brick steps of the ziggurat that had been built halfway into the mountain. It was over one hundred feet above the clearing where the worshippers congregated.

But there was no congregation this evening. Mikael was trying to avoid contact. He just wanted to slip into the lair of Ashtart as inconspicuously as possible.

When he arrived at the top, he saw several priests feeding the perpetual flames of the pit before retiring.

They noticed him as they were leaving the altar area. They whispered to themselves. They knew he was not supposed to be there.

So he immediately threw himself into the flames of the tophet. When the priests turned back, he was gone, disappeared. They walked back to the altar to see if he had gone back down the stairs. But they would not find their apparition that night. He was below them, having leapt through the fire that hid from sight a secret ledge outside of the flames below the tophet. Now, he was silently slipping through the long pillared hallway that was accessed through that secret ledge.

• • • • •

Gabriel and Raphael had avoided the front door in favor of a side entrance. They snuck through the ruins of a palace that used to be the guardian hall over this hidden tunnel. It had been the palace of Humbaba the Terrible who was conquered by Gilgamesh the king of Uruk right after the Flood.

The angels made their way through the ruins that had been burnt to the ground eons ago. Eventually, these too would be swept away with the sands of time.

They found the tunnel entrance and made their way through to the heart of the mountain.

• • • • •

Mikael reached the huge bronze doors that towered over him at the end of the pillared hallway. He knew this was the gateway to the assembly of the gods. He had been here once before a millennium ago, with Enoch the giant killer. All four of the angels had snuck into this most diabolical inner chamber with Enoch. He had been called by Yahweh to pronounce judgment on the two hundred Watchers and their evil progeny the Nephilim.

All five of them had walked right into the hornet's nest of evil, but had been translated into heaven before the fallen ones could get their hands on any of them.

But the archangels would not have that luxury today. This is why it was a good thing that the gods were not assembling at this time of year. This was a temple of supernatural wickedness, and Ashtart would have the upper hand. She would be stronger, faster, harder to overcome.

But there was something to the archangels' benefit in this location. Something Mikael thought Ashtart would regret for the rest of her eternity if they were able to capture her.

If they were able to capture her.

He pushed open the mighty doors with a heave and stepped into the wide opening. The vast rocky subterranean cavern hosted stalactites and stalagmites embedded with iridescent gems. They gave Mikael the impression of being in the mouth of an immense dragon.

He slipped silently through the labyrinth of rocky deposition and found his way to the clearing where the pantheon assembled before a throne. Between that throne and Mikael was a pitch-black lake that led to the Abyss. Its surface was perpetually aflame from the thick oozing substance.

This murky lagoon was where Noah ben Lamech and his comrades had jumped in to escape the clutches of assassin Nephilim in the antediluvian era. The Abyss led to Sheol and Sheol was the only place Nephilim were afraid of, so they did not follow.

Ashtart interrupted his thoughts with a booming voice. “Welcome to the assembly hall of your enemy, archangel. Welcome to your grave.”

Ashtart sat on the throne across the lake with a relaxed and confident demeanor. She knew angels could not die. But they were divine beings just like Watchers, so they could be bound into the earth in a living grave, which would be worse than death.

“I am a bit embarrassed. I did not have the time to change my wardrobe.” She was still dressed in her black leather fighting costume and painted white face that he had seen back at Edrei. “I have just been too busy preparing.”

She stepped off the throne and armed herself with her choicest weapons: A double set of straight swords sheathed behind her back for easy access, and her favorite, the scythe of death.

As she walked to him around the shore of the lake, he kept his eyes on her in silence, and matched her pace toward her.

It was a showdown of doom.

“I know you are a prince of angels, Mikael. But really, only you? I am a bit insulted. On the other hand, I will not complain about being handed an easy victory.” She looked up mockingly. “Thank you, Yahweh, for this meal I am about to eat.”

Mikael pulled his sword and used Ashtart’s true name. “Azazel, I condemn you in the name of the living god, Yahweh Elohim. For your crimes and evil against humanity and against your Creator, you are sentenced to imprisonment in the heart of the earth until judgment.”

They were almost upon one another.

Azazel said, “Come and bind me, archangel.”

He swung his scythe in an arc of preparation. Its sweeping curved blade at the base of a long handle twirled in his powerful hands like a windmill of death.

Mikael could hear the whistle of wind. Archangels as well as Watchers had preternatural senses. And those senses were heightened even more with the rising tension of confrontation.

But so were Azazel’s senses. So when he stopped in a ready stance for battle, he quipped, “That is more like it. Three against one. Now the odds are a bit more even.”

Azazel did not have to look behind him. He knew Gabriel and Raphael had moved out from the rocks to circle him from behind. Their weapons were drawn, their stances ready.

“Even so,” he said. “I will bury all of you.”

Azazel went on the offensive.

He swung in powerful arcs as he spun on his heels attacking all three angels in his dance of death.

Blades came in contact and sparked furiously.

The angels all carried shields, and it was a good thing too, because they needed the protection. Azazel was amazingly fast. He could fight all three simultaneously as if he were fighting one.

Raphael was having trouble keeping up with him. His shield was taking too many blows. The scythe was beginning to cut through it.

Raphael had to throw it down when it became useless. He had to be more guarded in his moves. More cautious.

That was exactly Azazel’s plan. He continued his relentless attack of blade against blades.

Now, Gabriel’s shield broke down under impact.

"I could do this all night," crowed Azazel, as he spun and struck. The angels dodged and weaved and guarded.

They were not unable to strike. They were playing their odds. Watchers were mighty, but they were not omnipotent. And all creatures tire, even divine creatures. They were wearing Azazel down until they could strike with efficiency and surety.

But Azazel was not going to give them that opportunity.

He suddenly dropped the scythe and bolted off amidst the rocks.

They followed.

This was Azazel's home. He knew the place intimately. All its nooks, crannies, oddities, and hiding places.

He was drawing them into his web.

He had disappeared into the shadows. They had to split up to look for him.

Azazel was separating them.

Mikael took the southern end. He moved slowly through a maze of rock and gems looking for any shadow of movement in the glow of the stones.

Gabriel took the western end. It had less of the jutting teeth-like stalactites and stalagmites. But it was also darker and harder to see in the shadows.

Raphael took the eastern end. This area had moss because it was near some water flow on the rocks.

He tread softly, his senses attuned to the darkness and silence. There were also fewer gemstones over here making it difficult to see.

But there were plenty of sounds.

The water trickled on the rocks. Some of it gurgling in small pools all about. Critters scraped across the rocky surfaces.

And then a new sound of movement drew his attention.

Bodily movement to his left near the wall of the cavern.

He cautiously moved around the rocks, hands gripping his sword, ready for a fight.

Back at the west end, Gabriel doubled back after sweeping his area. He made it to the shore where they had fought the goddess.

He noticed the scythe was gone.

Azazel must have circled back and picked it back up.

He decided to risk his position and yelled, "AZAZEL HAS THE SCYTHE!"

It echoed throughout the cavern.

He turned around, anticipating an attack.

But Azazel was not there.

Mikael decided they should not stay separated and yelled in return, "REGROUP ON THE WESTERN END!"

He heard Gabriel respond, "MOVING!"

Raphael did not respond. He knew he was near danger.

He could hear it clearly now. A sliding movement.

He crept around the large rock and stopped.

As his eyes adjusted to the darker area, he realized he had just walked into a nest of cave snakes.

There were hundreds of them. All at his feet, slithering around. One of them hissed at him, ready to strike.

It was all that was necessary to distract his attention.

He heard Azazel's voice suddenly behind him. "Goodbye, fool."

He did not even see the scythe blade as it swept through the air and cut him in half at the torso.

He screamed as he fell to the ground, his nerves alive with searing pain.

The serpents began to attack, striking his fallen body in the arms and torso.

Mikael and Gabriel ran to the sound of Raphael's voice.

When they arrived, they swatted the snakes away and pulled Raphael's torso to safety.

He was in shock. And shaking from the venom that ran through his upper body.

"Azazel has taken his legs," said Gabriel.

Azazel knew the angel would supernaturally regenerate if he had the chance to rejoin his severed halves. Angel flesh was Edenic in its abilities to regenerate tissue, nerves and function.

Raphael croaked through his pain, "Go get him. Leave me."

They hesitated.

"Leave me!" he repeated. "I am no danger to him now."

They all grasped wrists in unity.

They laid Raphael's torso down safely away from the serpents, and Mikael and Gabriel took off.

They burst out into the clearing of the shoreline to see Azazel at the lake's edge throwing Raphael's lower body into the waters of the Abyss.

"NOOO!" Gabriel screamed.

Azazel mocked him in return, "YEESSSS!" Then laughed wickedly.

Gabriel ran toward him.

Mikael yelled, "Gabriel, no! That is what he wants!"

But Gabriel was not listening.

He reached Azazel, threw his broken shield into the Abyss, and grasped his sword with both hands. He would engage his opponent with a double grasp technique. It would be a stronger strike to match the Watcher's own.

But Azazel reached behind him and pulled out his two swords.

Gabriel had double strength with his two-handed grip, but Azazel had double coverage with two swords.

They engaged.

Gabriel was driven by rage. His speed was lightning fast and relentless. He yelled with each hit.

He pushed Azazel back. Azazel blocked with Karabu grace, but each impact resonated through his body like a shockwave.

Rage made Gabriel sloppy. And Azazel saw his moment.

He blocked an overhanded swing with his swords crossed.

Azazel circled Gabriel's blade, locked it in his own, and jammed it into the ground.

Gabriel looked up in shock.

Azazel spun in a circle to get extra force, and struck out at Gabriel's neck to cut off his head.

But instead, his sword connected with Mikael's sword with a loud clang.

Mikael's strong steel sword.

And Mikael advanced against him. Their blades connecting like a whirlwind of metal, raining sparks that hit the lake and caused it to flame up.

Mikael backed Azazel up to the edge of the lake.

The Watcher pushed back with fear, because he now realized what they were planning on doing all along.

But it was too late.

Mikael screamed, "Now!"

Gabriel came at Azazel from the side. But he was not carrying his sword. He had Cherubim hair between his hands.

And the two archangels launched themselves at him, tackling the Watcher—right into the black ooze of the lake.

They landed with a splash of fiery pitch and began to sink.

Swords were gone.

It was now Watcher versus archangels wrestling for control.

They sank through the depths until they came through to a water layer and kept dropping.

But Watchers were weakened in water, so Gabriel and Mikael had managed to tie his hands in the indestructible binding.

Azazel panicked.

They held him tight.

They bound his feet with the Cherubim hair.

And then they breached the bottom of the Abyss and broke through into Sheol.

They landed on the ground. Gabriel looked up. The water of the Abyss was the ceiling of Sheol.

The air was dank and thick, barely breathable. It was a dark lifeless land of rock and dead gnarly tree roots sticking out of the ground as if the trees were inverted.

Within a short running distance was the Rephaim mountain that contained the pits of Tartarus.

Mikael said, "Let us get going before the Shades find out we are here."

They heard the chomping and grinding sounds of the Shades already finding their way toward them. These creatures had no eyes to see, but could smell and feel the presence of living things a mile away.

The Shades were the resident dead of Sheol. They were bodies whose innards were animated by worms and maggots that never died. They had lost all identity from the world above and were transformed into eating monsters with no eyes, but large chomping mouths that were always seeking flesh to eat, yet were never satisfied.

The living dead that they had encountered at Edrei were but pale reflections of the horror of the Shades of Sheol.

And the Shades were innumerable.

They picked up the inert form of Azazel together and sprinted their way to the small mountain.

They were carrying a Watcher, but archangels are powerful beings and can run like the wind.

When they arrived at the mountain cave, they entered, but found the Rephaim gone.

Not one to waste time figuring out why they were so blessed, Mikael led Gabriel over to the ledge of the pit. There were many of these, and some of them were already housing other Watchers that were imprisoned at the time of the Flood.

Azazel struggled, but he could not withstand the strength of the Cherubim hair.

He screamed, “NOOO! Please, do not. I will do anything. Anything. I will be your slave! I will repent!”

He wept like a frightened little child. A very selfish and devious little child.

“Tell Yahweh, I am sorry. I will grovel at his feet. Please!”

Gabriel and Mikael looked at each other with disgust for this pathetic fiend of deception.

Then suddenly, his tears stopped and he became lascivious.

"Do not forget, archangels, I am the goddess of sex. I could be your slave."

Mikael and Gabriel looked at each other. Then Mikael said, "No thank you, Azazel. You can spend the rest of your time groveling in the bowels of Tartarus."

With that, they heaved Azazel's body over the ledge and he fell into the depths. It was a hole that went on for miles of utter darkness and silence. There was no echo of Azazel's scream on the way down. The walls swallowed up the sound instead of echoing it.

When he hit the bottom, he would be at the farthest point in Sheol. Mikael's words were meant with irony. The fact was, Azazel would have no pleasure in the pit. His bindings were indestructible, and he would be unable to do anything for seventy times seven generations until the judgment.

What is more, he would be watched over by the mighty Rephaim. The very ones he had abandoned at the War on Eden. These were the mighty kings who were dragged down into Sheol by Rahab and her helpers, Leviathan and other creatures of the deep.

They would not be happy to see him. They had many eons of vengeance to make up for until the judgment.

CHAPTER 23

Rahab brushed her sister's hair when she heard the horns of Jericho announce the closing of the gate and the calling of the guard. It was not a good sign. Something was wrong. They never closed the gates and put up guards unless trouble was coming.

Rahab rushed out of her inn and made her way to the main gate. When she arrived she saw the guards posted along the main thoroughfare. Some of them forcibly led some travelers out of the city.

As she got closer, she saw the Chief Commander Alyun-Yarikh above the gates, looking out over the walls, and his Right Hand Jebir a short way from him.

She climbed the ladder to Jebir to find out what was going on.

"Greetings, Rahab," said Jebir. "I trust all goes well?"

She asked, "What is happening?"

She looked out and saw a train of traveling common folk. Hundreds of them. It was not a trading caravan. It looked more like refugees.

"Those are Amorites fleeing from Bashan. We cannot allow them refuge here. There are too many. And we fear they may bring an enemy upon us."

"The Habiru again?" she asked.

"Yes. I spoke to some of the refugees. Evidently, the Habiru have taken over the entire Transjordan."

A chill went down Rahab's spine.

She observed what the Commander was overseeing: a large display of the armed forces of Jericho engaging in battle exercises just outside the walls.

Jebir said, "They decimated Og of Bashan's forces. Cut off his head, burned his city, and cannibalized his body."

She doubted that last rumor. It was not like the Habiru to do so. She felt she knew these people just from her study of the several poems she held secret.

"After the fall of Og, they captured his sixty cities within a fortnight and secured all of Bashan. It is quite frightening."

"Quite frightening Indeed," said Rahab. Inside, she was filled with excitement.

"Does that include Gilgal Rephaim and Panias?" she asked.

"I am not sure. Most likely."

He added, "But these Habiru are monstrous. They kill every man, woman, and child. They leave no survivors, and strike down everything that breathes. It is utter destruction."

Because of her involvement with the Commander and other military officials, Rahab knew that this was the language of military conquest in their world. When a nation defeated an enemy they would often say that they utterly destroyed every living thing and left no survivors. It was a form of power hyperbole. A way of saying that the entire city or region was now under their king's fist of rule. It was not a lie or even an exaggeration, it was their way of expressing conquest.

But in any case, it gave her heart great joy to know that the inhabitants of Gilgal Rephaim had been conquered and brought under the rule of these Habiru and their god. It was a strange feeling inside her. It was not just that she was avenged. She also felt strange warmth in her heart for a deity she had not yet met.

Though she had been living as a woman without a tribe for a long time, she found herself rooting for this people and their advancement. She felt the curious thrill of what would happen if they came to Jericho.

She wanted to know this god.

It was a dangerous thrill. For she suspected the Habiru would most likely kill her along with all the others. But she had to know. She had to find out more. She had to see if these Habiru had truly liberated her from her past and from her perpetual fear of those who would track her down one day.

• • • • •

It was evening. The Amorites had camped a mile from the city. They did not know where they would go next.

Rahab disguised herself in a cloak and made her way to the camp.

There were a hundred tents and dozens of fires all haphazardly arranged. The refugees were from tribes all over Bashan with no central organization. It would be easy for Rahab to avoid detection because of the lack of tribal familiarity.

She walked through the camp trying to appear inconspicuous as she scanned for signs of refugees from Panias or Gilgal Rephaim.

She found none.

She decided to talk to someone. But who? Who could she trust to reveal herself to? Who would not become suspicious?

She saw a young girl, about eleven or twelve years old, standing alone by some vacant tents as if observing the people around her. Most of the people were gathered around the fires closer to the center of the camp.

She was wearing a modest robe that looked like something from the Heshbon area. She reminded Rahab of herself. She had that distant look in her eye, a look of separation from her own people. A look of wisdom beyond her age.

Rahab approached her.

The young girl looked up at her. Rahab pulled down her hood to be inviting.

"Hello, young girl."

"Hello."

"You look thoughtful this evening," said Rahab.

The little girl said nothing.

"My name is Rahab. What is yours?"

"Donatiya."

This was good. She was not fearful or suspicious.

"Which tribe are you from, Donatiya?"

"Heshbon."

Rahab had guessed right. She was confident she could read this girl well. She only hoped she was right about her being like Rahab.

"You look lonely out here all by yourself. Are you well?"

"Yes."

"Have you happened upon anyone from Rephaim Gilgal or Panias?"

Donatiya looked at her with curiosity. She knew Rahab was fishing for information. That she probably was not with the refugees.

Rahab tried to cover, "I have relatives there. I just want to know if they are well."

Donatiya shook her head no. Then she asked, "Were you kicked out of Jericho?"

Rahab could tell this girl was too clever to tell complete lies to. She would have to tell half-truths in order to appear believable.

"No. But I am a woman of ill repute."

"Would you take me with you back to the city?"

"There is no place to hide. They would discover you and exile you from the city."

"I could be one of your relatives."

So Rahab was also right about Donatiya being like her. Clever.

"I am sorry, Donatiya, but my house is already full of family."

"I could learn your trade. I would pay my way."

Rahab sighed. "My sweet dear girl. You are much too young for such things." Rahab could only think of how damaged her own soul was in losing her innocence at such a young age.

"I am twelve years old," she said. "I do not think I have much of a future with this rejected group of Amorites. The men have already been telling me how pretty I am."

She knew just how to strike at Rahab's heart. A clever girl indeed.

But Rahab could not risk it. She had suffered too much and had risked all to get to where she was. It was not merely her own safety that she might endanger. She had her entire family to protect as well. As much as it tugged at her heart, she could not take this girl with her.

"I am sorry, Donatiya. I cannot."

Rahab turned to walk away before she could change her mind. It ripped her apart.

She stopped for a moment. Turned to look back at the girl. Maybe she should try anyway. Maybe this Yahweh god would help her.

But Donatiya was gone.

Rahab turned back to leave the camp. She stopped in the face of a woman leaving a tent. She was older, graying. She had one glazed blind eye, and the facial tattoos of a sorceress—a sorceress of Gilgal Rephaim.

Rahab felt her breath knocked out of her. She had taken her hood down to talk to the young girl, but had neglected to pull it back up to disguise herself.

The woman stared at her. Her blind eye looked frighteningly into Rahab's soul.

"You are of the Habiru god," said the sorceress.

Rahab was genuinely shocked at the statement. She had certainly been drawn to the stories she had heard. She was definitely interested in learning more about the Habiru and their invisible god. But this sorceress had perceived that newfound interest and interpreted it in the extreme.

Before Rahab could process it all, the sorceress's eyes widened with realization and she said, "I know who you are."

"What are you talking about, sorceress?" hissed Rahab.

"I know who you are."

She pointed a bony finger at Rahab. It felt like she was stabbing Rahab in the heart, and cutting her open for everyone to see.

"You were with the Ob many years ago. He prophesied over you."

"You are mad, old lady," said Rahab.

But she would not back down.

"The serpent seer prophesied that out of your womb would come forth a great and mighty warrior, whose kingdom shall overthrow all kingdoms."

Rahab was speechless. The sorceress was right. Rahab had sought to forget that horrible experience and its frightening implications. She was running from it as much as she was running from the Clan of the Serpent.

She had told no one about it. And now, this sorceress would surely expose her. Everything she had done to hide her identity and protect herself and her loved ones, all her years of fighting for freedom and seeking to start anew, would be burnt to the ground. She and her family would be found out and slaughtered.

The sorceress grabbed Rahab's arm. For an old woman, she had an iron grip. And then Rahab saw her good eye and the woman's voice altered into a deep gravely growl.

"The chosen seed must die."

She was possessed by a demon.

Rahab flooded with panic. What could she do now?

There was only one thing she could do.

She reached in her cloak, withdrew her hidden dagger, and slashed the sorceress. The old woman released her grip on Rahab, grabbed her throat and faltered.

Rahab held her to keep her from falling. She whispered in the sorceress's ear, "You will speak no more of this Ob and his rambling. And carry your silence to Sheol."

Rahab dragged the sorceress's body to the side of the tent in the shadows where she would not be found until morning.

She backed away from the tent and looked around the camp. No one had noticed their exchange.

She had to get back to Jericho before anyone found out.

CHAPTER 24

The high place of Ba'al in Kiriath-arba was but a pale shadow of his palace on Mount Sapan in the far reaches of the north. But it would have to do for his base of operations in southern Canaan.

It was on the highest point of the ridge, built near the ancient circular megaliths. It had an outer courtyard about one hundred feet square fenced in with brick. A stone altar of sacrifice stood in the middle of the courtyard. The holy place was a fifty-foot square brick and pillared vestibule that led into a holy of holies that was also fifty foot square but a hundred feet high. A staircase led to the top roof where another altar was placed for special ceremonies.

Inside the holy of holies, Molech was frantic.

"I could not get here any sooner. The archangels chased me to Ammon. Thank the gods there is a treaty between Yahweh and the sons of Lot, or I would have been chained in Tartarus right now."

Ba'al did not care one whit about Molech. He was a sleazy and slippery eel who could not be trusted. For all he cared, let the child eater rot in Tartarus.

"But you are sure, they caught Ashtart and imprisoned her?"

"She told me that after she would vanquish the angels, she would travel to Kiriath-arba and join you in the war. She is long overdue. I had to wait until I knew the angels had left Moab and then I traveled a hundred miles circumventing the southern tip of the Dead Sea to get here. Ashtart would have been here by now."

Ba'al stared out into the distance. "They will come with the army of Yahweh. The Habiru have Yahweh's covering."

"These archangels are ferocious," warned Molech. "They laid waste an entire army of the undead. They did not stop coming at us."

"Let them come," said Ba'al. "I will give them war like they have never seen."

• • • • •

King Hoham and the Brothers Arba arrived at the temple of Ba'al. They had been summoned by the priests for consultation with the most high. Ahiman, Sheshai, and Talmai waited outside the holy place for their commands. Inside the holy of holies, the king genuflected prostrate on the floor before the graven image of Ba'al, now inhabited by the deity. Molech was to remain quiet; seen, not heard.

"I will prepare immediately, my King of kings," said Hoham.

"This is not a mere war of conquest," said Ba'al. "This is the War of the Seed prophesied in ancient days."

Hoham quivered, "But they are so few, my god. We are like cedar trees before mere grasshoppers."

"Those grasshoppers wiped out King Og of Bashan, last of the Rephaim, and took the Transjordan. If you do not want to be last of the Anakim, you had better prepare for the battle of your lifetime."

Hoham filled with pride. "It will be the honor of my lifetime to exterminate the Seed of Abraham that sought to exterminate our Seed of Anak. These Habiru have conquered the Rephaim. But they have not yet faced the might and power of the Anakim."

Ba'al said, "I want you to send out two of your most trustworthy spies on a mission."

"Name it, my Lord, and I will obey."

"Find out who this general Joshua ben Nun is. He leads the Habiru forces for the aged Moses. If he is the promised seedline of Eve, then we will kill him. If they are trying to cut off the serpent's head, then we will cut off the woman's feet."

Hoham smiled. "With pleasure my Lord. Where are they now?"

"They are quartered on the plains of Moab near Mount Nebo just across the Jordan from Jericho."

"That is hostile territory all around."

"The god Molech will guide your spies to Ammon, where they will be provided safe harbor and intelligence on the Habiru. If they confirm that Joshua ben Nun is the Seed, then I want them to strike. So the spies must also be your finest warriors."

"Excellent," said Hoham.

Ba'al said, "Bring me the head of this Joshua ben Nun."

Hoham said, "I have just the warriors for the task."

Ahiman, Sheshai, and Talmai rose from the floor when Hoham exited the most holy place.

Hoham said, "The War of the Seed is rising. Ahiman, begin preparation of our forces for the apocalypse. Sheshai and Talmai, I have a special mission for you."

CHAPTER 25

It took several days for Molech to lead the Arba brothers to Ammon on the eastern side of the Israelite settlement on the plains of Moab. They were in the area of Shittim, a fertile location of acacia meadows.

The Ammonites received Sheshai and Talmai with some caution due to the fact that they had in previous years eliminated the Zamzummim giants from their land. But when Molech explained through his priests that the sons of Anak were allies seeking intelligence to defeat the Israelites, they were given all the help they needed.

That help came in the form of two very important pieces of information.

A scribe named Sudru led Sheshai and Talmai through the Ammonite palace library. He was tall and lanky, effeminate looking, with a nasally voice. Talmai wondered to himself why so many scribes seemed to be one of two constitutions: scrawny and effeminate or fat and soft. He was glad he did not learn much to read and spent his time instead in the art of war.

Scribes were the keepers of knowledge and thus were most privy to all that pertained of importance to the priestly and noble classes. As they followed him through the halls and vaults of the library, Sudru explained to them an incident that had occurred not too long ago.

"As you may know, the Habiru had taken over the lands that had once been Moab's before King Sihon took them over. Well, a confederation of Moabite and Midianite tribes in the area had bound together in covenant led by the king of Moab, Balaak, son of Zippor. They wanted to curse these Habiru because they had become oppressive occupiers and they feared the Habiru would do to them what they did to the Amorites before them."

They entered the library area. It was a mundane series of shelves loaded with scrolls and tablets. It smelled musty to Sheshai's nose.

Sudru continued without pause, "So they sent for a Babylonian diviner, called a *baru*. His name was Balaam son of Beor, who resided in Pethor, a Mesopotamian city just south of Carchemish in the north."

All scribes seemed to be obsessed with petty details. It made Talmai impatient. But Sheshai followed closely because he knew that the gods were in the details.

"Balaak paid Balaam a handsome fee to curse the Habiru three different times. But word has it that this Balaam ended up blessing the Habiru three times instead, claiming that he could only proclaim according to what the god had told him."

Sheshai interrupted his flow of talk, "What god is that?"

"Allegedly, Yahweh."

Sudru was looking through the shelves. "Now where did I place those?"

Sheshai said, "Were his blessings copied down?"

Sudru stopped and looked up at Sheshai with an annoyed look. Then he quipped, "What do you think I am looking for, a children's lullaby?"

Sheshai was amazed at the arrogance of this little pipsqueak. He actually thought his access to knowledge gave him some kind of priestly superiority. Sheshai could crush him with one hand, and had they been in Kiriath-arba, he might have.

Talmai was thinking the same thing. But Sheshai gave him a look not to. It would be foolish for them to respond with such flagrant disregard for their host's gracious accommodations by pulverizing one of their privileged class.

"Oh, here they are," said Sudru. He had turned around and pulled out a few clay tablets from a shelf. "I accidentally put them on the shelf for astrological omens instead of divination."

He handed Sheshai the tablets, and said, "And please, be respectful of the clay. Do not treat it like it is one of your enemies on the battlefield."

Sheshai and Talmai looked at each other with more incredulity.

"Do you need help reading it?" asked Sudru.

"I speak and read four languages," boasted Sheshai. "Which one is it written in?" He could not kill the scribe, but at least he could humiliate him.

"Amorite," said Sudru with raised brow.

"Well, then, I will be fine."

Sudru harrumphed and muttered under his breath, "Educated barbarians."

It was loud enough for them to hear it. Talmai made a move toward Sudru. Sheshai held him back.

"Wait for us at a safe distance, scribe," said Sheshai, pointing a dozen feet away from them. "Unless you would like some education from a barbarian."

Sudru said with trembling, "I will be over there organizing shelves and manuscripts."

He quickly moved away from them to worry himself with the unending task of keeping the library in order.

Sheshai pulled the tablets over to a table to read them. Though the new form of parchment writing was becoming more widespread, cuneiform on clay tablets was still the basic standard for recording many important writings.

Sheshai began to eagerly read through the tablets. They were short. There were four oracles, one per tablet.

Talmai said, "Well, what does it say?" He was not as educated as his brother. He just did not have the patience to study the details of language like his more intellectual sibling could. He preferred the rigorous vitality of physical exertion in battle practice.

"Pretty standard oracle material. He calls the Habiru, "Israel" and "Jacob," which fits with what we know of our ancient prophecy of the Seed of Abraham through the line of his son Jacob."

He looked at another tablet. "Praises for Yahweh. He blesses those who bless the Seed of Jacob, and curses those who curse him."

He turned another tablet. "Oh, this is interesting. A reference to Jacob's seed being in many waters and his kingdom shall be exalted. He shall eat up the nations, his adversaries."

Talmai's muscles tightened.

Sheshai turned to the last tablet and was mesmerized.

"What? What does it say?"

Sheshai read as if in a trance,

"Come, I will let you know what this people will do
to your people in the latter days.
The oracle of Balaam the son of Beor,
the oracle of the man whose eye is opened,
the oracle of him who hears the words of El,
and knows the knowledge of Elyon,
who sees the vision of Shaddai,
falling down with his eyes uncovered:
I see him, but not now; I behold him, but not near:
A star shall come out of Jacob,
and a scepter shall rise out of Israel;
it shall crush the forehead of Moab
and break down all the sons of Seth.
Edom shall be dispossessed;
Seir also, his enemies, shall be dispossessed.
Israel is doing valiantly.
And one from Jacob shall exercise dominion and
destroy the survivors of cities!"

They were silent for a long moment.

Then it hit Sheshai. He called for Sudru, "Scribe, do you have any records of these Habiru, any of their own writings?"

Sudru came quickly and said, "I just may. Traders in the region are always looking to trade us manuscripts for food or materials which they foolishly consider of more importance."

Sheshai gave him a scolding look. Sudru said, "I will go check."

Seshai turned to his brother and said, "'A star shall come out of Jacob.' We know stars are deities. 'A scepter shall rise out of Israel.' So this deity will also be a king. He will dispossess and destroy everyone. He is also described as a lion in one of the other oracles. Who is this star, this scepter and lion?"

Sudru arrived with a leather parchment wrapped in a bundle with a strap. "We got this from a very respected Amorite trader. It has been verified to be from the Habiru."

Seshai grabbed it from him and opened it up. He unrolled the leather and began to read it.

"Very similar to the Edomite language." Seshai kept reading. "This is a copper mine of information. It looks like a blessing from the patriarch Jacob over his sons, who appear to be the very tribes of these Habiru."

He kept reading, occasionally mentioning the name whose blessing he was reading, "Reuben… Simeon…"

And then he stopped. He looked up at Talmai. "I found it, Talmai. I found the key."

He read the text out loud,

"Judah is a lion's cub;
he crouched as a lion and as a lioness;
The scepter shall not depart from Judah,
nor the ruler's staff from between his feet,
until Shiloh comes.
And to him shall be the obedience of the peoples."

And then Sheshai said, "Lion and scepter. The kingly seed we seek is the line of Judah within Israel."

Talmai said, "One out of twelve tribes. But that is still not as specific as we require."

Sheshai turned to Sudru, "Scribe, have you any intelligence on the military leader of these Habiru, Joshua ben Nun?"

"Well, why did you not ask me that?" said Sudru. "Of course we do. I have done the research myself on Joshua for the king."

Seshai could not believe his good fortune. This scribe was proving to be more useful than he had anticipated.

"Is he from the tribe of Judah?"

"No. Joshua is from the tribe of Ephraim."

Sheshai and Talmai were deflated. They had reached a dead end, only to discover that their dreaded enemy general was not the one they needed to kill for their long-term victory. The Chosen One must come from the tribe of Judah.

Sheshai said, "We must return to Hoham and alert him to this revelation. It could change everything."

Talmai added, "We will have to send spies into the Israelite camp to find out who is in that lineage of Judah."

"You may not need to worry about any of that," said Sudru.

The brothers looked at him curiously.

"The Habiru will not need to be defeated from without, because they are already being defeated from within."

"What do you mean?" demanded Sheshai.

Sudru smiled deviously. "Apparently, this Balaam seer was conscientious about earning his money. So after he spoke the blessing of Yahweh four times in favor of the Israelites, he gave the Midianites and Moabites some advice on how to undermine the blessing from within."

"Indeed," said Sheshai.

"Seduce them with women. The Israelites have developed a liking for Moabite and Midianite women, and with them their local deities. Their god Yahweh is a jealous god who demands exclusive allegiance to him and the destruction of all other gods. One can only imagine the anger he now has toward his own people."

Sheshai and Talmai were following his words closely.

"Word has it that this tyrant deity smote his own people by the hundreds and thousands when they rebelled against him in the desert. And now he is smiting them with a plague for their latest unfaithfulness."

Sheshai said with amazement, "We should thank this Yahweh then for helping us."

They all laughed.

Then Sheshai asked, "What god are these Israelites sleeping with now?"

"The god of Peor," said Sudru. And then he lifted his brow with a proud gossipy grin and said, "Ba'al."

It could not be more perfect. Ba'al, the very god of the Anakim, Israel's ultimate enemy, was already undermining Yahweh's inheritance through spiritual adultery, and they had not even yet faced off in confrontation.

"Well then," said Sheshai with a pleased smirk, "We must certainly let the influence of Ba'al do his work on these people, And we will see which god ends up dispossessing which people after all."

CHAPTER 26

Zimri ben Salu was an Israelite of the tribe of Simeon. He was a respected leader in the community. He had married a woman named Cozbi of the house of Zur, a tribal leader of the Midianites. The Midianites were a nomadic tribe that had recently found their home in Moabite territory.

The law of Yahweh delivered on Mount Sinai had demanded that Israelites not intermarry with the Canaanites because of their gods and abominable practices. They were to devote the peoples of Canaan to complete destruction and to show them no mercy. This was called *herem*, a holy ban on idolatry and its insidious effects.

But the way of man is to find loopholes to satisfy his appetite. And the loophole in this case was the fact that Yahweh named the seven nations of Canaan that they were to clear away. These were the Hittites, the Girgashites, the Amorites, the Canaanites, the Perizzites, the Hivites, and the Jebusites.

But Zimri had figured that the Midianites and Moabites were not a part of that ban since they were on the Transjordan side of Canaan and not a part of the herem. And after all, Moses had stayed with the Midianites for many years when he was AWOL from Egypt. His first wife, Zipporah, had been a Midianite.

But Yahweh was not concerned about the foreign people; he was concerned about their foreign gods. Most of the Midianites who joined Moses had sworn allegiance to Yahweh. Those who remained in Midian did not. As soon as Zimri found Cozbi and married her, she brought along her household gods, the teraphim, and her worship of Ashtart.

Cozbi had no problem with Yahweh. She would be willing to worship Yahweh as well as her local deities. They could all be one happy family of gods.

Zimri was one of many Israelites who could see the benefit of ecumenical coexistence. Yes, Yahweh was the chief of all gods. He would receive Zimri's highest worship. Zimri would continue to bring his sacrifices to the tabernacle as required, and keep the Sabbath and other laws of his people. But to appease his wife, he would also participate in the Midianite rituals and sacrifices.

It seemed to him a rational proposition, since some of the deities of the pantheon had specific realms of authority and power. For instance, Resheph, the god of plague, was a very appropriate deity to seek appeasement in time of plague. And that is what the Israelites were suffering under at this very moment. Hundreds were dying of the strange sickness throughout the camp, including some of Zimri's own family. It was an epidemic.

So this day, Zimri awoke and bowed down to Cozbi's little terra cotta statues, graven images of the gods in a home shrine, and prayed to Resheph for mercy. The plague was so terrible that Midianite priests told their people a sacrifice would be required to stay Resheph's mighty hand. Since the Israelites were the newcomers to the land, it could only be their fault for this calamity, so the god would require Israelites to bring an offering.

Cozbi had wept and pleaded with Zimri that she would be barren of children if they did not bring an offering to the high place on Mount Nebo, not far from camp.

Zimri had become despondent. He knew that Yahweh forbade offerings to other deities, and that he demanded exclusive sacrifice to himself. But he also knew that Cozbi had made sacrifices in the past that seemed to be accepted by her gods.

When they were married she made an offering of two turtle doves and a goat for fertility to Ba'al, and she became pregnant immediately. Later, a sacrifice of grain offering to Chemosh had healed their newborn son from sickness.

Cozbi's passionate pleading was evidence of a spiritual devotion that Zimri lacked in his own life. She would spend hours in prayer sometimes, singing and weeping. She would have the most contented presence about her when she spoke of Ashtart.

It had become apparent to Zimri that Cozbi had a more meaningful experience of her faith than he ever had of his. So who was he to deny such powerful experience? How could he demand his exclusive god when he did not experience even half of the emotional connection to Yahweh that Cozbi did with Ashtart? Maybe he needed to be more open-minded and tolerant, more inclusive in his beliefs.

He joined her in cutting himself before the household shrine in request for mercy. They took blades and made cuts that would bleed onto the floor with spiritual fervor.

Then Cozbi led them in a series of chants to Ashtart in order to draw down the deity into their bodies and inhabit them with her glorious splendor.

They would twitch and jerk as they felt a spirit enter them and fill their limbs.

Zimri felt lifted to the heavens. He felt possessed by the deity, by the spirit of Ashtart. It was as if clarity came over him and he could see, hear, and feel like a god himself.

They walked their family up to the foothills of Mount Nebo with a thousand other Israelites and their Moabite and Midianite spouses and concubines. There were some from every tribe of Israel who had embraced the foreign deities. It was a harmony that Zimri had not seen or felt for years as he grew up wandering in the wilderness.

He had seen how the tribes grumbled and complained, and how divisive they were amongst themselves, fighting for the best piece of land to place their tent, arguing over their limited resources of water and manna.

But here, there was such a mutual respect for one another's deities, and a harmonic convergence of unity within diversity. Whether you worshipped Ba'al, Chemosh, Molech, Ashtart or Resheph, everyone united in this beautiful moment before the high place that looked out over the valley below.

The Midianite and Moabite priests worked together in sacred unity to call upon the gods on their stone platform raised six feet above the ground. They made some burnt offerings to Ba'al, Chemosh, and Molech.

Their last appeal was to call out to the god Resheph to avert the plague that had consumed the land. The priests cut themselves as Zimri and Cozbi had done in private, and danced before their deity with abandon upon the raised dais.

They held their hands out to the Israelites and called out, "Now, may you bring your offerings unto Resheph that he might hear your cries and be satisfied with your sacrifice and turn this plague away!"

Zimri and Cozbi were crying. They knew what they had come to do. It was a difficult sacrifice to make. But it was a necessary one.

They took their newborn son, along with dozens of other Israelites and their infants, up to the altar to sacrifice them to the god of plague.

CHAPTER 27

The congregation of Israel had assembled around the Tent of Meeting in the aisles and open areas that stretched out from the center of the camp. They wept in repentance before Yahweh for their sin that had caused the plague upon Israel. Moses had led them in prayer at the opening of the tent. Joshua stood beside him, along with the priests Eleazer and his son Phineas.

Caleb watched and prayed from the front of the assembly with the elders, judges, and leaders of tribes. He could not comprehend why Israelites would take such pains to turn aside to the Canaanite gods that he and his Canaanite clan had taken such pains to turn away from. There was much crying and wailing throughout the camp for the suffering of the plague. Moses was weeping as much as the rest of them.

Joshua was angry. He had been in the tent when Yahweh commanded Moses what to do. He had seen the idolatry of Israel as it worshipped Ba'al and the other gods of the pantheon. They were not yet in their Promised Land of Canaan, and they were already playing the harlot with Ba'al of Peor. It was a form of spiritual adultery.

Yahweh had taken care of them in the desert wilderness these forty years until all the original gripers and complainers were dead. They had just conquered the Transjordan and the mighty Og of

Bashan as a prelude to Canaan. And still—still—these pathetic miserable backsliding wretches were already worshipping Ba'al like wanton idiots. They worshipped household idols and even engaged in human sacrifice on Mount Nebo to the god of plague.

The plague was therefore an ugly but fitting expression of a spiritual judgment. Afflicted Israelites would get puss filled boils and rashes in their private areas. Their excrement would be full of blood and excruciatingly painful. After a few days, if the victim did not get well, their body parts would turn black and rot. Within a week, the victim would be dead.

It disgusted Joshua. Not the plague so much as the spiritual and moral corruption that it pointed toward. These Canaanite gods of depravity inspired the debasement of every aspect of Yahweh's image in man. They bred perversions that violated all holiness. They defaced the body with occultic tattoos and mutilations. And they mocked the atonement of redemption with their human sacrifices.

Israel had become a festering cesspool of evil.

The only thing that made Joshua feel any better was knowing that he was to be the instrument for Yahweh's cleansing. Sin was a cancerous tumor. It had to be gouged out, not merely from those who hated Yahweh, but also from Yahweh's own people.

Moses spoke to the congregation, "Leaders of Israel, bring forth your clan heads from all the twelve tribes!"

The twelve clan leaders stepped forward with trepidation. They knew this could not be good.

"Hear O Israel, Yahweh our God is a holy God! And these leaders of the clans have not exercised their authority in honor of Yahweh's holiness! They have allowed Ba'al worship to thrive amidst their tribes!"

The twelve clan leaders looked at one another in fear.

Moses turned to Joshua and said, "Commence the judgment of Yahweh."

Joshua called forth a contingent of the army that had been situated by the side of the tabernacle.

They came forward and grabbed the clan leaders.

They dragged them over to a clearing and took twelve-foot long pikes and impaled the leaders on them. They hung them in the sun for all to see, that Yahweh might turn away his wrath.

Then Moses said, "Judges of Israel, each of you kill those of your men who have yoked themselves to Ba'al of Peor."

Women screamed and guilty men took off, trying to escape the swords that came after them. Men were hacked and hewn by the edge of sword and axe for their abominable practices in Israel's midst. Yahweh's zeal for holiness did not end with the Canaanite heathen. It applied as much to Israel as to anyone else. Yahweh would not compromise his glory.

At that moment, Phineas noticed Zimri was with his Midianite wife Cozbi among the congregation. Though many Israelites had also taken pagan women as their wives and concubines, they would not bring them in the congregation of the holy ones, because Yahweh had forbidden such contamination. But Zimri had become so brash as to parade his idolatrous wife in the presence of the holy.

Phineas saw Zimri pulling Cozbi away with him through the throng. He was getting away without being recognized.

Phineas grabbed a spear from a nearby soldier and made his way after them.

Phineas found Zimri and Cozbi in their tent hiding out in their bed together, and killed them both with his spear.

What Zimri had done that day was another terrible spiritual picture of the monstrous evil of idolatry.

And it was Phineas' cleansing act that stopped the plague. From that moment on, the sickness released its stranglehold on the Israelites and faded away. Phineas would receive a promise of perpetual priesthood, because that very day Phineas was jealous for Yahweh and made atonement for the people of Israel.

CHAPTER 28

Moses stood before Joshua, Caleb, and the commanders of thousands and hundreds and fifties in the war tent. He spoke with resolute firmness.

"Yahweh has commanded us to avenge the people of Israel upon the Midianites. My Midianite father-in-law Jethro would be ashamed of his own people if he were still alive. They have become a thorn in our side with their seduction of idolatry. Their god Ashtoreth is an abomination."

Ashtoreth was the name that the Israelites called Ashtart. It was an insult. By using the consonants of the name Ashtart, and combining them with the vowels from their word *bosheth*, which meant "shame," they created the name Ashtoreth.

Moses continued, "Yahweh wants you to kill all the kings of Midian: Evi, Rekem, Hur, Reba, and Zur, the father of Cozbi, whom Phineas killed. And you are to kill all the males along with them."

"How many troop divisions, my lord?" asked Joshua.

"Twelve," said Moses. "One from each tribe."

That would give them about a thousand men.

"And if you find this Balaam, son of Beor," said Moses, "execute him as well."

• • • • •

The troops of Israel took several days to rout out the Midianite tribes of the five kings that were in the land of Moab.

It was a bloodbath.

On the last day, they were trampling the clan of Zur. Caleb fought next to Joshua as he always did. But he had noticed a change in his commander with each battle. Joshua had lost the zeal of righteousness and had become more like a wild marauder.

This very day, Joshua and Caleb had cut down a unit of Midianite men all by themselves.

Caleb had stopped to catch his breath from their strenuous battle. He noticed Joshua standing over a fallen soldier, holding his blade in the Midianite's gut.

The Midianite was barely alive. He groaned with pain.

Joshua looked at him without a shred of emotion or soul. It was like a spider observing a fly caught in its web.

Joshua twisted the blade. The soldier cried out, "Mercy!"

Joshua twisted it again. The soldier pleaded, "I beg of you! Mercy!"

But Joshua was reveling in the soldier's misery.

He said with calm, "No mercy," and pushed the blade again.

The soldier cried out in anguish.

Until Caleb appeared and swiftly killed the soldier with his sword.

Joshua gave him an angry look.

Caleb diverted his attention, "Commander, we have found the prophet Balaam son of Beor. He is holed up in a cave."

Joshua turned to see the messenger who had brought the intelligence. He had not even heard the messenger's arrival. He had been swept up in the torture of his victim.

Then Joshua stiffened with resolve and marched right past Caleb like a predator zeroed in on blood.

Joshua and Caleb arrived at the foothills and got off their horses. There was a unit of soldiers standing guard. Hanging foliage disguised the opening from the casual observer.

They walked up to the captain who told them, "Balaam is in there with some women and children and elderly from the city. This appears to be one of the hideouts for the locals."

Joshua asked, "Are there any soldiers with them? Guards? Hostages?"

"We do not know, Commander."

Joshua walked to the cave entrance without pausing. He drew his sword and marched inward.

Caleb yelled, "Commander, what are you doing?"

He ran after him.

As Joshua's eyes adjusted to the darkness, he saw a trail of people cowering along the walls.

But some of them were men: farmers, elderly.

Others were not.

Two men stood in his way with swords. They were not soldiers; they were shepherds standing their ground to protect their innocent ones.

Joshua cut them down without losing stride.

A woman screamed.

Three other men approached him to negotiate.

But Joshua downed them as well.

"Commander!" yelled Caleb from behind. "This is unnecessary!"

But Joshua did not stop. He came upon a large group of people; men, women, and children surrounding a cloaked man at the back of the crowd.

It was the seer.

Joshua yelled, "Balaam son of Beor, your judgment has arrived! Prepare to pay for your deeds!"

The tunnel was too small for people to move out of the way. They were crammed in the space.

Joshua walked through the crowd, slashing and hacking at anyone in his way. Screams of pain echoed through the cave.

Caleb tried to stop Joshua, but he shoved Caleb to the ground and kept going; cutting, slicing, and killing men, women and children, until he arrived at the cowering form of Balaam.

The seer was wearing a cloak and had long white hair and a beard. He clutched a sack that apparently contained his wages of unrighteousness.

Joshua shoved his sword through Balaam and pinned him up against the wall.

He withdrew the blade and Balaam fell to the ground in pain.

And then Joshua began to hack at Balaam with his sword. The screams of the dying seer echoed through the cave.

Blood splattered against the wall and all over Joshua.

Balaam's screams ceased as his life left his body. But Joshua kept hacking like a madman in mindless fury until he was covered in gore.

A shudder went through Caleb because Joshua's visage reminded Caleb of Ashtart, the goddess of war drenched in the blood of her berserking terror.

This was not right.

"Joshua!" yelled Caleb.

But Joshua did not stop.

"JOSHUA!"

Caleb held Joshua's arm from another swing.

Joshua spun and shoved Caleb to the ground.

He then released his fury upon Caleb, who barely drew his sword in time to block the barrage of blows raining down upon him.

"Commander!" yelled Caleb.

But Joshua kept pummeling him, eyes filled with blinding rage.

Caleb would not return the blows. He would not fight his Commander, his friend.

Caleb's strength was not comparable to Joshua's. He was weakening. And he would not go on the offensive.

But then Joshua hit Caleb's sword out of his hands and it clattered against the rock wall.

Joshua raised his sword high to plunge it into his comrade.

In his eyes, Caleb saw the fury of madness.

Caleb yelled, "In the name of Yahweh, Joshua, stop!"

And Joshua stopped in mid-air.

His eyes suddenly filled with sanity.

He lowered his blade.

His conscience flowed over him.

His sword dropped to the ground.

He fell to his knees.

And he broke down weeping.

Caleb breathed a deep sigh of relief. He had been saved. Yahweh had spared him from the madness of his General, the man whom he now held in his arms like a crying child.

No words were needed. They both knew what had happened. Joshua had been overcome by his own righteous indignation. He had become so obsessed with Yahweh's war that he forgot he was a servant and not the sovereign. He became momentarily blinded by the delusion that he could do no wrong. And when his hatred for evil was projected outward, he was overwhelmed by his rage and forgot the evil in himself.

His momentary madness was the potential of every living person. This simple yet profound truth was what kept Caleb humble in his own perception of himself.

Being an instrument of Yahweh's wrath was a dangerous responsibility that was not without its damage to the human soul. This new age of iron was a violent and wicked world. The Creator, though being the foundation of all that is good and true and beautiful, had to confront that world of wickedness with the righteous fire of holy violence, otherwise evil would fester and cannibalize everything.

But the problem was that the instruments of Yahweh's wrath were still men. And the taking of human life, though morally justified, was still the destruction of man created in the image of Yahweh. And once you had taken human life, it changed you. You were no longer an innocent. You had stepped into a polluted river of pain that cried out for redemption, for atonement.

Joshua and Caleb stayed outside the camp of Israel for seven days of purification, along with Othniel and all the men who had killed anyone in the destruction of Midian. It was required of

Yahweh as a consecration of his holiness. Even the spoils that they captured would have to be purified.

They killed every male, adult and child, and every woman who had lain with a man, since these were the ones who had seduced the sons of Israel into their idolatry. The young girls who had not lain with men were taken as captives. These captives as well as their clothes, and personal items were all cleansed in the waters of baptism, along with the Israelite soldiers.

Thousands of sheep, cattle, and donkeys were also cleansed through water as spoils of war and divided among the peoples. So too the thousands of shekels of items of silver, gold, bronze, and iron were purified through fire and also apportioned out to the tribes.

On the final day of purification, Joshua and Caleb were getting ready to return to camp. They were in Joshua's tent eating a small meal of goat and bread.

Joshua took a sip of wine from his goatskin flask.

Caleb watched him closely. He had been watching Joshua closely these seven days.

Joshua looked refreshed. And he looked different. Like he was a changed man from the one whose pursuit of rigid excessive holiness rose to a crescendo of self-righteous vengeance and hate.

He had come to the end of himself and was crushed by his own unrighteousness. He had learned that his entire goal of being what Moses was not, a perfect man of obedience to the laws of God, was a delusion.

Joshua was a broken man.

All he had left was his faith in Yahweh.

And Caleb knew that was all he needed.

Joshua, however, was not so sure.

"Caleb, I do not know that I can face the congregation and Moses."

"Why not?"

"Because I failed them, and I failed my God."

"That is why we have atonement, Joshua. Or are you saying Yahweh does not know what he is doing?"

"Of course, not, my gadfly friend."

Caleb smiled at the remark.

But an ominous tone came over Joshua, "I have not told you everything."

Caleb waited for him to gather the courage to speak.

Joshua finally said, "When I was attacking Balaam, I saw who I really was. And I saw great darkness. I saw the Abyss."

"Welcome to the human race," said Caleb.

"No. This was more than mere sinfulness. I fear that the madness you saw was not temporary. It was who I truly am."

Caleb was silent.

"I am going to resign as general of the army upon my return to the camp. I will recommend to Moses that you are fully capable of replacing me—more than capable. More a leader than I."

"No," said Caleb. "That is not true, Joshua. You must not do this."

"There is nothing else I can do, Caleb. I am sorry for what I put you through. I have failed my people and my god. I have failed my truest friend. Let me make this right."

CHAPTER 29

The congregation of Israel gathered in the open areas and aisles around the tabernacle to hear Moses speak to them. He had recently been up to the heights of Mount Nebo to speak with Yahweh, so he was veiled again because of his transfigured brightness.

Joshua had not been available to assist him because he was outside the camp according to the laws of atonement. So Moses had asked Eleazer and his son, Phineas to accompany him. Eleazer was wearing his high priestly garments, with turban, blue garments, ephod, and breastplate of righteousness.

But today was the day that Joshua and his soldiers returned to camp after being purified. Joshua met Moses at the Tent of Meeting and the two of them embraced.

Joshua said with sad eyes, “Moses, I have to speak with you.”

Moses looked at Joshua. He could tell something was wrong with him. He looked troubled, like the fight had been beaten out of him.

“We will speak, Joshua,” said Moses. “But first, I have a word from Yahweh. There will be much of interest to you.”

Joshua sighed with discouragement. His spirit felt so heavy, he wanted to confess his tortured soul, release the burden, and accept his fading relevance into the mists of forgotten history.

He followed Moses to the open gateway of the tabernacle. He looked out upon the masses of Israelites, his brethren. Those he was sworn to protect with his very life. Every one of them, precious in the eyes of their shepherd, their father, their god.

They applauded and shouted praises to Yahweh, but also to his servant Moses and their deliverer Joshua.

It made Joshua sick to his stomach. He had failed them, and they held him in such high regard. It was a mockery of the truth. He could not wait to get it all over with.

But he also knew how fickle the masses were. They would worship you when you brought them success or food for their bellies, but they would impale you on a pole if you crossed them or failed to live up to their expectations.

The people were a mob.

Yahweh did not pick Israel because they were more righteous than the other nations, or for anything in themselves. He chose them as his people from his own mysterious sovereign will, for his own mysterious sovereign purposes.

Joshua's eyes met Caleb's. Caleb was watching his beloved commander with heartfelt concern. He smiled to assure Joshua he was with him in heart and soul, even if he disagreed with what Joshua was about to do.

Eleazer and Phineas stepped up next to Joshua. Three new young prophets of Israel were also brought by Moses to stand in this gathering of authority. The older prophets had died out over the forty years of wandering. They were not as needed since Moses spoke face to face with Yahweh. But these new ones were being raised up for when Moses was gone, which Caleb felt was imminent.

Moses pulled off his veil and his face shone with brazen light. His voice boomed over the camp with authority. Joshua remembered when Moses relied upon his brother Aaron to be his spokesman because he had no faith in his own abilities. What a difference from those earlier days.

"Children of Israel! I have been to the mountaintop of Nebo and I have spoken with Yahweh!"

It still amazed Caleb that Moses was the only man to ever speak face to face with Yahweh and live. He would probably be the only one who ever would.

"We stand on the threshold of entrance into Canaan, the land promised to our forefathers, Abraham, Isaac, and Jacob! I have seen this land from the mountaintop, and it is a land that Yahweh has told me I will not enter!"

The crowds murmured with gossip. How could this be? The very mouthpiece of Yahweh losing the reward after forty years of obedience?

Joshua had known of this. He was not surprised, nor was Caleb. They knew that Yahweh had vowed to withhold the promise from both Moses and Aaron for their act of consummate pride at Meribah.

Moses muttered to Joshua under the crowd's noise, "I asked him again if he would change his mind, and he got impatient and told me 'Enough!' I was not to speak of it ever again."

He turned back to the crowd. "My time is now at its end and I will be gathered to my fathers!"

More murmurs. Someone yelled, "No, Moses! You will live!"

Moses raised his hands to calm them down.

"I will die. As all men die! But Yahweh, the god of the spirits of all flesh, has appointed a new man over the congregation. He shall lead you out and bring you in so that you may not be as sheep without a shepherd."

Joshua broke out into a cold sweat. He suspected the worst. That he would be that man. For years he had sought the honor, but now that he was about to receive it, he knew he did not deserve it and was going to turn it down. He was so unworthy of the privilege. He looked at Moses with panic.

Joshua tried to shake his head enough for Moses to see, but not the congregation.

"That man will be a man in whom is the Spirit of Yahweh, Joshua ben Nun!"

The crowd broke out into wild applause.

Joshua took the opportunity to mutter to Moses under the din, "No, Moses, you do not understand. I cannot do this."

Moses said, "Neither could I."

"No. What I mean is that I will not do this. I was going to resign from my command this very night."

Moses said with a smirk, "I think Yahweh may have a difference of opinion with you."

The prophets nodded their heads in agreement with Moses' proclamation. Everyone it seemed was hearing from Yahweh except Joshua.

He laid his hands upon Joshua. "By the word of Yahweh, I invest in Joshua ben Nun my authority that all the congregation of the people of Israel may obey!"

More applause. The people loved ceremonies of such royalty.

Joshua made one last attempt, "I am unworthy of this commission."

Moses looked at him with pity. "My dear Joshua. Of course you are unworthy. But Yahweh declares you worthy. Will you finally give in and accept that you are wrong, if Yahweh himself tells you?"

Joshua looked dead into his eyes. He nodded. Yes, he would. He would have to. He could not argue with Yahweh's choice.

Moses said to Eleazer, "Bring forth the Urim and Thummim for the confirmation of the word of Yahweh."

Joshua's eyes went wide with fear.

Eleazer reached into his pouch that held the "Lights and Perfections."

He held them before Joshua who had dropped to one knee in reverence.

Eleazer said with a loud voice, "Almighty God, Yahweh Elohim, we beseech you to confirm the appointment of Joshua ben Nun as leader of this people!"

And then a miracle occurred. The entire congregation went silent. Their muttering and murmuring just suddenly stopped. It was as if they were all holding their breath.

A gust of wind seemed to flow over the three prophets alone, blowing their cloaks with ethereal movement. They began to chant a hymn of praise. But their voices sounded strangely divine and in perfect unison, as if they were *Bene ha Elohim* from the throne of Yahweh. They had become the representative witness for the heavenly host on earth.

Eleazer reached in his chest pouch and withdrew the two gemstones.

Those in the congregation could not see them for their size, but they could see the light that they produced.

They sparkled with the glory of the Lord, and Eleazer said, "Is Joshua your chosen leader for Israel to enter Canaan?"

The Lights and Perfections glittered and sparkled until a beam of their light settled on Joshua's face and he glowed in holy aura.

The crowd cheered. The prophets ceased their heavenly praise as one. Joshua looked over to see Caleb watching him with a proud smile.

So he was right again.

Moses said to Joshua, "When I am gone, these prophets will help you discern the will of Yahweh."

Moses then turned to the assembly of elders and judges, and the people behind them and gave them the charge to listen to the statutes and rules that Yahweh had given them that they would go in and take possession of the land that Yahweh was giving them.

"And beware lest you raise your eyes to heaven, and when you see the sun and the moon and the stars, all the host of heaven, you be drawn away and bow down to them and serve them, things that Yahweh your god has allotted to all the peoples under the whole heaven. But Yahweh has taken you to be a people of his own inheritance, as you are this day."

All covenants required witnesses. Moses called heaven and earth to witness against the people that if they obeyed his Law, they would be blessed, but if they did not and did what was evil in Yahweh's sight, they would utterly perish from the land instead of possessing it. Yahweh would scatter them among the nations.

He then read the Law that he had been writing down for so long. He recited it in the presence of the whole congregation before pronouncing a blessing upon them.

And then he concluded by saying to Joshua in the sight of all Israel, "Joshua ben Nun, be strong and courageous, for you shall lead this people into the land that Yahweh has sworn to their fathers to give them. You shall put them in possession of it. And know this: It is Yahweh who goes before you. He will be with you; he will not leave you or forsake you. Do not fear or be dismayed."

Joshua looked out upon the people before him. He was amazed that Yahweh would take a broken man and lead a broken people to be his own inheritance in a land of such adversity and hardship.

But there was something in the words of Moses that resonated within his soul. He had lost everything; his wife and family, his love, any shred of compassion, and had become a man of war. He felt like a pile of dead man's bones that was resurrected from the grave and animated with a new spirit. He would be strong. He would be courageous. He had nothing left to lose, and everything to gain by trusting his incomparable god, the god above all gods.

Caleb did not take his eyes off his beloved general and friend. He could not contain his smile. His heart was full of hope. He was eighty-years old, but he felt so young and virile in his health and strength.

All his life he had waited for this. Now they stood at the threshold of triumphal entry into the Promised Land. Yahweh had told him that he alone would enter that land along with Joshua, while all the others of his generation had perished.

He was the son of Jephunneh, a Kenizzite, and a convert to Israel. But he had always felt that he had to prove himself by vigilant deeds of faithfulness. He had hoped to earn his worthiness to be called an Israelite.

He remembered the day he and Joshua were captured by the Anakim near the caves of Machpelah. It was that day that he set his heart upon inheriting the land where Abraham was buried. There was no land more holy than this, no land more desirable to him. He knew the monsters that ruled that territory, but he was not afraid.

He would cut down every last one of them by the power of his god to claim his inheritance, his birthright.

Moses was weary from his speech. He was weary with life and with age. He was one hundred and twenty-years old. His eyes had not dimmed and his physical vigor had not abated. But his soul was weighed down with resignation. He had been the instrument of Yahweh's deliverance out of Egypt. He had shepherded an ungrateful people in the desert for forty years; he saw great and mighty signs and wonders. Yet he too was mortal. He too failed to uphold Yahweh as holy when he rebelled at the waters of Meribah. And for his disobedience, he would never enter the Promised Land.

To have come so far and through so much and yet not receive the reward had broken Moses' heart. He only found consolation in the fact that Yahweh was the great "I Am," the god of the living, not the dead. So Moses knew that he was one small but important part of Yahweh's plan to one day bless all the nations through the Seed of Abraham. Moses was but the planting of that seed that would ultimately blossom and grow into a tree that would fill all the earth with its glory.

Moses turned to Joshua and said, "Take me up to Mount Nebo again, to the heights of Pisgah. I would like to see the land that you will enter one last time."

• • • • •

Joshua, Eleazer, and Caleb stood at the peak of Mount Nebo. Moses was dead. An era was gone. The people would mourn for weeks. There had never been a prophet like Moses, who spoke with Yahweh face to face. And these men suspected there never would be another like him to come.

They would bury him in the valley in the land of Moab. But now, they looked out upon the land before them: Gilead to the north, the land west of the Jordan, past Jericho all the way to the sea, and the Negeb to the south.

Not a word passed between them. But the moment was filled with holiness. The spirit of the Lord came upon them.

And they knew that before them was the future of their people, their land of conquest.

Before them was the next battle in the War of the Seed: Jericho.

EPILOGUE

The body of Moses lay in a secret tomb somewhere in the valley of Moab. But it was not a secret to the unearthly Watcher and adversary of Yahweh, Mastema. He had been waiting for this moment for many years.

He had been planning for it.

He moved the large two-ton boulder at the entrance of the cave. The resting places of important figures in this part of the land would normally have megalithic markers over them, gargantuan rocks stood on end, or balanced in precarious ways to signify their presence.

But there were no megaliths on this unmarked grave. It was intended to protect against this very thing, the theft of a corpse.

Mastema stooped to avoid hitting the ceiling as he found his way down the catacomb to the body. His eight-foot height and sinewy musculature provided the image of him as a portrait of death itself.

And there it was, resting peacefully on a stone slab, the body of the mighty leader of Israel. The stench of death was a pleasing aroma to Mastema's nostrils. He breathed it in with eyes deliriously closed to focus his attention on his olfactory sense.

He breathed out with a sigh of delight, and lifted the body in his arms like cradling an old man. But this was no ordinary old man.

Moses had spoken face to face with Yahweh. When he was on Mount Sinai in the desert of exodus, something had changed in his physical being.

When Moses came down from the mountain carrying the tablets, he had no idea that the skin of his face was shining with light like burnished bronze. The Israelites were afraid at first, but Moses put a veil over his face to calm their fears.

It was a fading glory. As time passed, so would the shining of his skin. But it did signify a transformation of his body that no one really understood. No one, that is, except for the Shining Ones in Yahweh's presence, the *Bene Elohim*, or Sons of God.

Yahweh was light and dwelt in light, and the beings that surrounded his throne radiated light as well. Even the fallen Watchers who rebelled against heaven were still shining beings whose divine essence emitted from their bodies.

What had actually occurred was that Moses' body had been changed by the presence of Yahweh. His very genetic structure had been altered, transfigured by Yahweh himself into a hybrid being of heaven and earth.

Mastema wanted that transfigured flesh for his own purposes.

The corpse was very human and would eventually return to the dust from which it came. But because it had been transfigured, it contained the Edenic regenerative properties that, if nurtured with occultic sciences, might allow Mastema to create a new chimeric organism.

The Watchers had originally begun their program of unholy cross-breeding in antediluvian days, when the Sons of God mated with the daughters of men and bred the Nephilim. The Nephilim were the giant hybrid of human and angelic flesh that violated Yahweh's separated creation order. But the Great Flood had put a stop to that plan of corrupting the Seed of Eve.

Now that very Seed, in the form of the nation Israel, was about to enter Canaan and seek to wrest it from the Seed of the Serpent Nachash, or Mastema. If Mastema could revitalize that flesh and inhabit it with some of his *sheddim*, or demons, he hoped he could create a kind of "god puppet" of Moses that the Israelites would surely follow because of their naïve propensity to worship any god that could produce lights, bells, and whistles.

But he had to move fast before the body would become too decayed to be able to house the controlling spirit.

As Mastema stepped outside into the night, he was immediately surrounded by not four but all seven of the archangels. Mikael, Gabriel, Raphael, Uriel, Saraqael, Raguel, and Remiel.

Mikael stepped forward and announced, "Adversary, by what legal right do you desecrate this honorable grave and lay claim to the body of Moses?"

Mastema looked around at the seven mighty ones encircling him. He would not stand a chance against these highest of Yahweh's guardian archons—even if Ba'al were by his side.

Mastema simply stated, "I have a writ of Habeas Corpus."

Habeas Corpus was the legal demand to bring forth the body of the accused to face his charges. It was intended to keep criminals from being unjustly held from trial.

Mikael said, "That is ridiculous. What are you up to, you devil? This is a righteous grave. There are no criminal charges on Moses."

Mastema said, "I beg to differ, princely one. This lawbreaker never paid for the crime of murdering an Egyptian and hiding his body in the sand. He is under my jurisdiction to do with as I please."

"May Yahweh Elohim rebuke you," said Mikael. "He is atoned for. Yahweh will not allow your blasphemous designs upon his Chosen One. Hand the body over to us."

Gabriel and Raphael stepped forward to take the body from him.

Mastema thought of using a ruse to draw them down upon himself, suffer their beatings, and then cry victim and file charges of angel brutality in the heavenly court.

But today was not a day for games.

He muttered to Raphael, "I see you are not crawling around anymore."

He was making an insulting reference to the fact that Raphael had been cut in half by Ashtart's scythe and had his lower half tossed into the Abyss.

Fortunately, Mikael and Gabriel had recovered his lower part after they had imprisoned Ashtart in Tartarus.

Raphael showed no reaction. He and Gabriel received the body in their arms and backed away.

Mastema spit out at Mikael before leaving, "I will see you soon in court, Prince of Israel."

Mikael knew Mastema was always trying to manipulate the law in order to achieve injustice, but he had no idea about his latest machinations.

He would know soon enough.

The story is continued in the companion volume, *Caleb Vigilant.*

If you liked this book, then please help me out by writing an honest review of it on Amazon. That is one of the best ways to say thank you to me as an author. It really does help my exposure and status as an author. It's really easy. In the Customer Reviews section, there is a little box that says "Write a customer review." They guide you easily through the process. Thanks! — *Brian Godawa*

FREE DIGITAL BOOK

Get a Free eBooklet of the Biblical & Historical Research Behind the Exodus.

FREE

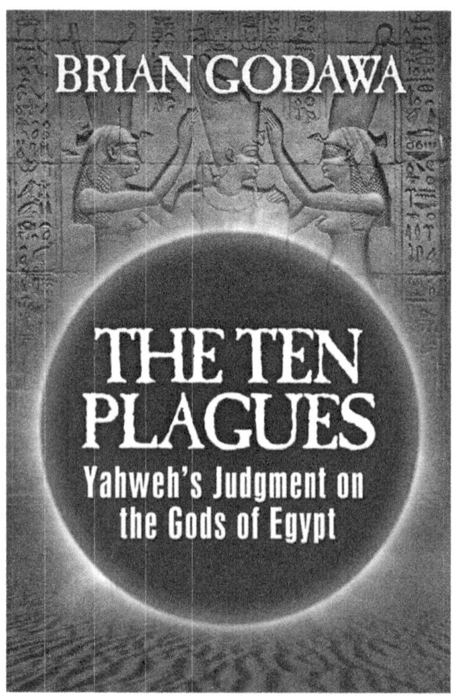

Limited time offer

Natural Disasters? Gods at War? De-creation?

Have you wondered what Yahweh meant when he said, "I will execute judgment upon the gods of Egypt"? Did you know that there is a connection between the plagues and Genesis 1? The answers may astonish you. Some of the research behind this novel can be found at the following link:

https://godawa.com/get-ten-plagues/

APPENDIX
MYTHICAL MONSTERS IN THE BIBLE

Perhaps one of the most unique creative elements of the *Chronicles of the Nephilim* series is its ability to interact with pagan mythologies within the context of retelling Biblical stories in such a way as to bring out universal and shared meanings. But it does so within the context of a Biblical worldview. So famous and infamous giants, monsters, and other creatures from pagan myths show up in the stories of Enoch, Noah, Abraham and others: The sea dragon of chaos, Gilgamesh the ancient Babylonian hero, the chimeric mushussu lion dragon, The demoness Lilith, and others all make their appearances in this theological Biblical fantasy.

Rather than being a syncretistic blending of all religions into heretical oneness, this technique more accurately is described in Narnian terms as a subversive submission of all stories under the lordship of Aslan.

But this is not a new phenomenon created by innovative Christian geniuses like Lewis and Tolkien; it is in fact a storytelling technique common to much ancient literature of imagination—including the Bible!

Leviathan and Behemoth

I have already written much about Leviathan and Behemoth as monsters of chaos in the Bible in appendices of previous Chronicles.[3] In those essays, I exegeted the Biblical texts where these monsters occurred. I debunked the notions that they are ancient descriptions of dinosaurs or other naturally occurring creatures, only to conclude that they bear the same characteristics of other ancient Near Eastern chaos monsters such as the Canaanite Leviathan and the Babylonian Tiamat. In passages such as Psalm 74 and Psalm 89, the historical event of the Exodus is mythopoeically presented as Yahweh fighting the waters and crushing the multiple heads of Leviathan or Rahab (another name for the same creature) in order to establish a new heavens and earth, his covenant order with Israel.

It is not that the Jews "copied" or "borrowed" such imagery from their pagan neighbors; but rather that, just as today, everyone of that time period used a common vocabulary of imagination to describe their worldviews. The Sumerians, Akkadians, Babylonians, Canaanites, Jews, and other ancient Near Easterners all described their gods' supremacy in terms of battling and overcoming the sea dragon of chaos so they could create order out of the chaos.

But this is just the tip of the ziggurat of other examples of Biblical authors poetically incorporating mythical elements into their writings about real people, places, and times of history.

Now things start to get hairy.

---

[3] See "Appendix C: Leviathan," Brian Godawa, *Noah Primeval* (Los Angeles, CA: Embedded Pictures Publishing, 2012), 325; and "Appendix: Retelling Biblical Stories and the Mythic Imagination in Enoch Primordial," *Enoch Primordial*, (Los Angeles, CA: Embedded Pictures Publishing, 2013), 352.

Satyrs and Centaurs and Demons, Oh My!

In my novels, *Joshua Valiant* and *Caleb Vigilant*, I write about a tribe called the Seirim people of Panias at Mount Hermon. They live in caves at the foot of the mountains and are led by satyrs; chimeric beings with the lower body of a goat and the upper body of a human. But this mythopoeic imagery is not a mere assimilation of ancient Greek myths about Pan, the satyr deity of nature and shepherding. The notion of satyrs or goat deities predates Greek myth and finds a place in Canaanite lore, and therefore, in the Bible as well.

Take a look at these prophecies of Isaiah referencing the destruction of Babylon and Edom.

> Isaiah 34:11–15 (The destruction of Edom)
> [11]But the hawk and the porcupine shall possess it, the owl and the raven shall dwell in it… [13]Thorns shall grow over its strongholds, nettles and thistles in its fortresses. It shall be the haunt of jackals, an abode for ostriches. [14]And wild animals shall meet with hyenas; the wild goat (*seirim*) shall cry to his fellow; indeed, there the night bird settles and finds for herself a resting place. [15]There the owl nests and lays and hatches and gathers her young in her shadow; indeed, there the hawks are gathered, each one with her mate.

> Isaiah 13:21–22 (The destruction of Babylon)
> [21]But wild animals will lie down there, and their houses will be full of howling creatures; there

> ostriches will dwell, and there wild goats (*seirim*) will dance. [22]Hyenas will cry in its towers, and jackals in the pleasant palaces; its time is close at hand and its days will not be prolonged.

The passages above speak of God's judgment upon the nations of Babylon and Edom (symbols of all that is against Israel and Yahweh). A cursory reading of the texts seem to indicate a common word picture of Yahweh destroying these nations so thoroughly that they end up a desert wasteland with wild animals and birds inhabiting them because the evil people will be no more.

Nothing about mythical monsters like satyrs there, right?

Wrong. Because the English translation of the Hebrew word *seirim* as "wild goats," obscures the full ancient meaning. If we look closer into the original Hebrew, we find a more expanded mythopoeic reference to pagan deities.

A look at the Septuagint (LXX) translation into Greek made by ancient Jews in the second century before Christ, reveals the hint of that different picture.

> Isaiah 34:13-14 (LXX)
>
> [11] and for a long time birds and hedgehogs, and ibises and ravens shall dwell in it: and the measuring line of desolation shall be cast over it, and satyrs shall dwell in it…[13] And thorns shall spring up in their cities, and in her strong holds: and they shall be habitations of monsters, and a court for ostriches. [14] And devils shall meet with satyrs, and

> they shall cry one to the other: there shall satyrs rest, having found for themselves *a place of* rest.[4]
>
> Isaiah 13:21-22 (LXX)
> But wild beasts shall rest there; and the houses shall be filled with howling; and monsters shall rest there, and devils shall dance there, [22] and satyrs shall dwell there.[5]

Wow, what a dramatic difference, huh? Of course, the LXX passages above are not in Greek, but are English translations, which adds a layer of complication that we will unravel shortly to reveal even more mythopoeic elements. But the point is made that ancient translators understood those words within their ancient context much differently than the modern bias of more recent interpreters. Of course, this does not necessarily make the ancient translators right all the time, but it warrants a closer look at our own blinding biases.

The LXX translates the word for "satyrs" that appears in these Isaiah passages as *onokentaurois* or "donkey-centaurs," from which we get our word "centaur." The *Greek-English Lexicon of the Septuagint* defines this word as "donkey-centaur, mythic creature (a centaur resembling a donkey rather than a horse)."[6]

In Isaiah 34:14 of the ESV we read of "the wild goat crying to his fellow," and in 13:21, "there wild goats will dance." But the underlying Hebrew (*seirim*) is not about wild goats, but satyrs, that were prevalent in Canaanite religion. Scholar Judd Burton points

---

[4] Lancelot Charles Lee Brenton, *The Septuagint Version of the Old Testament: English Translation*, Is 34:13–14 (London: Samuel Bagster and Sons, 1870).
[5] Lancelot Charles Lee Brenton, *The Septuagint Version of the Old Testament: English Translation*, Is 13:21–22 (London: Samuel Bagster and Sons, 1870).
[6] Johan Lust, Erik Eynikel and Katrin Hauspie, *A Greek-English Lexicon of the Septuagint: Revised Edition* (Deutsche Bibelgesellschaft: Stuttgart, 2003).

out that Panias or Panias at the base of Mount Hermon in Bashan was a key worship site for the Greek goat-god Pan as early as the third century B.C. and earlier connections to the goat-idol Azazel (see *Azazel* below).[7]

Satyrs were well known for their satyrical dance, the *Sikinnis*, consisting of music, lascivious dance, licentious poetry and sarcastic critique of culture.[8] This reflects the mockery of the "goats" dancing on the ruins of Edom and Babylon in Isaiah, and the Sikinnis finds its way also into *Joshua Valiant* of the Chronicles.

The Bible writers considered these pagan *seirim* deities to be demons and thus called them "goat demons." So prevalent and influential were these satyr gods that Yahweh would have trouble with Israel worshipping them as idols.

> Leviticus 17:7
> So they shall no more sacrifice their sacrifices to goat demons (*seirim*), after whom they whore. This shall be a statute forever for them throughout their generations.

> 2 Chronicles 11:15
> [Jeroboam] appointed his own priests for the high places and for the goat idols (*seirim*) and for the calves that he had made.

---

[7] Judd H. Burton, *Interview With the Giant: Ethnohistorical Notes on the Nephilim* (Burton Beyond Press, 2009) 19-21. "Regardless of his [Azazle's] origins—in pre-Israelite practice he was surely a true demon, perhaps a satyr, who ruled in the wilderness." Jacob Milgrom, *A Continental Commentary: Leviticus: a Book of Ritual and Ethics* (Minneapolis, MN: Fortress Press, 2004), 169.

[8] Gaston Vuillier, trans. Joseph Grego, *A History Of Dancing From The Earliest Ages To Our Own Times* (New York, NY: D. Appleton and Co., 1848), 27-28.

Not only did Israel fall into worshipping the *seirim* in Canaan, they were even committing spiritual adultery with them while in the wilderness! It is no wonder Yahweh considered them demons, a declaration reiterated in Moses' own prophecy that after Israel would be brought into Canaan by the hand of God, she would betray Yahweh by turning aside to other gods, redefined as demons.

> Deuteronomy 32:17
> 17 They sacrificed to demons that were no gods, to gods they had never known, to new gods that had come recently, whom your fathers had never dreaded.[9]

Demons and Goblins

Moving back to the prophecies of Isaiah 13 and 34 we find additional spiritual creatures of chaos that are connected to the satyrs. We read of hawks, ostriches, owls, and ravens was well as other unknown animals. But the English translations make it look like they are just more natural animals.

Not so in the Hebrew.

Let's take a closer look at the Hebrew words behind two more of these strange creatures, "wild animals" and "hyenas."

> Isaiah 13:21–22
> 21 But wild animals (*siyyim*) will lie down there, and their houses will be full of howling creatures; there

[9] The Psalmist also casts the gods of Canaan; Molech, Asherah, Ashtart, Ba'al, and others as demons as well in Psalm 106:37–38: "They sacrificed their sons and their daughters to the demons; they poured out innocent blood, the blood of their sons and daughters, whom they sacrificed to the idols of Canaan, and the land was polluted with blood."

> ostriches will dwell, and there wild goats will dance.
> 22 Hyenas (*iyyim*) will cry in its towers, and jackals
> in the pleasant palaces; its time is close at hand and
> its days will not be prolonged.
>
> Isaiah 34:14
> 14 And wild animals (*siyyim*) shall meet with hyenas; (*iyyim*) the wild goat shall cry to his fellow; indeed, there the night bird settles and finds for herself a resting place.

The Hebrew for the words "wild animals" and "hyenas" are not readily identifiable,[10] so the ESV translators simply guessed according to their anti-mythical bias and filled in their translations with naturalistic words like "wild animals" and "hyenas." But of these words, Bible commentator Hans Wildberger says,

> "Whereas (jackals) and (ostriches), mentioned in v. 13, are certainly well-known animals, the creatures that are mentioned in v. 14 cannot be identified zoologically, not because we are not provided with enough information, but because they refer to fairy tale and mythical beings. *Siyyim* are demons, the kind that do their mischief by the ruins of Babylon, according to [Isaiah] 13:21. They are mentioned along with the *iyyim* (goblins) in this passage.[11]

---

[10] "Siyyim," Francis Brown, Samuel Rolles Driver, and Charles Augustus Briggs, *Enhanced Brown-Driver-Briggs Hebrew and English Lexicon* (Oak Harbor, WA: Logos Research Systems, 2000), 850.
[11] Hans Wildberger, *A Continental Commentary: Isaiah 28–39* (Minneapolis, MN: Fortress Press, 2002).

The demons and goblins that Wildberger makes reference to in Isaiah 13:21-22 and 34:14 are the Hebrew words *siyyim* and *iyyim*, a phonetic play on words that is echoed in Jeremiah's prophecy against Babylon as well:

> Jeremiah 50:39 (ESV)
> [39] "Therefore wild beasts (*siyyim*) shall dwell with hyenas (*iyyim*) in Babylon, and ostriches shall dwell in her. She shall never again have people, nor be inhabited for all generations.

The Dictionary of Biblical Languages (*DBL*) admits that another interpretation of *iyyim* other than howling desert animals is "spirit, ghost, goblin, i.e., a night demon or dead spirit (Isa. 13:22; 34:14; Jer. 50:39), note: this would be one from the distant lands, i.e., referring to the nether worlds."[12] One could say that *siyyim and iyyim* are similar to our own play on words, "ghosts and goblins."

The proof of this demon interpretation is in the Apostle John's inspired reuse of the *same exact language* when pronouncing judgment upon first century Israel as a symbolic "Mystery Babylon."

> Revelation 18:2
> [2]"Fallen, fallen is Babylon the great! She has become a dwelling place for demons, a haunt for

[12] James Swanson, *Dictionary of Biblical Languages With Semantic Domains : Hebrew (Old Testament)*, electronic ed. (Oak Harbor: Logos Research Systems, Inc., 1997).

> every unclean spirit, a haunt for every unclean bird,
> a haunt for every unclean and detestable beast."[13]

Because of the exile under the Babylonians, Jews would use Babylon as the ultimate symbol of evil. So when John attacks his contemporaries in Israel for rejecting Messiah, he describes them as demonic Babylon worthy of the same judgment as that ultimate evil nation.

But regardless of one's eschatological interpretation, the "wild beasts" or "monsters" and "hyenas" of Isaiah and Jeremiah are interpreted as demons, unclean spirits and detestable beasts, along with the unclean animals that will scavenge over the ruins of the judged nation. The Old Testament "haunt of jackals" is the New Testament equivalent of the "haunt of demons." The "dwelling of hyenas and ostriches" is the "dwelling of demons."

In fact, even the Hebrew for "ostriches" is a word that is not all it seems. The actual Hebrew is *benot yaanah,* "daughters of ostriches," not merely "ostriches." Of course, this odd adjective did not make the translators comfortable because it pointed to something that may be other than ostriches, so they left it out.

The DBL says this Hebrew word phrase is "formally, daughter of greed, or daughter of wilderness… a kind of owl."[14] So they are not even sure it means an ostrich. Owls are connected to the underworld and spirits through all of ancient literature. But since there is no conclusive scholarship available on what this term really means, we will leave it as another possible reference to a

---

[13] Special thanks to Doug Van Dorn for this "revelation." Van Dorn, Douglas (2013-01-21). *Giants: Sons of the Gods* (Kindle Locations 3922-3925). Waters of Creation. Kindle Edition. In fact, his "Chapter 13: Chimeras" was helpful for more than one insight in this appendix.

[14] James Swanson, *Dictionary of Biblical Languages With Semantic Domains : Hebrew (Old Testament)*, electronic ed. (Oak Harbor: Logos Research Systems, Inc., 1997).

strange creature of the demonic wilderness in a passage of much debated strange demonic references.

Lilith

Another strange creature that occurs in Isaiah 34:14 is the "night hag," or "night bird" that "settles and finds for herself a resting place." The Hebrew word is actually *Lilith*, which the *Dictionary of Deities and Demons in the Bible* explains is a Mesopotamian demoness residing in a tree that reaches back to the third millennium BC.

> Here we find Inanna (Ishtar) who plants a tree later hoping to cut from its wood a throne and a bed for herself. But as the tree grows, a snake makes its nest at its roots, Anzu settled in the top and in the trunk the demon ki-sikil-líl-lá [Lilith] makes her lair.[15]

I've already written about Lilith in the appendix of *Enoch Primordial*,[16] but it is important that she shows up in this Biblical context connected with the satyrs and Azazel. The very next verse (Isa. 34:15) talks about the owl that nests and lays and hatches her young in its shadow. But lexicons such as the *Theological Wordbook of the Old Testament* and *Brown, Driver, Briggs Hebrew Lexicon* contest this Hebrew word for owl (*qippoz*) with more ancient interpretations of an "arrow snake."[17] If they are

---

[15] M. Hutter, "Lilith", in *Dictionary of Deities and Demons in the Bible*, ed. Karel van der Toorn, Bob Becking and Pieter W. van der Horst, 2nd extensively rev. ed., 520 (Leiden; Boston; Köln; Grand Rapids, MI; Cambridge: Brill; Eerdmans, 1999).

[16] Brian Godawa, *Enoch Primordial* (Los Angeles: Embedded Pictures Publishing, 2013), 349.

[17] 2050a, קִפּוֹז *Theological Wordbook of the Old Testament*, ed. R. Laird Harris, Gleason L. Archer, Jr. and Bruce K. Waltke, electronic ed., 806 (Chicago: Moody Press,

correct, then the poetry of the passage would be more complete as the NASB indicates.

> Isaiah 34:14–15 (NASB95)
> [14] Yes, the night monster (*Lilith*) will settle there And will find herself a resting place. [15] The tree snake (*qippoz*) will make its nest and lay *eggs* there, And it will hatch and gather *them* under its protection.

The snake of verse 15 would match the Lilith myth (v. 14) with the snake in the roots making its nest. The correlation is too close to deny that this is another Biblical reference to a popular mythic creature that the Bible writers refer to in demonic terms.

The Dead Sea Scrolls of Qumran evidence a preoccupation with demonology that includes reference to this very Isaianic passage. In *The Songs of the Sage*, we read an exorcism incantation,

> "And I, the Instructor, proclaim His glorious splendor so as to frighten and to terrify all the spirits of the destroying angels, spirits of the bastards, demons, Lilith, howlers, and [desert dwellers…] and those which fall upon men without warning to lead them astray[18]

1999). קִפּוֹזBrown, Francis, Samuel Rolles Driver, and Charles Augustus Briggs. *Enhanced Brown-Driver-Briggs Hebrew and English Lexicon*. electronic ed. Oak Harbor, WA: Logos Research Systems, 2000.

[18] 4Q510 Frag. 1. Michael O. Wise, Martin G. Abegg Jr., and Edward M. Cook, *The Dead Sea Scrolls: A New Translation* (New York: HarperOne, 2005), 527. Janet Howe Gaines, "Lilith: Seductress, Heroine or Murderer?" Bible History Daily, 08/11/2014,

Note the reference to "spirits of the bastards," a euphemism for demons as the spirits of dead Nephilim who were not born of human fathers, but of angels.[19]

Lion Men of Moab

As a side note, one other possible chimeric creature appears in the story of David's mighty men in 2Sam. 23:20. There it says that Benaiah, a valiant warrior, "struck down two *ariels* of Moab." The word "ariel" is a transliteration because scholars are not sure what it means. Lexicons explain the most likely meaning as "lion of god,"[20] which is why the King James and Young's Bibles translate these opponents of Benaiah as "lion-like men of Moab."

The ancient understanding of ariel as a lion-like hybrid humanoid finds support in a later Nag Hammadi text that speaks of a gnostic deity, Yaldabaoth, who was an ariel (spelled slightly different): "Ariael is what the perfect call him, for he was like a lion."[21]

The Lion Men of Moab will make their entrance in the coming Chronicle, *David Ascendant.*

But there is still more behind this hybrid creature concept of goat demons or satyrs than meets a cursory reading of the text. And

---

http://www.biblicalarchaeology.org/daily/people-cultures-in-the-bible/people-in-the-bible/lilith/, accessed 9/8/14.

[19] Loren T. Stuckenbruck, "The 'Angels' and 'Giants' of Genesis 6:1-4 in Second and Third Century BCE Jewish Interpretation: Reflections on the Posture of Early Apocalyptic Traditions," Dead Sea Discoveries, Vol. 7, No. 3, *Angels and Demons* (2000), pp. 354-37; Ida Fröhlich,"Theology and Demonology in Qumran Texts," *Henoch*; Vol. 32 Issue 1, June 2010, 101-129.

[20] Francis Brown, Samuel Rolles Driver and Charles Augustus Briggs, *Enhanced Brown-Driver-Briggs Hebrew and English Lexicon*, electronic ed., 72 (Oak Harbor, WA: Logos Research Systems, 2000).

[21] James McConkey Robinson, Richard Smith and Coptic Gnostic Library Project, *The Nag Hammadi Library in English*, 4th rev. ed., 173 (Leiden; New York: E. J. Brill, 1996).

it is something that ties in with *Chronicles of the Nephilim* with peculiar interest.

Azazel

In Leviticus 16, we read of the sacrificial offering on the Day of Atonement. Among other sacrifices, the high priest would take two goats for atonement of the people. One, he would kill as blood sacrifice on the altar, and the other, he would transfer the sins of the people onto the goat by confession and the laying on of his hands. This action of transferring the bloodguilt onto the "other" is where we got the concept of "scapegoat."

But that is not the most fascinating piece of this puzzle. For in verses 8–10 and 26, the priest is told to send the goat "away into the wilderness to Azazel" (v. 10)! You read that right: *Azazel.*

> Leviticus 16:7-10
> Then he shall take the two goats and set them before the Lord at the entrance of the Tent of Meeting. And Aaron shall cast lots over the two goats, one lot for the Lord and the other lot for Azazel.And Aaron shall present the goat on which the lot fell for the Lord and use it as a sin offering, but the goat on which the lot fell for Azazel shall be presented alive before the Lord to make atonement over it, that it may be sent away into the wilderness to Azazel.

The name Azazel is not explained anywhere in the Old Testament, but we've heard that name before in the book of

1Enoch.[22] Azazel was one of the lead Watchers who led the rebellion of 200 Watchers to mate with the daughters of men. And that Watcher was considered bound in the desert of Dudael.

The natural question arises whether this is the same sacrifice to goat demons that Yahweh condemns in the very Leviticus and Isaiah passages we already looked at. But a closer look dispels such concerns.

The first goat was "for Yahweh" and the second "for Azazel" (v. 8). But whereas the first goat was a sacrifice, the second was not. As commentator Jacob Milgrom claims, "In pre-Israelite practice [Azazel] was surely a true demon, perhaps a satyr, who ruled in the wilderness—in the Priestly ritual he is no longer a personality but just a name, designating the place to which impurities and sins are banished."[23]

Milgrom then explains that in the ancient world, purgation and elimination rites went together. The sending out of the scapegoat to Azazel in the wilderness was a way of banishing evil to its place of origin which was described as the netherworld of chaos, where its malevolent powers could no longer do harm to the sender.[24] This wilderness of "tohu and wabohu" or emptiness and wasteland was precisely the chaos that Yahweh pushed back to establish his covenantal order of the heavens and earth, so it was where all demonic entities were considered to reside.

So Azazel could very well have been considered the father or leader of the goat demons. In the book of 1Enoch, Azazel is imprisoned in an opening in the desert of Dudael (1Enoch 13:4–8).

---

[22] 1Enoch 8:1; 9:6; 10:4–8; 13:1–2; 54:5; 55:4; 69:2.

[23] Jacob Milgrom, A Continental Commentary: Leviticus: A Book of Ritual and Ethics, 169 (Minneapolis, MN: Fortress Press, 2004).

[24] Jacob Milgrom, *A Continental Commentary: Leviticus: A Book of Ritual and Ethics*, 169, 166 (Minneapolis, MN: Fortress Press, 2004).

But scholar Judd Burton argues that this unknown location might very well be connected to Mount Hermon, the original home of the Watchers when they came down to the earth (1Enoch 6:6). He points out that a very important "opening" existed near Hermon in the Grotto of Pan at the site called Panias. In the Hellenistic period (200 B.C.) the Greeks established a shrine to Pan, the satyr god of nature and shepherding, that became quite influential in the worship of Pan in the Greco-Roman period.

Judd then speculates that the shrine was originally to Azazel in antediluvian days because of the close similarities between Azazel and Pan. Firstly, both deities were associated with the goat. Secondly, Pan was driven by primal sexual lusts, just as Azazel lusted after human women and led the Watchers to mate with them. Thirdly, both Pan and Azazel were adept at war craft. The victory at Marathon in 490 BC was attributed to Pan, just as the art of making weapons and waging war was attributed to Azazel. And lastly, "with regard to the mystical, Pan and Azazel are also kindred spirits. The Greeks associated Pan with divination and prophecy, and Azazel himself took an active role in revealing the mystical knowledge of heaven to humanity."[25]

It was this cave grotto at Panias near Hermon that may be the mysterious Dudael location or the memorial to Azazel's imprisonment. The Seirim clan of Panias in *Joshua Valiant* and *Caleb Vigilant* embodies this spiritual and theological reality. And this is how I appropriated Azazel's original binding at the Flood in *Noah Primeval*, by having him bound in a desert called Dudael, but his final binding occurred at Mount Hermon in *Joshua Valiant*. It was a both/and theological unity.

---

[25] Judd H. Burton, *Interview With the Giant: Ethnohistorical Notes on the Nephilim* (Burton Beyond Press, 2009) 20.

The Serpent Clan of Gilgal Rephaim

Throughout the *Chronicles of the Nephilim*, Bashan, "the place of the serpent," plays an important part of the storyline of the Watchers because it seems to have an important role in the spiritual history of the region. Bashan is where Mount Hermon, the touch point for the Watchers, resides (1Enoch 6:6), as well as the Seirim tribe of satyrs at Panias. The very land of Canaan around Mount Hermon that was called Bashan was described as the "land of the Rephaim" (Deut. 3:13), whose inhabitants were described as tall giants like the Anakim (Deut. 2:11, 20) and were related to Goliath the giant (1Chron. 20:4–8). It was also the domain of the mighty giant, Og of Bashan, the "last of the Rephaim" (Josh. 12:4; Deut. 3:11), who was Joshua's last impediment to entering the Promised Land. The ancient Jewish book of Jubilees adds some more details about these giant Rephaim ("Raphaim") and their territory to corroborate the Biblical record:

> Jubilees 29:9–10
> [9] But formerly the land of Gilead was called "the land of Raphaim" because it was the land of the Raphaim. And the Raphaim were born as giants whose height was ten cubits (15 ft.), nine cubits (13.5 ft.), eight cubits (12 ft.), or down to seven cubits (10.5 ft.). [10] And their dwelling was from the land of the Ammonites to Mount Hermon and their royal palaces were in Qarnaim, and Ashtaroth, and Edrei, and Misur, and Beon.[26]

---

[26] James H. Charlesworth, vol. 2, *The Old Testament Pseudepigrapha and the New Testament, Volume 2: Expansions of the "Old Testament" and Legends, Wisdom, and*

But there is more to this region that has been unearthed in recent decades. The Hivites, one of the seven Canaanite peoples marked out for annihilation (Ex. 23:23), resided "under Hermon" (Josh. 11:3) "on Mount Lebanon, from Mount Baal-hermon as far as Lebo-hamath (Jdg. 3:3). Though the Bible tells us no particulars about these people, there are some interesting factoids that illuminate some possibilities.

The Hebrew word for Hivite has the same consonants as another common word for snake,[27] and they are descendants of the cursed line of Canaan, son of Ham (Gen. 10:17; 1Chron. 1:15).

About 20 miles south of Mount Hermon is a serpentine ravine about a mile long bearing the marks of manmade engraving that do not match its surrounding natural formations. It's like a huge snake cut into the earth. And then about seven miles southwest of there lies a large serpentine mound that may date back to ancient days.[28]

And right near that serpentine mound lays Gilgal Rephaim.

Gilgal Rephaim is a large monument of megalithic stones set in concentric circles with a tomb ("tumulus") at the center and an outer diameter of about 520 feet. The ruins are anywhere between eight and fifteen feet tall and amount to forty thousand tons of stone. The name means, "Circle of Giants," and it lays 25 miles northwest of Edrei, the city of Og of Bashan, in the land of the Rephaim, the territory ruled by Og. Scholars have conjectured that this site, much like other circular megalithic sites around the world,

---

Philosophical Literature, Prayers, Psalms and Odes, Fragments of Lost Judeo-Hellenistic Works, 111 (New Haven; London: Yale University Press, 1985).

[27] Michael S. Heiser *The Myth That is True*, p 186. Available online at www.michaelsheiser.com

[28] Van Dorn, Douglas (2013-01-21). *Giants: Sons of the Gods* (Kindle Locations 3074-3076). Waters of Creation. Kindle Edition.

was used for religious astronomical/astrological purposes.[29] Other sites like it include the famous Stonehenge, as well as the newly discovered ancient Gobleki Tepe in Turkey, the world's oldest known religious monument, dating as far back as 9000 B.C.

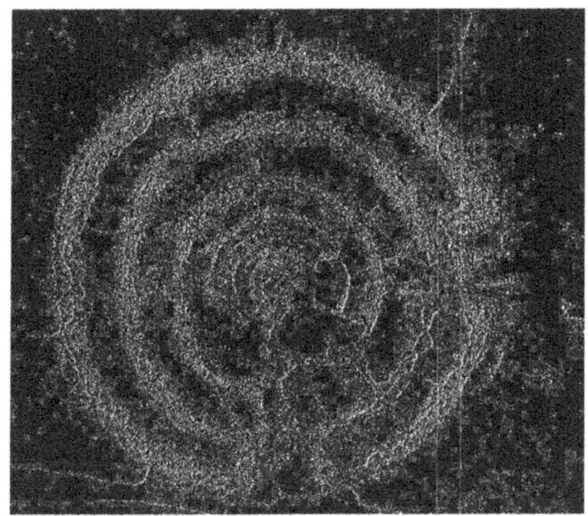

Aerial view of Gilgal Rephaim

But the connections are all there between a cult of the serpent in the land of the Rephaim and Bashan, the place of the serpent. Thus, the Serpent Clan of Gilgal Rephaim, from which Rahab the prostitute originates in *Joshua Valiant.*

Winged Fiery Serpents

In *Joshua Valiant* I tell the infamous story of Nehushtan, the bronze serpent, from Numbers 21. As Moses leads the people of Israel through the Negeb desert on their way to enter the Transjordan, the Israelites grumble and complain yet again about their lack of food and water. Yahweh responds by sending serpents to punish them.

[29] Anthony Aveni and Yonathan Mizrachi, "The Geometry and Astronomy of Rujm el-Hiri, a Megalithic Site in the Southern Levant," *Journal of Field Archaeology*, Vol. 25, No. 4 (Winter, 1998), pp. 475-496.

> Numbers 21:6–9
> Then the LORD sent fiery serpents among the people, and they bit the people, so that many people of Israel died. [7] And the people came to Moses and said, "We have sinned, for we have spoken against the LORD and against you. Pray to the LORD, that he take away the serpents from us." So Moses prayed for the people. [8] And the LORD said to Moses, "Make a fiery serpent and set it on a pole, and everyone who is bitten, when he sees it, shall live."
> [9] So Moses made a bronze serpent and set it on a pole. And if a serpent bit anyone, he would look at the bronze serpent and live.

The Hebrew word for "fiery serpents" used in this text is *seraph*, which is the same word used for the winged serpentine guardians of Yahweh's throne in passages like Isaiah 6:2.[30] There are several different Hebrew words that can be used for serpents, so the choice of this word here should clue us into the deliberations of the writer. While the notion of "fiery" can refer to the venomous sting of a desert snake such as a viper or cobra, there may be more going on here than a mere poetic description of snake bites.

The picture of *seraph* snakes having wings shows up in two other passages from Isaiah.

> Isaiah 14:29
> [29] Rejoice not, O Philistia, all of you, that the rod that struck you is broken, for from the serpent's root

[30] Timothy R. Ashley, *The Book of Numbers*, The New International Commentary on the Old Testament (Grand Rapids, MI: Wm. B. Eerdmans Publishing Co., 1993), 404–405.

> will come forth an adder, and its fruit will be a flying fiery serpent.
>
> Isaiah 30:6–7
> [6] An oracle on the beasts of the Negeb. Through a land of trouble and anguish, from where come the lioness and the lion, the adder and the flying fiery serpent...[7] Egypt's help is worthless and empty; therefore I have called her "Rahab who sits still."

Both of these prophecies against Philistia and Egypt respectively use the idea of a "flying fiery serpent" as a poetic description of the evil or dangerous nature of those nations. Though they are not required to be literal existing creatures for the prophecy to be legitimate, they nevertheless use the same Hebrew reference to fiery serpents that was used in the more historical passage of Numbers describing the "fiery serpents."

Additionally, the Isaiah 30 passage describes these flying fiery serpents as the beasts of the Negeb, the same location for the fiery serpents of Numbers 21.

Jacob Milgrom argues that the bronze or copper snake that Moses put on the pole was a winged serpent. He concludes this from the link of the Hebrew *seraph* to the Egyptian *uraeus* serpent.

> Egypt is the home for images of winged serpents. For example, the arms on the throne of Tutankhamen consist of two wings of a four-winged snake (uraeus), which rise vertically from the back of the seat. Indeed, the erect cobra, or uraeus, standing on its coil is the symbol of royalty for the

> pharaoh and the gods throughout Egyptian history. Winged uraei dating from the Canaanite period have been found, proving that the image of the winged serpent was well known in ancient Israel.[31]

Scholar Karen Randolph Joines adds more to the Egyptian origin of this motif, by explaining that the usage of serpent images to defend against snakes was also an exclusively Egyptian notion without evidence in Canaan or Mesopotamia.[32] And Moses came out of Egypt.

But the important element of these snakes being flying serpents or even dragons with mythical background is reaffirmed in highly respected lexicons such as the *Brown, Driver, Briggs Hebrew Lexicon.*[33]

The final clause in Isaiah 30:7 likening Egypt's punishment to the sea dragon Rahab lying dead in the desert is a further mythical serpentine connection.[34]

---

[31] Jacob Milgrom, *Numbers*, The JPS Torah Commentary (Philadelphia: Jewish Publication Society, 1990), 459.

[32] Karen Randolph Joines, "The Bronze Serpent in the Israelite Cult," *Journal of Biblical Literature*, Vol. 87, No. 3 (Sep., 1968), 251.

[33] Francis Brown, Samuel Rolles Driver, and Charles Augustus Briggs, *Enhanced Brown-Driver-Briggs Hebrew and English Lexicon* (Oak Harbor, WA: Logos Research Systems, 2000), 977. Wilhelm Gesenius and Samuel Prideaux Tregelles, *Gesenius' Hebrew and Chaldee Lexicon to the Old Testament Scriptures* (Bellingham, WA: Logos Bible Software, 2003), 795. See also, James Swanson, *Dictionary of Biblical Languages with Semantic Domains : Hebrew (Old Testament)* (Oak Harbor: Logos Research Systems, Inc., 1997).

[34] "This final clause uses the name Rahab (51:9; Job 9:13; 26:12; Ps 87:4; 89:11), the great sea monster from ancient Near Eastern legends, as a symbol for Egypt. The final cryptic clause, "Rahab the Do-Nothing" (NIV), interprets "Do-Nothing" as a sarcastic name for this supposedly powerful monster. Beuken prefers to interpret this as Rahab "who sits still," meaning that Egypt will not come to assist Judah in her conflict with Assyria.[133] Another possible translation is Rahab the dead one. All these warnings argue for a policy that does not depend on Egypt. It makes no sense to trust in a political policy that is sure to fail. It is futile to follow a plan that God opposes." Gary V. Smith, *Isaiah 1–39*, ed. E. Ray Clendenen, *The New American Commentary* (Nashville: B & H Publishing Group, 2007), 513.

But the Bible and Egypt are not the only places where we read of flying serpents in the desert. Hans Wildberger points out Assyrian king Esarhaddon's description of flying serpents in his tenth campaign to Egypt in the seventh century B.C.

> "A distance of 4 double-hours I marched over a territory… (there were) two-headed serpents [whose attack] (spelled) death—but I trampled (upon them) and marched on. A distance of 4 double-hours in a journey of 2 days (there were) green [animals] [Tr.: Borger: "serpents"] whose wings were batting."[35]

The Greek historian Herodotus wrote of "sacred" winged serpents and their connection to Egypt in his *Histories*:

> There is a place in Arabia not far from the town of Buto where I went to learn about the winged serpents. When I arrived there, I saw innumerable bones and backbones of serpents... This place… adjoins the plain of Egypt. Winged serpents are said to fly from Arabia at the beginning of spring, making for Egypt... The serpents are like water-snakes. Their wings are not feathered but very like

[35] Hans Wildberger, *A Continental Commentary: Isaiah 28-39* (Minneapolis, MN: Fortress Press, 2002), 136. Quoting from James Bennett Pritchard, ed., *The Ancient Near East an Anthology of Texts and Pictures*, 3rd ed. with Supplement (Princeton: Princeton University Press, 1969), 292.

the wings of a bat. I have now said enough concerning creatures that are sacred.[36]

The notion of flying serpents as mythical versus real creatures appearing in the Bible is certainly debated among scholars, but this debate gives certain warrant to the imaginative usage of winged flying serpents appearing in *Chronicles of the Nephilim*.[37]

Giants in the Land

There are some monsters that I want to address here that are not as mythical as the ones we have looked at, but they are nevertheless as demonic and worthy of comment. These are the giants of Canaan: the Rephaim and the Anakim.

A cursory reading of the conquest narrative certainly results in the discovery of giants in the land of Canaan, but a closer look at the sacred text brings out just how important they are to the cosmic storyline of the Wars of Yahweh.

In *Joshua Valiant* we see two kings of the Transjordan that must be overcome in order for Israel to secure a safe entry point into the Cisjordan to begin their conquest of the Promised Land: Sihon of Heshbon, and Og of Bashan.

These are not fictional characters. They are from the text. But Sihon is not described as a giant, only as a mighty king of the area whose colonial ambitions were so well known that he had a ballad

---

[36] *Herodotus, Herodotus, With an English Translation* by A. D. Godley, ed. A. D. Godley (Medford, MA: Harvard University Press, 1920) Histories 2:75.1-76.3. Thanks to my editor, Don Enevoldsen, for this reference.

[37] Scholars who acknowledge the evidence for mythical flying serpents, but argue against it: Wilhelm Gesenius and Samuel Prideaux Tregelles, *Gesenius' Hebrew and Chaldee Lexicon to the Old Testament Scriptures* (Bellingham, WA: Logos Bible Software, 2003), 796; R. Laird Harris, "2292 שָׂרָף," ed. R. Laird Harris, Gleason L. Archer Jr., and Bruce K. Waltke, *Theological Wordbook of the Old Testament* (Chicago: Moody Press, 1999), 884.

penned for him about his subduing of the Moabites under his power. A ballad that finds its way into the novel as well.

> Numbers 21:26–29
> For Heshbon was the city of Sihon the king of the Amorites, who had fought against the former king of Moab and taken all his land out of his hand, as far as
> the Arnon. [27] Therefore the ballad singers say, "Come to Heshbon, let it be built; let the city of Sihon be
> established. [28] For fire came out from Heshbon, flame from the city of Sihon. It devoured Ar of Moab, and
> swallowed the heights of the Arnon. [29] Woe to you, O Moab! You are undone, O people of Chemosh! He has made his sons fugitives, and his daughters captives, to an Amorite king, Sihon.

Last of the Rephaim: Og of Bashan

Og of Bashan is another Biblical story in need of a closer look. The Bible says that he reigned in the northern region of the Transjordan and ruled out of Ashtaroth over sixty cities of Bashan (Deut. 3:4; Josh. 9:10).

These two kings, Og and Sihon are depicted in the Bible as the enemies to overthrow in the Transjordan, so God gives Israel their victory over them (Num 32:33; Deut 1:1–8).

But then the text adds an important note about Og. It says that he was the "last of the Rephaim," a species we have seen elsewhere to be giants (Deut. 2:10–11, 20–23). It says that his territory, Bashan was called "The land of the Rephaim" for its population of giants (Deut. 3:13). It says his bed, or sarcophagus was at least thirteen and a half feet long. His size was so impressive that the bed had become a museum trophy piece in Israel years later.

> Deuteronomy 3:11
> [11] (For only Og the king of Bashan was left of the remnant of the Rephaim. Behold, his bed was a bed of iron. Is it not in Rabbah of the Ammonites? Nine cubits (13.5 feet) was its length, and four cubits (6 feet) its breadth, according to the common cubit.)

In the original Hebrew, Og's "land of the Rephaim" is an ambiguous wording that could equally be translated as "the 'hell' of the Rephaim."[38] Bashan was a deeply significant spiritual location to the Canaanites and the Hebrews. And as the *Dictionary of Deities and Demons in the Bible* puts it, Biblical geographical tradition agrees with the mythological and cultic data of the Canaanites of Ugarit that "the Bashan region, or a part of it, clearly represented 'Hell', the celestial and infernal abode of their deified dead kings," the Rephaim.[39]

Mount Hermon was in Bashan, and Mount Hermon was a location in the Bible that was linked to the Rephaim and ruled over by Og (Josh. 12:1–5), but it was also the legendary location where the Sons of God were considered to have come to earth and had

---

[38] K. van der Toorn, Bob Becking and Pieter Willem van der Horst, *Dictionary of Deities and Demons in the Bible DDD*, 2nd extensively rev. ed., 162 (Leiden; Boston; Grand Rapids, Mich.: Brill; Eerdmans, 1999).

[39] "Bashan," *DDD*, p 161-162. "According to *KTU* 1.108:1–3, the abode of the dead and deified king, and his place of enthronement as *[Rephaim]* was in *[Ashtarot and Edrei]*, in amazing correspondence with the Biblical tradition about the seat of king Og of Bashan, "one of the survivors of the Rephaim, who lived in Ashtarot and Edrei" (Josh 12:4)."

sexual union with the daughters of men to produce the giant Nephilim.[40]

As I explained in previous Chronicles' appendices, the Rephaim have an extra-Biblical tradition in Ugarit that is also tied to the land of Canaan. One of the corpus of texts unearthed at Ugarit just north of Canaan within the last century was what came to be known as the Rephaim Texts. These texts and others talked about a *marzih* feast that involved royalty traveling distances in their chariots to participate, wherein the "most ancient Rephaim of the netherworld" are summoned to assemble as the "council of the Ditanu, (or Didanu)."[41]

As Ugaritic scholars Levine and Tarragon sum up, "the Rephaim are long departed kings (and heroes) who dwell in the netherworld, which is located deep beneath the mountains of that far-away eastern region where the Ugaritians originated."[42]

There are two places in the Bible that hint at the Rephaim being warrior kings brought down to Sheol in similar language to the Ugaritic notion of the Rephaim warrior kings in the underworld:

> Is. 14:9
> Sheol beneath is stirred up
> to meet you when you come;
> it rouses the shades [The Hebrew word *Rephaim*]

---

[40] The non-canonical book of Enoch supports this same interpretation: "Enoch 6:6 And they were in all two hundred [sons of God]; who descended in the days of Jared on the summit of Mount Hermon, and they called it Mount Hermon, because they had sworn and bound themselves by mutual imprecations upon it."

[41] William W. Hallo and K. Lawson Younger, *The Context of Scripture*, (Leiden; New York: Brill, 1997-) 356-58.

[42] Baruch A. Levine and Jean-Michel de Tarragon, "Dead Kings and Rephaim: The Patrons of the Ugaritic Dynasty," *Journal of the American Oriental Society*, Vol. 104, No. 4 (Oct. - Dec., 1984), pp. 649-659

> to greet you,
> all who were leaders of the earth;
> it raises from their thrones
> all who were kings of the nations.
>
> Ezek. 32:21
> They shall fall amid those who are slain by the sword… The mighty chiefs [*Rephaim*] shall speak of them, with their helpers, out of the midst of Sheol: "They have come down, they lie still, the uncircumcised, slain by the sword."

Hebrew scholar, Michael S. Heiser concludes about this connection of Rephaim with dead warrior kings in Sheol and Bashan:

> That the Israelites and the biblical writers considered the spirits of the dead giant warrior kings to be demonic is evident from the fearful aura attached to the geographical location of Bashan. As noted above, Bashan is the region of the cities Ashtaroth and Edrei, which both the Bible and the Ugaritic texts mention as abodes of the Rephaim. What's even more fascinating is that in the Ugaritic language, this region was known not as Bashan, but *Bathan*—the Semitic people of Ugarit pronounced the Hebrew "sh" as "th" in their dialect. Why is that of interest? Because "Bathan" is a common word across all the Semitic languages, biblical Hebrew included, for "serpent." The region of Bashan was

known as "the place of the serpent." It was ground zero for the Rephaim giant clan and, spiritually speaking, the gateway to the abode of the infernal deified Rephaim spirits.[43]

Sons of Anak: Ahiman, Sheshai and Talmai

But the real enemy to overcome in Canaan was the Anakim, a powerful giant clan that seemed to dominate the southern region of the hill country. In fact, when the spies went on their forty day reconnaissance of the country, they came back with a report that told of the "Sons of Anak," who were giants that apparently had genetic roots in the original Nephilim before the Flood.

> Numbers 13:32–33
> "The land, through which we have gone to spy it out, is a land that devours its inhabitants, and all the people that we saw in it are of great height. [33] And there we saw the Nephilim (the sons of Anak, who come from the Nephilim), and we seemed to ourselves like grasshoppers, and so we seemed to them."

These Anakim are referred to as being "of great height" making the Israelites feel "like grasshoppers" (Num. 13:33), their height was a standard of tallness that other giants are compared to (Deut. 2:10, 21), a people "great and tall" who had a reputation for being so mighty that no one could stand before them (Deut. 9:2).

---

[43] Michael S. Heiser *The Myth That is True*, p 169. Available online at www.michaelsheiser.com.

> Deuteronomy 9:2–3
>
> [2] a people great and tall, the sons of the Anakim, whom you know, and of whom you have heard it said, 'Who can stand before the sons of Anak?' [3]

Joshua 14:15 adds that the city of Kiriath-arba, (later changed to the name Hebron), was founded by Arba, "the greatest among the Anakim." In Joshua 15:13 we discover that "Arba was the father of Anak," the original descendant of the Anakim. That is why I placed Arba many generations earlier as the founder of Kiriath-arba during the time of Abraham in the previous novel *Abraham Allegiant*. Since Abraham spent many of his years at the Oaks of Mamre, only two miles away from Kiriath-arba (Gen. 35:27), it was not too much of a leap to think that he had some contact with Arba, and maybe that was where a blood feud arose between the two peoples.

But then the Bible says that there were three very important Anakim who Caleb had ousted from Kiriath-arba when he conquered that key Anakite city. (Judg. 1:9–10)

> Joshua 15:13–14
>
> He gave to Caleb the son of Jephunneh a portion among the people of Judah, Kiriath-arba, that is, Hebron (Arba was the father of Anak). And Caleb drove out from there the three sons of Anak, Sheshai and Ahiman and Talmai, the descendants of Anak.

But there were also some interesting Jewish legends that added Ahiman as being the mightiest of the three.[44] Rabbinic tradition records Ahiman as challenging passers-by with the taunt, "Whose brother will fight with me?"[45] Sheshai and Talmai were said to make deep furrows or pits in the ground with their footsteps.[46]

I used these names of Sheshai, Ahiman, and Talmai, as brothers of a ruling Anakim family and chief villains in *Joshua Valiant* and *Caleb Vigilant*. These warriors must have been the most difficult to overcome for Israel since they received such a special mention in Scripture several times for their mighty prowess (Josh. 15:13–14; Num. 13:22; Judg. 1:9–10). This was the basis for my focus on these three in the novels as the ones to beat for Joshua and Caleb.

How Tall Were the Giants?

Most of the giants in *Joshua Valiant* and *Caleb Vigilant* are between eight and twelve feet tall. While some writers on the Nephilim have conjectured giants in Canaan to be as tall as thirty feet and higher, I think that is without Biblical, historical, or archaeological justification.[47]

---

[44] b. Yoma 10A - Jacob Neusner, *The Babylonian Talmud: A Translation and Commentary*, vol. 5a (Peabody, MA: Hendrickson Publishers, 2011), 31.
[45] in Num. R. xvi. and Tan., Shelaḥ, 7, ed. Buber, 11 — Isidore Singer, ed., *The Jewish Encyclopedia: A Descriptive Record of the History, Religion, Literature, and Customs of the Jewish People from the Earliest Times to the Present Day*, 12 Volumes (New York; London: Funk & Wagnalls, 1901–1906), 552.
[46] b. Yoma 1:1, III.20.C-E: "C. Ahiman: the most skilled among the brothers. D. Sheshai: for he made the ground on which he walked into pits. E.Talmai: he made the ground full of ridges."
[47] Some interpreters take the obviously poetic phrase of the giants being "the height of the cedars" quite literally (Amos 2:9), and claim some giants could have been thirty six feet high or so. This kind of literalistic interpretation is naïve.

The only sizes of giants that are specified in the Bible are that of Goliath ("6 cubits and a span" or 9½ feet tall),[48] Og of Bashan (his bed of nine cubits long or 13½ feet),[49] and an unnamed Egyptian giant "of great stature, five cubits tall" (7½ to 8 feet).[50] These numbers are based on the cubit size in Scripture as being the "common" cubit of Canaan, which most scholars agree is about eighteen inches. But the definition of a cubit in that day was the span of a man's elbow to his forefinger, which was not uniform like we have today. So in reality, those sizes are only approximations and could more likely be a bit larger.[51]

A further complication arises when one considers the fact that Moses had been raised and educated as royalty in Egypt. So he and the Exodus Israelites no doubt used the Egyptian royal cubit in their measurements. The question then is whether or not the Biblical text translated that cubit measurement to the smaller Mesopotamian/Levantine cubit or not. There is an indication in other Biblical texts of the awareness of this cubit difference. The writer of the Chronicles (written much later in Israel's history during the exile) makes this distinction when describing the dimensions of Solomon's temple. He writes that the "the length, in cubits *of the old standard*, was sixty cubits, and the breadth twenty cubits" (2 Chron. 3:3). Ezekiel, describing the measurements of the

---

[48] 1Sam 17:4. Some scholars point out that the Septuagint (LXX), Dead Sea Scrolls and Josephus after them describe Goliath at only four cubits and a span, which would make him more like six feet six inches tall. But scholar Clyde Billington has pointed out that the DSS and Josephus took their cue from the LXX, which was written in Egypt, whose royal cubit was consistently at 20.65 inches. The result would then be over 9 feet tall. So rather than the Bible exaggerating for mythic effect, the later translators adjusted numbers to fit their local Egyptian measurements. Clyde E. Billington, "Goliath and The Exodus Giants: How Tall Were They?" *JETS*, 50/3 (September 2007) 489-508.

[49] Deut. 3:11.

[50] 1Chron. 11:23.

[51] John H. Walton, Zondervan *Illustrated Bible Backgrounds Commentary* (Old Testament): Joshua, Judges, Ruth, 1 & 2 Samuel, vol. 2 (Grand Rapids, MI: Zondervan, 2009), 347.

temple in his vision, also makes this distinction of cubit difference as well when he writes, "the altar by cubits (the cubit being a cubit and a handbreadth)" (Ezek. 43:13). He later calls this a "long cubit" (Ezek. 41:8). So these parentheticals written by authors around the time of the exile indicate that during that time, there was still an awareness of the older and longer Egyptian cubit as if they had been still using it up until that date.[52]

If we apply this longer cubit measurement to Goliath's 9 cubits and a span, we get a height of about 10 1/2 feet tall![53] The Egyptian giant warrior that was killed by Benaiah (1 Chron. 11:23) was then 8 1/2 feet tall. Og of Bashan, whose bed was 9 cubits long (Deut. 3:11), would be 13 or 14 feet tall by this longer cubit. But the text says his measurement was made "according to the common cubit," so Og was more likely the shorter height of about 11 to 12 feet.

A few extra-Biblical sources add some more context to the size of Canaanite giants. The pseudepigraphical *Book of Jubilees*, when speaking of Og's kingdom of Rephaim, measures the giants from the size of 10 feet to 15 feet tall.

> Jubilees 29:9
> But before they used to call the land of Gilead the land of the Rephaim; for it was the land of the Rephaim, and the Rephaim were born (there), giants

---

[52] Conservative scholars claim that Moses wrote the Pentateuch during the time of the Exodus, so that would most likely mean that the older longer cubit was used in those texts. Critical scholars claim that Moses did not write the Pentateuch, but that it was mostly written and/or compiled during the time of the Exile which would mean they most likely used the newer shorter cubit in the Pentateuch, but then made some reference to that older cubit in Chronicles and Ezekiel to remind their readers of the changeover.

[53] If this is the case, then the Septuagint translators misunderstood the cubit of the Hebrew text as being the smaller cubit, when in fact it was the larger Egyptian cubit. They would then be translating the number incorrectly downward.

> whose height was ten, nine, eight down to seven cubits. [10 1/2 feet to 15 feet tall]

One thirteenth-century Egyptian papyrus describes bedouin nomads in Canaan as being "four or five cubits (7 to 9 feet) from their nose to their foot and have fierce faces."[54]

First century Jewish historian Josephus wrote about the giants in Hebron or Kiriath-arba of Canaan as giants

> who had bodies so large, and countenances so entirely different from other men, that they were surprising to the sight, and terrible to the hearing. The bones of these men are still shown to this very day, unlike to any creditable relations of other men.[55]

Josephus also wrote of a Jew named Eleazar during the time of Tiberius who was 7 cubits tall (10½ feet).[56]

Pliny, the Roman historian wrote of a giant during the time of Claudius named Gabbaras, who was over 9 feet tall.[57]

Greek historian Herodotus (ca. 430 B.C.) wrote of ancients finding a coffin ten feet long with human bones in it to match.[58]

---

[54] Edward Frank Wente and Edmund S. Meltzer, vol. 1, *Letters from Ancient Egypt*, Writings from the Ancient World, 108 (Atlanta, GA: Scholars Press, 1990). This measurement assumes that longer Egyptian cubit.

[55] Antiquities 5.125. Flavius Josephus and William Whiston, *The Works of Josephus: Complete and Unabridged* (Peabody: Hendrickson, 1987).

[56] Josephus, *Antiquities* 18.4.5.

[57] Pliny the Elder, *The Natural History* 7.16, ed. John Bostock (Medford, MA: Taylor and Francis, Red Lion Court, Fleet Street, 1855), 2157.

[58] Herodotus (ca. 430 B.C.) *The Histories* 1.67–68. Quoted in Mayor, Adrienne (2011-07-27). *The First Fossil Hunters: Dinosaurs, Mammoths, and Myth in Greek and Roman*

A Greek geographer, Pausanias (ca. A.D. 150) wrote of Roman soldiers diverting the river Orontes in Syria finding a coffin more than 16 feet long with a corpse the size of it inside. The Orontes flows through Mount Hermon in the land of Bashan, where the Rephaim king Og ruled.[59]

Scholar Adrienne Mayor analyzes many other ancient accounts of the discovery of coffinless giant bones, some as big as sixty cubits tall, in her book *The First Fossil Hunters: Dinosaurs, Mammoths, and Myth in Greek and Roman Times.* She analyzes them only to reveal that most of them are mammoth and other ancient extinct fossils innocently misinterpreted as buried bones of giants by ancient man unaware of such prehistoric beasts.

In light of these ancient descriptions, I kept my giants within this more realistic range of 7 to 12 feet tall, with Ahiman being an anomaly of 15 feet high.

But the Bible does not merely mention giants as being generic bad guys in the land just because they are tall and mean. Joshua seems to be on a systematic search and destroy mission for the Anakim in particular, which as noted earlier in Numbers 13:33 was because they had direct ancestral ties to the evil Nephilim giants wiped out at the Flood.

> Joshua 11:21–22
>
> [21] And Joshua came at that time and cut off the Anakim from the hill country, from Hebron, from

---

Times (New in Paper) (Kindle Locations 4672-4678). Princeton University Press. Kindle Edition.

[59] Pausanias, Guide to Greece, 8.29.1-4 referenced in *Mayor, Adrienne (2011-07-27). The First Fossil Hunters: Dinosaurs, Mammoths, and Myth in Greek and Roman Times (New in Paper) (Kindle Locations 4770-4778). Princeton University Press. Kindle Edition.*

> Debir, from Anab, and from all the hill country of Judah, and from all the hill country of Israel. Joshua devoted them to destruction with their cities. [22] There was none of the Anakim left in the land of the people of Israel. Only in Gaza, in Gath, and in Ashdod did some remain.

But since the Anakim were theologically tied to the Nephilim of Genesis 6, whose bloodguilt was partially responsible for the Flood, it makes sense that God would engage in a mop up operation on their giant descendants later. Interestingly, the giants left in Gaza and Gath, the land of the Philistines, would cause much pain for Israel in the time of the Judges and be wiped out finally by David, the symbolic type of Messiah, who would be the ultimate victor over the principalities and powers of this present darkness in the heavenly places. Christus Victor. But that is for the upcoming novels to reveal.

For additional Biblical, historical and mythical research related to this novel, go to www.ChroniclesoftheNephilim.com under the menu listing, "Scholarly Research."

If you liked this book, then please help me out by writing an honest review of it on Amazon. That is one of the best ways to say thank you to me as an author. It really does help my exposure and status as an author. It's really easy. In the Customer Reviews section, there is a little box that says "Write a customer review." They guide you easily through the process. Thanks! — *Brian Godawa*

More Books by Brian Godawa

See https://godawa.com/ for more information on other books by Brian Godawa. Check out his other series below:

Chronicles of the Nephilim

Chronicles of the Nephilim is a saga that charts the rise and fall of the Nephilim giants of Genesis 6 and their place in the evil plans of the fallen angelic Sons of God called, "The Watchers." The prelude to Chronicles of the Apocalypse. Learn more here. (paid link)

Chronicles of the Apocalypse

Chronicles of the Apocalypse is an origin story of the most controversial book of the Bible: Revelation. An historical conspiracy thriller trilogy in first century Rome set against the backdrop of explosive spiritual warfare of Satan and his demonic Watchers. Learn more here.

Chronicles of the Watchers

Chronicles of the Watchers is a series that charts the influence of spiritual principalities and powers over the course of human history. The kingdoms of man in service to the gods of the nations at war. Completely based on ancient biblical, historical and mythological research. Learn more here.

•••••

Biblical & Historical Research

For additional free Biblical and historical scholarly research related to this novel and series, go to Godawa.com > Chronicles of the Nephilim > *Scholarly Research.*

GREAT OFFERS BY BRIAN GODAWA

Get More Biblical Imagination

Sign up Online For
The Godawa Chronicles

www.Godawa.com

Updates and Freebies
of the Books of Brian Godawa
Special Discounts,
Weird Bible Facts!

CHRONICLES OF THE NEPHILIM

Nephilim Giants, Watchers, Cosmic War. All in the Bible.

www.Godawa.com

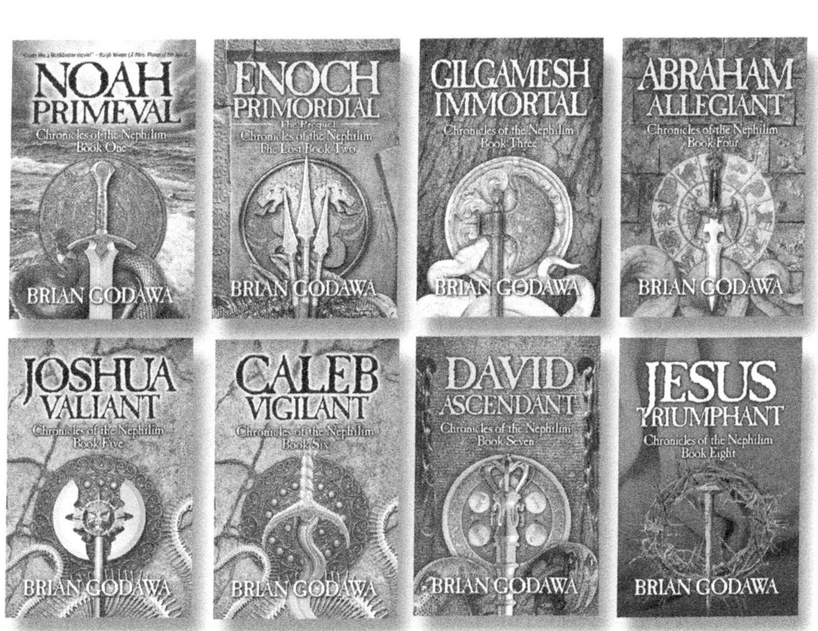

CHRONICLES OF THE APOCALYPSE

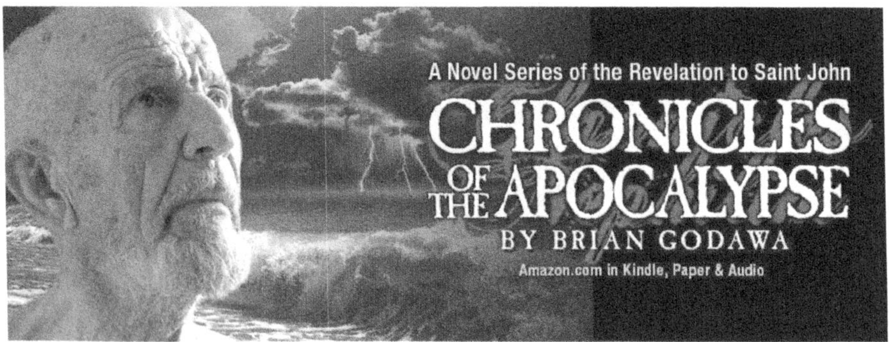

A Novel Series About the Book of Revelation & the End Times. A Fresh Biblical View.

www.Godawa.com

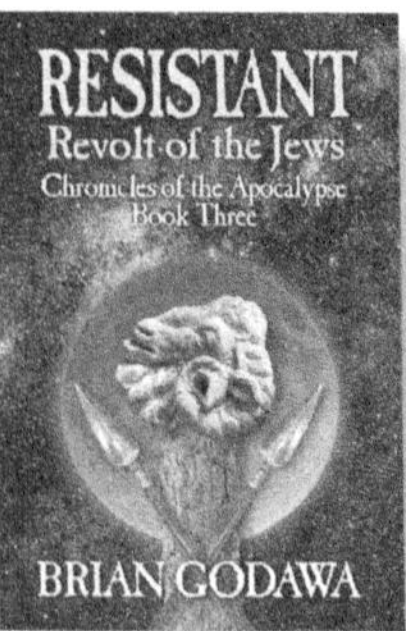

VIDEO LECTURES

The Book of Enoch: Scripture, Heresy or What?

This lecture by Brian Godawa will be an introduction to the ancient book of 1Enoch, its content, its history, its affirmation in the New Testament, and its acceptance and rejection by the Christian Church. What is the Book of Enoch? Where did it come from? Why isn't it in the Bible? How does the Book of Enoch compare with the Bible?

Available on video.

Chronicles of the Nephilim: The Ancient Biblical Story

Watchers, Nephilim, and the Divine Council of the Sons of God. In this dvd video lecture, Brian Godawa explores the Scriptures behind this transformative storyline that inspired his best-selling Biblical novel series Chronicles of the Nephilim.

Available on video.

To download these lectures and other books and products by Brian Godawa, just go to the STORE at:

www.Godawa.com

GOD AGAINST THE GODS

How God Captures the Imagination

This book was previously titled *Myth Became Fact: Storytelling, Imagination & Apologetics in the Bible.*

Brian Godawa, Hollywood screenwriter and best-selling novelist, explores the nature of imagination in the Bible. You will learn how God subverts pagan religions by appropriating their imagery and creativity, and redeeming them within a Biblical worldview. Improve your imagination in your approach to glorifying God and defending the faith.

Demonizing the Pagan Gods
God verbally attacked his opponents, pagans and their gods, using sarcasm, mockery, name-calling.

Old Testament Storytelling Apologetics
Israel shared creative images with their pagan neighbors: The sea dragon of chaos and the storm god. The Bible invests them with new meaning.

Biblical Creation and Storytelling
Creation stories in the ancient Near East and the Bible both express a primeval battle of deity to create order out of chaos. But how do they differ?

The Universe in Ancient Imagination
A detailed comparison and contrast of the Biblical picture of the universe with the ancient pagan one. What's the difference?

New Testament Storytelling Apologetics
Paul's sermon to the pagans on Mars Hill is an example of subversion: Communicating the Gospel in terms of a pagan narrative with a view toward replacing their worldview.

Imagination in Prophecy & Apocalypse
God uses imaginative descriptions of future events to deliberately obscure his message while simultaneously showing the true meaning and purpose behind history.

An Apologetic of Biblical Horror
Learn how God uses horror in the Bible as a tool to communicate spiritual, moral and social truth in the context of repentance from sin and redemptive victory over evil.

For More Info
www.Godawa.com

THE IMAGINATION OF GOD

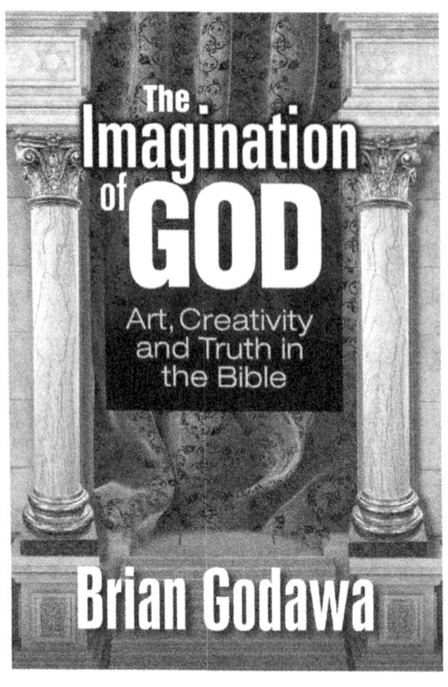

Art, Creativity and Truth in the Bible

In his refreshing and challenging book, Godawa helps you break free from the spiritual suffocation of heady faith. Without negating the importance of reason and doctrine, Godawa challenges you to move from understanding the Bible "literally" to "literarily" by exploring the poetry, parables and metaphors found in God's Word. Weaving historical insight, pop culture and personal narrative throughout, Godawa reveals the importance God places on imagination and creativity in the Scriptures, and provides a Biblical foundation for Christians to pursue imagination, beauty, wonder and mystery in their faith.

This book was previously released with the title, *Word Pictures: Knowing God Through Story and Imagination.*

Endorsements:

"Brian Godawa is that rare breed—a philosopher/artist—who opens our eyes to the aesthetic dimension of spirituality. Cogently argued and fun to read, Godawa shows convincingly that God interacts with us as whole persons, not only through didactic teaching but also through metaphor, symbol, and sacrament."

— Nancy R. Pearcey,
Author, *Total Truth: Liberating Christianity from its Cultural Captivity*

"A spirited and balanced defense of the imagination as a potential conveyer of truth. There is a lot of good literary theory in the book, as well as an autobiographical story line. The thoroughness of research makes the book a triumph of scholarship as well."

— Leland Ryken, Clyde S. Kilby Professor of English, Wheaton College, Illinois
Author, *The Christian Imagination: The Practice of Faith in Literature & Writing.*

For More Info
www.Godawa.com

ABOUT THE AUTHOR

Brian Godawa is the screenwriter for the award-winning feature film, *To End All Wars,* starring Kiefer Sutherland. It was awarded the Commander in Chief Medal of Service, Honor and Pride by the Veterans of Foreign Wars, won the first Heartland Film Festival by storm, and showcased the Cannes Film Festival Cinema for Peace.

He also co-wrote *Alleged*, starring Brian Dennehy as Clarence Darrow and Fred Thompson as William Jennings Bryan. He previously adapted to film the best-selling supernatural thriller novel *The Visitation* by author Frank Peretti for Ralph Winter (*X-Men, Wolverine*), and wrote and directed *Wall of Separation,* a PBS documentary, and *Lines That Divide*, a documentary on stem cell research.

Mr. Godawa's scripts have won multiple awards in respected screenplay competitions, and his articles on movies and philosophy have been published around the world. He has traveled around the United States teaching on movies, worldviews, and culture to colleges, churches and community groups.

His popular book, *Hollywood Worldviews: Watching Films with Wisdom and Discernment* (InterVarsity Press) is used as a textbook in schools around the country. His novel series, the saga *Chronicles of the Nephilim* is in the Top 10 of Biblical Fiction on Amazon and is an imaginative retelling of Biblical stories of the Nephilim giants, the secret plan of the fallen Watchers, and the War of the Seed of the Serpent with the Seed of Eve. The sequel series, *Chronicles of the Apocalypse* tells the story of the Apostle John's book of Revelation, and *Chronicles of the Watchers* recounts true history through the Watcher paradigm.

Find out more about his other books, lecture tapes and dvds for sale at his website www.godawa.com.

Made in the USA
Las Vegas, NV
26 February 2024